C0-AWR-608

Female Playwrights and Eighteenth-Century Comedy

Female Playwrights and Eighteenth-Century Comedy

Negotiating Marriage on the London Stage

Misty G. Anderson

palgrave

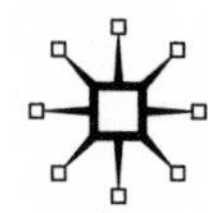

FEMALE PLAYWRIGHTS AND EIGHTEENTH-CENTURY COMEDY

First published 2002 by PALGRAVE™
175 Fifth Avenue, New York, N.Y.10010 and
Houndmills, Basingstoke, Hampshire RG21 6XS.
Companies and representatives throughout the world

PALGRAVE is the new global publishing imprint of St. Martin's Press LLC Scholarly and Reference Division and Palgrave Publishers Ltd (formerly Macmillan Press Ltd).

ISBN 0–312–23938–6 hardback

Library of Congress Cataloging-in-Publication Data
Anderson, Misty G. 1967-
Female playwrights and eighteenth-century comedy : negotiating marriage on the London stage / Misty Anderson.
p. cm.
Includes bibliographical references (p.) and index.
ISBN 0–312–23938–6
1. English drama—18th century—History and criticism. 2. Women and literature—Great Britain—History—18th century. 3. English drama—Women authors—History and criticism. 4. Theater—England—London—History—18th century. 5. English drama (comedy)—History and criticism. 6. Courtship in Literature. 7. Marriage in literature. 8. Women in literature.

PR708.W6 A53 2002
822'.0523099287'09033—dc21 2001036573

A catalogue record for this book is available from the British Library.

Design by Letra Libre, Inc.

First edition: February 2002
10 9 8 7 6 5 4 3 2 1

Printed in the United States of America.

To Andy and John,
who laugh at my jokes.

Contents

Acknowledgments

This book was researched and written with the financial support of an NEH Dissertation Fellowship, two International Scholar Awards from the P.E.O. Sisterhood, a University of Tennessee Professional Development Award, and a summer fellowship from the John C. Hodges Better English Fund. I thank the librarians at Vanderbilt University's Alexander Heard Library, the University of Tennessee's Hodges Library, the New York Public Library's Berg Collection, and the British Library for their kind assistance over the years. From the beginning of this project, Margaret Doody believed in my ability to say something intelligent about women and comedy. She taught me to think of the eighteenth century not as a period but as a periodical, which continues to publish. She also allowed me to transform her living room into a literal stage to bring some of these comedies to life through the Eighteenth-Century Players reader's theater company at Vanderbilt University. Thanks to all the fearless souls who took part in that project, especially Marilyn Allison, Elaine Phillips, Phil Phillips, Phil Nel, Karin Westman, Gary Richards, Roger Moore, Jonathan Rogers, Ted Mulvaney, Eric Bledsoe, Arnold Schmidt, Julia Fesmire, Adrienne Stewart, Ann MacDonald, and Allan Bourassa. As this manuscript evolved, Paul Helton, Steven Sparks, Maria Bibbs, Darren Hughes, and especially Audrey Tinkham helped me manage the thousands of tasks that cascade in the writing of books. Mark Schoenfield offered his astute readings, his generous intellect, and his friendship at the most crucial moments, for which I am forever grateful. Valerie Traub taught me about the historical and theoretical terms of gender, lessons that are exceeded only by what she taught me about being a colleague and a teacher. John Zomchick has greatly enriched my intellectual life at the University of Tennessee and has given me sage advice on contract law, the eighteenth century, and finishing books. I owe special thanks to Marilyn Gaull, who took an interest in this project and helped me bring it to completion by offering me her editorial experience, her timely insights about the profession, and her warm and welcoming collegiality. Thanks to all those who have read drafts, commented on talks, or challenged me through their conversation: Jay

Clayton, Vereen Bell, Nancy Walker, Robert Mack, Steve Miskinis, Kenny Mostern, John Evelev, Emma Lipton, Heather Hirschfield, Jay Dickson, Randi Voss, Allen Dunn, Stanton Garner, Elizabeth Sutherland, Julie Crawford, and Devoney Looser. Thanks also to the friends and family who have sustained me and mine in myriad ways throughout this project: Jen Shelton, Julia Fesmire, Paul Alexis, Michael Phillips, Trevor Jefferson, Sandra Moutsios, Frank Tirro, Charlene Tirro, Kelli Anderson, Chris Anderson, Charles Anderson, and Gale Anderson. Anderson Tirro, whose life has been spanned by this project, has enlivened my work with his joyful and loving ways. My greatest debt, though, is to John Tirro, partner, spiritual guide, and bard. He has negotiated a commuter marriage with panache while weaving the garlands of work and home, proofreading and childcare, and theory and practice, with the steady understanding that these things are all part of our very good bargain.

The text of the *Sylvia* cartoon "Gender Based Differences in Humor" appears with the kind permission of Nicole Hollander.

Introduction

In a Nicole Hollander cartoon entitled "Gender Based Differences in Humor," which prefaced the 1988 volume *Last Laughs: Perspectives on Women and Comedy,* the heroine, Sylvia, composes the following quiz while lounging in a bathtub: "Are you a man or a woman? Check the things you find funny: Larry, Moe, and Curly; Men dressed up as women, but with their unshaven legs showing; The disparity between the ideal and the real. Send quiz and stamped self-addressed envelope to find out."[1] To "pass" Sylvia's test as a woman, one must think like a comic theorist. The first two choices in the cartoon present a Hobbesian position of superiority over someone who has failed to master the terms of social interaction, physical discipline, or gender performance. In the tripartite joke structure of the cartoon, these options are tagged as wrong answers. The third choice, the punch line, is the contradiction of all comedy that William Hazlitt called "the difference between what things are, and what they ought to be."[2] The "correct" answer points the reader to a gendered perspective on comedy within a world of contradictions, rather than a seemingly objective position of mastery. This cartoon, with its comic theorist in the bathtub, provides an anachronistic point of departure for my study of stage comedies by women in the long eighteenth century.

In *Female Playwrights and Eighteenth-Century Comedy: Negotiating Marriage on the London Stage,* I explore the popular comedies of Aphra Behn, Susanna Centlivre, Hannah Cowley, and Elizabeth Inchbald, the most commercially successful Restoration and eighteenth-century British women playwrights. These playwrights and their heroines measure the disparity between idealized marriage narratives and the real circumstances of characters in history through the gendered scripts of comedy. Behn, Centlivre, Cowley, and Inchbald found in comedy a narrative where the economic future, erotic possibility, and public visibility of women merge, and they were able to engage generations of theatergoers in their versions of that story. Marriage held out the promise of sexual fulfillment and social adulthood to women, in spite of the legal and economic inequalities between men and women that marriage and property law reproduced. The successes of these playwrights' careers outline a cultural conversation about marriage and rights that corresponds to the liberalization of marriage law through the principles of contract and then to the subsequent return to coverture at the end of the century. Susan Staves has traced these changes in her study of marriage and property law, which provides the legal framework for my argument about stage comedy.[3] The historical changes in marriage law over the course of this period put female dramatists in a unique position to negotiate women's new relationships to the old scripts of courtship and marriage. These two categories, gender and genre, frame my study as they framed the reception of plays for Restoration and eighteenth-century audiences.

I treat comedy both as a generic marker that describes a story about marriage and as a designation of a performance that the audience expected to find funny. My study examines the relationship between comic closure, which tends to be predictable, and comic events, where the more local jokes and comic conflicts of the comedies play out. Playwrights use the tension between comic events and comic structures to navigate between an ideal plot that the genre reiterates and the impediments or alternatives to that plot along the way to the comic destination, marriage. At the risk of ruining jokes, I take these comic events seriously as the crisis moments within comedy's overdetermined representation of marriage. These are not plays about resisting marriage, but about negotiating the terms, literal and figurative, under which Restoration and eighteenth-century women existed within the institution. The audience's and the playwright's conflicting investments in both conservative endings and more progressive models of modern marriage animate these comedies. Comic events establish positions of authority for the negotiating heroines of these plays, while comic closure assures the audience that marriage will survive these negotiations.

The patterns that emerge in the comic events of these plays articulate the terms in which women might represent themselves as subjects rather than objects in marriage negotiations. Scenes of circulating contracts and letters in Susanna Centlivre's *The Busy Body* allow heroines to write themselves into their married futures, rather than to disappear under coverture. Her couples, who trick their way around the will of bad guardians, contract with each other for more equitable terms that allow them to share in the financial benefit of their marriages. Similarly, Hannah Cowley invokes national identity as the basis for the legal agency of her heroines. The art auction in *The Runaway*, in which no one knows the provenance of or the stories portrayed in a series of continental historical paintings, is a joke on the collapse of identity without nationality. Cowley imagines a British nationalism that trumps foreign decadence and guarantees the place of married women as citizens who share in the liberties of civil society. These comic events are in dialogue with the plot, but they cannot be reduced to the foregone conclusions of comic closure, which ends the independence of the witty heroine and celebrates the economic victory of elite families. Comic events refer to the history outside of the comic text, an outside that was part of the audience's experience of marriage.

Behn's, Centlivre's, Cowley's, and to a lesser extent Inchbald's plays make marriages work by suggesting that although something may be wrong with the institution, it can be made right. As a group, these playwrights are more optimistic about the social and legal implications of contract thought for women than many of their male colleagues. Otway's *The Soldier's Fortune* (1680) and Southerne's *The Wives' Excuse* (1691) both represent with great sympathy wives driven to adultery or to the brink of it, while Vanbrugh's *The Provok'd Wife* (1697) and Farquhar's *The Beaux's Stratagem* (1707) close with wives hoping for legal separation from Chancery court.[4] These plays are more cutting indictments of women's legal status than either *The Feign'd Courtesans* (1679) or *The Busy Body* (1709), in which Behn and Centlivre respectively imagine heroines who are free to make contracts, choose husbands, and seize their portions. I point out these differences to clarify that this group of successful women writers did not have a clear proto-feminist agenda, though they were committed to happy endings for their heroines. The popularity of these plays suggests that Restoration and eighteenth-century audiences enjoyed these hopeful visions of female agency.

The playwrights in my study support their heroines' ability to make contracts and secure places in the community through a comic rhetoric that bribes the audience with their own pleasure to take the heroine's side. Comedies, like contracts, usually have a clear end in sight; the interesting part is the negotiation. I do not suggest that endings are irrelevant, but rather that they must be read in light of the comic events that precede them. Comedies end on the same cloying note with few variations: happily ever after, order restored. The security of this repetitive narrative offers pleasures of its own, but the laughter comedies generate comes from comic events that tap into cultural anxieties about the problems with happy endings. After Hellena makes Willmore swear "never to think—to see—to Love—nor Lye—with any but thyself" she declares "what a wicked Creature I am, to damn a proper Fellow" (III.i, 482). Her joke draws its force from the problem it exposes: Willmore is a notorious rake who will probably not be faithful to Hellena after the comic ending. Twenty lines later, his indiscriminate sexual desire subtends another comic exchange with Belvile, in which Willmore ignores Belvile's conversation, then wrongly assumes Belvile is pining after Hellena:

Willmore: Why dost thou know her?
Belvile: Know her! Ay, Ay, and a pox take me with all my Heart for being Modest.

Willmore: But hearkey Friend of mine, are you my Rival? and have I been only beating the Bush all this while?
Belvile: I understand thee not—I'm mad—see here—(*Shews the picture*)
Willmore: Ha! whose Picture's this!—'tis a fine Wench! (III.i, 482)

Willmore's comic incompetence in this exchange is also a serious reference to one of the main problems in Behn's comedies: women are too easily exchanged, and their erotic specificity can be undermined by careless lovers like Willmore to whom they nonetheless find themselves drawn. The comic events underscore the problems of the comic structure and call readers and characters alike to be alert to the specific conditions necessary for the comic ending to be a happy one for all parties.

In the case of comedy, where audience laughter or the lack thereof could determine the fate of a play, the author's identity played an important role. My first chapter takes up the questions of social control that are embedded in the psychological operations of humor and their relationship to these very visible women writers. While comedy as a genre proved welcoming to women, the politics of humor and joking put women in a rhetorically complex situation. According to Freud's otherwise compelling *Jokes and Their Relation to the Unconscious,* women can't be funny, at least not intentionally; most Restoration and eighteenth-century literary theorists concurred in the face of evidence to the contrary. Working from the feminist insights of Regina Barreca, Nancy Walker, and others who have challenged Freud's assumptions about women and comedy, Eileen Gillooly and Audrey Bilger argue that late-eighteenth- and nineteenth-century female novelists created feminine and occasionally feminist strategies to address social injustice, particularly as it concerns gender.[5]

Bilger's and Gillooly's studies carefully show the ways that gender inflects humor and comic style, but my focus on stage comedy raises a different set of generic and historical questions. In contrast to the novel, stage comedies demand public laughter. While I cannot reproduce that laughter or any comprehensive accounts of audience response, I sketch the response of the audience throughout my study in my attention to popular plays that survived in repertoire. Female playwrights were able to keep their audience, but they had to negotiate for their comic authority in prefaces, prologues, and letters, where they argued for their right to entertain people for profit. The comic novels of Burney, Austen, or Gaskell aimed at private enjoyment and did not require the immediate consensus of public laughter that theaters demanded (though the manuscripts of Burney's and Austen's howlingly funny comedies and farces prove that they could have written for the stage). Stage comedies also take shape through a more fixed set of generic expectations that did not admit such experiments in tone and structure as Burney's

Camilla or Austen's *Mansfield Park,* which shade the marriage plot with dark jokes and caustic comic reflections. Female playwrights offered subtle rereadings of marriage that had to fit within the parameters of genre and the theatrical market.

In the second chapter, I discuss the contradictions within early modern contract theories as they relate to the status of women in marriage in the Restoration and eighteenth century. The three primary categories of contracts, the social compact, commercial contracts, and the marriage contract, raise questions about the nature of the individual and her, or his, social authority. The social compact, renegotiated in the wake of the Restoration and the Bloodless Revolution of 1688, vested inalienable powers of contract in civil subjects, who could renegotiate the social compact if it proved faulty or unjust. This political logic built the liberal model of civil society on the property that individuals have in themselves and on their ability to make contracts that distribute wealth and power. But Restoration and eighteenth-century political philosophers and judges were unable to decide whether women possessed or lacked this basic form of property at the level of the social compact and how much, if any, of this self-possession survived in marriage. The ambiguous legal status of women informs their relationship to the marriage contract, which may or may not subsume the identity of a particular woman. The courts also vacillated between liberal interpretations of the similarities between these types of contract and more hierarchical interpretations of the fundamental difference between them.

The subsequent chapters of the book trace the development of comic strategies in the careers of these four playwrights as they respond to historical changes in the concepts of marriage and gender. In chapter three, I examine the landmark career of Aphra Behn, which set the professional standard for women writers in the long eighteenth century and provided a sexual outer limit to the content of their plays. Although it is fair to say, counter to her critics, that Aphra Behn was no more bawdy than her male contemporaries, she takes a special interest in the female body as both subject and object. Behn suspects contract logic of undermining royalist principles of identity, and she rails against the anonymity of exchange in its fully commercial form as a Whiggish plot to crush her heroines' erotic appeal. Her strategy, then, is to direct her audience away from the mercantile calculus that makes women equal to some given exchange value and toward the particular woman in question. The attention she gives to the erotic lives of her heroines and their desires re-materializes women in the marriage plot. Although Behn in her later career grows more cynical about the ability of anything to stem the rising bourgeois tide and the alienations that are its inheritance, she continues to pursue an elusive erotic embodiment in which her heroines are *active* objects of desire.

In contrast, as I argue in chapter four, Susanna Centlivre's heroines embrace the language and culture of commercial exchange. Centlivre's optimism about modern British liberalism and the logic of possessive individualism likely contributed to the extraordinary popularity of her plays, which held the stage for 200 years. No other playwright of the eighteenth century could boast as many plays in repertoire, and her most popular comedies remained in the nineteenth-century repertoire.[6] Unlike Behn, the Whiggish Centlivre relished the idea of free markets and saw them as part of a larger project of liberating English society from arbitrary modes of power. She took a great personal interest in the early stock exchange and spoke of the "Publick Good" of free trade policies supported by the house of Hanover.[7] Judging from the box office, audiences liked her comic argument that egalitarian contracts should be open to men and women in civil society. Centlivre emphasized the social and economic possibilities of contract thought in her comedies, and only reluctantly acknowledged its limitations. Her heroines use the comic circulation of words, letters, papers, and legal contracts to parlay their ambiguous legal status into contractually binding economic security. Her interest in contracts coincides with what Susan Staves has termed the first stage of contract logic in Restoration and eighteenth-century marriage law, in which equity courts were hospitable to the idea that husbands and wives could make contracts with each other.[8] But Centlivre's arguments for a more egalitarian private sphere led her into the heart of the paradox of women in contract thought. Contracts may offer theoretical equality to women, but the social compact and the marriage contract reiterate the bars to their full subjectivity.

In chapter five, I consider the strongly nationalist plays of Hannah Cowley, the first woman to achieve sustained popularity after David Garrick's career ended. In 1776, her first hit, *The Runaway,* was edited and sponsored by Garrick, but her greatest successes came after his patronage ended. Cowley tapped the larger audiences of the 1770s and 1780s by satisfying middle-class demands for sexually tame comedies that celebrated sexual abstinence and filial duty, while also catering to the laboring-class audience that had new access to the theaters under Garrick's pricing schemes. Cowley's stage comedies make Englishness the ultimate aphrodisiac and the source of gender equity. Her comedies exploit popular ideas about individual liberty, developed by the philosophical and political individualism of Enlightenment thought and enforced through years of international trade and British military success. A healthy sprinkling of English soldiers, jokes at the expense of other countries, and funny rather than bumbling servants help her plays maintain a strong populist bent as they take up the threads of Centlivre's conversation about contract. Cowley allows her heroines to claim a share in the natural right of self-possession by virtue of their nationality, but by the end of her career, the once-progressive Chancery courts were becoming more reluctant to maintain a married woman's right to make contracts with her husband. In the later plays, such as *Which Is the Man?,* Cowley finds nationalism an insufficient bulwark against the greed that undermines both national and individual identity for male and female characters.

Elizabeth Inchbald's more conservative comedies appear as British marriage law retreats from contract logic and as Britain responds to the French Revolution. The colonial settings of many of her plays reiterate the nationalism of Centlivre and Cowley, but Inchbald focuses on the legal complications of marriage and divorce in her comic events. Her disinterest in courtship shifts the emphasis from empowering heroine-subjects to protecting them from the sexual and economic threats of failed marriages. Without taking the side of adulterous wives, she represents their situations sensitively and points to the realities of divorce, which, like marriage itself, gave the legal and economic advantage to husbands. Inchbald's heroines can secure their identities only through bonds of affection, beyond the letter of the law. Inchbald's communitarian hopefulness keeps the female adulterers, maligned wives, and gambling daughters of her plays within the scope of society, even when the marital contracts and social compacts that had defined their places fail. Inchbald exposes the limits of liberal individualism for late-eighteenth-century women as British property law began to close the avenues to independent existence that earlier eighteenth-century marriage law had created. Her comedies have unusually dark and provisional endings that unsettle generic expectation. These plays betray a pessimism about the contractual equality that Centlivre and Cowley mapped in their comedies; in its place, Inchbald proposes a model of identity grounded in community. She moves away from individualism and toward a self created and secured through meaningful relations, though community, as her heroines discover, sometimes comes at the price of autonomy.

My close readings of these plays eschew the summary methodology of Northrop Frye, but not his insights about comedy's investment in and optimism about marriage. My approach also turns from Jameson's Marxist priority on innovation and revolutionary intervention but embraces his dialectic of structural norm and textual deviation. I am interested in the more immediate narrative struggle between closure and comic event, which provides a way to read the history of marriage that women translated for the stage. My reading of comic events against comic structures is ultimately not specific to plays by women, though it is an approach well adapted to illuminate their deft negotiations of the genre. I am interested in this structuralist insight precisely because it cannot be supported through structuralist claims; instead, it returns the local moments of these comedies to history as it considers the relationship of those local events to the history of the comic marriage plot. I also provide some account of comic pleasure in this book. To talk about pleasure as a literary historian requires both some sense of the tastes of Restoration and eighteenth-century audiences, sketched throughout by my selection of comedies that were long-term popular successes, and attention to the pleasures of the comic text, which can often lead back to distressing social realities. My work tries, like Pope's less charitable descriptions of plotting women, to "trick . . . off in air" the pleasures of these plays as well as their function in the period's debates about gender and power. Some of these comedies come to life only when their historical context becomes clear; others continue to sparkle because they speak to anxieties about identity, contract, and marriage that have followed Anglo-American culture into the twenty-first century. In other words, I think this study is important because, for better or worse, some of this is still funny.

CHAPTER ONE

Funny Women

What do critics and playwrights mean when they call a play a comedy? I begin my inquiry into the first staged comedies written by British women with this deceptively simple question. Fredric Jameson asserts that "genres are essentially literary institutions, or social contracts between a writer and a specific public" that promise to identify the appropriate use of a text or artifact.[1] His functional insight about genre provides a first answer to my question: playwrights promise their audience a particular kind of play when they put comedy on the title page. Behn jokes about this promise in the preface to *The Dutch Lover,* where, "having inscrib'd Comedy on the beginning of my Book, you may guess pretty near what peny-worths you are like to have, and ware your money and your time accordingly" (*Works* V: 160). The difficulty for literary critics and historians is in ascertaining what that social contract meant at a particular moment in history.[2] The most likely promise made to the audience in that generic contract after Shakespeare is the guarantee of a play that culminates in a marriage that affirms the community. While there are comic narratives and plays that incorporate marriage before the Reformation and before Shakespeare, the familiar rubrics of comedy and tragedy may not, as Brian Corman and Glynne Wickham argue, have been the primary categories of plays for earlier audiences.[3] After Shakespeare, most writers of stage comedies turned to the Greek New Comedy for their plots, which placed a greater emphasis on courtship and marriage than Aristophanic, satiric, or Jonsonian comedies had. Imperfect as this description is, it identifies the narrative thrust of most stage comedies in Restoration and eighteenth-century England.

Comedies about marriage in this period, as I will argue in my next chapter, reflect historical changes in marriage law that elevated and then diminished women's standing as agents within the institution. But marriage is only part of the comic contract. Comedy also refers to scenes, events, or exchanges that offer their viewers and listeners concentrated moments of pleasure through witty dialogue, jokes, farce, and repartee. The happy ending and the comic scenes or events of a play work together to generate the kind of dramatic experience audiences, critics, and playwrights called good comedy. My dialectic of comic events and comic structures illuminates some of the psychological mechanisms of comedy. The witty exchanges of couples, the discussions about money, the comparison of successful with failed lovers, the weddings, and the engagements provided comic marriage lessons to audiences who were bribed with their own laughter to assent to the logic of the comic event.

Following the lead of the critical conversation in the period, which focused on the comic rather than the narrative definition of comedy, I begin with a brief history of comic theory to reassert the place of the comic within studies of the genre. Comic events, in the estimation of Hobbes, Fielding, Shaftesbury, Shadwell, and others, were potential sites of danger as well as sources of pleasure for the audience. Their arguments that the writer of comedy had an obligation to uphold social standards clash with the pronouncements of Behn and Centlivre, who positioned themselves as populist writers seeking to entertain and please their paying audience. When Cowley and Inchbald entered the theatrical conversation later in the century, they inherited the terms of comic pleasure, populism, and financial gain that Behn, Centlivre, and their critics had established along with the older didactic arguments about the comic playwright's responsibilities. Prologues, prefaces, and reviews had created the "woman's comedy," and subsequent critical elaboration of the category left them either to celebrate or to distance themselves from it. The audience's experience of those comedies was framed by reminders that the audience was watching (or reading) a woman's play. What was funny, appealing, or subversive about it was in part a function of the author's gender.

The female playwrights who succeeded commercially in the genre used the formal qualities of comedy to explore the crises of marriage before they made good on their guarantee to the audience that the social order would be preserved and even strengthened by comic closure. Their humorous arguments for female agency in comic events capitalize on the genre's attention to heroines' desires. The playwright who refuses to grant authority to the desires of female characters turns a constrained but ultimately successful Miranda or Anne Lovely into a tragic Clarissa. The formal importance of female desire to these stage comedies conflates a generic with an historical question: under what circumstances can a woman's will be meaningfully acknowledged before and after marriage? The most popular plays by these playwrights worked through this knotty question in comic tropes that turned the contradictions of civil law into opportunities for female agency, and in comic plots that had already promised the audience their happy ending.

Comic Danger, Comic Pleasure

The motley history of comic theory is something of a shaggy dog story; Aristotle lost the second book of *Poetics,* somebody lost the *Margites,* and what is lost on most comic theorists is this great joke of history. The lack of a text to balance Aristotle's theories of tragedy left the future generations of Western literary critics to supply or, more often, ignore comic theory. Aristotle makes the most general pronouncements about comedy: comedy imitates persons below our world; comedy is not the same as lampoon; and comedy usually ends without death. He uses the *Margites,* a burlesque attributed to Homer, to justify his claim that Homer "was the first to mark out the main lines of comedy. . . . [A]s are his *Iliad* and *Odyssey* to our tragedies, so is the *Margites* to our comedies" (*Poetics* 17: 4.12). The inability of later generations to consider the import of this lost comedy has foiled not only consensus on the bases of comic theory but the possibility of even knowing key moments in its lineage in the West. Comedy, even in Aristotle's time, was always already in a state of neglect; until 465 B.C., the chorus for comedy was composed of volunteers as opposed to professionals. Aristotle admits that much of comedy's history, including its earliest poets, prologue writers, and innovators, is not known "because it was not at first treated seriously" (*Poetics* 21: 5.3).

Northrop Frye, C. L. Barber, Fredric Jameson, and others have contributed to the critical discourse on comedy by separating comedy as a narrative category from questions of the comic or humorous, which allows them to elaborate on the shapes and values of comedies. But the division overlooks the way that comic narratives and comic events or moments are intertwined, particularly in stage comedy, which depends on both elements for success. The lack of a single entry under "humor" or "laughter" in Frye's *Anatomy of Criticism,* the dry assessment of sub-genres in studies by Nicoll and Hume, and the serious account of early eighteenth-century comedy by Krutch are a few examples of this genre-driven sensibility.[4] Their insights about form come at the expense of more disruptive and fleeting comic pleasures. The risks that comic playwrights take, which are necessary to make people laugh, gamble on the audience's response to the visual and textual jokes that get the reader to the promised ending. I will return to the structural and narrative dimensions of comedy, but first I sketch a brief history of humor, its function in comic events, and its volatile relation to gender.

Contrary to this twentieth-century critical trend, Restoration and eighteenth-century critics were most likely to discuss the humorous moments of comedies and caution writers of their volatile pedagogical potential. Prince

Hoare, in his 1809 introduction to Elizabeth Inchbald's "Essay on the Stage" in *The Artist,* quotes "an observation in one of Reynold's excellent comedies, that 'the most *serious* thing in nature is a *joke*'" (3). Samuel Johnson registered that sense of danger in *The Rambler* when he called wit "the unexpected copulation of ideas," a particularly threatening metaphor for the female comedian.[5] The strong sense that comic events are up to something, or that their pleasures might be dangerous, is the doppelgänger of Horace's utilitarian argument that comedy can delight and instruct. Horace's insights in *Ars Poetica* dominated discussions about the use of comedy and the definitions that grew from the supposition that it should do something more than please. But the danger of bad instruction seemed greater than the benefits of good comic lessons.

One of the most important early modern meditations on the dangers of the comic is Thomas Hobbes's 1651 entry on laughter in *Leviathan.* Hobbes describes laughter as rooted in the passion of "Sudden Glory," which causes the physical response of a "grimace" or laugh. Laughter comes "by some sudden act of their own, that pleaseth them; or by the apprehension of some deformed thing in another, by comparison whereof they suddenly applaud themselves" (125). Hobbes's account of laughter as superiority reflects the general tenor of the assumptions in *Leviathan* about human competitiveness, cruelty, and selfishness in the state of nature. In his catalogue of the passions, laughter falls on the side of evil or "turpe"; the laughing party indicates that he or she has a weaker character than the great mind whose mission it is to free others from scorn. Hobbes's moral analysis urges his readers to resist laughter *qua* scorn as an abuse of power, which leaves little place for the comic in a good society.

Working with variations on Horace's plea for "*miscuit utile dulci*" (blended usefulness and pleasure), Dryden, Congreve, Farquhar, Shaftesbury, and others claimed that comedy existed to naturalize correct social behavior by mocking faults.[6] Congreve declares that humor is "either to be born with us, and so a Natural Growth; or else to be grafted into us, by some accidental change in the Constitution, or revolution of the Internal Habit of Body." Humor, for Congreve, "shews us as we are," while for Dryden, it paints "some extravagant habit, passion, or affectation; particular (as I said before) to some one person: by the oddness of which, he is immediately distinguish'd from the rest of men."[7] The implication of both claims is that comedy, through humor, has the potential to correct error. Congreve returns to this normalizing comic pedagogy in his late-career assertion that it is "the business of Comedy to render Vice ridiculous, to expose it to public Derision and Contempt, and to make Men ashamed of Vile and Sordid Actions."[8] Congreve called on playwrights to use their comic powers for good rather than evil by limiting humor to instructive comparisons. Dryden argued for particularly nationalist uses of comedy as part of the work of creating an English cultural tradition and disseminating cultural values to the population. Dryden valued the repartee of comic dialogue, something he claims the English do best in his *Essay on Dramatic Poesy,* but the main stream of his thought sees good theater as a means to cultural and political ends. Farquhar's point that "an English Play is intended for the Use and Instruction of an English Audience," was one among many in the eighteenth century that furthered Dryden's plan to establish an English literary tradition, with comedy as its centerpiece.[9]

Shaftesbury's 1711 treatise, *Characteristics of Men, Manners, Opinions, Times, etc.,* picked up the nationalist banner of comic theory. Shaftesbury's Lockean intellectual disposition and his Whig politics frame his argument within the terms of Enlightenment ideologies of improvement: "'Tis the habit alone of reasoning which can make a reasoner. And men can never be better invited to the habit than when they find pleasure in it. A freedom of raillery, a liberty in decent language to question everything, and an allowance of unraveling or refuting any argument, without offense to the arguer, are the only terms which can render such speculative conversations any way agreeable" (1: 49). Shaftesbury's "raillery" will correct those who stray from the normative path of "reason." To illustrate his point, he imagines a "native of Ethiopia" who comes to Europe for the first time during the carnival season and laughs at the fantastic celebration. If the Ethiopian also laughed at the "natural face and habit," Shaftesbury claims, he would be guilty of "carrying the jest too far; when by a silly presumption he took nature for mere art, and mistook perhaps a man of sobriety and sense for one of those ridiculous mummers" (1: 57). The comic, for Shaftesbury, cannot give way to confusion of national and cultural norms; the Ethiopian "other" and the Catholic carnival must bow to the sensible, natural, and unfunny European. Genial raillery, assures Shaftesbury, will render the divisions between the natural and unnatural self-evident, even to a cultural outsider, though his example suggests the local quality of the social order. To stabilize the uses of laughter, Shaftesbury holds both audience and actors to the universality of Great Britain's bourgeois, Protestant, and colonial values.

Fielding's 1742 preface to *Joseph Andrews* distinguishes the comic from the burlesque, although his theatrical narrative style (particularly the farcical night adventures episode of chapter 14) blurs the distinction. The difference between the comic and the burlesque, according to Fielding, is that the comic expresses a more realistic vision of class. In the burlesque, he finds confusion about class and economics: " . . . were we to enter a poor house and behold a wretched family shivering with cold and languishing with hunger, it would not incline us to laughter (at least we must have very diabolical natures if it would); but should we discover there a grate, instead of coals, adorned with flowers, empty plate or china dishes on the sideboard, or any other affectation of riches or finery either on their persons or in their furniture, we might then indeed be excused for ridiculing so fantastical an appearance" (11). The affectation and the "fantastical . . . appearance" justifies his scorn for these hypothetical poor but pretentious people. While they are literally suffering from their misapprehension of wealth as display rather than as a means for survival, they are participating in the same cultural logic that any upwardly mobile middle class family of the time might use. What comedy must do, says Fielding, is encourage proper class and social identifications. Comedy can teach readers or viewers the "natural" discernment of class behaviors through the corrective of laughter. His concern updates Horace's aesthetic plea, "Let each style keep the becoming place allotted it," with this social addendum: let the comic characters keep their places as well (459: 91–92). Fielding reminds us that the didactic dimension of comic theory should not be separated from the political and economic content of the plays, which interpolate audiences into the social order.[10] The subject matter of comedy, the courtship and marriage of wealthy young people within their own social class, frames the critics' calls for plays that uphold the social order.

The arguments about the positive uses of comedy to correct and educate the public find their opposites in the religiously conservative and anti-monarchical critics of the theater. In the late seventeenth-century backlash against Restoration theater, John Tillotson, Richard Baxter, and Jeremy Collier resurrected Cromwellian objections to the theater and joined them to classical arguments about the uses of art to rail against the sexual content of comedies, which they perceived to be a threat to public morality. Tillotson, who gained the admiration of John Dryden for his prose, argued that the instructional value of plays was lost in the current theatrical climate, where instead plays "do most notoriously minister both to infidelity and to vice. By the profaneness of them, they are apt to instil bad principles into the minds of men, and lessen the awe and reverence which all men ought to have for God and religion; and by their lewdness they teach Vice, are apt to infect the minds of men, and dispose them to lewd and dissolute practices."[11] Richard Baxter had likewise argued that plays represent "sin in a manner to entice men to it, rather than to make it odious, making a sport and a mock of sin."[12] Even Shadwell (however disingenuously) criticized what he perceived as a moral problem in the theater in his preface to *The Royal Shepherdess:* "I find, it pleases most to see Vice encouraged, by bringing the Characters of debauch'd People upon the Stage, and making them pass for fine Gentlemen, who openly profess Swearing, Drinking, Whoring, breaking Windows, beating Constables, &etc."[13] Shadwell's immediate target was the libertine license of men like Rochester and Sedley, made more glamorous by Etherege and Wycherley. Like Baxter and Collier, Shadwell expresses a desire to mold public opinion, but he fears that comic playwrights are already doing this work. The commentaries try to center this didactic function on the question of vice, but, like the most morally ardent of these tracts, Collier's *A Short View of the Prophaneness and Immorality of the English Stage,* Shadwell's argument fragments into diatribes on class and social order. His concern that comedies encouraged bad behavior is secondary to the fear that "debauch'd people" were mussing up the category of "fine Gentlemen."

Collier, who refuses to quote from the plays in question because "'Tis my business rather to kill the Root than Transplant it," attests to the power of comedy, which would gain force and fresh life through any quotation, even if the context were damning. He hides his nervousness about the hydralike comic behind complaints about the need for more sophisticated comedies that distinguish between the lewd and the socially inferior: "Some People appear Course, and Slovenly out of Poverty; They can't well go to the Charge of Sense. They are Offensive like Beggars for want of Necessities. But this is none of the *Plain Dealer's* case; He can afford his Muse a better Dress when he pleases."[14] The danger of comedy, in addition to its ability to bloom where planted, is that it encourages slumming. His first general complaint, that "The Poets make Women speak Smuttily" and his second that "They Represent their single Ladys, and Persons of Condition, under these Disorders of Liberty" assume male playwrights have neglected their comic responsibility to write female characters who are more chaste and less free (15; 19). These (male) playwrights have been unmanly in pandering to low audiences and have, as John Dennis suggested, prostituted their talents and thus become more like women. Collier's paranoid treatise makes visible the connection between the agency of comedy and the market forces of the modern theater that put the playwright at the service of public pleasure.

James Beattie's 1764 *On Laughter and Ludicrous Composition* takes a less puritanical tone and advocates the social uses of comedy, but he also maintains that the danger within comedy must be tamed. He distinguishes between the ludicrous, a pure source of laughter, and the ridiculous, which is full of the contempt and cruelty that makes men "monsters." Without moral limits, the power of comedy is too anarchic. Beattie interprets laughter as evidence of the human capacity for delight, which is "beyond the reach of every other animal" but which does not in its purest form entail feelings of superiority over other people (298). He challenges Thomas Hobbes's account of the implicit power arrangements of laughter with his own sociological observations about pride: "persons of singular gravity [are] often suspected of that vice, but great laughers seldom or never. . . . If laughter arose from pride, and that pride from a sudden conception of some present eminency in ourselves, compared with others, or compared with ourselves as we were formerly, it would follow—that the wise, the beautiful, the strong, the healthy, and the rich must giggle away a great part of their lives . . ." (310). Beattie opens the field of the comic to authors and spectators who do not have positions of power, but who are still able to make humorous observations about the incongruities of life. In the tradition of Tillotson and Collier, Beattie claims that comedies such as *The Provok'd Wife, The Old Bachelor,* and *The Beggar's Opera* are dangerous because they might lead the audience to imitate their attractive reprobates. He assumes, however, the good humor and good sense of the audience, whose laughter is a sign of their cheer and their sound judgment. Even though Beattie aims at the general subject, laughter and laughable compositions, he emphasizes the sociality and social function of laughter through references to the theater. The rhetorical relations of authors, actors, and spectators are all part of the comic equation, though the responsibility for managing the results falls squarely on the author.

The array of comic treatises in the long eighteenth century, including the comic theory put forward in prologues and prefaces, generally agree that comedy is potentially dangerous, that it can be useful, and that it shapes public attitudes toward gender and class. Comedy's alleged instructional work had everything to do with the preservation of class prerogatives and of the role that women played in the transmission of wealth in marriage, particularly in its narrative or structural demands.[15] But the implicit and explicit situation of comedy as theatrical in arguments as diverse as Collier's, Shaftesbury's, Fielding's, and Beattie's had less to do with narrative structure and more to do with the local comic events that pleased audiences. Comedy's pleasures, to which Behn, Centlivre, Cowley, and Inchbald seemed particularly attuned, threatened to overtake its more normative social functions of improving and regulating behavior. While a comedy's ending might affirm marriage and familial duty, its plot might also be overrun with vivacious, witty women who challenge the principle of coverture that declares women legally absorbed into the personae of their husbands. Female characters were at the heart of the comic pleasures and dangers that obsessed eighteenth-century critics.

Aphra Behn entered the London theater world in 1670 with *The Forc'd Marriage* 28 years before Collier penned his critique. Even though she predates the Collier controversy, she still managed to unsettle critical norms by defying the Horatian tradition of useful comedy in favor of the pleasurable populism that Collier and others feared. In the preface to *The Dutch Lover,* she declares that she has hung out the sign "comedy" and "inscrib'd Comedy on the beginning of my Book," which makes her work a popular effort to please rather than a pedantic effort to teach:

> And as for Comedie, the finest folks you meet with there, are still unfitter for your imitation, for though within a leaf or two of the Prologue, you are told

> that they are people of Wit, good Humour, good Manners, and all that: yet if the Authors did not kindly add their proper names, you'd never know them by their characters . . . even those persons that were meant to be the ingenious Censors of the Play, have either prov'd the most debauch'd, or most unwittie people in the Companie. . . . I take it Comedie was never meant, either for a converting or a conforming Ordinance: In short, I think a Play the best divertisement that wise men have: but I do also think them nothing so, who do discourse as formallie about the rules of it, as if 'twere the grand affair of humane life. This being my opinion of Plays, I studied only to make this as entertaining as I could. . . . (*Works* V: 161–62)

The alleged instructional benefit of imitating good characters breaks down, Behn says, in the contract between playwright and audience for comic pleasure. Although she also claimed that plays were "secret instructions to the people," she had little patience with "converting or conforming" through moral comedy. She mocks critical language in her references to "Indiscerpibility and Essential Spissitude (words, which though I am no competent Judge of, for want of Languages, yet I fancy strongly ought to mean just nothing)," just the sort of overblown and laughable seriousness that critics, not playwrights, generate (*Works* V: 160).

Centlivre echoes Behn's populism in a letter to Robert Boyer: "I think the main design of Comedy is to make us laugh. . . . [I]f the Poet can be so happy as to divert our Spleen, 'Tis but just he should be commended for it."[16] In her preface to *Love's Contrivance* (1703), she complains that classical standards have nothing to do with dramatic success, which depends on "Wit and Humour" and the talents of the players (*Works* I). In her polemical dedication to *The Platonic Lady* (1707) she believes that even her "spleenetic" critics will be "pleased against their Will" by her comedy, whether they will admit it or not (*Works* II). Her jibe suggests that her critics were uncomfortable with pleasure, particularly comic pleasure, as a criterion for judging plays. Their resistance to the pleasures of comedy also comes from their understanding of the distribution of power in the theater; they know that audiences, not critics, could buoy or ruin a show by expressing their pleasure and their sense of the play's entertainment value.[17] As Farquhar noted: "To make the Moral Instructive, you must make the Story diverting; the Spleenatick Wit, the Beau Courtier, the heavy Citizen, the fine Lady, and her fine Footman, come all to be instructed, and therefore must all be diverted; and he that can do his best, and with most Applause, writes the best Comedy, let him do it by what Rules he pleases, so they be not offensive to Religion and good Manners. . . . [T]he rules of English comedy don't lie in the compass of Aristotle or his followers but in the pit, box, and galleries" (*Works* II: 378).

Farquhar's life-long poverty forced him to please the paying public rather than the aesthetic elite. His disenfranchisement, relative to playwrights with more cultural or financial capital, such as Vanbrugh, Congreve, Cibber, or Steele, aligned him with the most successful women writers. Though he tries to walk the line between use and pleasure, he is a part of the new breed of literary professionals who looked to public taste rather than aesthetic principles and critical validation for their artistic direction.

The ability and willingness to reject aesthetic standards proved enabling for Behn and Centlivre, who shared a lack of formal education. Centlivre claimed her "Disadvantage of Education, and the Privilege of my Sex" in her dedication of *A Bold Stroke for a Wife* to Phillip, second marquis of Wharton. Behn regarded the Greek and Latin underpinnings of the critical tradition with some suspicion, and she chose to challenge them rather than to be intimidated by them, though she had mastered French and read Descartes.[18] Behn's exclusion from formal education made her "common" understanding a gendered as well as a populist issue. She gestures to the opposition of comedy and theory in the epilogue to *Sir Patient Fancy:* "Your learned Cant of Action, Time and Place,/ Must all give way to the unlabor'd Farce." Farce, she argues, takes over the bodily reserve of the spectator, demanding laughter and a temporary suspension of the rules of rationality. She describes a process similar to the Freudian "release" theory of comedy, which claims that jokes allow a person to make absurd or socially inappropriate connections that the psyche would normally prevent. The pleasure one feels from a joke or comic event is a surplus of energy, due to the momentary relaxation of the psyche's self-policing activities. "Unlabor'd Farce," which undercuts the unities, also challenges the authority of normalizing, socially conservative models of the comic (like Congreve's, Shaftesbury's, and Fielding's) that present themselves in the language of aesthetics.

Behn's and Centlivre's thoughts on comic theory, which emphasize pleasure over aesthetic purpose, find a modern advocate in Susanne Langer's 1953 *Feeling and Form: A Theory of Art.* Langer claims that comedy is impious, risqué, and full of energy, positions that Behn affirms in her plays and prefaces. Langer conceptualizes the comic as force that preserves the impulse to life in an inanimate universe, a position with similarities to Henri Bergson's. Bergson's *élan vital* or vital impulse remains outside the purview of logic. This crucial conceptual space is part of Bergson's resistance to the mechanism of nineteenth-century thought in *Le Rire* or *Laughter,* even though he could not entirely escape mechanical structures. He returns a mystical (as opposed to rational) dimension to the comic that values the lightness and movement of comic energy above any logical structure or formula. The pleasure created through this comic energy, however, raises questions of artistic quality and propriety. Comedy, it seems, will do anything for a laugh, and Langer retreats from the populist call of the comic by invoking aesthetic standards. Langer cautions would-be authors that comedy's sensuous qualities make it "tempting to command an audience by direct stimulation of feeling and fantasy, not by artistic power" (349). She tries to contain the pleasurable work that comedy does by juxtaposing "artistic power" to "direct stimulation" and by separating comedy's affective appeal from the aesthetic qualities of "true art." Built into Langer's assumptions, however, is a hierarchy of aesthetic values that presupposes comedy's inferiority to tragedy.

James Beattie's theory of comic pleasure, which is contemporary with the plays in this study, avoids the value-laden discussion of aesthetic merit and turns instead, as Behn had, to the question of how comic pleasure operates. He anticipates Freud's insight in his 1905 *Jokes and Their Relation to the Unconscious* that comic pleasure comes from the liberating experience of connecting ideas that we normally separate. Beattie argued that laughter, which tends to come from comic events in which individuals, verbal exchanges, or situations strike the audience as comic, requires the viewer to recognize an alternative logic that engages the spectator by drawing her or him into an assessment. He claims that comic objects call for "a sort of Ironical Reasoning, not easily described, which would seem to derive the ludicrous character from a surprising mixture of Plausibility and Absurdity" (333). Examples of this reasoning include mistaking effects for causes, discovering that unrelated objects are related and uniting incongruous objects through contiguity. These comic responses are the effects of a mental comparison that leads to the "agreeable emotion," laughter. The existence of such a form of reasoning that leads to laughter sets up a comic unconscious, through which audiences could make connections together that might otherwise be suppressed.

Freud's original title, *Der Witz,* and its operative term, "wit," suggest a greater congruity between his and Beattie's studies than the translation "joke" implies. Freud's English translator Strachey renders *witz* as "joke" to avoid the connotation of intellectual humor and urbane sophistication that "wit" carries in English. The choice, however, obscures the mental function that the German word implies, replacing it instead with the notion of a concrete product, the "joke."[19] Freud describes the witticism (or joke) as something that conserves psychical energy by providing a mental "short cut" from one idea to another. The short cut saves the energy that is otherwise necessary to keep concepts separate in the conscious mind. He elaborates several different joking techniques, including condensation, substitution, repetition, and double meaning, which create an acknowledged parallel between Freud's *Interpretation of Dreams* and his work on jokes. He concludes "all these techniques are dominated by a tendency to compression, or rather to saving. It all seems to be a question of economy. In Hamlet's words: 'Thrift, thrift, Horatio!'"(42). The joke exemplifies some of the same unconscious processes that dreams do in circumventing the repressive force of the conscious mind. Behn's and Centlivre's discussions of comic pleasure, while they decline to elaborate on its mechanisms, emphasize its ease. Behn, in the preface to *The Dutch Lover,* juxtaposes the true comedy of pleasure and ease with classical definitions of comedy, particularly the unities. She claims that she "studied only to make this [comedy] as entertaining as I could . . ." and adds that with so many ridiculous people in London, writing comedies is not that difficult (*Works* V: 162). Similarly, Centlivre claims in the preface to *Love's Contrivance* that classical rules for comedy cause playwrights unnecessary trouble, when the audience "relishes nothing so well as Humour lightly tossed up with Wit, and dressed with Modesty and Air" (preface, *Love's Contrivance, Works* I). Behn's anti-intellectual reproach of "serious" comedy and Centlivre's comic salad are the pattern of Beattie's and Freud's insights; the dividend of comic pleasure takes the spectator away from conscious, rational paradigms of knowledge and allows for greater freedom of play and association.

The comic freedoms that Behn and Centlivre celebrate are different, however, than the witticism or joke model in that they take place in a sustained and predetermined narrative structure. Freud applies his principle of economic savings and evasion of psychological restrictions to his specific investigation into the comic. The comic unfolds more gradually than the burst of the joke or the instant of the witty remark. The comic, like jokes, can overcome internal obstacles (repression) and external obstacles such as authority figures and social restrictions, giving pleasure to viewers as vicarious participants in the victory. According to Freud, it entails a comparison of something less known with something better known: "Every such comparison, especially of something abstract with something concrete, involves a certain degradation and a certain economy in expenditure on abstraction" that brings pleasurable relief through the energy liberated from repression, though the comic relief is not as rapid as that of the joke (210). He also locates the comic within the realm of human society; the comic springs from observing human social relations, human movement, and an implicit judgment that an observer makes on the comic spectacle.[20] Beattie's emphasis on the social implications of laughter and Shaftesbury's account of raillery as the basis for sociality itself provide important historical contexts for Freud's theoretical insights about comic pleasure.

"Ironical reasoning" in stage comedies happens first in the space of the theater, where comic risks have to be tempered by a sense of what the audience in general rather than the individual psyche will bear. Playwrights must enlist the audience in comparisons and the implicit norms behind them through comic events that inflect the marriage plot. When Centlivre's Anne Lovely strikes back at her Puritan guardian, Mrs. Prim, in *A Bold Stroke for a Wife,* she uses a joke to enlist the audience in her cause. Mrs. Prim chides that Anne's fashionable clothes and patches are unnatural and frightening, but Anne retorts: "If it shou'd turn your Inside outward, and show all the Spots of your Hypocrisy, 'twou'd fright me worse" (V.i, 51). Anne targets Mr. and Mrs. Prim's closeted erotic lives, which lurk behind the veneer of purity, to speak into consciousness the sexual motives that Anne and the audience know are at work in the plot. The joke gives the audience permission to complete the connection and to join in the laugh at the Prim's expense. Unlike the novel, where reflection in tranquility characterizes the reading process, stage comedy's success depends on the swift response of the audience. This responsiveness gives playwrights opportunities to normalize their points of view by subjecting the behavior of characters who undermine their heroines' choices to public ridicule.

Cowley and Inchbald comment cautiously about the normalizing power of laughter, which they also learned to tap. Their pronouncements are close to Langer's suspicion of the comic, but they make clear the playwright's status as commercial entertainer. Cowley, in "The Present State of the Stage," written for *The Pocket Magazine,* laments that character development is losing to the tyranny of laughter. "LAUGH! LAUGH! LAUGH! is the demand. Not a word must be uttered that looks like instruction," though she admits that she writes these words after her active career as a playwright: "I have *made* such things, and I blush to have made them."[21] It was perhaps easier for Cowley to recant in this more conservative late-century moment after her ties to the box office were severed. Inchbald offers a more general complaint about writing for the stage, drawn from her own successes with the comedy. "The Dramatic Writer exists but under a despotic government—Passing over the subjection in which an author of plays is held by the Lord Chamberlain's office, and the degree of dependence which he has on his actors—he is the very slave of the audience. He must have their tastes and prejudices in view, not to correct, but to humour them."[22] Inchbald represents the tension between aesthetics and comic pleasure as a contest always decided in favor of the public's demand for comic pleasure. Cowley and Inchbald made these statements late in their careers and at a time of conservative reaction to the French Revolution, which displayed the force of populism in the most politically immediate terms. Their responses, especially Cowley's, suggest a concern about being read as inappropriate or pandering to public taste. But Cowley and Inchbald were also frustrated by their inability to change public taste. Comedy, more than any other literary mode, is a form in which an author can find herself struggling over generic expectations and the limits of her comic contract with the audience. The public expectations of the past, reproduced through repertoire plays, shape the public expectations of the present, and the playwright who seeks to change comedy labors against the force of these repetitions.

The concept of the comic event as the impetus to laughter helps to clarify the psychological power of stage comedy. The comic event instructs viewers and readers with their own laughter in perspectives that may challenge or alter the overt lessons of the comic plot. In plays, these joking moments are refracted through the performer and situated by the narrative context of the play as a whole, conditions which distinguish comic events from isolated jokes. But comic events still offer the "bribe" of jokes, the momentary permission to think across boundaries and to entertain logical or social impossibilities. Considered in relation to Freud's psychoanalytic model of the joke's aggressive pleasures, comic events give female playwrights and their characters the power to articulate social norms within the boundaries of what the audience will entertain. The popularity of these four female playwrights in their own eras and in repertoire testifies to their ability to satisfy the audience's taste, but they also pushed and prodded with their own forms of comic pedagogy. The jokes and comic events that female characters orchestrate in these plays provide important leverage against the weight of the marriage ending. These events help to build the comic authority of female characters who can negotiate the terms of their marriage contracts, and they open the larger discussion of what those negotiations might look like.

"Because a Woman's"

When Aphra Behn lamented that her play *Sir Patient Fancy* had been attacked as bawdy because "*from a Woman it was unnatural,*" she gestured both to the gender battles fought by early professional women writers and to the theoretical problem that women writing comedy generated. Most ancient and modern theories of comedy insist on the unmarked and universal position of the joker who creates comic speech, a position that Behn and other women could not automatically occupy. Congreve, who put the matter starkly in his "Concerning Humour in Comedy," declared:

> . . . methinks something should be observed of the Humour of the Fair Sex; since they are sometimes so kind as to furnish out a Character for Comedy. But I must confess I have never made any Observation of what I Apprehend to be true Humour in Women. Perhaps Passions are too powerful in that Sex, to let Humour have its Course; or may be by reason of their Natural Coldness, Humour cannot Exert itself to that extravagant Degree, which it often does in our Male Sex.[23]

The lack of humor in women comes, he speculates, from some essential difference between men and women. But his explanations for this difference, either too much passion or too much coldness, are contradictory. Women fall out of the register of humor, just as they tend to be disqualified as valid jokers in most comic theory. Like Reginald Horace Blythe, who claimed that "women are the undifferentiated mass of nature from which the contradictions of real and ideal arose and they are the unlaughing at which men laugh," most comic theorists have taken as read that women are comic objects, not comic subjects.[24] Critics and practitioners from Lucian and Rabelais to Wycherley and Smollett tend to valorize the aggressive and the smutty, masculine prerogatives for jokers with the social license to take risks. For Hazlitt, Freud, and other theorists of comedy, "to modify humor meant to compromise it," to emasculate it and fit it for women, who were not heirs to its domain (Gillooly 4). Congreve's voice is one among many over the last 400 years which have asserted that women are not in themselves funny, regardless of evidence to the contrary.

G. W. F. Hegel and, more recently, Susan Purdie have positioned the joker as a dominating figure whose body and circumstances do not impinge on *his* comic speech. Hegel insists that comedy depends on the position of complete mastery that the comic writer or speaker enjoys. In his *Philosophy of History,* he asserts that "comedy is a world in which man has made himself, in his conscious activity, complete master of all that otherwise passes as the essential content of his knowledge and achievement. . . . Infinite geniality and confidence capable of rising superior to its own contradiction and experiencing therein no taint of bitterness or sense of misfortune whatever."[25] This lack of what Purdie has called "implicating context" keeps comedy floating free from worldly concerns, which would bring the comic vision crashing back down to earth (81). The use that Behn, Centlivre, and Cowley make of contracts *de presenti* and clandestine marriages are ways of wishing away the "implicating context" of marriage law and parental prerogatives in elite marriages. But the position of neutrality for the writer of comedy eluded these writers, who brought their perspectives as women to bear on their comic plots. Purdie makes this point inadvertently when she identifies the exchange of women as one of her three categories of comic exchange, reminding her readers that lack of implicating context requires a male body in most situations.

Freud claims that viewers or readers could find a scene or play comic without knowing its author, but the bodies, or at least the gendered identities, of the first female playwrights became a part of their comedies. The fact that the plays can, contrary to the eighteenth century's fascination with authorship, be enjoyed without knowing the identity of the author contradicts the fact that they usually were not. While an author's name was not always posted on playbills, the prefaces, prologues, and epilogues of plays from 1660 to 1800 do attend to the gender of the author. Between gossip in the pit, newspaper reviews and, most importantly, prologues, the gender if not the identity of a playwright was usually established by opening night. In this sense, it is information that functions, like genre, to frame a reading. Joseph Addison observes in the *Spectator,* no. 1, that "a Reader seldom peruses a Book with Pleasure, 'till he knows whether the Writer of it be a black or a fair Man, of a mild or cholerick Disposition, Married or a Batchelor, with other particulars of the like nature, which conduce very much to the right understanding of an Author."[26] Addison identifies a strong biographical component of interpretation that he connects to a reader's pleasure. Without biographical information, says Addison, readers do not know how to identify with an author, but once they have it, they can relax into a pleasurable relationship of knowledge that enables their reading. The author imbues his or her text with meaning through his or her identity; no reading is, by this logic, autonomous, and no reading can be pleasurable without the information about the author that grounds the reading process. This process of placing a text *vis à vis* the author has everything to do with finding a comedy pleasurable, and it dominated the reviews and prefatory materials of women writers, such that the gender of the author became the most important "fact" one could know about a play. The stress that the theatrical apparatus placed on the importance of the author's gender to the play functioned as another dimension of generic expectation. The audience and the critics read the sex of the author as part of the comedy, even though it is a fact technically outside the plot.

Playwriting placed female authors in a public sphere of negotiation, performance, and commerce, unlike the more private worlds of novel and poetry writing. A commercially successful stage comedy, the most popular theatrical form, meant extraordinary benefits, particularly after Garrick introduced more careful bookkeeping practices and regularized charges owed to theater management. But it also put women into very direct competition with their male counterparts. Their sexual difference, which reviewers and theatergoers never tired of discussing, framed their public role as agents in this entertainment marketplace. For women, the commercial relationship of author to audience carried sexual connotations that painted the dramatist as a prostitute to the audience's pleasure. In Behn's case, the analogy became a staple for her detractors.[27] Wycherley declared that "Now Men enjoy your parts for Half a Crown,/ Which, for a Hundred Pound, they scarce had done," though he ends with a nod to the full house for *The City Heiress.* William Attwood suggested that Behn's "lustful Rage/Joyns to Debauch the too Effem'nate Age."[28] Attwood's concern goes beyond the subject position of the female author to fears about writers pandering to public appetite.

Churlish male critics and playwrights seized on the analogy between female playwrights and prostitutes to discredit professional women writers individually and en masse. In *A Comparison Between the Two Stages* (1702), the surly character Critic asks: "What a Pox have the Women to do with the Muses? I grant you the Poets call the Nine Muses by the Names of Women, but why so? not because the Sex had any thing to do with Poetry, but because in that Sex they're much fitter for prostitution."[29] The comment, which betrays as much anxiety about the rise of professional writing as it does about female authorship in general, echoes Gould's famous criticism of Behn's career, which equates female writers with prostitutes.[30] Women playwrights seemed both to possess and to lack the ability to make comedies in the eyes of their male colleagues. Dryden's support of Behn, though most of it was posthumous, and Farquhar's support of Centlivre balance the scales of critical opinion, but the criticisms continued to circulate and, in the case of Behn, to proliferate.[31]

Though their successes galled their critics, Behn, Centlivre, Cowley, and Inchbald share the distinction of succeeding both with their first audiences and in repertoire amid, as Judith Phillips Stanton describes it, "the most public and immediate of literary consequences: live audiences, payment on the third night, real applause, real derision."[32] The nature of their genre required them to please an audience that could either close a play or see it into repertoire, and their successes speak to their ability to fulfill the comic contract with the audience. Behn was second in popular success only to Dryden as a Restoration playwright, and Centlivre was the only playwright, male or female, with four plays among the most popular repertoire offerings of the eighteenth century. The 1695–1696 London season featured plays by women as 33 percent of its offerings, and women constituted roughly 10 percent of the new professional playwrights in the 1788–1790 seasons in London, which included Cowley and Inchbald.[33]

While the theatrical market was unpredictable and much less lucrative for Restoration and early-eighteenth-century writers, it held great rewards for later contributors. Behn made as little as £10 from the sale of a play manuscript, and between £20 and £30 for volumes of poetry and prose.[34] Generally, playwrights took the box-office receipts after expenses under the third-night system.[35] Behn's career was largely over by the time this regularized benefit was in place, so it is difficult to estimate her profits from the "full Third Day" performances she alludes to in the preface to *The Lucky Chance.* The incomplete records of Restoration theaters compound the difficulty. Like many other popular Restoration playwrights, she died in poverty. No receipts are recorded for Centlivre's benefit nights, though she would have received the house receipts minus £40 in costs. Link estimates that she made between £50 and £100 in box office receipts and £10 on the sale of each of the eight early plays, and between £100 and £150 in box office receipts and £21 apiece from Curll on the sale of *The Wonder, The Cruel Gift,* and *The Artiface.*[36] Contrary to Mr. Centlivre's complaint that he "barely [gets] his dinner" from Susanna's writing, her profits compare favorably with his £60 a year as yeoman of the mouth.

Hannah Cowley enjoyed the regularized charges of benefit nights from the beginning of her very successful career. Her first play earned over £719 in benefit nights. Though she made only £70 on the popular farce *Who's the Dupe?*, *The Belle's Stratagem* cleared more than £500. *The London Stage* records four benefit nights for *Which Is the Man?*, which brought in an estimated £500, and three benefit nights for *A Bold Stroke for a Husband*, which should have brought Cowley at least £400.[37] Inchbald, who left an estate of over £6,000 at her death in spite of her impoverished childhood and early widowhood, excelled at making money in the theater and the stock funds, where she religiously lodged her earnings. Robinson, who had published most of her plays, paid £200 for *A Simple Story* in 1791, but her earnings from original and translated stage plays outpaced profits from her novel writing, as the following figures show:

The Mogul Tale	£300
Appearance Is Against Them	£300
I'll Tell You What	£101 plus £200 from the sale of the script
Such Things Are	£900
Everyone Has His Fault	£700
Wise Man of the East	£500
To Marry or Not to Marry	£600
The Midnight Hour	£130
Animal Magnetism	£130
The Child of Nature	£50
The Married Man	£100
The Wedding Day	£200
Lover's Vows	£150

Inchbald made more money and made it at a faster rate as a playwright than as a novelist, and she took some pleasure in recording her successes.[38] *The Revels History of Drama* has put forth the opposite logic, that novel writing was more lucrative for women, as a general truism, citing Frances Burney's subscription profits on *Camilla* at £2,000.[39] While some novelists did command large sums, including Fielding's £1,000 for *Amelia*, Burney's subscription revenue was stunning for a novel in general and particularly for a woman, even one of her stature.[40] At the height of her popularity, Burney made only £250 from *Cecilia*, all of which was commandeered for "investment" and mismanaged into nonexistence by her father.[41] The top price Jane Austen received was £300 for *Emma*, well into her career. Burney's and

Austen's financial rewards for these novels, which took more time to write than *The Mogul Tale* or *Such Things Are,* were on par with or below Inchbald's earnings in the same time period.

Because of their considerable success, the public and the critics knew the gender of these four playwrights, though some attempted brief periods of anonymity. Reviewers tended to call attention to their sex, most often to damn with faint praise the light, natural, or, when they strayed from expectations, the unnatural efforts of the fair sex. The immediate tasks before a female playwright in this climate were to negotiate the terms of comic authorship for herself and to turn critical attention to her gender to her advantage. A swelling chorus of female authors lamented that the public could use their sex against them to dismiss their work as "a woman's comedy," a dismissal with immediate financial implications in the case of the third night benefit system. Behn claimed that rumblings about the sexual content of her plays have everything to do with her sex. She writes in the preface to *The Lucky Chance,* "if they find one Word that can offend the chastest Ear, I will submit to all their peevish Cavills; but Right or Wrong they must be Criminal because a Woman's" (7: 215). Her direct attack on the sexist discrimination against her comedies connected comic license and financial loss for her readers. Though she stretches the truth when she implies that *The Lucky Chance* is a chaste play, its merits and sexual mores are commensurate with comedies that preceded it by only a few years, such as Wycherley's *The Plain Dealer* (1676) and Shadwell's *The Virtuoso* (1676) and *Epsom Wells* (1672).

Behn's edgy representations of women and female desire challenge the Cartesian (and Platonic) truism that the soul or thinking self is distinct from the body it masters; it matters a great deal that her heroines are women who cannot transcend their bodies. Gallagher's insight that Behn's persona as prostitute also made her "nobody" should not obscure Behn's refusal of a disembodied or neutral position as a writer. The prologue to her first play, *The Forc'd Marriage,* challenges:

> Can any see that glorious Sight and say (*Woman pointing to the Ladies*)
> A Woman shall not Victor prove today?
> Who is't that to their Beauty would submit,
> And yet refuse the Fetters of their Wit? (5: 8)

The prologue complicates the notion of woman as object by allotting to women (and in particular Behn) the power of wit. Professional women in the theater, both in their spectacular object positions as players and their more distinct subject positions as writers, challenged the previously male profession at the same time that they provided it a boon by offering themselves as objects of desire to a paying public. In keeping with this productive tension, the prologue argues for a woman's "active valor" along with her passive attractions. Behn remains aware of the importance of who is speaking in the prefatory materials to her plays, an awareness that comic theory in general affirms. Behn freely used her sexual identity to promote and defend her plays. In all but one case, either the prologue, epistle, or epilogue to her plays mentions her sex, and most, whether in terms of reception or content, insist that her sex plays a significant role in her work as a writer.[42]

After Behn, the theater was theoretically more open to women writers, but the moral backlash of the 1690s, represented by Collier's *On the Immorality and the Profaneness of the Stage,* positioned women writers as sexual suspects as well as trespassers in a male preserve. In 1706, Susanna Centlivre "came out" as a woman after five years as a presumptively masculine "anon." with *Love at a Venture,* followed by *The Platonic Lady.* She addressed the issue of her sex by dedicating her second play "To all the Generous Encouragers of Female Ingenuity," echoing Behn's self-defense in the preface to *The Lucky Chance,* in which she claims the privilege for her "Masculine Part, the Poet in me." Centlivre, like Behn, was stung by gendered attacks on her plays, and argued that the best plays suffer the fate of being dismissed: "But, if by chance the Plot's discover'd, and the Brat found Fatherless, immediately it flags in the Opinion of those that extoll'd it before, and the Bookseller falls in his Price, with this Reason only. *It is a Woman's.* Thus they Alter their Judgement, by the Esteem they have for the Author, tho' the Play is still the same" (Preface to *The Platonick Lady, Works* II). Her personification of the play as a baby echoes Dryden's epilogue to Behn's *The Widow Ranter, or the History of Bacon in Virginia,* which calls the play "an Orphan Child, a bouncing Boy" in need of the audience's charity for his "keeping." And like Dryden's, Centlivre's anthropomorphized play raises questions about inheritance. Inheritance law established legitimacy through the male line, an imperfect parallel to the idea of authorship, which now had to accommodate the woman writer who creates and "parents" her text. The mothered but unfathered text becomes a bastard brat, though Centlivre's dedication disputes the logic with the claim that the play is the same, whether by a man or a woman. Here, Centlivre departs from Behn's performative gender politics in favor of the more liberal point, "for since the Poet is born, why not a Woman as well as a Man?" Centlivre's desire to posit not a male part but a female poet with equal talent reflects the sense of urgency with which she approached the Lockean contract crisis; if a male person is possible, why not a female person? Using the logic of individualism and the public persona of Queen Anne, "this Miracle, the Glory of our Sex," she makes the claim for a female subject in contract relations. Her strategy, however, is stymied again and again. Her liberal subject, the female playwright or heroine who can make contracts with either the audience or the hero, cannot escape her gender. The implicit exchange of cash for entertainment between audience and author unfolds in light of Centlivre's sex. As much as she would like to posit it, there is no neutral position from which she can make her comic contract with the audience and no neutral "Judgement" for her comedies. They are always gendered, and she is always tied to them.

The praise of the *Biographia Dramatica* for Centlivre as a "self-taught genius" and a female writer second only to Behn interweaves discomfort with her popularity in its praise. *The Busy Body* "forced a run of thirteen nights; while Mr. Congreve's *Way of the World,* which perhaps contains more true intrinsic wit, and unexceptionable accuracy of language, than any dramatic piece ever written, brought on the stage with every advantage of recommendation, and when the author was in the height of reputation, could scarcely make its way at all."[43] Francis Gentleman's *The Dramatic Censor* (1770) refers to Centlivre's "pretty, whimsical talent" and her productions as "more of froth than solidity; they may divert but cannot improve." Of *The Busy Body,* he writes: "if we search for solidity of sentiment, or purity of language in this comedy, our enquiry will be fruitless; yet there is a pertness of dialogue and a womanish whim of incident, that must ever tickle the lighter passions."[44] The easy causal connection between Centlivre's sex as a writer and the deficiency of her plays was part of a gendered aesthetic that challenged writers' claims to authorship, as it did in the charges of plagiarism leveled at Behn and Centlivre.[45] As Janet Todd, Jacqueline Pearson, Laura Rosenthal, and others have argued, Restoration and early-eighteenth-century women found it difficult if not impossible to own their writing publicly without also taking on the stigma of sexual immodesty or prostitution.[46] But perhaps the more insidious challenge to female authorship was the dismissal of their style.

The most pervasive tendency on the part of eighteenth-century critics was to soften their assessments of women's intellectual and creative efforts as feminine themselves. When Steele praises *The Busy Body* in Tatler, no. 19, May 24, 1709, he speaks of the "Subtilty of Spirit which is peculiar to Females of Wit" whose love stories are "the Effect of Nature and Instinct" rather than invention or skill. Sewell, in his prologue for Centlivre's *The Cruel Gift,* asserts her strengths, "Intrigue, and Plot, and Love," but undercuts his praise by exclaiming "The Devil's in it, if the *Sex* can't write/Those Things in which They take the most Delight." The common use of "the Sex" to refer to women in the Restoration and eighteenth century codes women as both more tied to their physical sex and more interested in sex, or at least intrigue, the "things" in which they delight to write. Sewell's chain of associations contaminates "the Sex" with connections to the devil, delight, and pleasure, all of which map onto women's writing in general and Centlivre's plays in particular. In this description, neither she nor her plays can escape her embodied position. Her body is both the secret to her success and the bar to full authorship, the unmarked position of (masculine) mastery.

Centlivre, who appreciated the nod from her fellow Whig, also registered her frustration with the sexist dismissal of her work. She reminds her readers that her greatest successes to date had been her anonymously presented plays, *Love's Contrivance* and *The Gamester.* She argues that she chose anonymity, hoping "to find some Souls Great enough to protect her against the Carping Malace of the Vulgar World." She illustrates her point with the anecdote of the spark who admired *The Gamester* and was on the verge of buying the book: "Having bought one of the Books, [he] ask'd who the Author was; and being told, a Woman, threw down the Book, and put up his Money, saying, he had spent too much after it already and was sure if the Town had known that, it wou'd never have run ten days."[47] Centlivre argues that women have excelled "in all Arts, in Musick, Painting, Poetry; also in War. . . . The mighty Romans felt the Power of Boadicea's Arm; Eliza made Spain tremble; but ANN, the greatest of the Three, has shook the Man that aim'd at Universal Sway." She argues that women are social subjects suited to tasks such as political leadership and professional writing, but she does so as Congreve, Addison, and Steele were nervously trying to define the professional writer. According to Jonathan Kramnick, their mainstream critical conversation invokes the feminine, first as a civilizing force and then as the threat of commercialization and the emasculation of national culture. The resulting hierarchy of masculine writing (independent, satiric, and intellectual) and feminine scribbling (popular, soft, and natural) opposes literary greatness to feminizing commercial success.[48] At the level of content, marriage stories contrasted with the heroic themes of "great" literature, and at the level of popular function, their status as mere commercial entertainment opposed an abstract and masculine category of timeless art.

Evaluations of Cowley's and Inchbald's plays as sentimental, artless, and gentle continued to separate women's writing from men's in a critical climate Ellen Donkin deems more hospitable to women. In the later eighteenth century, a critic who openly attacked a woman writer might be called illiberal, and the idea of female genius seemed more tenable to most critics (Donkin 20). James Boaden recalls the audience's response to Inchbald's *The Mogul Tale* upon discovering the sex of the author: "some thunder 'Bravo,' and some gaze and bless her! Young maidens wave their kerchiefs, and old women silently weep for joy."[49] But critics were still willing to be disparaging and patronizing. The prologue to *Appearance Is Against Them* compares Inchbald to a race horse who has won at smaller tracks and now tries "Newmarket's plain," a reference to this her first play at Covent Garden. Thomas Vaughan's prologue to *Such Things Are* refers to Inchbald as "Mrs. Scribble," who "dares *again* invade" the literary space of the theater. These references mark off playwriting as masculine, thus forcing female authors to supplicate, challenge, or invade as the first condition of their authorship.

Other prologues and epilogues that framed Cowley's and Inchbald's plays were less flattering. Garrick's prologue to Cowley's first play, *The Runaway,* advertises:

> O list! a tale it is, not very common;
> Our Poet of to-night, in faith's a—Woman . . .
> How she could venture here I am astonished;
> But 'twas in vain the Mad-cap I admonished . . .

Garrick's prologue is one of many that maintain the pretense of continual surprise that women do indeed write plays, which could not have been much of a surprise to anyone in 1776. Yet the rhetorical relationship of professional women to the theater seems to have been that of perpetual outsider, such that Joanna Baillie could describe her career in 1798 as "this new-found path attempting."[50] Part of this phenomenon had to do with the openly misogynist response of some writers to the presence of women in the professional theater, but a softer discourse of gendered private and public spaces also made the gender of these playwrights a topic of discussion. The tendency to represent women as trespassers, another variant of this type, intimates that women have encroached where they are not welcome and must beg a special day pass from the audience. Frances Sheridan, who penned her own prologue to her 1763 *The Discovery,* takes up this cliché when she describes herself as "a female culprit" confessing her "trespass" on poetic grounds:

> The fault is deem'd high-treason by the men,
> Those lordly tyrants who usurp the pen!
> Then try the vile monopoly to hide
> With flattering arts, "You ladies, have beside
> So many ways to conquer—sure 'Tis fit
> You leave to us that dangerous weapon wit!"[51]

Sheridan's dig at the male "monopoly" satirizes the various arguments in prologues and reviews which explain why women should "be debarr'd the use of pen and ink," like state criminals.

Sheridan's prologue embraces a more aggressive stance against misogyny, a stance that Hannah Cowley also took 16 years later in 1779. When the expected prologue did not appear for *Who's the Dupe?,* Cowley wrote her own, in which she laments that the modern "Learned Men" abuse and even invent women's faults in order to be witty:

> Sure then 'Tis fair one hour to give—
> 'Tis all she asks—a Woman leave
> To laugh at all those learned Men!

Like Sheridan's prologue, Cowley's describes the loaded and gendered terms of theatrical address. While this prologue was not spoken the first night, it identifies Cowley as a female comedian getting her day in the sun rather than as Garrick's "Mad-cap" protégé who can't be talked out of folly. The unknown authors of the prologue to *A Bold Stroke for a Husband* celebrate the "female sense" and "female virtue" that flow from Cowley's "female pen" in a relatively innocuous address that is nonetheless careful to keep the sex of this now-established writer before the audience.

Praise of female authors at the end of the century was also complicated by implicit as opposed to explicit sexual content, as in Colman the Younger's prologue to Inchbald's *I'll Tell You What,* which asserts:

> Our Author, is a Woman—that's a Charm
> Of Power to guard herself and Play from harm.
> The Muses, Ladies Regent of the Pen,
> Grant Women Skill, and Force, to write like Men.
> Yet they, like the Aeoleian Maid of old,
> Their Sex's Character will ever hold:
> Not with bold Quill too roughly strike the Lyre,
> But with the *Feather* raise a soft Desire.

The last erotic image recycles the playwright as prostitute analogy from Behn's career, though this time a male colleague evokes the connection as flattery. The female author can raise "soft Desire" because she knows how to use her pen, which is to say she uses the feathery part rather than the quill. This eroticized female writer writes like a man, but only thanks to the muses, the "Ladies Regent," who grant her power because of her sex. The image keeps Inchbald's creativity and genius at a distance from her person through a series of mediating relationships. The muses, like the prince regent in 1785, are at a distance from the real political or aesthetic center of things, and thus from real political power. The prologue then turns to "the Aeoleian Maid," a reference to Sappho of Lesbos, part of the Aolean chain of islands. Horace called Sappho "Aeolae Puellae," or the Aeolean girl, in Ode 4.9, line 12, identifying both her region of origin and the dialect, "aeolic," in which she wrote her poetry. Sappho, a figure of both female wit and literary eroticism, stands alternately for Inchbald and all women. Sappho wrote lyric, referenced here with the image of the lyre and characterized by softness and lesser themes in comparison to the martial epic or the ode. Sappho's poetry, like the domestic materials of Inchbald's stage comedies, was on the side of the culturally feminine.[52] It might be art, but it was gendered art.

Sappho, Inchbald, and the general category of women come together through the mediating term "character," which brings dual connotations into play. As in Pope's *Moral Essays,* character ("Most women have no characters at all") refers to a fixed identity, but it connotes sexual character or reputation. Character in this line deploys both of these senses of the term and layers yet another; Inchbald is like a character in a play, as she had been just the season before in her own *The Mogul Tale.* The connection to theatrical character implicates the playwright as an actor in a sexual drama in which she raises the audience's desire with the more sensual end of her quill. We are once again at the old label of playwright as prostitute, which Behn both created and dodged but which emerges here as a complicated and tendentious joke. According to Freud, the tendentious joke requires three parties: the speaker, the object of the joke's hostility (usually a woman), and the listener "in whom the joke's aim of producing pleasure is fulfilled."[53] The prologue unfolds before a more general audience of men and women, however, which only makes its tendentious dimension more cutting. All women in the theater are implicitly identified with Inchbald as a writing woman, and all are marshaled into the space of the joke's object, who must accept the insult as a compliment to the erotic source of women's talent as writers. The Freudian model of the positions in a tendentious joke underscores what a difference the speaker makes; Behn was the subject of her own joke about prostitution, while Inchbald was the object of Colman's.

Genre

The sustaining feature of the more vicious and the more welcoming climates for female playwrights is that both introduce sex as a critical factor for audiences and the reading public. This information, so regularly supplied to audiences and readers, qualifies as a type of generic expectation. Like other horizons of expectation, the "woman's comedy" became part of the reception history and the reading process for these plays. At a superficial level, critics associated the domestic concerns and the lightheartedness of comedy with women writers, many of which were strategies used by male and female comic playwrights. But there were substantive differences between men's and women's comedies that guide my reassessment of genre. Richard Alleman's 1942 *Matrimonial Law and the Materials of Restoration Comedy* points out that the manners comedies by Etherege, Wycherley, Congreve, Vanbrugh, and Farquhar only occasionally used clandestine, tricked, and mock marriages while Behn and Centlivre show tremendous interest in these irregular legal situations.[54] Of Behn's comedies, 37.5 percent make use of clandestine marriage, while another 37 percent have tricked marriages; for Centlivre, the figures are 69.2 percent and 15.4 percent.[55] Etherege, Wycherley, Congreve, Vanbrugh, and Farquhar average 23 percent in each category. The evidence is more revealing in real numbers; as a group, these male playwrights have six clandestine marriage comedies and six tricked marriage comedies, while Behn has six of each on her own and Centlivre has nine and two respectively.[56] While Alleman's study does not make claims about gender and authorship, it foregrounds Behn and Centlivre at a time when they received little scholarly attention.

Jacqueline Pearson's line counts in *The Prostituted Muse* (1988) show that female characters speak more lines (one-third of the total) in plays by women. In 27 of these plays, women speak more than half of all the lines, while they have an average of one-fourth of all lines in plays by men. Her survey includes closet dramas by Margaret Cavendish, which inflate the ratios in favor of women, but the trend to write more developed female characters, to have them open the plays, and to give them more substantial speeches were strong features of Behn's, Mary Pix's, and Centlivre's plays, all of which were staged.[57] Later in the eighteenth century, successful plays by men increase the proportional number of lines for women to a century average of 29 percent, a change due in part to the availability of talented actresses like Anne Oldfield, Frances Abington, Kitty Clive, and Sarah Siddons for women's parts. Betterton, Farquhar, Cibber, Garrick, and Colman (the Elder) devote an average of 35 percent of their lines to women. Their attention to female characters reflects the shift in theatrical personnel, an interest in domestic entanglements, and the influence of Restoration and early eighteenth-century female playwrights, whose popular plays proved that audiences were interested in outspoken female characters. Female characters garnered closer to 33 percent of the dialogue in the most popular repertoire comedies by men (excluding Shakespeare) for the whole of the century.[58] These statistics suggest that the most successful male playwrights of the eighteenth century were following the lead of their first female colleagues in creating more dialogue and more complex roles for women.

In spite of the statistical differences between comedies by men and women, the plays themselves are more alike than different in the most general terms: plot, complication, blocking characters, witty women, and marriage. The generic move toward the romance plot is part of what makes Restoration and eighteenth-century comedies so similar to each other. Character names like Hellena, Belvile, Doricourt, Dorimant, Fopling, Foppington, and Flutter cycle through plots and repeat conflicts between lovers, fathers and children, and old and young men. Moving away from Aristophanic and humours comedy, the eighteenth-century's bourgeois version of the Greek New Comedy-style marriage plot foregrounds romance, love, and marriage. The ascendancy of Shakespeare's romantic comedies, particularly *As You Like It, The Merchant of Venice, Much Ado about Nothing,* and *The Tempest,* over Jonson's comedies in the Restoration and eighteenth-century repertoire gestures to the appeal of romantic comedies concerned specifically with marriage.[59] As Brian Corman has argued, this shift is not a complete one but a case of Dryden's "mix'd way" in its dialectic of Jonsonian wit and Fletcherian intrigue and romance, which are themselves conceived in terms of longstanding generic patterns.[60]

The most popular Shakespearian plays in the Restoration and eighteenth century were, in fact, the tragedies, but the comedies that Northrop Frye would later idealize as "the mythos of spring," or the heart of comedy, are the plays that are most in vogue in the eighteenth century. The most popular comedies from 1659 to 1779 include *The Tempest* with 292 performances, *The Merry Wives of Windsor* with 274, *As You Like It* with 219, *The Merchant of Venice* with 217, and *Much Ado About Nothing* at a respectable 119. By way of comparison, Jonson's *The Alchemist* was staged 158 times, *Epicoene* 97, and *Bartholomew Fair* 30 in the same period. *Volpone* all but disappears from the repertoire. Jonson still had a place in the theaters of the period, but the new comedies reflect more romantic, Shakespearean concerns. The most successful original stage comedies of the period, including *The Rover, The Conscious Lovers, The Busy Body,* and *The Beaux' Stratagem,* focused even more closely on the conditions that make marriage sexually and socially fulfilling for their characters.[61]

The repetition of the marriage plot in these plays creates two critical temptations that I try to avoid. On the one hand, marriage can be a structuralist assumption, relatively timeless and impervious to historical variation, as Frye and Jameson variously assert; or on the other, it can be a field of expression for histories other than its own. Both of these approaches yield their insights at the expense of marriage; it becomes either the transparent medium of genre or the canvas of history. Structuralist arguments obscure the ways that comedies such as Centlivre's or Inchbald's, which debate the effects of contract thought and divorce law on marriage, are both about and structured by marriage. But critics who approach marriage as an historical allegory, as in the most recent discussions of Aphra Behn's plays, are also prone to bypass marriage as a subject. Robert Markley, Susan J. Owen, and Elizabeth Bennett Kubek have examined the political allegiances of Behn's plays and her role as a Tory propagandist and playwright who often conducted political battles in the language of sexuality.[62] Without denying the political content of Behn's plays or the importance of such politically focused criticism, my return to the significance of marriage in its own right in the plays of women begins with the question of its naturalization as the stuff of stage comedy in the long eighteenth century. While they were not the only comedies to do so, the women's plays I examine here use the constitutive tension between comic events and comic structures to imagine the terms under which the marriage contract would indeed be the happy ending for the heroine.

Those who have theorized the structure of comedy most cogently (Barber, Frye, and Jameson) have tended to reduce comedy's drive toward wish fulfillment *to* sexual union in marriage, making it difficult to discuss the historical function of comedy beyond what Frye termed "romance." When genre studies focus primarily on plot and closure, they find themselves telling the same story—happy ending, order restored, community confirmed—as the truth of comedy. Northrop Frye's short definition of comedy reflects some of the limitations of this overview: "What normally happens is that a young man wants a young woman, that his desire is resisted by some opposition, usually paternal, and that near the end of the play some twist in the plot enables the hero to have his will. . . . At the end of the play the device in the plot that brings hero and heroine together causes a new society to crystallize around the hero. . . ." (163). Frye's core definition of comedy, drawn from C. L. Barber's *Shakespeare's Festive Comedy,* is firmly grounded in the heterosexual marriage plot viewed from a male perspective.[63] And as Regina Barreca argues, "being the girl the boy 'got' so that he can then found a nice little society around himself is not her happy ending."[64] The myth of structuralist objectivity in which Frye's study participates depends on plots (69 in all) abstracted to a safe set of common structures that reduce the comic to its most predictable and arguably least interesting moments. Notably, no works by women are included in his study. Barber's and Frye's tendency to see marriage as the reward for the hero, along with the absence (until very recently) of most women's plays from the field of genre studies, produces a fairly untroubled norm of comic structure from the point of view of heterosexual male desire.[65]

While Frye's particular brand of formalism no longer occupies critical center stage, his structural reading of genre and his assumptions about community and marriage have fundamentally shaped genre criticism. In *English Stage Comedy 1490–1990: Five Centuries of a Genre,* Alexander Leggatt includes many examples from Behn, Centlivre, Cowley, and Inchbald, and displays a refreshing sensitivity to the comic spirit of stage comedy. But the discussion ranges so quickly from play to play that narrative differences and textures become difficult to trace.[66] Even Jameson's theoretically circumspect *The Political Unconscious* reproduces the trajectory of this gendered plot in the language of Freudian psychoanalysis. He argues that "the classical conflict in comedy is not between good and evil, but between youth and age, its Oedipal resolution aiming not at the restoration of a fallen world, but at the regeneration of the social order." The Oedipal narrative, while not bound to reproduce symbolic gender in actual plots, obscures the range of social interests and actors in comedy.[67] Jameson calls for a historicized narrative and genre theory attentive to the repressed "Real" of class struggle, but his analysis of comedy reproduces the symbolic function of heterosexual union as the mechanism of narrative without questioning its content. The Oedipal narrative situates the story on fathers and sons as the bearers of social authority. The story requires a female object of desire for its resolution, but it does not necessarily entail her story. Jameson's move normalizes the priority of the male hero, a critical sleight-of-hand that leaves the sexual narrative of comedy right where Frye found it.

Any structuralist reading that follows in Frye's path has the benefit of his basic insights about the marriage plot. But these insights also make it difficult to see that the content of comic resolution is a function of social and historical scripts, which change over the course of the long eighteenth century. A rakish Restoration comedy such as *The Country Wife,* which defies the marriage ending in its main plot, cannot be easily grouped with Goldsmith's *She Stoops to Conquer,* in which the conventional antagonism between generations melts into a joint effort between Mr. Hardcastle and daughter Kate. While both plays reflect the turn toward the Greek New Comedy plot, their different sexual and familial politics mark the force of historical change on generic structures. *The Country Wife* satirizes ideologies of masculinity at the expense of marriage, while *She Stoops to Conquer* presents the happy complicity of generations in bringing about the ideal companionate marriage.

While Frye and Barber wrote their studies of comedy without considering plays by women, the field of genre studies is no longer so exclusive. Recently, Brian Corman's *Genre and Generic Change in English Comedy, 1660–1710* and J. Douglas Canfield's *Tricksters and Estates* both include women writers in their analyses of the genre and its representations of marriage. Canfield, more in the model of cultural studies, proposes an ideological look at the estate and class warfare in Restoration comedy that shares my interest in thinking about the comic moments of comedies, a surprisingly rare critical move. His multiple categories of tricksters make plenty of room for the plays of Behn, but his interest in taxonomies, which is "not ontological but heuristic," emphasizes the defining force of a play's ending (6). The conclusions of comedies provide a way to distinguish comedies from one another, and scholars before Canfield, including Scouten, Hume, and Fujimura, have used them to elaborate types of Restoration and eighteenth-century comedies, including comic satire, farce, social comedy, subversive comedy, the comedy of manners, and wit comedies. All of these scholars, however, have confessed to the difficulties and pitfalls of their projects, citing the prescriptive dimension of such labels and their proliferation into subspecies.[68] Even the most satiric comedies of the 1670s, as Rose Zimbardo has noted, tend to celebrate "old-fashioned" values of chastity, virtue, and marriage in their plot outcomes; their "bite" lies elsewhere.[69] I share Canfield's interest in endings, but my critical intervention in this debate has to do with the dialectic of comic events and comic structure. Comedies are not made of endings alone, and reading comic events and jokes against comic structures or plots is a way to register the rhetorical nervous systems of comedies without the heuristic of categories. The marriage ending and the affirmation of dominant-class values always coexist with comic events that inflect and shape those endings with conflicting versions of marriage, gender, and contract culture.

Brian Corman's study draws on the repertoire plays in representative seasons from 1660 to 1710. His argument for "the mix'd way" of comedy that moves into a more sympathetic, romantic version of the Greek New Comedy coincides with the advent of professional women playwrights and actresses on the British stage.[70] I pursue this historical parallel and use the light it sheds on the rhetoric of marriage in plays by women. Without positing a causal relation between these events, I argue that the women who were successfully writing this plot brought to it what Paula Backscheider called "the experience of being bartered," through the "mix'd way" of the romantic comedy and the comic dialectic it fostered. But I also extend Corman's caution against the tendency for genre to become prescriptive. The regularizing force of genre theory has obscured some critics' discomfort with the themes and strategies of female playwrights. A woman playwright's perspective on marriage and the hazards of childbirth, or more baldly the "pack of repentance," as Behn's Hellena puts it, that sex could bring might complicate the heroine's implied or expressed relationship to the marriage ending. Backscheider noted the implications of a masculine *qua* normative vision of comedy in Maximillian E. Novak's response to Ariadne's *She Ventures and He Wins,* which failed, he argued, "due to its feminist reversal of sexual roles."[71] His assertion that Lovewell "has suffered a complete humiliation" maps twentieth-century expectations about roles and sexual politics onto a Restoration psyche.

Important studies that have framed modern critical understandings of the drama have not, however, always excluded women. Allardyce Nicoll's 1923 history provides some groundbreaking analysis of Behn, Centlivre, and others, but he paints his moral disgust at the bawdier Restoration works, particularly Shadwell's, onto Behn through comparisons and general judgments.[72] He maintains that her plays show range, variety, and some quality, but he nervously assures his readers that she wrote like a man. Robert Hume's *Development of the English Drama in the Late Seventeenth Century* (1976) includes Behn and Centlivre, but the descriptions of their work echo the earlier chorus of moral disapprobation. Other critics continue in these veins, placing female playwrights outside of "high" comic categories such as the manners comedy, categories that are late nineteenth- and twentieth-century heuristics.[73] These studies suggest a very consistent model of comic plot that affirms community *qua* patriarchal renewal, while exiling challenges to the domains of satire or farce. By turning away from generic subcategories and exploring instead the dialectic within the plays as it unfolds in history, I hope to map new territory for genre studies that focus on the social function and social vision of comedy.

Reading comic events against comic structures can repoliticize the discussion of comedy, which is too often stripped of its critical force by generic rubrics that bracket off satire and farce, or that consider plays only in terms of their endings. Northrop Frye's distinction between satire and irony as the "mythos of winter" as opposed to comedy's spring and romance's summer establishes a generic distinction between satire and stage comedy that later critics such as Claude Rawson (*Satire and Sentiment, 1660–1830*) and Stuart Tave (*The Amiable Humorist*) continue. Even Canfield's hybrid category, satiric comedy, nods to the basic difference between the terms. Brian Connary and Kirk Combe's introduction to their volume *Theorizing Satire* captures the contradiction of the attempt to keep the terms separate. They refer to satire both as a genre of its own and as a strategy whose "formlessness forces it to inhabit the forms of other genres" (5). These contradictory definitions reflect the problems of trying to keep the terms comedy and satire separate. The contradiction makes an a priori assumption that romantic comedy is a coherent category with which to oppose satire, when in practice the most paradigmatic comedies of the period, such as *The Beaux' Stratagem* and *The Rivals,* are full of satiric moments.

My approach to stage comedy through narrative theory illuminates the strategies of writers who might have a stake in alternative versions of comic narrative. Mrs. Sullen's critique of arranged marriages in *The Beaux' Stratagem* ("Were I born an humble Turk, where Women have no Soul nor Property there I must sit contented—But in England, a Country whose Women are its Glory, must Women be abus'd? where Women rule, must Women be enslaved? nay, cheated into slavery . . .") balances the unions between Aimwell and Dorinda, and Archer and Cherry, through which the audience can imagine a better marriage (though Aimwell and his beloved Dorinda do not speak to each other until the end of the play) (IV.i). Similarly, Aphra Behn renders explosive scenes with the armed Angellica, and yet still assures her audience of a marriage between Hellena and Willmore, which is the first thing to go in *The Second Part of The Rover.* Behn's abrupt abandonment of the marriage that the first play worked so hard to broker admits that her comic endings are as much nods to generic demand as they are meaningful resolutions. There is no room for a married Willmore, and thus no room for Hellena in a new comic narrative. Indeed, Hellena's death seems like a relief to Willmore, who reclaims his title as the "careless wild Inconstant . . . Rover" in pursuit of La Nuche (I.i, 234). The play concludes with La

Nuche's promise to follow Willmore "without the formal foppery of Marriage," and Willmore closes the play with a gesture to generic constraint: "So tho by several ways we gain our End,/ Love still, like Death, does to one Center tend" (V.iv, 294; 297). Elizabeth Berry, who played both Hellena and La Nuche in the first runs, provided some continuity to the two plays' vision of marriage, even as the second pressed further on the social possibility of a happy ending without a marriage. But Behn's two-part critique of the marriage plot relies on comic events, most importantly the moments in which Hellena, La Nuche, and the two "Jewesses" undo the assumption that all women want to marry.

From the point of view of narrative theory, repetitions in the period's comedies present us with a version of the Freudian death drive, which most genre critics have read as libido or eroticism. The narrative of repetition in Freud's *Beyond the Pleasure Principle* concerns his infant grandson's staged scenarios of loss and recuperation with his toys that enabled him to master his mother's departures. Using this story as a model for narrative, Peter Brooks argues in *Reading for the Plot* that narrative repetitions, which take us over the same ground as readers, are attempts to master the ending that we know to be inevitable (Brooks 97–105). The repetition of plots about marriage speaks to a cultural desire for mastery in the midst of legal and ideological changes in the institution. The structural repetitions of genre, as Jameson has argued, function like a contract between audience and playwright; the playwright agrees to provide familiar, generically readable comic material laced with new comic events (or at least new combinations), and the audience agrees to laugh. Playwrights invite audiences to identify with the characters' desires that shape the plot in order to participate in the reward-fantasy of its ending. While the particular attractions of characters vary in significant ways, the structure of desire, identification, and reward defines the genre and shapes the expectations of the audience. The bribe to the audience is tremendous: this erotic and economic future is a reward for these plots played out by these kinds of people. The interlocking patterns of desire and aesthetic expectation in comedy work a bit like the comic short-circuit in the process of cultural education that Pêcheux and Žižek describe: "no wonder you were interpellated as a proletarian, when you are a proletarian" (Žižek, *Sublime* 3). Through the lens of these narrative and psychoanalytic insights, marriage is the object of repetitions that, like the Freudian death drive, seek to master it.

The narrative structure of comedy traces the outlines of the social fantasies of theatergoers who sought out the genre as entertainment and who preferred some plays to others. Even though their responses may be opaque or inaccessible, these narrative remains, the comedies themselves, can illuminate the expectations and pleasures of their first audiences. The tension between the narrative drive toward closure and the impediments to closure that all stories entail corresponds to the distinction between pleasure and desire that Lacan makes in "Of the Subject of Certainty:" "Desire, more than any other point in the range of human possibility, meets its limit somewhere. . . . Pleasure limits the scope of human possibility—the pleasure principle is a principle of homeostasis. Desire, on the other hand, finds its boundary, its strict relation, its limit, and it is in the relation to this limit that it is sustained as such, crossing the threshold imposed by the pleasure principle."[74] Read through Lacan's formulation, the homeostasis of the comic ending, which Barber, Frye, and others have described as the inauguration or restoration of community, is the pleasure principle at work. Comic events, in contrast, can occasionally "cross the threshold" of the comic structure. Such is the case when Angellica breaks from the comic narrative of *The Rover* to challenge the faithless Willmore with a gun, or when Mrs. Sullen explains to a young women how to roast her husband's amputated leg in *The Beaux' Stratagem.* These instances of violence take the comic energies of their respective plays into dangerous territory, where women have momentary revenge on the men and the social codes that cheat them of their due. But the comedies are grounded by their endings, repetitions of the homeostatic community that reproduces itself through marriage.

This comic repetition at the structural level is a social reiteration of what Žižek calls "*la condition humaine* as such: there is no solution, no escape from it; the thing to do is not to 'overcome,' to 'abolish' it, but to come to terms with it, to learn to recognize it in its terrifying dimension and then, on the basis of this fundamental recognition, to try to articulate a *modus vivendi* with it" (5). *La condition humaine* can be either tragic or comic, but comedy emphasizes the sociality of the human condition and the possibility of finding others with whom to live it out. Comedy is a social form that turns not to the individual psyche and its struggles but to the social order itself in its focus on the ability of individuals to create bonds with others. Conversely, tragedy's focus on the fall of the individual and her or his suffering entails a solipsism that is rare if not impossible in comedies. Stage comedies work within social rules, even at their most aggressive, to provide palatable solutions for characters and viewers who cannot transcend their historical circumstances. These are stories about living in a present freighted with both generic and legal history but open to comic negotiation.

The comic events in the works of each playwright fall into repetitive patterns and tropes that are symptoms of the dis-ease of women within the law and their limited existence within the social compact, commercial contracts, and the marriage contract. These comic symptoms, the sexed body for Behn, written contracts for Centlivre, nationalism for Cowley, and marriage law itself for Inchbald, reflect on the failure of Enlightenment culture to deliver the promise of possessive individualism to women. Žižek, in his analysis of the Lacanian *sinthome,* argues that the symptoms of social or psychological disease become paradoxical solutions as the psyche turns to them again and again for answers. The symptom persists beyond its immediate relation to the problem and into fantasy, where it becomes the *sinthome,* "a certain signifying formation penetrated with enjoyment: it is a signifier as a bearer of *jouis-sense,* enjoyment-in-sense. . . . In other words, symptom is the way we—the subjects—'avoid madness,' the way we 'choose something (the symptom formation) instead of nothing (radical psychotic autism, the destruction of the symbolic universe)' through the binding of our enjoyment to a certain signifying, symbolic formation which assures a minimum of consistency to our being-in-the-world" (75).

The *sinthome* transforms psychic and social rupture into pleasure as it locates the individual in a social order, a place of "being-in-the-world" that assures the subject's existence, which was a matter of some legal urgency for Restoration and eighteenth-century women. Though Žižek eventually found the *sinthome* to be too limited a concept for his project, it provides a rubric that mediates between the psychological claims of jokelike comic events and the narrative demands of genre. In the comedies of the four writers in my study, comic events articulate the psychological and political symptoms of gender inequity and propose to resolve the inequity on those same terms. While the comedies are also "about" other political and historical concerns of the moment, their comic symptoms make consistent reference to the potential legal nothingness of daughters and wives and also articulate the terms in which women could secure a place in the shifting and shifty discourse of marriage.

The symptom turned *sinthome,* through which anxiety becomes pleasure, does psychological work similar to that of jokes or comic events, but it unfolds within the comic plot and its horizon of marriage. The comic events that display these symptoms present both possibilities for more empowered heroines and critiques of the developing legal and social culture of liberalism, which come to crisis for women at the moment of marriage. Their bodies, their access to contract, their status as citizens, and their relationship to the law all impinge on the ability of women to enter fully into the social order of eighteenth-century England. Comic events turn these symptoms of injustice into sites of pleasure as heroines reiterate their comic mastery of the sociopolitical conversation in the world of the play. Centlivre's Isabella and Violante repeatedly argue for the "Faith, Truth, and Honour of a Woman" by making and keeping promises with each other. Felix, who is at first suspicious of their ability to make contracts honestly, eventually sees his error and declares at the play's close that "Man has no Advantage but the Name" (V.i, 79). Their comic scenes play with the problem of women's access to contract by mastering the objections of the men around them through their own comic performances. The comic symptom, in this case the problem of access to contract within marriage, emerges as the pleasurable *sinthome* fueling the comic events that lead heroines as well as heroes to the pleasures of the comic ending.

The tropes that characterize the comic events of these plays are historically responsive ways to "avoid madness . . . [to] choose something . . . instead of nothing" in relation to the marriage contract, as in Hannah Cowley's *The Belle's Stratagem.* Once Letitia Hardy has made her betrothed fall in love with her as a continental incognita, she must return him to the realities of marriage, while still retaining some of the erotic content that courtship has produced:

> *Letitia:* You see, I *can* be any thing; choose then my character—your Taste shall fix it. Shall I be an *English* Wife?—or, breaking from the bonds of Nature and Education, step forth to the world in all the captivating glare of Foreign Manners?
>
> *Doricourt:* You shall be nothing but yourself—nothing can be captivating that you are not. . . . (V.v, 81)

Letitia's appeal to nationalism is a way to "choose something" when faced with legal and erotic nothingness. Her theatrical claim to identity, the bold "I *can* be any thing," proposes the multiple identities from which she has negotiated her marriage compact with Doricourt, but these identities also function as commodities. She offers Doricourt his choice of this girl or that one. Letitia has been made too much like nothing through the betrothal and the body of property law that surrounds marriage, but she uses that absence to construct an identity as an English subject, a legal and erotic "somebody" whom Doricourt can love and respect. Doricourt's reply signals the tension between nothingness and "somethingness" that Letitia has been trying to navigate through her nationalism: "nothing can be captivating that you are not." Cowley's play creates the positive condition of wifely presence out of a national failure to provide a stable subject position for married women. Like other comedies, hers does not present a utopia, but rather a hopeful resolution to her heroine's existential dilemma in an imperfect world.

The symptom played a progressively greater role in Lacan's critical work, where it was eventually formulated as the dilemma of woman as symptom of man. While I find his insight unpersuasive in isolation, it proves useful when it is thought through in this historical context. "Symptomatic" thinking moves from individual cases to the history they try to negotiate. My analysis brings Lacan's universalized explanation of the crises of sexuality into dialogue with the elite or merely propertied eighteenth-century Englishwoman's dilemma as a subject in the marriage contract, an object of the marriage exchange, and a demi-subject in the social compact. Female playwrights have no uniform point of view on the quandaries of contract that stage comedy represents, but the arc of popular plays by women suggests they saw in comedy the space to argue for a better version of marriage, one in which women were subjects in their own right. The shape of the genre in the Restoration and eighteenth century provided the strategy. The form mixed its assurances of marriage with anxious joking about the impediments to and arguments against marriage that were also sources of pleasure for the audience. To borrow a thought from Lacan, the comic letter may reach its destination, but it may have an alarming postmark. Behn's, Centlivre's, Cowley's, and Inchbald's plays are balanced between the foregone conclusions of genre and the possibility for innovation, just as they mediate between the legal freight of coverture and the new principles of self-possession that shaped chancery cases concerning married women. The moral of the comic story, at least in the plays of Behn, Centlivre, Cowley, and Inchbald, is that you get what you can negotiate.

CHAPTER TWO

REPETITION, CONTRACT, AND COMEDY

Lord Fitzgerald: And now my amiable Sophia condescend to marry me. (*He takes her hand and leads her to the front*)
Stanly: Oh! Cloe, could I but hope you would make me blessed—
Cloe: I will. (They *advance*)
Miss Fitzgerald: Since you, Willoughby, are the only one left, I cannot refuse your earnest solicitations—There is my Hand.
Lady Hampton: And may you all be Happy!

(Jane Austen, *The Visit,* II.ii, 51–52)[1]

The ending of Jane Austen's very brief *The Visit* captures the formulaic sense of romantic comedy at the end of the eighteenth century. In this skit from Austen's juvenilia, no one breathes a word about marriage until it pounces upon the reader in the last five lines. The abrupt ending parodies the predicable long-form romantic stage comedy. The transition "And now my amiable Sophia" is all the narrative logic the farce provides, but it is all that is necessary. Austen and her readers already know how this story ends. Talk of bed sizes, immoderate drinking, and odd foods (the dinner fare includes tripe, liver, crow, and red herrings) displace any specific conversation about romance with an off-key version of the domestic, in which young women get drunk at country houses and men find themselves controlled by female relatives. Lord Fitzgerald is a slave to his deceased grandmother's furniture specifications, with short beds and no extra chairs, while Lord Hampton silently surrenders to Lady Hampton, who speaks for him and orders his food. The final joke, reproduced above, clarifies the absurdity of the marriage ending as comic closure. It seems to have nothing to do with the comic events that precede it, and yet it is itself thoroughly predictable. The comic events in the skit are not so much at odds with the closure as apart from it.

The parody comments on the tension in the "serious" comedies, in which the comic agency of plotting characters, especially women, must be wrenched into agreement with the generic closure of marriage.

The rules of genre and in particular the preceding 120 years of comedies enable Austen's comic perspective in *The Visit.* The generic shift toward marriage as both the theme and the form of comedy, which I discussed in the previous chapter, occurs during a period of struggle over the definition of marriage in British law. New ideas about contract placed emphasis on the potential agency of both parties to make agreements with each other, while more strictly patriarchal ideas about inheritance, property, and the legal status of women continued to find support in common law and the cultural imagination. As a *feme sole,* a woman had the ability to make contracts with other parties, but marriage changed her legal status and thus altered her relationship to property and by extension to other people. The competing logic of contract and the common law principle of coverture render this implicit contradiction of eighteenth-century liberalism explicit. Susan Staves, Carole Pateman, and Michael McKeon have all argued that legal and popular ideas about marriage in the period preserve features of an older ideology of family and kinship while they also present marriage as a contract between individuals, in which women were full parties.[2]

At a time when the institution of marriage and the political culture of England were undergoing egalitarian reforms, the legal terms of property transfer preserved and strengthened a psychology of male exchangers and female units of exchange in the move from classic to modern "contractual" patriarchy.[3] As James Thompson has summarized, "if owning is juridically gendered, so too is subjectivity."[4] My use of the term patriarchy here is not meant to suggest an unvarying history of male privilege but a shifting discourse in which authority in marriage, over children, and over property was subject to negotiation. Margaret Ezell has cautioned scholars that accounts of a continuous or assumed patriarchy based on literary example do not survive historical scrutiny, and she offers an impressive range of historical materials that nuance any simple understanding of patriarchy in seventeenth century England.[5] With Ezell's caution in mind, I bring theatrical and legal accounts of marriage into dialogue to show the shifts, variations, and negotiations of marriage's meaning in the late seventeenth and eighteenth centuries, a period that ultimately shored up the legal authority of husbands at the expense of wives. The marriage ending of comedy, which became more predictable in eighteenth-century British theater, affirmed the settled character of marriage that the courts sought through a uniform body of marriage law governed by the principle of coverture. But comic events negotiated and occasionally challenged the assurances of the play's ending, suggesting the negotiability of marriage for women who could find ways to articulate the terms of their authority.

The periods of initial success for the women in my study, from 1670 to 1720 for Behn and Centlivre and from 1776 to 1800 for Cowley and Inchbald, were the most welcoming years for female playwrights in general. The lull between these two blocks of time included the general decline in new plays after the 1737 Licensing Act and the Garrick years of selective mentorship for new female playwrights.[6] These periods also correspond to two stages of legal argument that reconsidered marriage in light of a more liberal model of the modern state. Abridgements and public legal treatises from 1660 to 1700, including *Baron and Feme* (1700) and *A Treatise of Feme Coverts: The Lady's Law* (1732), drew from the property law elaborated in *Coke on Littleton* (1628) and began to map the modern procedures of civil law. Some of the most significant cases establishing married women's separate property in the first three decades of the eighteenth century followed the publication of these texts, intended for lay readers. Later, after the appearance of Blackstone's *Commentaries on the Laws of England* (1765–1769), lawyers and printers provided a steady stream of legal literature that summarized the law and provided case histories for the reading public. The output of legal treatises was part of a larger movement to reconcile competing bodies of law from the various jurisdictions that flourished until the later seventeenth century. Susan Staves surveys this literature, which included Charles Fearne's *An Essay on the Learning of Contingent Remainders and Executory Devices* (1772), John Fonblanque's revision of Henry Ballow's *Treatise of Equity* (1793–1794), Charles Watkins's *Treatise on Copyholds* (1797–1799), R. S. Donnison Roper's *Revocation and Republication of Wills and Testaments: Together with Tracts upon the Law Concerning Baron and Feme* (1800), and Edmond Gibson Atherley's *Practical Treatise on the Law of Marriage and Other Family Settlements* (1813). These lay texts paid great attention to married women's property from 1770 to 1830, elaborating the fiscal implications of marriage and the struggles for ownership between couples and their heirs that were endemic to middle- and upper-class unions. They also insisted on a uniform logic to, in the words of Charles Watkins, "reconcile the jarring and discordant cases" that comprised the body of existing case law.[7] While the post-Blackstone era of equity cases began with support for a woman's ability to make contracts with her husband, later cases retreated to the logic of coverture.

The two periods of my study are also bisected by Lord Hardwicke's 1753 Marriage Act, which reconciled canon and civil law somewhat belatedly after Charles II's 1660 abolition of the 1653 Civil Marriage Act technically annulled civil marriages contracted between 1653 and 1660 and forced the question of the difference between canon and civil law. Lord Hardwicke (Philip Yorke) sought to address this and other irregularities by creating a much needed uniform legal standard for marriages. While he was Lord

Chancellor, he supported the principle that wives can make and enforce contracts with their husbands for separate property. His general investment in contract logic expressed in the 1753 Marriage Act extended a general legal emphasis on contracts to marriage, though it vested parents with authority over those contracts. The act protected the interests of wealthy families by raising the age of consent for a girl from a troubling 12 to a late 21 and enforcing the same age of consent for males. These higher ages of consent curtailed the ability of their children to make their own marriage contracts, as did a more uniform system of registering marriages. Lord Hardwicke asserted that "the law has intrusted parents with the marriage of their children" in *Harvey v. Ashley,* a case that upheld the prerogative of a father who had arranged his minor daughter's marriage. The challenge to his legal right to bind her to ancillary agreements about property came after her widowhood, but Hardwicke ruled in favor of the father as the authority over his daughter and in favor of the principle of contract, which should not alter with circumstances.[8] The 1753 act allowed families to have greater control over the extensive provisions for inheritance in common law, provisions for which Blackstone admitted "there is no foundation in nature or natural law" (Bk. II, ch. 1: 2). The act favored the interests of parents over the liberty of children, but the principle of uniformity that shaped the 1753 act also foreclosed on some of the negotiable legal questions created by the competing jurisdiction of ecclesiastical, manorial, equity, and common law courts. The ascendance of coverture via common law reinforced the function of married women as conduits for consolidating property. Common law inheritance, which recognizes women's difference from men at the most basic level of legal identity, was designed to settle real property on eldest males and is thus built on the anonymity of women, the *femes* on whom the baron's children are begotten. Somewhat ironically, marriage, the form of contract that erased a woman's subsequent identity in the social compact or in many commercial contracts, was also the only form of contract in which a woman was recognized as a specifically *female* subject capable of making contracts.[9]

The evolving body of eighteenth-century marriage law both promised greater equality under the law for married women and made married women all but invisible as legal subjects in their own right. While women writers did not necessarily think the same things about marriage, comedies, or women, the form required them to reflect minutely on the mechanics of courtship and marriage in light of the contradictions in the legal representation of married women. As the newly arrived, women writing stage comedy tended to take up the domestic narrative of comedies and to give credibility to female characters who question romance narratives. Behn's Hellena in *The Rover* and Cornelia in *The Feign'd Courtesans* both replace feminine fidelity with promises to be "mistress-like" partners who defy the model of respectable marriage in order to sustain their erotic authority over their men after the wedding. Nearly one hundred years later, Bella's parting shot in Cowley's *The Runaway* critiques the marriage vow: "Love, one might manage that perhaps—but *honour, obey,*—'tis strange the Ladies had never interest enough to get this ungallant form mended" (V.i, 72). Bella's assessment of the ladies' lack of "interest" or political clout provides the implicit explanation; marriage law has been written by and tends to serve the interests of men. Women may participate in this contract, but in the legal sense, they do not compose it. Their situation as a group defined by law and yet as a group whose specific claims are not represented in the law is the liberal paradox with which power minorities continue to struggle in contemporary Western societies.[10] In this climate, marriage as a theatrical subject contained (both in the sense of included and attempted to limit) the contractual crises of modern civil society, but it also raised the question of how women were to negotiate this emotionally and economically crucial contract.

The Funny Thing About Contract

The Civil Marriage Act of 1653, which reflected a Protestant interpretation of marriage as a civil contract rather than a sacrament, reassigned control over marriage from ecclesiastical courts to the state. The Cromwellian act redefined marriage as a type of contract that draws its force from civil society and the range of voluntary contracts that civil societies can support. Susan Staves has argued more pointedly that the secularization of marriage law had everything to do with political challenges to monarchy: "as the rights of subjects against the monarch increased, so the rights of inferiors within the family also increased."[11] Locke would later articulate the political nature of these challenges, built on individual rights, in his *Second Treatise of Civil Government* (1689).

In the wake of the Civil Marriage Act and the discourse of possessive individualism, the ideal of marriage as a contract between a man and a woman chipped away at patriarchal authority on several fronts. Before the Civil Marriage Act, Edward Coke had, as John Zomchick explains, "pitted the common law against the prerogative of the crown, thus enlarging civil freedoms and modernizing the law itself."[12] Coke's elaboration of a body of common law that could limit the domains of canonical or ecclesiastical law and royal prerogative moved England closer to its modern civil state, but subsequent legal changes were neither straightforward nor consistently progressive. The tug of war between civil law and the ecclesiastical courts, which also had to respond to decisions from manorial and equity courts, created a Byzantine body of case law. Among the complications were the protectorate-era marriages that parliament was obliged to declare legal after the Civil Marriage

Act, which were used by justices later in the eighteenth century justices as precedents for their legal opinions about marriage. This hybrid civil/canonical body of marriage law reeled between the poles of legal subjectivity for wives, who were invested with the right to make contracts with their husbands, and the extremes of coverture, which denied a wife's separate existence. These legal contradictions mask even more disturbing currents in the lived experiences of seventeenth- and eighteenth-century women, who also had the burden (or the benefit) of local statutes from manorial courts and the demands of their own families with which to contend. Coke's systematization of law, including marriage law, in the interest of a more equitable civil society, stands in stark contrast to his own behavior as a parent. He forced his fourteen-year-old daughter Frances to marry a violent man (who was later declared insane) by tying her to the bedpost and whipping her until she consented.[13] The liberal promise of civil law collapsed in the face of such domestic brutality. The gap between Coke's theoretical position and his domestic practice serves as a reminder that the structures of the law are at a remove from the lived experience of men and women, though such examples of familial cruelty often mirrored legal contradictions.

The contradictions within marriage law in late seventeenth-century England, beyond the specific consequences of the Civil Marriage Act, sprang from the same contest that animated political theory in the period: the struggle between a monarchist vision of the social compact and a liberal, Protestant compact between individuals with property in themselves. The former vested power in the monarch and proposed that the relationship of individuals to the state was one of obligation to a sovereign, in whom they vest their natural-law rights for the sake of protection. In this Hobbesian vision, contract still plays a part, but it is a one-time contract that gives birth to civil society *qua* monarchy. Subjects voluntarily surrender their natural law rights to the sovereign and agree to submit to the sovereign's power for the sake of protection, even if their submission is produced under duress. They have no subsequent claims on the sovereign and hence cannot rebel. The strong monarch created a peaceful state and stable trade, which were the ends of Hobbes's sociological analysis.[14]

Lockean accounts of civil society depended on the consent of the governed, their ability to own property, and their right to rebel against an arbitrary government. Locke imagined not a Hobbesian state of nature in which lawless subjects battled one another but rather a placid, quasi-agrarian state of nature, in which subjects accumulated property. P. S. Atiyah describes Locke's *Second Treatise of Civil Government* as "the moral justification needed to satisfy the consciences of the propertied classes of the eighteenth century" (45). His argument locates the basis for civil society in ongoing contractual negotiations rather than in one original compact. Locke believed that people could and should rebel against a government when it abused its property rights or broke its contract with its citizens. Such was the Whig representation of the Glorious Revolution of 1688, in which James II's ouster was evidence that he had broken his contract with the people. Civil society for Locke exists for the protection and enforcement of property rights, and civil subjectivity originates in the individual having property in him *or* herself. The relationship between property and civil society was, by the end of the eighteenth century, fundamental. A conservative-sounding Wollstonecraft declared in 1790 in *A Vindication of the Rights of Man,* "Security of property! Behold, in a few words, the definition of English liberty."[15] Property in the self, as the cornerstone of civil society, seemed to provide the basis for universal enfranchisement and a foundational social equality.

The contractual concept of marriage, which recognized women's role as legal agents with interests in the marriage contract, was the proving ground for the legal status of women in modern liberalism. Locke presumed a basic equality between man and woman as parties who seek the mutual benefits of the marriage contract: "conjugal society is made by a voluntary compact between man and woman; and though it is necessary to its chief end, procreation, yet it draws with it mutual support and assistance" (*Two Treatises* 159). While these philosophical principles did not resolve the ambiguous status of women in civil society, they provided the legal logic for tracts such as *A Treatise of Feme Coverts: Or the Lady's Law* (1732), which claimed that women were civil subjects able to make contracts. *The Lady's Law* appeared anonymously, though Elizabeth Nutt, widow of the printer John Nutt, whose firm published the treatise, may have been one of its authors.[16] The treatise describes women as legal subjects and contrasts the clarity and rationality of contract thought to legal remedies from earlier times. While most of the treatise pragmatically explains the logic of particular cases of concern to women, the author takes glee in the following absurd example of a premodern widow's penance for having born a bastard and thus forfeited her estate. Before the rise of civil marriage law, the treatise emphasizes, she had to depend on arbitrary remedies. She could redeem all if she entered her lost manor, riding on a black ram, and pronounced the following lines:

> *—Here I am,*
> *Riding upon the Back of a black Ram,*
> *Like a Whore as I am;*
> *And for my* Crincum Crankum,
> *I have lost my* Binkum Bankum;
> *And for my Tail's Game,*
> *Have done this worldly Shame,*
> *Therefore pray,* Mr. Steward, *let me have my Land again.*

> Upon this Penance she is restored to the Possession of her Estate, for that Time (128)

The theatricality of this legal remedy reads like a scene from a farce, which shores up the author's claim that marriage and marriage law ought to be a modern and rational contract. Elsewhere, the treatise insists that marriage is a rational contract, as in the following: "A Marriage Contract is an Agreement between a Man and a Woman, to live together in a constant Society. . . . And nothing more is requisite to a compleat Marriage by the Laws of *England,* than a full, free and mutual Consent between Parties, not disabled to enter into that State, by their near Relation to each other, Infancy, Precontract or Impotency; for Marriage is of Divine Institution, to which only the Consent of the Parties is necessary, though the Solemnizing of it is a Civil Right, regulated by the Laws and Customs of Nations" (25). *The Lady's Law* emphasizes the mutual position of men and women in relation to the marriage contract. Though marriage had always depended on the exchange of vows, late seventeenth- and eighteenth-century treatises underscored the contractual authority of promises between bride and groom as the legal core of marriage.

While some basic notion of mutual consent had always been a part of a valid marriage, the status of women in relation to the marriage contract turned on the question of whether their property in themselves was alienable or not. Common law still rendered a woman a *feme covert* after marriage, which implied her loss of property in herself and thus a loss of civil subjectivity, but legal decisions that established forms of married women's separate property suggested that coverture was negotiable. Such was the verdict when Lord Hardwicke ruled in *Grigsby v. Cox* (1750) that "where anything is settled to the wife's separate use, she is considered as a feme sole," a decision which upheld a wife's right to separate property and to the legal selfhood that allowed her to claim it.[17] Blackstone further defined the limits of a husband's right to his wife's movable property when he maintained that the husband must specifically negotiate for or otherwise claim property other than real estate. "For, unless he reduces them to possession, by exercising some act of ownership upon them, no property vests in him, but they shall remain to the wife, or to her representatives, after the coverture is determined" (Bk. II, ch. 29: 433). According to Blackstone, the husband does not automatically absorb her movable possessions, even in the absence of a contract for separate property or pin money. The husband has to lay specific claim to her stocks, her jewels, or any other forms of portable property she may own in order to establish his right of ownership. Blackstone's legal analysis illustrates the effect contract law had on traditional property arrangements without mounting a full challenge to the common law principle of the *feme covert.*

Ultimately, however, the eighteenth-century ideal of possessive individualism failed to translate into general legal and economic equality for women. The narrative of modern contract presumes, as Carole Pateman argues, the subordinate status of women as the inhabitants of a pre-civil domain that structures the civil space of contract: "For all the classic writers (except for Hobbes) a difference in rationality follows from natural sex difference. . . . Only masculine beings are endowed with the attributes and capacities necessary to enter into contracts, the most important of which is ownership of property in the person; only men, that is to say, are individuals" (5–6). Pateman's broad generalization overlooks the range of private contracts available to women, including stock ownership and employment contracts. Amy Louise Erickson, in *Women and Property in Early Modern England,* has shown that women of many economic backgrounds inherited and earned personal property from the fifteenth to the seventeenth centuries. While common law, which gained authority over the course of the eighteenth century, kept the transfer of property between men, competing precedents from ecclesiastical and manorial courts supported daughters' and widows' claims to property, especially portable property and cash. Pateman does, however, identify the moments in Locke, Hardwicke, and Blackstone that coincide with the more inflexible interpretation of coverture in the developing standard of common law. The reconciliation of competing bodies of law included definitions of women as natural subordinates and undermined their right to possess property under the logic of early liberal capitalism. Without independent property, they were less able to assert that they were themselves persons, capable of ownership. The economic tautology is similar to Locke's description of servants and laborers in the *Second Treatise of Civil Government,* whose poverty compromises their personhood. Women defined in these terms cannot be fully self-possessing persons. In a Hobbesian understanding, which Locke supports on this point, they have already exchanged obedience (hence will) for protection and thus have limited proprietary relationships to themselves and to other forms of property.[18]

The philosophical problem for both feminist critics and theorists of political history that springs from Locke on this point is twofold: first, Locke does not explicitly extend rights to women. While women, and in particular professional women writers, could take part in the conversations of the public sphere, the customary definition of familial authority compromised their legal and political status a priori. Locke invites his reader to consider "a master of a family with all these subordinate relations of wife, children, servants and slaves, united under the domestic rule of a family; which, what resemblance soever it may have in its order, offices, and number, too, with a little commonwealth, yet it is very far from it, both in its constitution, power, and end. . . ."[19] Locke, as his contemporary Mary Astell and, later,

Carole Pateman argue, retracts the possibility of women's full participation in civil society when he places women in pre-civil society. As pre-civil persons, they are subject to male rule because rule, says Locke "should be placed somewhere, [and] it naturally falls to the man's share, as the abler and stronger" (*Two Treatises* 161). The contradiction in the category of "women" within Lockean social and economic theory has especially befuddled Anglophone feminisms seeking to describe agency through a post-Lockean model of civil society. The proliferating types of relationship in Locke's private and public spheres belie the fact that a woman's designation as a subordinate within the family returns to the gendered category of "paternal power" as the natural basis of government. In so doing, Locke abandons his earlier definition of "parental power" as an analogy for civil society (146). His telling conditional statement about the family, "if it must be thought a monarchy," is a prelude to his separation of the domestic realm from the civil as fundamentally different species of society (162). Civil contractual society *seems* to provide the necessary legal remedies to balance power in the public sphere, but women and families remain rhetorically and legally private.

The second category of difficulty in Locke's formulation comes from his notion of inalienable property in the self, which marriage undercuts. The cultural and legal institution that preceded and survived Locke maintained that a woman was only a temporary possessor of property in herself by virtue of her sex. She fully possesses herself for the brief (fictional) moment between father and husband, only to surrender her legal identity in a contract that leaves her status ambiguous at best. Lockean thought, in concert with a historical shift to common law as the rationalization of competing ecclesiastical and manorial law, proposed a neutrality that in practice was a form of discrimination. As Patricia J. Williams has argued with respect to race, the seeming neutrality of the law can mask its investments in the viewpoints that it empowers, which it justifies through the claims of private property. The problem, which has persisted into the twenty-first century, is that individual attitudes about gender, race, ethnicity, and other attributes mark the "neutral" category of the civil subject and shape the contracts that make some subjects more equal than others, both within and beyond the law. This legal neutrality ignores difference as a matter of justice, creating the blind legal culture through which "children are taught not to see what they see; by which blacks are reassured that there is no real inequality in the world, just their own bad dreams; and by which women are taught not to experience what they experience, in deference to men's ways of knowing."[20] The neutral subject proves to be a fiction that holds the concrete individual hostage to its assumptions. Liberal critical perspectives that draw on a discourse of rights *pace* Locke posit a seemingly neutral subject who exercises rights based on the principle of property in the self. This presumptive neutrality, however, is at odds with the distinctions that the law and individuals in liberal society make between persons who are vested with varying quantities of cultural and economic capital.

Locke's analysis is particularly modern in that it does not reflect the range of contractual arrangements women made just a generation earlier and could, in some cases, still make. Earlier ecclesiastical and manorial courts upheld women's claims to property within and after marriage as well as their right to take their cases to court. Amy Erickson estimates that up to one quarter of all Chancery (or equity) litigants from the fifteenth to the seventeenth centuries were women, while many marriages were negotiated by mothers due to widowhood or prior experience.[21] Erickson's account of early modern women and the law suggests a legal landscape in which women had more opportunities to act as agents under the law than their eighteenth-century counterparts. Early modern women could and did make bonds with their husbands that are not part of Chancery litigation. "A simple bond—of the type that the Sussex rector Giles Moore bought pre-printed by the dozen—obliged a man to provide his wife with certain specified property. His obligation took one of three forms: to pay a certain amount to the wife upon his death, which property (or the equivalent value thereof) the wife had brought into marriage; to pay the portions of her children by a previous marriage, since the property she brought to marriage incorporated her husband's previous estate; or to pay to a third party a sum of money for the wife's use, and/or allow her to make a will while married" (Erickson 130). The wife herself could not sign, but the husband and men or unmarried/widowed women who acted as securities for both parties could. Erickson finds an overall rate of 10 percent of all married men's probate accounts included such bonds or obligations, which suggests the practice was much more widespread than previous studies of aristocratic and upper gentry marriages revealed (131). Later arrangements for pin money and other forms of separate property held out limited forms of ownership for women against the general principle of coverture, but coverture ultimately overrode the legal precedents for married women's separate property that emerged in the seventeenth and early eighteenth centuries.[22] The possibility of negotiation both in the terms of ecclesiastical and manorial courts and through the confusion of competing legal discourses shrank as the consolidation of legal authority in common law proceeded though the eighteenth century. Ecclesiastical and manorial courts lost significant influence by the mid-seventeenth century, while the Court of Chancery remained out of the reach of most people.[23]

Astell's famous response to Locke targets the inequity within the legal and Enlightenment principles of universal equality writ large in marriage law: "If all Men are born free, how is it that all Women are born slaves? as they must be if the being subjected to the inconstant, uncertain, unknown arbitrary

Will of Men, be the perfect Condition of Slavery?" (*Reflections,* 1706: xi). The hypothetical answer is a tautology: the new economic order (liberal capitalism) colluded with the most restrictive version of the old order (classic patriarchy expressed as common law) to make them so. In other words, they are slaves because the men who write the rules say they are. Astell, a Tory and a believer in monarchical succession, challenged the Lockean distinction between men and women on the basis of its politics: "If absolute sovereignty be not necessary in a state, how comes it to be in a family? . . . For if arbitrary power is evil in itself, and an improper method of governing rational and free agents, it ought not to be practis'd anywhere: Nor is it less, but rather more mischievous in families than in kingdoms, by how much 100,000 tyrants are worse than one" (*Preface).* Her rationale exposed a contradiction within Enlightenment thought that was the point of entry into debates about gender and power for Catherine Macaulay, Mary Wollstonecraft, and other early feminist thinkers. The priority of rationality as the basis of intellectual and social good should level the cultural playing field of its gendered biases. But as Macaulay notes in her *Letters on Education* nearly ninety years after Astell's *Reflections,* the "false bias" of men who wield social power over women undermines the emancipatory dimension of Enlightenment thought as "mind and body yield to the tyranny of error" (47).

The struggle between a generalized, egalitarian rationality and the concrete experiences of inequality under the law framed Mary Wollstonecraft's and Mary Hays's reflections on how little had changed for women at the end of a century of alleged enlightenment, rights talk, and contract logic. Hays argued that " . . . men, by breaking through laws of equal authority, with those by which they endeavor to enslave the other sex; with all their boasted superiority, set women a very bad example, both in principle and practice" (6). Divinely justified male dominance, she claims, "falls with the first pair to the ground" (7), but the institutional limits placed on her and her contemporaries continue to shape an unequal and unjust world: "It is a melancholy truth, that the whole system raised and supported by men, tends to, nay I must be honest enough to say hangs upon, degrading the understandings, and corrupting the hearts of women; and yet! they are unreasonable enough to expect, discrimination in the one, and purity in the other" (59). The public institutions of eighteenth-century British culture shaped the private spaces that women were to inhabit in what Hays insists is a corrupt cycle. Hays maintains that these confusions, coupled with the uneven education of women, produce the ethical and legal complications that women lived through their marriage contracts.

The liberal fantasy of "equal freedom of everybody before the law and in the marketplace" fractured on the legal contradictions of marriage contracts that juggled women between the private and public spheres.[24] Common law preserved women's legal difference from men, while Chancery courts affirmed the equal freedom of bride and groom to make contracts. Nancy Armstrong and Michael McKeon situate this liberal dilemma in the context of the analogy between family and state, which gave structure to eighteenth-century social institutions. Armstrong, in a literary historical argument that parallels Pateman's thesis on political theory, claims that the founding paradox of modern patriarchy is the development of a liberal civil society separate from the private realm of familial authority. This private realm of the family grounds the modern liberal state by giving definition to the public.[25] McKeon, building on their work, argues that the separation of private from public in discourses like Locke's entailed the separation of the terms *sex* and *gender* from each other. The distinction reifies sex as inalienable and inevitable even as the complementary social category, gender, seems to provide an open and variable model of subjectivity. In practice, however, the split tied sex and gender to the same orbit, as conduct books, periodical essays, and medical texts insisted that appropriately gendered behaviors were evidence of appropriately sexed bodies. Following Judith Butler's theoretical insights, McKeon concludes that sexual difference as it circulates in the discourse of liberalism is nothing less than "what renders the system systematic."[26] The performative domain of gender is, in the absence of a more radical notion of rights, a means to regulate the status of particular sexed bodies, to wit, women.

The Economics of Genre

If the novel was the genre in which class-crossing was possible, if dangerous, in works like *Pamela, Moll Flanders,* and *Fanny Hill,* then the stage comedy was the form in which class prerogatives were generally maintained. The generic tools of comedy and the strategies of particular playwrights polish the ideology of elite marriage to a glossy sheen by playing up the choice of the young people and assuring audiences that the young man and, even more importantly, the young woman are choosing freely. At the same time, the conversation about marriage and money becomes more frank over the course of the century, despite the notable increase in "delicacy" associated with the rise of sensibility. Shakespeare's comedies rarely mention money as a factor in the marriages they celebrate; the exceptions, such as *The Taming of the Shrew,* illustrate the rule. When Baptista offers to double Katherine's dowry ("The wager thou hast won, and I will add/Unto their losses twenty thousand crowns/Another dowry to another daughter" [V.iv]), Shakespeare underscores Baptista's need to rearticulate his daughter's worth in this extraordinary case. Beatrice and Benedick, the most Restoration-style couple in Shakespeare's comedies, have only to negotiate "our own hands against our hearts" (V.iv); however manipulated they may be by their contemporaries, there appear to be no financial pressures shaping their elite arrangement.

In contrast, comedies in the long eighteenth century are obsessed with the wealth exchanged in marriage. Restoration allusions to capital in the form of Millamant's undisclosed fortune in *The Way of the World* or Harriet's portion in *The Man of Mode* give way to the later eighteenth century's explicit accountancy. Melinda in Farquhar's *The Recruiting Officer* is worth £20,000, and Biddy Tipkins in Steele's *The Tender Husband* has £10,000 in money, £5,000 in jewels, and £1,000 annually from lands. Lydia Languish of *The Rivals* has enough stock to pay off the national debt, we are told, which is later joined to her lover Thomas's fortune of £3,000 a year. In Cibber's *The Non-Juror,* Maria's father will augment her £5,000 with £3,000 to £4,000 more when she marries; Hannah Cowley's *The Runaway* estimates Lady Dinah's personal wealth at £40,000, and her *Which Is the Man?* reveals that Lady Bell Bloomer is worth £20,000. The focus on fortune, which has been widely noted in Jane Austen's comic novels, is even sharper in stage comedy. These fantastic sums indicate an anxiety about and a fascination with mercenary marriages, which Sir William Temple lamented: "Our marriages are made, just like other common bargains and sales, by the mere consideration of interest or gain, without any love or esteem."[27] The emphasis on specific amounts of money equates heroines with that money, rendering them abstractions of economic value and threatening to erase their status as individuals.

The high rollers on the stage, however, did not often mirror the circumstances of the audience. It is difficult to ascertain a very accurate picture of audiences for the period, but the one point of agreement for theater scholars is that they were not monolithic.[28] Harry William Pedicord has argued that the late seventeenth-century audience included merchants, middle-class tradesmen, soldiers, Freemasons, and apprentices, as well as royalty, gentlemen, and ladies.[29] The records assimilated in *The London Stage* show a range of ticket prices. Later in the century, aftermoney or discounted tickets sold after the third act made the theater accessible to journeymen and workers. While Pedicord argues that a shilling would have been prohibitively expensive for the laboring "masses," the half-price option opened the theater to some of that population, who could still enjoy the afterpiece, usually a comic skit, as well as the balance of the mainpiece.[30] Aristocratic patrons comprised a greater share of seats in the Restoration, but Pepys's January 1662 report that "the house was full of citizens" and references to the range of classes in the audience in prologues paint an audience of mixed composition.[31] Speaking of the changes he perceived between 1660 and 1668, Pepys mused that "I do not remember that I saw so many by half of the ordinary 'prentices and mean people in the pit at 2s. 6d. a-piece as now" (quoted in *London Stage* I:

clxvi). The gist of prologues that anatomized the audience into pit, boxes, and galleries suggest an increasingly diverse audience, which grew with the seating capacity of the patent theaters over the century. Scouten estimates that the total capacity for the London theaters in the early eighteenth century before the Licensing Act was around 4,160 per night, with the patent theaters accounting for about 2,860.[32] Later in the century, after the size of theaters was increased yet further, attendance rose to roughly 1,500 a night in each of the four main theaters in 1790 (over the 1750 average of 1,000 a night) for a comparative total of 6000 spectators per night (*London Stage* V: ccix).

The attractions of stage comedy include the fantastic identification of the audience with the witty and wealthy romantic couple, but the particular behaviors and lessons being taught through the ending alone could not have been very literal. For most people who married in the period, little wealth was transferred at the time of marriage. According to Joseph Massie's 1759 calculations, 1,193,500 families, or roughly 80 percent of his population estimate of 1,474,570, claimed a family income of £49 or less, with 718,000 of those under £24 a year.[33] Amy Erickson, who considers the economic lives of "ordinary people" with incomes between £40 and £500, finds that these individuals and families had both some disposable income and wealth sufficient to warrant wills and probate cases. These figures, along with similar estimates from Malachy Postlethwayt and twentieth-century revisions by historians P. H. Lindert and J. G. Williamson, describe a population in which many could imagine themselves aspiring to the middle class and attending the theater occasionally, but few could hope for the outrageous portions and jointures that stage comedies portrayed.[34] Even among elite families, second sons and younger daughters had very different marriage expectations than their older siblings, and for most theatergoers, the estates and settlements under consideration were likely so unrealistic as to lie beyond meaningful analogy.

For all but the wealthiest 3 percent with incomes over £200 a year, what was gained in marriage was affection and additional labor capacity in the home or in a trade. Most women who married transferred only small amounts of wealth. Portions such as the £30 Thomas Gaunt left to his two daughters, Susan Spaldinge's £20, and Margaret Greave's £22 were more likely the sort of wealth that most English women brought with them in marriage. Their labor as housekeepers, shopkeepers, textile workers, and mothers, however, was very economically significant. Household manuals printed well into the seventeenth century instructed women in a range of activities, including managing dairy and brewery trade. By the mid-eighteenth century, notes Erickson, the "mistery and sciencs" once attributed to housewifery had largely disappeared, a change attributable in part to the privatization of many of the functions once in the purview of individual households (55). Nonetheless, the success of businesses and the operation of households continued to depend on the labor and intelligence of women.

The basic concept of dowry, which governed the cultural logic of marriage in England, still based a woman's worth on the amount of wealth or potential wealth she might bring to the new family, but that worth could include the ability to negotiate and conduct business. Female shopkeepers were often unpaid wives, like the bookseller James Lackington's wife, who was "immoderately fond of books" and who tended his shop when he was away.[35] The world of publishing held many such opportunities for women, which ranged from unpaid labor to ownership. Olwen Hufton estimates that roughly 50 percent of the publishing houses in Great Britain were family businesses that employed wives, while 10 percent "were in the hands of women alone, usually widows."[36] Bridget Hill notes that a substantial number of widows chose to take on their husbands' businesses rather than sell them, and did so with success,[37] which suggests a level of prior involvement in these businesses.

Women's contributions to marriage in these cases are no less imbricated in economic matters than the wealthy matches of the stage, but for the merchant- or aspiring middle-class audience, the witty heroine may well have represented another sense in which women's value is abstracted as a unit of exchange. The intelligent and contractually adept Hellena (*The Rover*), Miranda (*The Busy Body*), Elizabeth Doiley (*Who's the Dupe?*) and Miss Dorrillon (*Wives As They Were*) would have been fine examples of women who could help to run a business. While the dilemmas of wealthy heroines and their lovers bore little resemblance to the economic conditions of the audience, they exaggerated a larger public's experience of marriage: the continued importance of negotiation, unequal access to property, sexual double standards, and the paradoxical position of women in this special form of contract. These questions energized comedies by appealing to the contradictions of British culture in this early phase of modern civil society, contradictions that extended beyond the theatergoing population.

The shift away from a physical notion of the estate as real property and toward an abstract notion of estate as monetary value also reshaped marriage negotiations for families and young people. This historical movement, most of which was accomplished over the course of this period, made it possible for women to imagine themselves as legal actors who manipulate wealth at the same time that it threatened to abstract them as exchange values. Daughters had long been likely to inherit cash and personal property from their parents, while real property devolved to sons, with few exceptions.[38] These personal goods or "moveables" were also often of greater relative value for ordinary people in that they depreciated slowly, were more durable, and by nature more saleable, while land values were (until the mid-eighteenth century) slow to appreciate (Erickson 66). But their dual status as subject and object of the marriage contract rewrote their legal status in increasingly draconian terms as common law proved ascendant over the more flexible arrangements of ecclesiastical and manorial courts. As both legal subjects in the marriage contract and as conduits of heritable property in that same contract, the elite women represented in stage comedies were caught in the philosophical and legal paradox of contract thought that governed inheritance law for the eighteenth century. They were subjects in their marriage contracts, but their bodies were also the objects of that contract.

The logic of the marketplace, which shapes both the social compact and commercial contracts, demands a purpose for the marriage contract. As Bishop Gilbert Burnet, a supporter of the Glorious Revolution, summarized in his 1699 *An Exposition of the Thirty-Nine Articles of the Church of England,* marriage was a contract for the purposes of making children: "For the end of Marriage being the ascertaining of Issue, and the Contract itself being a mutual transferring of the Right to one another's Person, in order to that End; the breaking of this Contract and destroying of the End of Marriage does very naturally infer the Dissolution of the Bond."[39] The modern discourse of commercial productivity thus becomes a domestic discourse of marital reproductivity. Burnet's use of "ascertaining" suggests some of the assumptions about marital property that the logic of production masks. The production of children is possible without marriage, but the "ascertaining" of parentage as either legitimate or illegitimate requires a legal mechanism, however imperfect, to enforce a husband's claims over the reproductive capacity of women. *The Lady's Law* alludes to this purpose when it mentions impotence as a disability that would prevent marriage or possibly provide grounds for divorce. *The Lady's Law* argues that impotence from the beginning of the marriage could be grounds for dissolving or invalidating the marriage contract, but that impotence that develops in the course of the marriage is not (27–28). The legal logic of consummation completes the marriage contract and underwrites the husband's proprietary interest in the wife's body, which exceeds the claims of the wife and the commercial logic of (re)productive marriage.

In his 1705 *Essays Upon Several Moral Subjects,* Collier describes the social difference between male and female sexual sin in terms that expose the asymmetrical positions of men and women in the marriage contract: "When a woman proves perfidious, the Misfortune is incorporated with the Family, the Adulterous Brood are fed upon the Husband, and it may be run away with the Premisses. But when the Man goes astray, the Wife can't pretend to such great Damages" (112). Collier's observation draws on the connection between women and their bodies through which English culture attempted to inscribe inheritance laws on the bodies of women. But the meaning of female chastity is something that Collier has to naturalize in the shadow of contract thought. Contract opens up a range of possible relationships and financial arrangements regarding children, since it represents those relationships as negotiable rather than natural. The seeming materiality of a wife's infidelity and the immateriality of the husband's is only an effect of inheritance law, which polices the wife's sexuality as though she were the property of the husband, a relationship that is not reciprocal. If inheritance were reckoned in the male line but based solely on the firstborn of any man, regardless of marriage, only the man's infidelity would matter as a drain on the family's consolidated wealth.[40] Pregnancy makes apparent a wife's infidelity, but the husband's infidelity also has the potential to create children who do not always disappear. Thus, the claim that the man can go "astray" but that woman's perfidy has more permanent economic and social implications is entirely an effect of property law and not the "natural" consequence of biological difference. A woman's infidelity might introduce a bastard into the family, but inheritance law, not material principle, determines the status of that child. In fact, Collier's claim masks the allegedly more common situation of bastard children fathered by wayward husbands; much like Jane Austen's "truth universally acknowledged," Collier states as obvious what is in fact constructed by law and subject to debate. Elite men, such as Richardson's fictional Mr. B., accepted certain conventional if not fully legal responsibilities for the bastard children they fathered, which required familial resources. Hillaria, the heroine of Ravenscroft's *The Careless Lovers* admits that having a husband is necessary "to save the trouble of being ask'd questions o're and o're, as who's the Father, who got it? and besides, what Children the Gallant gets, the Husband must keep" (V.ii 172). She jokes that by marrying her "Gallant," she will force him as a Husband to keep his own children, but the joke only makes sense in light of a social expectation that gallants are supposed to be responsible for the keeping of their bastards.

What lies behind Collier's self-evident truth is the power of female sexuality either to stabilize or to disrupt the trajectory of property in the marketplace. Pateman, who reads the marriage contract as a potential instrument of force, argues that "Women, their bodies and bodily passions, represent the 'nature' that must be controlled and transcended if social order is to be created and sustained. . . . [W]omen's bodies must always be subject to men's reason and judgement if order is not to be threatened" (100–101). One such attempt at control was a 1699 act to make female adultery punishable by a £100 fine; the legislation failed, but the attempt signaled a new phase in the social accounting of female sexuality. The act encountered a woman not as a special category of property, as criminal conversation suits for damage did, but as a legal agent with the responsibility for her own body. As a potential producer of bastards as well as heirs, she bears the responsibility for insuring the upwardly mobile fortunes of the new consumer society through her body.

It is in this context that we should read Dr. Johnson's famous dictum on infidelity and illegitimate birth: "Consider, of what importance to society, the chastity of women is. Upon that all the property in the world depends. We hang a thief for stealing a sheep; but the unchastity of a woman transfers sheep, and farm and all, from the right owner" (quoted in Boswell, V: 209). Notably, in Johnson's formulation the woman does not actively transfer the property; rather, it is her "unchastity" that stands in as the agent. The threat of women's latent agency *qua* sexuality poses such an economic problem that Johnson must hold it at bay grammatically. Rousseau is more direct in *Emile* when he claims that an unfaithful wife "dissolves the family and breaks all the bonds of nature. In giving the man children who are not his, she betrays both. She joins perfidy to infidelity. I have difficulty in seeing what disorders and crimes do not flow from this one" (361). These famous statements about women and marriage naturalize the legal status of her body as a conduit for male property while also making her an agent. Johnson's and Rousseau's calls to police female sexuality correlate to the newfound legal authority of women as negotiating, contractual subjects.

The dual status of women as negotiators and makers of contract and as the material objects of those contracts shaped the lives of elite and more ordinary women alike. The tension was writ large in stage comedy, where the heroine's freedoms cannot overcome it. Even the witty Restoration heroine, such as Etherege's Belinda, who seems to circumvent parental edicts, must submit to a marriage that will enlist her body in the further transmission of wealth through heirs. Mirabell's famous conditions for Millamant in the proviso scene of *The Way of the World* include the prohibition against straight-lacing "when you shall be breeding," lest his son (of course) should be deformed. Mirabell's control over Millamant focuses on her body and her reproductive capacities, which he uses contract to contain; Millamant's provisos are all defensive attempts to control some private space. Steele's crude pragmatist Cimberton in *The Conscious Lovers* parodies this control when he examines his prospective bride Lucinda, "And pregnant undoubtedly she will be yearly. I fear, I shan't, for many years, have discretion enough to give her one fallow season" (III.i, 112). The play only questions the degree to which market logic should be applied to marriage, not the transfer of estates through reproductive young women. Lucinda, who objects to being "thus survey'd like a steed at sale" nonetheless knows that her mother expects her to obey in her choice of a husband, who will be "chosen" for her. Lucinda explains her mother's policy on courtship: "the first time you see your husband should be at that instant he is made so" (III.i, 113; 109), a policy the play does not endorse but from which its values cannot be absolved. Steele's comic representation of bad marriage options draws its force from cultural anxieties about the ambiguous state of daughters as contractual subjects.

They are necessary participants in the contract, but they can do little to change its terms or impose their wills on the plot without breaking with the terms of femininity. Indiana's passivity bears an uncanny resemblance to the daughterly obedience that Fordyce, Chapone, and other conduct book writers recommend, while the "sale" of Lucinda is only an exaggerated reading of the same principles.

While early- and mid-eighteenth-century courts were more open to the premise that women could make contracts with their husbands, the practice was still limited to elite women who managed to come to agreeable terms before the nuptials. Laetitia Pilkington, whose marriage was a disaster, reflects cynically in her 1749–1754 *Memoirs* on the loss of economic power and the vulnerabilities to which marriage exposed women who found themselves with cruel husbands: "As for our being endow'd with the worldly goods of our husbands 'tis known they are so little apt to share with us, that it has always been found necessary, in a marriage-settlement, to stipulate for pin money, a very useful clause even to the husband, and it is much better his wife should have a share of his fortune, than be obliged to a gallant for a trifle, which gratitude may make her repay in too tender a manner" (115). The distinction between the private space of the family and the public world of law and contract appears to Pilkington a dangerous fiction that puts women at economic and sexual risk. Women, she argues, need to negotiate private contracts or marriage settlements before the wedding to ensure their private comfort and safety, since their legal and economic interests are not automatically insured by marriage. The ideology of companionate marriage, what Pilkington describes as the happy state "where she is to be lov'd, honour'd, cherish'd, nay, even worshipped," masks the reality of private miseries that contracts could avert (114).

Pilkington's experience illuminates the ways that marriage is both like and unlike other contracts. It involves the exchange of promises between parties, it is legally binding, and it recognizes the transactional force of words. But the permanence and the inequality that characterize it make marriage a contract that leaves elite women with less than they brought to the contract in significant legal and material senses. The radical difference of power between husband and wife is a function of both conventional power arrangements and submerged arguments for the social utility of marriage. Blackstone's definition of contract as "an agreement, upon sufficient consideration, to do or not to do a particular thing," identifies the importance of three elements: the agreement itself; the thing to be done (or not done); and the middle term, the consideration, usually something with a market value, such as labor or money, which made a contract valid (Blackstone 1766, I: 442). The element of consideration, a slippery but acknowledged moment in most other contracts, is particularly ambiguous in the marriage contract, which seems to depend on the labor or wealth of the woman as the tacit assumption of marriage. Consideration validated the contract by making reference to a material world for evidence that the verbal agreement has merit. Labor, understood as consideration, would itself require an employer to pay his employee. In the case of marriage, the materiality of the woman's reproductive body and the wealth exchanged in the contract served as consideration, albeit uneasily.

The tension in eighteenth-century law between women as objects of contractual consideration and women as subjects of contracts abstracts female identity in opposite directions. On the one hand, the older system of male primogeniture to determine land inheritance defines wives as chattel, while families were identified with their land by place names and economic relations. In this system, women were themselves consideration, but they could also depend on the legal guarantees of dower, jointure, and the "reasonable third" (the widow's guarantee of a third of the estate for herself and another third for her children) that grew out of the same body of feudal law. Her legal disenfranchisement comes with the benefit of legal protections. The modern notion of contract, in which consideration played a diminished role, made marriage the exchange of promises between two civil subjects, even though strictly interpreted common law challenged the ancillary contracts between husband and wife that were a part of elite marriages. The influence of contract logic in the development of married women's separate property meant greater economic power for elite women within marriage, though their ability to take advantage of this logic depended on their access to Chancery. Pin money extended a married woman's role as owner from clothing and jewelry to cash and stocks that were not subject to a husband's control. Provisions for separate property allowed women to participate in the stock market, where they had garnered 25.4 percent of bank stock by 1744; stocks were not taxed and were admissible as a married woman's personal estate, factors that made these instruments attractive (Ingrassia 30). But with these more contractual principles and the range of transactions they enabled came the loss of her former protections, for which she now had to negotiate. As English wealth grew more abstract over the period, women experienced the potential for greater autonomy as individuals in the new understanding of contract and greater abstraction as property in this more capacious model of exchange if they could not secure a position as a negotiator.

Stage comedies offered versions of the legal moment of marriage as a bond secured though the technical mechanism of sex. In *The Way of the World*, Mirabell must have a witness that Waitwell is "Married and Bedded" to assure that he is truly married and thus safe for his plot to seduce Lady Wishfort. Similarly, Behn's codger Sir Feeble declares he is anxious to have "Livery and Seisin" of the young Letitia's body in order to secure the bargain (III.i,

245). Consummation both affirms the mutuality of the contract and affirms the delivery of the "goods," the female body, which seals a homosocial bargain between generations. Women's fears of being turned into an exchange value surface in stage jokes by miserly uncles or guardians who threaten to sell their charges to bad husbands; such jokes abound in *The Busy Body* between the "Guardee" Sir Jaspar and his "Chargee" Miranda, and in *A Bold Stroke for a Wife,* where Tradewell wonders "if when cash runs low, our Coffers t'enlarge,/We can't, like other stocks, transfer our charge?" Later in the century, the threats turn serious; in *Everyone Has His Fault,* Lord Norland proposes to marry off Miss Woodburn without her consent. In *Wives As They Were, Maids As They Are,* the jealous Lord Priory insists on a degree of obedience from Lady Priory that culminates in Lord Bronzely's rape attempt.

The ability of comic heroines to trade, negotiate, and act as economic agents balances the threat that Inchbald renders all too clearly; by the end of the eighteenth century, British women had lost legal authority in marriage. The old legal protections of traditional dower rights had been undermined by modern marriage contracts, and their identity as agents within the marriage contract established by separate maintenance agreements in equity courts had been undermined by cases heard at King's Bench by Lord Chief Justices Mansfield and Kenyon. Their decisions in *Lean v. Shutz* (1778), *Corbett v. Poelnitz* (1785), and *Marshall v. Rutton* (1798–1800) affirmed the principle that husband and wife are one under the law and thus cannot make contracts with each other. In this treacherous legal territory, British women found themselves without the old protections of dower or the new authority of modern contract. Inchbald captures this frustrating and precarious situation in the plights of her heroines, who find that they can depend only on the affective claims of the love relationship for protection and self-definition within marriage as they retreat from the law that refuses their claims to selfhood. But the continued appeal of comedies by Behn, Centlivre, and Cowley suggests that the negotiating heroine still held some fascination for these theatergoers, male and female.

Writing the Good Marriage

Restoration and eighteenth-century comedies had to adjudicate between the contractual ideal of the companionate, loving marriage at the level of plot and the legal inconsistencies in women's legal status throughout the play's events. Comedies in the period usually satisfy these contradictory demands by granting nubile young women striking forms of agency or by staging accidents in which nature and narrative conspire to give young women the young men they deserve. The plot often includes a bad prospective husband who is deemed economically advantageous by parents or guardians but who is ill-suited to the heroine and who has no real regard for her. The initial match, which highlights her presence as a commodity in the circuits of exchange, gives way to another match with a wealthy, witty, and handsome partner who admires her. Such is the pattern in *The School for Scandal,* in which the socially advantageous match between Maria and the hypocritical Joseph Surface gives way to a marriage based on love between Maria and Charles Surface, whose good heart confirms his sincerity. Similarly, Bevil Junior's match with Lucinda Sealand in *The Conscious Lovers* proves a mere pretense to appease parents until he can propose to the defenseless Indiana and his friend Myrtle can court his beloved Lucinda. Indiana, as the daughter and heir to Sealand's fortune, will enrich Bevil's family, a fact that Sealand underscores in the last act when he refers to her as "this object." By presenting the temporarily powerful heroine with the man of her dreams (or something like him), comedies can give the illusion of greater female agency or authority than the general culture allows even as they contain female desire within a civil plan that depends on woman as property.

In spite of the limits they place on heroines, most comedies of the period take a critical stance on strict arranged marriages. Comedies by men and women build on the generational conflicts that are part of the bone structure of stage comedy from Aristophanes to Shakespeare. These generational struggles pertain to men and women, but the power to negotiate an agreement between the marrying and the wealth-controlling generations is most often in the hands of grooms, as it is in *The Man of Mode, The Way of the World, The Beaux' Stratagem,* and *The Clandestine Marriage.* Dryden's Palamede laments in *Marriage a la Mode,* "my old man has already married me, for he has agreed with another old man as rich and covetous as himself . . . and yet I know not what kind of woman I am to marry" (I.i, 15), but his basic right to object is never in question. Any challenge to Palamede's status as a legal subject would feminize a prospective groom. Steele's Bevil Junior conscientiously obeys his "tender obligations" to "the best of fathers," but he still tries to thread the needle of contractual and arranged marriage: "You may assure yourself I never will marry without my father's consent. But give me leave to say too, this declaration does not come up to a promise that I will take whomsoever he pleases" (I.ii, 336). These are questions that pertain to men and women, but the active negotiation of an agreement between the marrying and wealth-controlling generations is most often in the hands of grooms. The control that male characters exert in these plays is both ideological and realistic; they affirm the existing gender scripts that shape and, in turn, reiterate the law.

As comedies elaborated the logic of modern marriage, they moved further into the contradiction between contract thought and the priority of husbands' and fathers' claims. Playwrights tend to resolve the contradiction in favor of the latter. *The Conscious Lovers,* an example of the sentimental turn in stage comedy, is not long on plotting women. Indiana is a limp and defenseless orphan waiting on Bevil and her Daddy Warbucks, Mr. Sealand, to rescue her. Lucinda, who cries out against the merchant mentality of her mother and father, does very little to alter the plot. These limitations, although Steele exploits them here, are endemic to the heroine's role. Congreve's female characters, who are among the most witty and authoritative in the period's popular comedies, are usually powerless to make plots of their own. Even the independent-minded Angelica in *Love for Love,* who has her own fortune, has little influence in Congreve's story line, which focuses on the struggle between Sir Sampson and his son Valentine. Other strong women, such as Mrs. Sullen in *The Beaux' Stratagem,* Mrs. Friendall in Southerne's *The Wives' Excuse,* Lady Brute in Vanbrugh's *The Provok'd Wife,* and Althea in Sedley's *The Mulberry Garden,* are part of a substantial Restoration and early eighteenth-century chorus who criticize unhappy and forced marriages from a woman's point of view. But their sharp and insightful critiques do little to change the comic narrative.

In contrast to Etherege's, Congreve's, Farquhar's, Southerne's and Colman's heroines, Behn's and Centlivre's plotting Hellena (*The Rover*), Julia (*The Lucky Chance*), Miranda (*The Busy Body*), and Violante (*The Wonder*) use knowledge of their economic value to maneuver through the courtship narrative to a better marriage. Hellena can challenge her brother's plan to send her to a nunnery because she knows that she has a separate inheritance of 300,000 crowns coming from an uncle. Miranda taunts Sir George Airy for his love of her and "my thirty-thousand pounds," and knows to secure herself and her "writings, the most material part" of her future with George (IV, 52). Letitia Hardy in Cowley's *The Belle's Stratagem* takes her place as a trader alongside her father, and even the mild Donna Victoria of *A Bold Stroke for a Husband* passes as a man to retrieve the deeds that her husband has given away to his mistress. These comic events, where characters produce their authority by their wits, show how comic negotiations might inflect the foregone conclusion of the plot.

Goldsmith's *She Stoops to Conquer* and Cowley's *The Belle's Stratagem,* two plays that allow their heroines to manage the seduction and capture of their husbands, exhibit different attitudes toward female plotting in spite of their strong similarities. In each play, a young woman is betrothed to a young man who is reticent to marry, so the young woman takes on disguises to woo her future husband, who ultimately falls in love with her for her wit and understanding as well as her beauty. But in *She Stoops to Conquer,* Mr. Hardcastle declares to Kate that he "shall have the occasion to try your obedience" in his choice of Sir Charles Marlow (I, 112). Even though he assures her that "I'll never controul your choice," he dictates her dress, and Kate assures her father, "I find such a pleasure, sir, in obeying your commands, that I take care to observe them without ever debating their propriety" (III, 158). In contrast, Letitia Hardy of *The Belle's Stratagem* disguises herself first as a bumpkin and then as a worldly continental woman, leaving her father Mr. Hardy to chuckle his resignation: "I forsee Letty will have her way, and so I sh'an't give myself the trouble to dispute it" (I.iv, 19). These differences in attitude between Goldsmith's and Cowley's plays suggest the different power arrangements possible within a social and generic plot. Both stories accept the transfer of wealth through women, but they depart in the ways their heroines negotiate the terms of that ending. The terms of the marriage contract include the legal and extralegal negotiations through which wives and husbands imagine the new union. Cowley's heroine reigns as she proclaims to her lover Doricourt, "you see, I can be anything," to which he vows she shall be "nothing but yourself." Goldsmith's Marlow, on the other hand, exits the stage lamenting, "Zounds, there's no bearing this; it's worse than death," as Kate teases, a less promising beginning to a marriage supposedly founded on the mutual regard of husband and wife.

The problem these playwrights pose is at once legal, cultural, and psychological: under what terms does a woman exist within marriage as a self-determining individual rather than an abstraction or exchange value? The answers begin with Behn's appeal to a modified female libertinism. Behn's political affiliations put her plays at odds with an emerging discourse of rights, which provides the basis of most feminisms. Behn has little patience with the rhetoric of equality, which she was likely to parody as Dutch nonsense, as she did in *The Lucky Chance:*

> *Gayman:* Holland's a commonwealth, and is not ruled by kings.
> *Ralph:* Not by one, Sir, but by many. This was a cheesemonger. . . . (I.i, 225)

Behn's comedies are, in the broadest sense, uncomfortable with equality, both as a Whiggish political value and as a mathematical concept that makes people (especially women) equal to one another and, in an extreme reading, interchangeable abstractions. While she values the access that men *and* women have to desire, her erotic rhetoric keeps difference alive whenever possible. Exchanges that seem to be equal, such as Angellica's bargain with Willmore for "thy love for mine" turn out to be shams, while more viable promises, like Hellena's paradoxical vow to be "Hellena the Inconstant," involve a surplus that keeps women from being fully exchangeable and hence without identity. The erotic and narrative dynamics of the plays work against the state of loss that rights were meant to redress by positing the heroine's plenitude. Behn's heroines are active objects who try to teach their lovers this libertine lesson through comic events.[41] Behn reconciles libertine pleasures to the heroine's greater need of marriage because of her pregnable rather than impregnating body, which forces her into a different relationship to the Restoration libertine ethos. Her guarded optimism about female agency celebrates the erotic appeal of the female body. Her comic events keep this erotic difference alive, but her later plots move into dark territory, where the weight of commercial exchange undermines the unique claims of her individual lovers and leaves them with comic endings in which marriage ceases to be a viable resolution.

For Centlivre, the discourse of rights was as liberating as it was problematic for Behn. Centlivre reinterprets Behn's heroines through the lens of contract in the early eighteenth century, when equity courts were most hospitable to contract logic. *Williams v. Callow* (1717), *More v. Freeman* (1725) and *Moore v. Moore* (1737) all supported the premise that wives were individuals with rights, capable of making claims to property within marriage.[42] Centlivre, in 1709, challenges the objectification of female sexuality through her comic portrait of Sir Francis Gripe, the unethical guardian of Miranda, who tries to short circuit the "free market" of marriage exchange by marrying her himself. Centlivre embraced the free market and the rhetoric of independence it offered women with tales of self-determining women who make their own marriage contracts. Miranda in *The Busy Body* uses this market logic to write her own marriage contract. She unromantically proposes to George: "our Time's but short, and we must fall into Business: Do you think we can agree on that same terrible Bugbear, *Matrimony,* without hastily Repenting on both sides?" (V.iii, 52). Her most popular play and one of the most popular plays of the century, *The Busy Body* captured the public's imagination with its distinctly modern romance. Miranda uses the heat of the comic moment to negotiate her terms; the contract itself is quite mundane, but Miranda's role as an agent on her own behalf is remarkable. Her later plays struggle to make women subjects rather than objects of contracts, but Centlivre maintains the ideal of mutual contract as the grounds for the good marriage in the face of counterpressures that undermine her heroines' access to contract.

Hannah Cowley, who modeled her women after Behn's and her politics after Centlivre's, refigured the problem of women's uneven access to the marriage market as a failure of national principles. After Hardwicke's Marriage Act of 1753, the newly reconciled law and the higher age of consent made the tricked or clandestine marriages of Behn's and Centlivre's plays much less likely. In the wake of these legal changes, Cowley tried to prop women's uncertain status as a contractual subject on the discourse of nationalism. Her nationalist tone reinvents Centlivre's relish for soldiers and her John Bull-ish sensibilities for the 1770's, when England was embroiled in colonial conflicts. Like Frances Burney's *Evelina,* Cowley's plays pit the morally flawed

French (or pseudo-French) and their faulty liberties against the true natural English ideal in comic events that confirm the mutual authority of hero and heroine. Cowley's appeal to English identity as the basis of her heroine's contractual authority reaches its most optimistic tone in *The Belle's Stratagem,* but it becomes progressively less stable over the course of her career. Her uncertainty follows the general pattern in the careers of all these playwrights, but it also mirrors specific anxieties about the state of the nation. The Hastings trial, the war with the American colonies, and the ongoing conflict with France tarnished the great political hope of the Enlightenment, a rational and just system of government that would gain assent from ever-widening populations.

In the 1780s Inchbald takes on nothing less than the issue of the law's ability to provide the support that modern marriages required. In her late-century perspective, the law is not sufficient to support the equality that contract had promised. Neither is it sufficient to protect women from the pitfalls of regarding marriage as a contract, which opens the door to divorces that penalize women in her plays, as divorces did in most contemporary documented cases. Divorce laws prove prejudiced in favor of the powerful and wealthy men who control the communities of her comedies, and so she calls for relationships that exceed the letter of the law. Her plots identify women as subjects in a community of affective relationships that sustains them when the law and marriage fail them, as they inevitably do. Her liberal cynicism looks forward to the legal assumptions of the nineteenth century, which closed down some of the ambiguities in English law that had been sites of flexibility and creative interpretation for earlier playwrights and earlier women.

In these plays, the social as well as more psychical fantasies of adulthood and reconciliation that are the infrastructure of comedy meet the threat of alienation and the loss of identity for the heroine. These playwrights use the genre's focus on women and marriage, as well as its constitutive balance of comic events against comic closure, to imagine ways for their heroines to participate in marriage's fantasy of personal and social fulfillment. Historical debates about a woman's relationship to civil society animate these comedies, even as the playwrights reflect on the limits of those debates in their later plays. These terms—female desire in Behn, contracts in Centlivre, nation in Cowley, and the law in Inchbald—are the "hysterical symptoms" to which their plays return again and again in their comic events as they try to keep women from disappearing in the social and legal process of courtship and marriage.

CHAPTER THREE

YOU IRREPLACEABLE YOU

Behn's Unalienable Bodies

"What Man would endure to be so plagu'd as I have been. I have parry'd with my best Skill the most dangerous Thrusts that ever were made at me. To tug at an Oar, or dig in a Mine in Peru, is Recreation to it: But the first time to offer Marriage to me! I sweat to think on it. It made me tremble twice, for fear she should have forc'd my Neck into her muddy Noose of Matrimony"

(Betterton, *The Amorous Widow,* I.i, 17).

"What do you fear a longing Woman Sir? . . . Why stand you gazing Sir, a Woman's Passion is like the Tide, it stays for no man when the Hour is come—"

(Behn, *The Lucky Chance,* III.iii, 249).

Thomas Betterton and Aphra Behn share with most Restoration playwrights an interest in sexuality, even though they represent female desire in radically different ways. Lovemore, the rake who speaks the lines above in Thomas Betterton's *The Amorous Widow* (1668–1670), calls female desire a "dangerous Thrust" that he must work against and compares himself to a slave mining gold in Peru.[1] Like Rochester, who raved, "Let the porter and the groom, /Things designed for dirty slaves, /Drudge in fair Aurelia's womb, / To get supplies for age, and graves," Lovermore's libertine vision of sex must be free from the implication that he is anything less than a master seeking pleasure.[2] Warren Chernaik refers to such a dynamic as the "zero-sum game" of seventeenth-century libertinism, in which "the assertion of freedom by one participant means the deprivation of freedom for another."[3] A whiff of agency on the part of the woman concerned, or any hint that her willingness has become desire, disrupts that fantasy of the male libertine's "natural" sexual dominance as a subject in a world of objects.

By comparison, Aphra Behn's Julia puts a very different face on female desire in *The Lucky Chance* (1686). Julia, young and attractive, has unfortunately contracted a loveless and mercenary marriage with the much older Sir Cautious Fulbank. In the passage above, Pert, Julia's maid, lures Julia's former lover Gayman into a mysterious assignation with her lady, the "longing woman" whose identity remains unknown to him. Though Gayman does not know how to read it, Julia's sexual desire is neither comic nor frightening; instead, it allows her to participate as an agent in the sexual exchanges of comedy and to challenge her circulation in a monetary economy. Behn's " . . . do you fear a longing woman . . . ?" counters Betterton's anxiety about female desire with an erotic female sexual subjectivity that challenges the assumption that desiring women are objects of derision.

The newly coeducational stage of Restoration London added the presence of actresses and the female playwright to theatrical conversations about gender and power. Male and female playwrights were suddenly able to write more developed women's roles for women.[4] Behn's theatrical body consciousness, as Elin Diamond has argued of *The Rover,* took advantage of the fetishistic possibilities of the Restoration stage and the body of the actress on it, and created a physical counterpart to her textual comic politics.[5] But as playful and inventive as Restoration representations of women could be, the most critically heralded playwrights tended to serve up the same character types. The widowed Lady Laycock belongs in a parade of sexually active older women whose names (Laycock, Cockwood, Loveit, Wishfort) speak volumes about the anxiety that female desire provokes.[6] In *She Would If She Could,* Etherege punishes Lady Cockwood's desire for Courtall. Courtall manipulates her in order to gain access to her cousin Gatty, and her husband, Sir Oliver, orders his wife to make way for the prostitutes he brings home: "Go, we have sent for a civil person or two, and are resolved to fornicate in private" (II.ii). Sir Oliver later tells Courtall that "a poor fiddler, after he has been three days persecuted at a country wedding, takes more delight in scraping upon his old squeaking fiddle than I do in fumbling on that domestic instrument of mine" (III.iii). Lady Cockwood, whose name indicates her alleged desire to have a "cock" as well as to cuckold, becomes, like Lady Laycock, a site of alienated labor, where men work for the profit of another. The similar fates of Mrs. Loveit in Etherege's *The Man of Mode,* Mrs. Woodly ("jilting, unquiet, troublesome, and very Whorish") in Shadwell's *Epsom Wells,*[7] and Lady Fidget and her entourage in Wycherley's *The Country Wife* all portray women's sexual desires as comic when they exist independently of men's. Janet Todd has argued that the seventeenth century had a stake in female sexual pleasure, even if few people thought it was as important as male sexual pleasure. Humoural theory, still the reigning medical discourse, suggested that female orgasm was necessary for reproduction (*Secret Life,* 200). But the attitudes on display in the playhouse painted female desire as a potentially dangerous and unfeminine sign of independence.

As desiring and desirable women, Behn's heroines use the dual status of women as both property and possessors of property in themselves to generate erotic agency. This strategy appealed to the theatergoing public much more than the cynical though insightful sexual politics of plays like Wycherley's *The Gentleman Dancing Master,* Dryden's *Mr. Limberham,* Otway's *Friendship in Fashion,* Southerne's *The Wives' Excuse,* and Congreve's *The Double-Dealer,* none of which were notable popular successes.[8] While Southerne's Mrs. Friendall thoughtfully conveys the condition of most women in bad marriages in her fifth act resignation, "I must be still your Wife, and still unhappy," Behn's Julias in both *The False Count* and *The Lucky Chance* manage to escape their ridiculous husbands through highly unlikely fantasy divorces. These happy endings do not make Behn's plays more critical of sexual ideology than Southerne or Wycherley; in fact, they are more ideologically complicit in the development of companionate marriages. But Behn's optimistic iconoclasm and her erotic pedagogy succeeded with audiences well beyond the Restoration. Her most performed comedies, *The Rover, The Feign'd Courtesans, The False Count, The City Heiress,* and, to a lesser extent, *The Lucky Chance* continued to appear on the eighteenth-century stage despite criticism from Collier, Pope, and others. I am interested in these plays because of their popularity and because of Behn's comic negotiation of a place for her heroines as desiring and desirable women.

Of all the playwrights in this study, Aphra Behn has received the most critical attention. Most Behn scholars see her as an early feminist, loosely defined, on the basis of her plays' differences from those of her peer dramatists.[9] In particular, Jacqueline Pearson's discussion of Behn's celebration of active, bold women in prefaces, prologues, and epilogues, with the clarification that her sentiments are not uniformly feminist, set the tone for subsequent scholars, who have tried to grapple with Behn's relationship to sexual ideology.[10] Working in very different argumentative models, Patricia Gill, Laura Brown, and Nancy Cotton all conclude that Behn's approach to gender and marriage sets her comedies apart from those of her contemporaries Wycherley, Etherege, and Congreve. Gill argues persuasively that Behn is uninterested in the "vicissitudes of male subjectivity" and that she represents men through the eyes of her female characters.[11] Catherine Gallagher makes the broader claim that women's plays in the period generally manifest the persistent imbalance of powers between the sexes, as well as an anxious sense of authorship and dispossession. For Behn, this nexus of sexual identity and exchange authenticates her prostitutes as more honest than "honest" women and becomes the basis for her own authority as the "poetess-punk."[12] Robert Markley, Heidi Hutner, and Susan Green have similarly argued for the importance of a feminine model of desire that challenges the construction of women as passive objects in her plays.[13] For Markley, the struggle is a political one that celebrates Tory rakes and repudiates sexually repressed Roundheads and Whigs. For Hutner, Behn's celebration of the body of the "other" woman, the colonial, non-European women in *The Rover,* parts I and II, is most significant. For Green, the semiotics of the female body, in a historical relationship to the Renaissance stage, highlights the contradiction between a construction of femininity and an essentialized female body. While my argument shares their interests in questions of subjectivity, an overview of the most popular plays does not support some of the theoretically supple arguments that they offer. Without contesting their conclusions, I want to try the role of the body in Behn's comedies in the courts of public opinion and generic expectation, where Behn makes use of the object status of the body without being confined to it. The tension between subject and object in her most successful comic strategies clears a space for an embodied female self who cannot be displaced.

Behn's dedication of *The Feign'd Courtesans* to Nell Gwyn argues for the agency of women as active objects. Deborah Payne has argued that the dedication subverts the economic authority of the patron relationship; to her insight I add that it also subverts the subject/object relationship of heterosexual desire.[14] Gwyn's public persona captured the spirit of Behn's sexy royalism; she is both the king's mistress and the woman whom Behn called an argument against misogyny: "Succeeding ages who shall with joy survey your history shall envy us who lived in this, and saw those charming wonders which they can only read of, and whom we ought in charity to pity, since all the pictures pens or pencils can draw, will give 'em but a faint idea of what we have the honour to see in such absolute perfection" (*Works* VI: 86). Gwyn is a prototype for the fantasy of non-negotiable female identity in the comedies. This dedication does not deny that some sort of sexual economy is necessary; rather, it claims that Gwyn's value resists displacement and anonymity. Gwyn's authority is constructed by the desires of others for her, but Behn also touts her subjective power without contesting the status of Gwyn as a sexual object.

Behn is a political paradox only if one accepts the post-Cartesian principles of Enlightenment rationality and their insistence on distinct rational subjects and the world of objects. Behn had read Descartes in her study of Copernican and Ptolemaic science, in which she asserted the ability of "naïve" readings of scientific and biblical scholarship to move beyond philosophical dogma, such as the clear division between subject and object or mind and body.[15] Descartes's dualism between mind and body establishes the grounds of scientific objectivity crucial to Enlightenment culture. The Cartesian withdrawal of the soul or the "I" from the body is the condition of knowledge in his philosophical system. Descartes's "I" reflects on the body as an object like any other "unthinking thing." The body, as a part of the material world, must remain separate from the mastering mind even in the process of perception: " . . . bodies are not strictly perceived by the senses or the faculty of imagination but by the intellect alone, and . . . this perception derives not from their being touched or seen but from their being understood; and in view of this I know plainly that I can achieve an easier and more evident perception of my own mind than of anything else" (*Meditations,* 2.22–23). Descartes's anxiety about the body and its senses centers on the unreliable knowledge that sensation provides, an anxiety that has its heirs in the intellectual self of Locke, the immaterialism of Berkeley, and the skepticism of Hume. But Descartes resolves the anxiety at the expense of the body, preferring instead a neutral category of mind to sensual or bodily knowledge. Descartes's logical leap inaugurated an epistemic shift in seventeenth-century science and philosophy. In his wake, Sprat, Hooke, and Newton moved English culture closer to thinking of a world of objects that could be mastered and appropriated as property by those who were rational masters of their own bodies. It was both the philosophical cornerstone of rational thought and a means to distinguish subjects from objects in the early culture of possessive individualism.

Twentieth-century feminisms have been haunted by this split, rendered as the sex/gender split, in which sex approximates a purely physiological category of self, and gender stands for the acculturated, socialized self and its learned behaviors. Toril Moi has returned to the work of Simone de Beauvoir to address the debilitating features of the sex/gender split, which renders the body (sex) an inaccessible object on which gender is mapped. The split denies what Moi reads as the true spirit of Beauvoir's claim, "one is not born, but rather one becomes a woman," which is to understand the body as a situation. The historically situated body disappears, she argues, from post-structuralist accounts such as Judith Butler's, in which Moi insists that "sex is the inaccessible ground of gender, gender becomes completely disembodied, and the body itself is divorced from all meaning" (74). While she reads Butler somewhat reductively, Moi's critique is instructive when paired with the disappearance of the body in liberal feminist legal accounts, such as the work of Mary Ann Case.[16] When contemporary critics refer to Behn as a feminist, they risk reading Behn's fascination with the body through this problematic sex/gender split. Behn's interest in the body is closer to Beauvoir's model of subjectivity, which defies the subject and object division. Her revision of the sexual vocabulary of libertinism and of contemporary science challenged the prerogatives of the penetrative male who moves through a world of feminized objects, in spite of her awareness of what Patricia Gill calls the "latent cruelty" of rakish vitality (150). In contrast to a world of objects and subjects, Behn presented her audience with a plan for mutual pleasure through male and female characters who are themselves both subjects *and* objects.

Intriguing Bodies

The Rover. Or, The Banish't Cavaliers (1677), the biggest commercial success of Behn's early career, is also one of the most discussed Restoration plays in late-twentieth century criticism.[17] One of its greatest attractions is Behn's deft trickster, Hellena. Hellena's energetic desire for Willmore and her skepticism about sexual purity, which she nonetheless finds an economic necessity, move the main plot forward. Hellena begins the play by making a joke of the construction of the sexually innocent woman:

> *Hellena:* 'Tis true, I was never a Lover yet—but I begin to have a shreud Guess, what 'tis to be so, and fancy it very pretty to sigh, and blush and wish, and dream and wish, and long and wish to see the Man; and when I do, look pale and tremble; just as you did when my Brother brought home the fine *English* Colonel to see you—what do you call him? Don *Belvile.*
> *Florinda:* Fie, *Hellena.*
> *Hellena:* That Blush betrays you. . . . (I.i, 455)

Hellena's joking exposes Florinda's feminine modesty as a ruse. Behn accentuates the artifice of the "good" sister and the honesty of the transgressive Hellena. When Florinda warns Hellena not to be so wild and curious about love, Hellena points at Florinda, the model of femininity, as illogical and dishonest. In contrast, Hellena makes her desire *for* desire licit, open, and harmonious with her character, with which the audience must identify to tap the play's comic pleasures.

Hellena's conquest of Willmore, the eponymous Rover, depends on witty exchanges that owe something to the banter of Beatrice and Benedick. Her tendentious jokes lead Willmore through an argument about what it means to be in a female body. Willmore relishes these erotic-comic lessons and, like Longvil in Shadwell's *The Virtuoso,* "would not have the body without the mind,"[18] though his sexual appetites are stronger and his bent less satiric. It is Hellena, however, who controls the conversation:

> *Willmore:* . . . I'l neither ask nor give a Vow,—tho' I cou'd be content to turn Gipsie, and become a left-hand bridegroom, to have the Pleasure of work-

> ing that great Miracle of making a Maid a Mother, if you durst venture; 'tis upse Gipsie that, and if I miss, I'l lose my Labour.
>
> *Hellena:* And if you do not lose, what shall I get? a cradle full of noise and mischief, with a pack of repentance at my back? can you teach me to weave Incle to pass my time with? tis upse Gipsie that too.
>
> *Willmore:* I can teach thee to Weave a true loves knot better.
>
> *Hellena:* So can my dog. (V.i, 517)

Willmore's not-so-veiled reference to sexual intercourse meets with no batting eyelashes. Hellena reduces his alleged sexual skill to an unattractive animal level (the "miracle" of sexual reproduction) while also making it clear that Hellena doesn't need to be taught. As comedian Elayne Boosler once said in response to the "miracle of birth" argument in right-to-life rhetoric, "Popcorn is a miracle, too, if you don't know how it's done."[19] Behn's substitution of dog for man identifies the animal nature of sex. The retort demystifies the play of female innocence and sexual knowledge that Restoration comedies ranging from *The Country Wife* to *The Way of the World* use to keep female characters outside the sphere of action.[20] Behn and her heroines have little use for women who know nothing of sex, yet who exist within a socioeconomic system fixated on female sexuality.

Behn's attention to sex and reproduction in such comic events imposes a female point of view on the comic structure of marriage and reproduction. Hellena knows that her body is necessary to the future of the social order, and she refuses to hide what she knows about the "female condition." Hellena's joke about reproduction gestures toward the material realities of life beyond the romance. *She* must attend to the legal status of their sex acts not out of some arbitrary sense of propriety but because, as a woman, she may find their consequences written on her body. In a dark comment on what can happen beyond the ending, *The Second Part of the Rover* opens with Hellena already dead after only a month of marriage, and the sexually voracious Willmore on the prowl. Willmore wishes for "women in abundance" a few lines after he calls Hellena "a saint to be adored on holy days," employing a disembodied, rigid language to describe her that has nothing to do with the character from *The Rover* (I.i, 235; 234). Even more disturbingly, Willmore calls her "too good for mortals," while the stage directions instruct the actor to deliver the line "with sham sadness" (I.i, 235). In this sequel, Behn questions her ability to create comic plots that reflect enduring material changes for female subjects; she proves that she can trick her way through the courtship plot with a witty heroine, but maintaining her authority after marriage is another matter. As Pateman has noted, the making of social or sexual contracts is not a problem; the enforcement of them is (58). Willmore's resistance to location, in contrast to Hellena's potentially disastrous location as an unmarried mother, makes the point. Willmore wants to avoid commitment, while Hellena knows it is her only option as a sexually active adult. Hellena responds to Willmore's particular instabilities by mirroring them, provided she can have her sexual adventure without progeny.[21] Behn's awareness of this asymmetry in gender relations inflects the narrative end of the genre, marriage, with a female point of view.

Hellena handles the cultural contradiction between sexual innocence and knowledge so expertly that she runs circles around the witty Willmore. Willmore's offer of "free love" only sets up Hellena's "cradle full of noise and mischief, with a pack of repentance at (her) back," the punch line of their comic exchange. Hellena is hardly the first character on the Restoration stage to mention the consequences of sexual intercourse, but her response does the work of comic truth-telling. She offers the audience the pleasure of release for following the joke of a sexually aware young woman. Hellena presses her comic advantage further when Willmore asks her for a kiss: "One kiss! how like my Page he speaks; I am resolv'd you shall have none, for asking such a sneaking sum—he that will be satisfied with one kiss, will never dye of that longing; good Friend, single kiss, is all your talking come to this?—a kiss, a caudle! farewel Captain, single kiss" (V.i, 517). Her joke reverses the hierarchy of male desiring subjects and female objects by objectifying Willmore's desire and finding it lacking. His request for "such a sneaking sum" does not match her longing or her vision of a relationship continually animated by desire on both sides. When he announces his name is "Robert the Constant," Hellena scoffs "A very fine name; pray was it your Faulkner or your Butler that Ch[r]istened you? do they not use to Whistle when they call you?" (V.i, 517). Her steady banter keeps Willmore's lines to a minimum when they play together and helps her maintain agency within their plot.

In contrast to Hellena, Angellica, the city's famous courtesan, is at the mercy of her beloved Willmore, though she enjoys a more general and public form of power over other men.[22] Angellica's position as a sex worker should establish her object status as a woman who must attract the male gaze. Instead, her extreme beauty, figured by the portraits that advertise her availability, makes men objects, who "put on all their Charms to appear lovely in her sight . . . while she has the Pleasure to behold all languish for her that see her" (I.ii, 465–66). Angellica doubles the logic of exchange in a way that seems to undo the female conundrum of sexual objectivity. Pregnancy disappears as a factor for Angellica, who instead inhabits the paradox of a woman who is both outside and yet forever on the sexual market. Angelica enjoys sexual pleasure, but she cannot be a slave to it because the exchanges she orchestrates are temporary. As Laura Rosenthal has argued, *pace* Pateman, prostitutes doubly destabilize contractual relations because they do not fully inhabit the position of the individual who makes legitimate contracts, and because they are necessarily "jilting" in that they never become completely subordinate to their lovers (112). Angellica profits from this instability when she accumulates financial capital instead of relinquishing it through sex, but she loses control over her body and her wealth at the moment when Willmore persuades her to fix her value as woman-in-love. Her affective economic contract at the end of act II with Willmore ("the pay, I mean, is but thy love for mine") deprives her of the power she had as the self-possessed "almighty courtesan," who could determine her own value.

Angellica's angry retreat outside the comic plot signals her failure as a libertine woman, but it is a productive failure. She illustrates the paradox that faces the women of Behn's plays: women become individual subjects when they articulate their desire, but when they enter contracts, they become a known quantity, "tried and impressed in the mint," as Gay's Mrs. Peachum sings in *The Beggar's Opera*, and are thus subject to exchange and substitution. Angellica believes that love cannot be bought, but she has been duped into accepting the contractual false promise of Willmore, unlike Hellena who vows, paradoxically, to be "Hellena th' Inconstant." Angellica's unresolved rage haunts the ending that unites Hellena to Willmore and Florinda to Belvile. Angellica remains, according to Suz-Anne Kinney, where "the theatre apparatus (the actress and the female playwright), and the social struggle (an analysis of the commodification of women) intersect."[23] Angellica's armed confrontation with Willmore is not easily reconciled with the comic spirit of *The Rover*'s sexual playfulness, but it is crucial to Behn's comic pedagogy. Angellica has learned that men and women are not equals in love, and that the struggle for power is an ongoing one for women in the sexual marketplace:

> All this thou'st made me know, for which I hate thee.
> Had I remain'd in innocent security,
> I shou'd have thought all men were born my slaves;
> And worn my pow'r like lightening in my Eyes,
> To have destroy'd at Pleasure when offended. (V.i, 513)

Once her sexual power is undermined by the false promise of romantic love and fidelity, she is free to expose the nearly impossible space of feminine desire; she can exist only in the interstices between subjectivity and objectivity.

Rape, the shadowy twin to Behn's libertine sexual politics, also haunts this comedy. Unlike the tragic but opportunistic use of rape in Nicholas Brady's *The Rape; or, The Innocent Imposters* (1692) and D'Urfey's *The Injured Princess* (1682), Behn's approach avoids the titillating display of the sexual victim and instead highlights the anonymity of sexual violence. Florinda, already known to spectators as Hellena's sister and Belvile's sweet intended, is reduced to her body through rape, a "mere" woman without claim to identity.[24] In the first potential rape scene of the play, Florinda mistakes Willmore for her intended Belvile when he stumbles into the walled garden where she is to meet Belvile. The erotically coded scene opens as she enters the garden "*in an undress, with a Key, and a little Box*" (III.iii, 486). The box contains her "jewels," also slang for genitalia, which she has brought to fund an escape with Belvile. Her plan to hide them "in yonder Jessamin" only futhers the set of connections between the eroticized jewels and her sexualiy. The comic slippage between her literal jewels and her genitalia codes her as an alienable, commodified body. Willmore, assuming she can be purchased, offers her a pistole and then wrestles with her when she rejects his offer. His ability to narrate her as a body of female genitals rather than an embodied self suggests that she can be exchanged indefinitely; Florinda, unknown as an individual, "means" flower, female, genitals, sex, jewels, and cash equally. If he can reduce her not only to an anonymous genital sexuality but then further to an implied cash value, then "Florinda" no longer exists in that economy; an unmarked "she," Florinda must rely on the kindness (or cruelty) of strangers to give her body meaning. Her sexual reserve only facilitates the equation of her body with an exchange value. Behn gives her audience hope for a comic resolution to the rape scene in spite of Florinda's real bodily danger; they know that her virtuous lover Belvile is on his way. This information makes Behn's darkly comic circulation of Florinda's passive body tolerable but still critically pointed. Female sexuality figured as a polite, proto-bourgeois absence can be filled by any number of externally supplied meanings. When Kemble edited the play for his 1790 version, *Love in Many Masks,* he omitted all possible references to rape and whores (including this scene), undercut Angellica's role substantially, and reformed Willmore into an only slightly rakish bourgeois husband to make it succeed with late-century playgoers.[25] The violence of the rape was, it seems, no longer tolerable to late-eighteenth-century audiences, even though the cultural logic that objectifies Florinda and Angellica was more pervasive, as I will argue in chapter six.

The second attack on Florinda is even darker and more difficult to accept as comic, yet it too depends on the strategies of farce, physical comedy, and comic substitution. Blunt misreads the sexual economy of Naples and believes the whore Lucetta to be "a person of Quality" because of her clothes. Blunt reads social rank through sumptuary codes, which no longer carry legal force. Beverly Lemire notes that all legal prohibitions on dress in England were removed from the law by 1604, but that there remained some official sanction against upper class fashions spreading to the lower ranks. This sanction was not firm, and since it was unsupported by specific sumptuary law, it was unevenly and rarely enforced.[26] Blunt's inability to understand new models of class and his politically suspect wealth feminize him in relation to the other Cavaliers. Instead of giving him "free" sex, Lucetta steals his money and his clothes. A furious Blunt swears his revenge on all women just as Florinda walks into his rooms, seeking protection from her brother. Blunt seizes her and raves: "I will kiss and beat thee all over; kiss, and see thee all over; thou shalt lye with me too, not that I care for the injoyment, but to let thee see I have tain deliberated Malice to thee, and will be revenged on one Whore for the sins of another" (IV.iv, 505). His parodic anger is a real threat to Florinda. Blunt tells Florinda he will "strip thee stark naked, then hang thee out at my window by the heels, with a Paper of scurvy Verses fasten'd to thy breast, in praise of damnable Women" (IV.iv, 505). Blunt needs to make Florinda a sign that he can control, a sign that will affirm that women are exchangeable, non-specific topics for bawdy poems and thereby announce his mastery over them.

Blunt's attempt to separate her body from her identity without according any value to that body is a graphic misreading of the play's erotics. He lacks the libertine bonhomie that celebrates sexual desire, and he tries to supply this lack with sexual force. He is about to rape Florinda when Frederick enters the room and nonchalantly offers to join in the attack; a diamond ring and Belvile's name allow Florinda to thwart the rape by supplying her missing identity:

> *Florinda:* Sir, If you find me not worth *Belvile's* Care, use me as you please; and that you may think I merit better treatment than you threaten—pray take this Present—[*Gives him a Ring: He looks on it.*]
>
> *Blunt:* Hum—a Diamond! why, 'tis a wonderful Virtue now that lies in this Ring, a mollifying Virtue; adsheartlikins there's more perswasive Rhetorick in't, than all her Sex can utter.
>
> *Frederick:* I begin to suspect something; and 'twould anger us vilely to be trust up for a rape upon a Maid of quality, when we only believe we ruffle a Harlot. (IV.iv, 506)

Florinda must represent herself through a commodity, a ring whose mobility and marketability underscore her own place as a commodity. Her salvation preserves a comic tone de facto while it indicts a culture that cannot distinguish between whores and maids of quality yet alleges that these labels determine the plot of a woman's life.

The Rover's bold yet comically readable investigation of sexual identity continued as a stock repertoire piece into the nineteenth century, though as *Love in Many Masks* after 1790. Its appeal suggests that the basics of Behn's sexual politics were palatable to audiences beyond the Restoration conversation about Royalism and sexuality that structures the play.[27] The sexually desiring female characters of *The Rover* set the tone for a string of comedies that explore the courtesan and female characters who mimic their comic mobility. Behn's 1678 *Sir Patient Fancy* capitalized on these themes in a partisan cocktail of Dissenting Whigs, Puritans, hypocrisy, cynicism, and impotence. Inspired by the recent translation of *Le Malade Imaginaire,* Behn wrote this tightly plotted, farcical, and bawdy comedy with an impotent rich Puritan in the title role.[28] The effort, however, with its defense of a woman writer's right to "Sense and Sacred poetry" in the epilogue and its argument for bawdy plays in the prologue proved too much for theater audiences in the late 1670s. Already troubled by anti-Catholic grumbling that would grow into the tempest of the Popish Plot nine months later, the London theaters were vulnerable to Catholic associations due to the Tory base of their support and because of their pageantry. The fact that the sheriff of London, also a prominent merchant and Whig, was named Sir Patience Ward could not have helped matters. Behn drew fire for plagiarizing from Molière and for bawdiness, tenable charges that are best tempered by Behn's defense: "had it been owned by a Man, though the most Dull Unthinking Rascally Scribbler in Town, it had been a most admirable Play." As Janet Todd notes, men were also attacked for bawdy, but the criticism of Behn anticipates the attacks that were yet to come for Ravenscroft, Otway, and others who would feel the heat of criticism during the Popish Plot and from Jeremy Collier. Behn's critics called her out before the tide had officially turned. Behn would not return to such direct political tactics or to a device as risky as impotence until *The Lucky Chance,* the last of her plays she saw produced.

Behn wrote a commercially unsuccessful but interesting sequel to *The Rover* in 1681, which did not make it to a third night or to later revivals. Behn created a fantastic cast of female bodies, including transvestite women, giants, dwarves, and "jewesses," and reprised the roles of Ned Blunt and Willmore. Blunt and his friend Featherfool share the fantasy of transforming their intendeds (a dwarf and a giant) into nubile fifteen-year-olds with the help of the magic bath that Willmore and his sidekick Harlequin peddle around Madrid. The promise of being normalized into a male fantasy of femininity, however, is no improvement for the She-Giant. She tells Featherfool directly that she would rather have a man to match her size than to change her body: "Not that I would change this noble Frame of mine, cou'd I but meet my Match, and keep up the first Race of Man intire: But since this scanty World affords none such, I to be happy, must be new created, and then shall expect a wiser lover" (III.i, 259). The comic force of her situation comes from the juxtaposition of the She-Giant's strength and "masculine" presence with Featherfool's "feminine" timorousness. After he receives a sound beating at La Nuche's house, his cowardice culminates in his wishful soliloquy: "to be a Woman, to be courted with Presents, and have both the pleasure and the profit—to be without a Beard, and sing a fine treble—and squeak if the Men but kiss me—'twere fine—and what's better, I am sure never to be beaten again" (V.iii, 288–89). Featherfool wishes for the disempowered female body that the She-Giant resists; she prefers an active model of female subjectivity that is the opposite of his feminine fantasy. This bold experiment with gender roles and the possibilities for embodying female agency that the She-Giant and the new female lead La Nuche presented fell flat, however, with audiences. The harsher, more drunken Willmore; the rough, satirical farce; and the scathing critique of marriage made it a difficult play for theatergoers who were uncertain about the future of the crown in the early 1680s. James, duke of York, had suggested the sequel to Behn, but he later requested the first *The Rover,* with its more attractive Willmore and its slightly sunnier vision of marriage, for two command performances at court when he was king.[29]

The popular heir of *The Rover's* economy of pleasure was *The Feign'd Courtesans* (1679). Although it was slow to take off with audiences, it returned to the stage in 1716 and 1717 for a respectable revival. Behn's dedication to the "Protestant whore" Nel Gwyn may have offered some cover in the politically charged days after the Popish Plot, which had driven away much of the theatre's audience. Her focus on prostitution explores a sexual economy that defies the objectifying forces of elite marriage. Marcella and Cornelia, sisters posing as courtesans, clearly understand the importance of money to their survival and understand as well that their sexuality determines their access to money. But they struggle to create an economy of pleasure with their lovers that transcends "necessary trash," the money that Cornelia rejects in her guise as a courtesan. Behn turns the usually devastating plight of women who must make money from sex into a comic fantasy of sexual pleasure without sexual risk; "La Silvianetta," the great courtesan whom all the men in the play seek, is the rarest of creatures, a courtesan and a "zitella," or virgin. Marcella, Cornelia, and their cousin Laura Lucretia all take advantage of this identity to preserve their virginity while "playing" the whore. Through this mythical creature, Behn revisits the critique that Hellena provides as the sexually knowing virgin and presses on its limits. Marcella tries to seduce the unassailable Fillamour, and Cornelia leaps from role to role to escape consequences. The circulation of identities, which draws formally on the Spanish intrigue plot, sets up the highest test for these lovers: they must know each other well enough to make it through the maze of the plot. Theatrically, Behn accomplishes this end with some of her most physical comedy as well as a casting joke in the first run. Actress Betty Currer, who played the sweet Marcella, brought to the role her comic talents as well as her off-stage reputation for sexual escapades, which created another site of comic dissonance in the very consonance of Currer and Euphemia, Marcella's courtesan alter-ego. With disguises and identities flying, this play can be difficult reading at times, but these confusions translate, as Jane Spencer and Dawn Lewcock have pointed out, into exciting comic theater.[30]

Economic questions pervade the play and structure Behn's critique of sexual exchange. While Fillamour argues for "lawful enjoyment," which he claims deepens pleasure while upholding necessary moral obligations to women and their families, Galliard, in Rochesterian fashion, encounters women and sex through the "generous law of nature, to enjoy 'em as we do meat, drink, air, and light," under which women are "free" commodities. Like his predecessor sensualist Willmore, Galliard wants easy access to women. Galliard claims that men and women can both be commodified and happily imagines himself as an erotic object, "as staple a commodity as any's in the Nation,—but I wou'd be reserv'd for your own use! faith take a sample to Night, and as you like it, the whole piece" (III.i, 116). Cornelia's rejoinder, that his over-liberality might have "spoiled the sale of the rest" of his samples, ascribes to him the problems of female commodification; he too may lose his value as a sexual object if he is too available. Her quip comes with the sexual barb that he should include love and constancy to "inch out" his lack of honesty. Mere sex, it seems, is not enough to impress Cornelia. Galliard jokingly imagines sexual exchanges that do not exist in relation to money as a third term, a utopic vision of a world where women and men could be subjects and objects without regard to money. While Cornelia interjects the need for love and constancy, qualities that protect women in the real sexual economy, his utopia offers the pleasures of the commodity without the fetishism. His commodified sexuality brings mobility, access, and recurrent pleasure because he refuses to substitute the meager pleasures of value for the pleasures of the thing itself.

The commodity exchanges that do attend the "feigned" courtesans of the play are part of a running joke in Behn's oeuvre: real men don't have to pay for sex. Men like Sir Signal Buffoon and his prototype Blunt, who do pay, announce their lack of erotic appeal, an extension of their Whiggish and unmanly obsession with money. By act I, Sir Signal has given the trickster Petro an undisclosed amount to meet "Donna Silvianetta"; Tickletext, his tutor, parts with 20 crowns for La Silvianetta in act I; In act II, both fools are robbed by Petro, posing as a civility master; in act III, Sir Signal announces he has given 500 crowns; 70 lines later he gives another 500. Fittingly, when he introduces himself to Cornelia in act IV, it is as "Sir Signal Buffoon, sole son and heir to eight thousand pounds a year" (131). His money must stand in for his body, but it is a phallic ruse that only confirms his lack. Sir Signal's obsession with money is a function of his education by the xenophobic low-churchman Tickletext, who prefers plain English university buildings to Roman cathedrals. Tickletext, who claims to hate prostitutes, "worse than [rosary] beads or holy water," proves hypocritical in his secret whoring, which he tries to explain as missionary work. In addition to their lack of individual appeal, their relations with women fail miserably because they deal only with Petro, Galliard, and Fillamour, who cheat them time and again. But their failures are crucial to the plot; the money they give to Petro to secure "La Silvianetta" supports Marcella and Cornelia and, ironically, allows them to preserve their virginity.

Tickletext and Sir Signal are eager to enter into bargains with courtesans, but their distance from actual women underscores their sexual inexperience and their politically coded alienation from their own bodies. The only direct conversation they have with a woman is with Cornelia, who has been expecting Galliard and who is "resolved . . . to be Reveng'd on 'em for this disappointment" (IV.i, 130). The comic event reverses the power dynamic between Florinda and Blunt: a woman takes her revenge on two men not because she makes no distinctions between men (as Blunt refuses to distinguish between women) but because they are the wrong men who seek her out as a general sexual commodity. Their beatings, a standard punishment for Whigs in Behn's plays, brings them back to the immediacy of the body even as it exiles them from the world of sexual pleasure. The viewer who would dare to identify with their economic politics would find him or herself in a similarly uncomfortable position as the comic object whose body is a thing rather than the comic master whose body is the means to erotic subjectivity.

Behn tests her erotic economy when she puts Galliard in dialogue with Sir Signal. Sir Signal resolves to take a "delicious young harlot" by force, ignoring the fact that courtesans are sexually available by definition. Galliard mocks Sir Signal's threat of force when he speaks longingly of ancient Rome, "when Noble Rapes, not whining Courtship, did the Lovers business" (III.i, 119). Sir Signal's misreading of sexual subjects and objects (like Blunt's in *The Rover*) misses the subtle shadings of Behn's sexual economy. He substitutes masculine economic force for mutual pleasure in his reply to Galliard, "[P]sha[w] Rapes, man! I mean by force of mony, pure dint of Gold, faith and troth." In his suspect equation, money and sexual force are both substitutes for what Galliard already has, erotic powers of attraction. Behn's Royalist ideology of natural sexual prerogatives is built on the premise of mutual attraction; the need to use force, whether Sir Signal's "gold" or Blunt and Frederick's directly physical attack on Florinda in *The Rover,* is a sign of masculine failure to attract a woman "naturally." Galliard's satiric joke plays on the difference between rape and Royalist sexuality, but Behn remains suspicious enough of her male characters, even her beloved Royalists, to keep them from explaining the finer points of her sexual politics.

Marcella and Cornelia expose the contradiction of female sexual honesty; in order to be considered honest (chaste), they must be dishonest about their sexual desires. "Honest," like "ruined" and "fortune," means different things for men and women; these terms link sexual activity and economic viability for women, while for men they mean economic credibility and economic viability.[31] Cornelia imports the notion of credibility into her definition of honesty to build her case for her sexual agency. When Cornelia argues with her sister Marcella, she points out that a rich woman should be able to be honest in the masculine sense:

> *Marcella:* A too forward Maid, *Cornelia,* hurts her own fame, and that of all her sex.
>
> *Cornelia:* Her Sex, a pretty consideration by my youth, an Oath I shall not violate this dozen year, my sex shou'd excuse me, if, to preserve their fame, they expected I shou'd ruin my own quiet: in choosing an ill-favoured husband such as Octavio before a young, handsome lover, such as you say Fillamour is . . . life Sister thou art beautifull, and hast a Fortune too, for which before I wou'd lay out upon so shamefull a purchase as such a Bedfellow for life as *Octavio;* I wou'd turn arrant keeping Curtizan, and buy my better fortune. (II.i, 102–3)

Like Hellena in *The Rover,* Cornelia commits her comic heresy directly; women are fools to destroy their lives for some abstract notion of feminine chastity. Logically, her solution turns to economics; women are bought by men all the time, so why shouldn't rich, beautiful, and truly honest women find ways to be agents as well? Cornelia's serious joke puts the key term "fortune" into circulation against the term "fame." Marcella has a monetary fortune, the form of fortune most often associated with women, but Cornelia encourages her to use it to buy a better "fortune," or fate, like a man seeking his fortune in the public sphere. The play of the term suggests that women can appropriate the system of sexual circulation as agents rather than conduits if those women can lay claim to their sexual choices.

Marcella and Cornelia understand that money can give them social freedom when they approach it as courtesans, even if they only "play" at exchanging sex for money. The conditions that lead them to such heavy play, however, are serious; the sisters are out of money and face real prostitution if they cannot find another source of cash. When Marcella claims they must sell their jewels, Cornelia rejoins, "When they are gone, what jewel will you part with next?" in a pun that repeats the dangerous conflation of genitals and precious stones that leads to Florinda's near rape in *The Rover.* The bad logic of the sexual contract, which renders women as indistinguishable values while it also locates them in bodies they cannot transcend or reinterpret, structures both Cornelia's joke and the assault on Florinda. Through these scenes, Behn asks this dark political question: what can keep all women from becoming the same counters in an infinite exchange? Her answer returns to female sexuality and sexual objectivity: the erotic object must produce her own subjectivity within the power relations of Restoration sexuality. Following the logic of capital, which according to Marx both produces alienation and class division and also creates the conditions for their abolition, Behn argues that female sexuality can both alienate women from themselves and provide the cultural logic of their self-possession and agency.

In keeping with Behn's challenging sexual politics, Marcella, as the courtesan Euphemia, is relatively unconcerned with her lover Fillamour's faithfulness but very interested in his erotic sensibilities. When he fails to recognize her, Marcella makes him pay a price for his unrakish gullibility: "Not know me, and in love! punish him Heaven for falsehood! but I'le contribute to deceive him on, and ruin him with perjury" (II.i, 107). As Fillamour tries to argue her into a more virtuous life, Marcella retorts, "Virtue itself's a dream of so slight force,/ The very fluttering of Love's wings destroys it/ . . . In men a feeble Beauty, shakes the dull slumber off" (IV.i, 127). She claims that the virtue of men, not women, disappears in the sexual marketplace of courtship. Behn's reversal draws comic force from a truth more universally acknowledged: virtue is a man's dream about women that he must also wish away in throes of his own desire. Virtue based on female self-denial provides the emotional architecture of the chaste marriage, but it must collapse when a woman feels some sexual desire as a prelude to marriage. Euphemia and thus Marcella prove comic masters of this contradiction that shapes the social order. Social conventions, especially those concerning women's behavior, are overdetermined by sexual relations, which is the insight that Fillamour wants her to repress by submitting to "honesty." To taunt him for his preaching, Euphemia/Marcella imagines Fillamour in the pulpit as the sexually compelling priest of abstinence who raises the desire of his (female) flock. The meta-joke, however, is that Marcella, who is no libertine, understands the terms of her own circulation and can argue against them.

Marcella works out the dilemma of Angellica with a vengeance. She can critique the economics of marriage while retaining her place in the social order. She can thus afford to rage when Fillamour offers her money to reform without falling out of the register of femininity because multiple masks protect her.[32] Euphemia rejects the "Unconscionable" fiscal irresponsibility of taking herself off the open market; "—Oh t'were to cheat a thousand!/ Who between this and my dull Age of Constancy,/ Expect the distribution of my Beauty . . . / 'tis a Mas[s] wou'd Ransome Kings!/ Was all this Beauty given, for one poor petty Conquest[?]" (IV.i, 128–29). Marcella recasts Fillamour's language of gallantry as the language of economics to make plain the power relations that his "reform" presupposes. She asks, "was it for that you sent two thousand Crowns[?] / Or did believe that trifling sum sufficient,/ To buy me to the slavery of honesty[?]" (128). Her comically inverted claim, that the amount she is paid for sex (a hefty 2,000 crowns) is not nearly enough to purchase her freedom and make her submit to marriage, equates marriage with slavery, while sex remains in the realm of freedom. Galliard's "Hold there, my brave Virago!" indicates how close Marcella strikes to the truth of both libertinism and a more conservative ideology of marriage. Though Fillamour argues with complete sincerity, his interest in Marcella's fortune shapes his definition of female honesty.

The play's critique of alienation through commercial exchange returns to images of the inexchangeable women, the mythical "La Zitella" and the real Cornelia and Marcella, whose desire and attractiveness keep them in sexual circulation without sex. Their desirability as sexual objects, which must be produced and reproduced through theatrical devices, gives them authority as self-determining agents in the plot. Behn plays with sexual identities heavily in *The Feign'd Courtesans,* challenging the division between subject and object positions by having her heroines act out sexually aggressive alter egos. But *The Feign'd Courtesans* also shows the strain of maintaining female characters as desiring objects as well as objects of desire in its ending. Cornelia has to "reason" Galliard into marriage, whereas Willmore, however inconstant, was eager. The play also closes with Donna Laura awkwardly reconciled to her intended Julio after her pursuit of Galliard. The ending avoids the tragic taint of Angellica by providing Laura with a man who is better than she thought, if not exactly what she wanted. In these final ambiguities, Behn steps back from the exuberance of *The Rover*'s ending to consider, however briefly, the limitations of her erotic politics. Behn's plots depend on constant, vigorous, yet malleable male sexual desire; without it, her desiring women find it difficult to negotiate the terms of their futures as married women.

Cynicism, Politics, and the Disappearing Woman

Behn's political identity made her transition into the theater of the 1680's a bumpy one. The tide that supported her pro-loyalist *The Rover* turned with the partisan and religiously charged debates of the Popish Plot in 1678. But in spite of the controversy, political plays still succeeded.[33] The political unrest of the times, including Charles II's dissolution of Parliament at Oxford in 1681, were discussed, not repressed, in works like *Absolom and Achitophel, Venice Preserv'd,* and *City Politiques.* Of the four plays that Behn wrote between 1681 and 1682, the two that succeeded were the overtly political plays, *The False Count* and *The City Heiress.* Although theaters and playwrights were convenient political targets in this period, it is a mistake, as Robert Hume argues in *The Rakish Stage,* to assume that Restoration comedies, with their political and sexual content, were driven off the stage by more sentimental plays. The theaters in general were not doing well in the 1680s and 1690s. The merged United Company of 1682 marked these troubled times and was itself a factor in reducing the number of plays that could reach the public. In the 1680s, tragedy was the most successful stage fare. Plays such as Otway's *Venice Preserv'd* (1682), Dryden and Lee's *Oedipus* (1679), and Lee's *Lucius Junius Brutus* (1680) displaced some of the more raucous and cynical comedy of the 1670s, such as *Love in a Wood* (1671), *The Gentleman Dancing Master* (1672), *The Country Wife* (1675), *The Man of Mode* (1676), *The Plain Dealer* (1676), and *Mr. Limberham* (1678). The reasons for the ascendance of tragedy over comedy gestures toward the growing anxieties about political power and authority that audiences in the 1680s shared, but the economics of the theaters and the scale of this shift cannot be reduced to anti-sex sentimentality.

Behn's response to this theatrical environment was to craft rougher, more impoverished rakes and older, more sexually ridiculous male blocking figures. One of her greatest gambles with this formula was *The False Count,* a delayed success after its initial one-night run. *The False Count* was Behn's third most popular play, after *The Rover* and *The Emperor of the Moon,* and it enjoyed a renaissance after 1715, for a total of seven different productions, including a Covent Garden revival in 1762. The play's attack on the merchant Francisco and his hoyden daughter Isabella undercut the prologue, which slyly announces that Behn has turned Whig. Francisco has snatched the beautiful heroine Julia away from her beloved Carlos, governor of Cadiz. Francisco also plans to marry Isabella off to the worthy Antonio, who is in love with Clara, Julia's sister. The couples—Julia and Carlos, and Clara and Antonio—conspire with Guiliom the chimney sweep to trick Isabella and her father into thinking he is a count and thus distract her from Antonio.

Guzman, Carlos's gentleman, also plays the trickster by inventing a second piece of theatrical business, a staged Turkish invasion of Francisco's ship on his departure from Cadiz. During this episode, the Grand Signior (Carlos in disguise) threatens Francisco with castration and forces him to "Pimp for [his] own Wife" and cajole her into Carlos's arms (V.i, 347). Behn drew Isabella's and Guiliom's plots from Molière's *Les Précieuses Ridicules* (1659) and likely borrowed the Turkish incident from his *Les Fourberies de Scapin* (1671), but she works these materials into her own critique of mercenary marriages and social climbing. Those who ignore passion for the sake of money or status meet with comic punishments that challenge the conventions of the comic ending. The marriages and the suspended marriages of the last act press on the legal assumptions of the family patriarchs, Francisco and Baltazer, and the narrative boundaries of comedy.

Francisco has a predictable blocking figure role, but the twist in this play is that he has already married the heroine. Behn frames Julia's marriage to him as a transaction between Baltazer, her father, and Francisco, a "shoo-maker" who is older than her father. Baltazer admits, "Wou'd I never marryed her to this Sott" (I.ii, 31), but the force of parental will has already played out when the play opens. Julia makes no explanation of her marriage except to tell her maid Jacinta "witness heav'n with what reluctancy I forc't my breaking heart. . . . My life I hate, and when I live no more for Carlos, I'll cease to be at all, it is resolv'd" (I.ii, 308). The situation, in which Julia seems bereft of options, raises questions about genre that creep into the dialogue. Jacinta, in an attempt to cheer Julia, replies, "Faith, Madam, I hope to live to see a more Comicall end of your Amours," and proposes that she, Julia, and Clara get to work on the plot: "Hang't, why shou'd we young Women pine and Languish for what our own Natural invention may procure us; let us three lay our heads together, and if *Machavil,* with all his Politicks, can out-witt us, 'tis pity but we all lead Apes in Hell, and dy'd without the *Jewish* blessing of consolation" (II.i, 316). Comedy, which has everything to do with a woman's ability to make her own sexual and marital choices, might still be possible for Julia if she is prepared to write her own script. Jacinta's oblique references to virginity suggest that Julia's comic plot means finding a way to lose her true virginity to Carlos. "The Jewish blessing of consolation" recalls the story of Jeptha's daughter, who was sacrificed by her father to fulfill his promise to God. She is allowed, however, to bewail her virginity before her death, which Willmore mentions to Hellena in *The Rover* as an argument for sex. The biblical reference, which Behn made repeatedly, gives some historical if not moral credence to the idea that good, chaste women can desire sex without being hypocrites or sexual deviants. Without female sexual desire, Behn argues, there is no comic plot and no good marriage.

The events of the play and the discussion of genre highlight the relationship between comic freedom and comic closure. In the next scene, Antonio and Carlos explain to Guiliom, "our Design is onelly Comical," though apt to turn tragic if Guiliom's identity as a chimney sweep is prematurely exposed (II.ii, 318). And later, concerned that Francisco will die from fright during their staged Turkish invasion, Carlos warns his gentleman Guzman to be cautious, lest he "make a Tragedy of our Comedy" (IV.ii, 339). To her previous definition of romantic comedy, Behn adds the need for suspended consequences. This discussion of genre unfolds within Behn's own description of the play as a farce, a moniker that is true to the raucous spirit of the play but that belies its fundamentally comic plot concerns. Jacinta's hope for a "Comicall end" and Carlos's "Comical" design can be fulfilled only if Behn can rewrite Julia's story as a comedy, with an ending in the spirit of her desires.

The play's value system skates close to Whig ideology by selectively celebrating class mobility. A good merchant, Antonio, is Clara's romantic interest; a chimney sweep successfully poses as a viscount; and Julia carries herself with grace as a shoemaker's wife. But Behn distinguishes between healthy and unhealthy attitudes toward money. Carlos, in a chance encounter with

Julia, explains that though love and money may be hopelessly intertwined in metaphor and in practice, there are ways to resist the ratios of economic thinking:

> *Julia:* But should we be unthrifty in our Loves,
> And for one moment's joy give all away,
> And be hereafter damn'd to pine at distance?
> *Carlos:* Mistaken Miser, Love like Money put
> Into good hands increases every day,
> Still as you trust me, still the Summ amounts,
> Put me not off with promise of to morrow,
> To morrow will take care for new delights,
> Why shou'd that rob us of a present one? (II.ii, 319–20)

Carlos's libertine *carpe diem* argument still uses economic metaphors to convert Julia's miserly logic into a notion of erotic investment. But the scale of value exists only between the lovers; they mutually validate each others' worth and pleasure without reference to a third term that would make them or their passion commodities. Putting off pleasure or hoarding the moment in hopes of a better future converts pleasure into units of exchange, in which the "moment's joy" becomes something one can trade. Carlos implores Julia to think of their affair through a libertine logic of the present instead of the Whig economy of surplus value, in which she will always be an object of exchange and consumption. Francisco, by comparison, calls his Julia "duckling" and "chicken." He routinely relates Julia to other forms of property, particularly food. He is capable of jealousy at the thought of any other man taking "his" Julia, but he can make no investment, sexually or psychically, in Julia as herself. Francisco, who encounters Julia as a possession he consumes metaphorically, can only parody the passion that makes Julia and Carlos lovers.

Appetite unfolds with greater complexity as a libertine trope in the exploits of trickster Guiliom, who observes that "a man's Appetite increases with his Greatness." Even though Guiliom's performance is originally for the sake of the lovers Antonio and Clara, it takes on a life of its own as he promises to "wench without mercy; I'm Resolv'd to spare neither man, Woman, nor Child" (III.i, 327). His line echoes Rochester's "The Disabled Debauchee," in which the narrator boasts of an evening so dedicated to appetite that the most passionate kiss determined "whether the boy fucked you, or I the boy."[34] Behn had either read the manuscript of the poem or the posthumous 1680 *Poems by the Right Honourable the E of R,* in which the poem appeared. Janet Todd, speculating on his appeal for Behn, comments that "Rochester, misogynist as he so often sounded, made sex funny," a strategy that Behn also uses to undermine the authority and seriousness of sexual mores (194–95). Her elegy on Rochester's death in July 1680 glossed over the dangers of libertinism that she had explored in *The Rover* when she eulogized him as a god bestowing "the charms of Poetry, and Love" on his public. Rochester's literary libertinism shaped Behn's, even if it did not fit her experience or her plays precisely. What is clearer is that his "shock jock" playfulness helped clear a space for Behn's dramatic conversation about sexuality.

Behn returned to the project of renegotiating libertine appetite in *The False Count* at a time when she was discovering new struggles with her body. Behn was suffering from joint pain and symptoms of depression by 1680, and she likely turned to the ideas of Thomas Tryon, who had also traveled to the Caribbean, for a remedy. Tryon's advice on diet was published as his *Way to Health, Long Life, and Happiness* (1683), and Behn supplied the commendation. Tryon advocated a diet without meat, tobacco, or alcohol as a means to restore health lost in self-indulgence and to correct the sin of killing animals.[35] Behn reflected on Tryon's prelapsarian vision in "The Golden Age," which celebrated a world without want and a nature "Who yielded of her own accord her plentious Birth." Her idealized nature maintained its ecological, social, and aesthetic balance because it is a world before repression, property, avarice, and alienation.[36] Appetites, to the extent that they exist in this world, are natural and healthy, but they can be abused and deformed by greed. Guiliom tips the balance between natural appetite and socially constructed appetites; he "plays" the libertine and develops his hungry nature as a function of his performance.

Behn uses the objectifying force of Whig economics to distinguish between healthy and corrupt appetites; any system in which people too easily become commodities is based on a corrupt model of appetite. Behn punishes Francisco and his daughter for believing that they can buy love and respect by making them victims of their materialist logic, which turns people into things and, in extreme cases, food. The "invasion" of the last acts, in which the pretend-Turks threaten Isabella and Francisco with cannibalism and sexual violation, humiliates and threatens daughter and father with a parody of their own materialism. Guzman tells Isabella and Julia they are "Dishes to be serv'd up on the board of the *Grand Signior*" and asks for "a slice of each" so that he can make up his mind (IV.i, 338). In act IV, Isabella is impatient to be raped as long as her attacker is the Grand Signior ("none shall ravish me but the Great Turk"), while Francisco cries out "will nothing but raw flesh serve his turn?" (IV.ii, 343) as he prepares to prostitute Julia to avoid castration. Their excesses clarify Behn's libertinism; true libertinism distinguishes between life-affirming desire and the appetite for power, which is a sign of weakness. Her critique touches on the excesses of Charles II as well as the limits of libertine discourse as social and sexual policy.

The confusion of objects and subjects in *The False Count* extends to conversations about Francisco's sexuality, in which the sex of the parties concerned becomes less and less stable. Julia teases Francisco about his sexual incompetence and his snoring: "I find no fault with your Sleeping, 'tis the best quality you have a-Bed" (I.ii, 313). In response to her jokes that make clear his sexual inadequacy, he calls her "thou wicked Limbe of Satan," an epithet that makes her both an object-part of Satan and a subject-agent who acts upon her husband. He meekly calls himself "a good Tenant that payes once a quarter," in sexual services, to which Jacinta replies, "Of an hour do ye mean Sir [?]" (313). His equation of sex with a tenant's payment further alienates him from his role as husband and opens his sex acts to quantifiable scrutiny. Their insults end when Francisco locks up Julia, persuaded that a man (and any man proves a threat to Francisco's fragile domestic authority) is coming. The intruder turns out to be Isabella, the daughter who is not a "real" woman but a lady in drag who must "have [her] Peticoats lac'd four Storyes high; wear [her] false Towers, and Coole [her]self with [her] Spanish Fan" (I.ii, 314). Her father's assessment of her class-crossing reads as an indictment of her gender performance and the fetishistic supplements she uses to construct herself as a woman. Objects in *The False Count* multiply around those who lack more authentic selves.

Gender instabilities resurface in a similar joke at her next entrance. Jacinta, Julia's maid, questions Francisco's jealousy of a "petticoat," or female friend, to which he replies: "Peticoat, Come, come, Mistress *Pert,* I have known as Much danger hid under a Peticoat, as a Pair of Breeches. I have heard of two Women that Married each other—oh abominable, as if there were so Prodigious a Scarcity of Christian Man's Flesh" (II.i, 317). Francisco's suspicions of lesbian activity, a comic reinvention of Behn's "To the Fair *Clarinda,* who made Love to me, imagin'd more than Woman," extend his jealousy of Carlos to all of Julia's relationships. Behn played with cross-dressing and transgender relationships in *The Dutch Lover* and *The Rover,* but here, crossing happens in Whiggish contexts that have already inverted the "natural" order, an association Behn will use again in *The Roundheads.* Francisco's paranoia gives voice to the possibility that female desire might displace heterosexual plot lines. After Francisco's diatribe against the dangers that petticoats hide, Isabella, the woman in drag, enters on cue. Francisco's subsequent interactions with women devolve into a series of visual jokes about gender instability. He assures Clara she will be safe on the walk home at night because "look ye, I go Arm'd, (shows his Girdle round with Pistolls)" (II.i, 317). Francisco's revelation of his pistol-girdle draws attention to the insufficiency of his body; the substitute phalloi announce to the audience that his own masculinity is a sham. The joke was augmented in the first run by the presence of James Nokes, the first Francisco. Nokes was both a great comedian and a former boy actor who had played women's roles briefly after the 1660 reopening of the theaters.

This feminine association, as well as the range of cuckolds, older husbands, and foolish "cits" that were his comic stock-in-trade, furthered the comic association of his body with faked manhood.

Because the play opens after the marriage of Francisco and Julia, his cuckolding is a necessary object of the comic plot; contrary to Eve Sedgwick's insight about the homosocial function of the term, however, it is also something that women do in Cadiz. In the first act, Carlos swears revenge on Francisco by using "all the Arts and Ways I can, to cuckold him" (306), but Julia and Jacinta also discuss cuckolding as a woman's prerogative:

> *Jacinta:* Wou'd I were in your room, Madam, I'd cut him out work enough I'd warrant him; and if he durst impose on me, i'faith I'd transform both his Shape and his manners; in short, I'd try what Woman-hood could doe. And indeed, the revenge wou'd be so pleasant, I wou'd not be without a jealous Husband for all the world, and really, Madam, Don Carlos is so sweet a Gentleman.
>
> *Julia:* Ay, but the Sin, *Jacinta!*
>
> *Jacinta:* A' my Conscience Heav'n wou'd forgive it, for this match of yours, with old *Francisco,* was never made there.
>
> *Julia:* Then if I wou'd, alas what opportunities have I, for I confess since his first Vows made him mine—
>
> *Jacinta:*—right—that lying with old *Francisco* is flat Adultery—.(I.ii, 308)

Neither woman says the word "cuckold," but the talk of Julia's "revenge," her "opportunities," and Francisco's transformation intimates that cuckolding is something that women do as well. Francisco's plea to Julia later in the play to "cuckhold him a little bit" to save him from the castrating cannibal Turks finally makes her the grammatical agent. To justify her actions, Julia and Jacinta appeal to vows or *contracts de presenti* that Julia and Carlos exchanged. His vows have made him *hers,* and she has a right to "that charming Body" which she refuses to see in her sister Clara's arms. In contrast to her lack of control in her marriage to Francisco, Carlos is both the object of *her* desire and the man who makes her a subject in their mutual plot to find a life together.

The staged Turkish invasion of the last act distinguishes between healthy and unhealthy relationships to the world of objects. Isabella, after being passed over for ravishment by the grand Turk, makes up with Guiliom and begs him to make her "Vicountess *de Chimeny Swiperio*" (III.ii, 331). Guiliom, who has seen to it that the documents authorizing Isabella's marriage portion have been signed and notarized, is happy to oblige. Jokes about Guiliom's profession and his body have been building throughout the play; Guiliom asks Isabella to suffer "the Broom of my Affection to sweep all other lovers from your heart" and swears to her that "the rustling Pole of my affection is too strong to be resisted" (331). These jokes detonate in Guiliom and Isabella's discussion of consummation:

> *Guiliom:* Come, Madam, your Honour and I have something else to doe—before I have fully dub'd you a Vicountess.
> *Isabella:* Ah Heav'ns, my Lord, what's that?
> *Guiliom:* Why, a Certain Ceremony, which must be perform'd between a pair of Sheets,—but we'll let it alone till Night.
> *Isabella:* Till night, no; whate'er it be, I wou'd not be without an Inch of that Ceremony, that may Compleat my Honour, for the World; no for Heav'ns sake let's retire, and Dub me presently. (V.i, 350–51)

Isabella translates the imaginary ceremony with Guiliom into "inches"; he is her commodified lord who will further her incremental claims on a world of objects. Guiliom also grammatically displaces intercourse as a subjectless act that concerns things and not people. The ceremony "perform'd between a pair of Sheets" is something that might be done by people or by the sheets themselves, further confusing the world of embodied subject and objects. Once Guiliom reveals himself, he teases the furious Isabella with her own claim that Guiliom was more than a thing to her: "'twas my own sweet self you lov'd, my amiable sweet and charming self" (V.i, 354). The danger of Guiliom as a character rests in his pliability, through which he remains curiously unalienated from himself or his work. He is "honest Guiliom the Chimney sweeper," yet he also secures the marriage portion that will allow him to transform himself into "as pretty a fluttering Spark as any's in Town" (354). Isabella's reward is that she has married a social climber who performs his class position better than she performs hers. In Guiliom, Behn comes close to legitimating the social mobility she excoriates elsewhere in order to condemn Isabella's pretensions.

Julia's relationship to the comic ending is complicated by the fact that she has "consummated" with Francisco, though her ultimate reward is double; she is cleared in the eyes of her jealous husband and she gets Carlos. She resists her husband's requests that she cuckold him only to torment him with the fear of castration, but this is enough to prove her honor to Francisco: "I know thy vertue, and will no more be jealous, believe me Chickin I was an old Fool" (V.i, 352). Carlos confirms that she is chaste, highly unlikely after their suggestive exit "to Shades/Where onely thou and I can find an enterance" (IV.ii, 344). Francisco's fantasy surrender of Julia is still marked by the commercial world of objects and goods, but in this last comic inversion, it is his claim to possess Julia that allows him to give her away: "she's my Wife, my Lumber now, and, I hope, I may dispose of my Goods and Chattels:—if he takes her we are upon equal terms, for he makes himself my Cuckold, as he has already made me his . . ." (V.i, 353). Francisco reinstates a definition of cuckolding as an act between men, even though he has put the power to cuckold in Julia's hands just hours before. His traditional definition squares with his equation of women with commodities, which provides Julia a way out of this marriage. Julia ends the play free to be with Carlos, though she must be "given away" as used merchandise.

The farcical elements of the play and its homage to Molière underpin its legally unlikely conclusion, in which the marriage of Julia and Francisco easily dissolves in favor of the prior contract with Carlos. The play also goes further than *Les Précieuses Ridicules* in marrying the parvenu to the chimney sweep, which Molière only threatened. *The False Count* uses raucous comic events to objectify those who impede good feminine desire and those who fail to recognize sexual values over economic ones. The play registers the ability of an emerging, commodity-driven merchant mentality to disrupt Behn's carefully crafted comic worlds, where women and men challenge the logic of subjects and objects with their own versions of sexual subjectivity. Behn must use the most outrageous comic events in this farcical comedy to authorize her conclusion, which has more fantasy than reality to it.

Behn found success again with her brand of politicized sex comedy in *The City Heiress* (1682). She wrote that the play "had the luck to be well received in the Town; which (not for my Vanity) pleases me, but that thereby I find Honesty in fashion again, when Loyalty is approv'd and Whigism becomes a Jest where'er 'tis met with;" Langbaine simply called the performance well-received.[37] The triumph, however, was not without a critical backlash; Thomas Shadwell, Robert Gould, William Wycherley, and others accused Behn of bawdiness, plagiarism, or both.[38] While the plagiarism charge was insubstantial, the accusation of bawdiness, as in the case of *Sir Patient Fancy*, is hard to dismiss out of hand. In act IV, Tom Wilding and Lady Galliard enter the stage from her bedroom in a state of disarray, as Lady Galliard complains bitterly of her ruin. The scene prompted Shadwell to satirize "Poetess Aphra" for whom Otway must pimp. Robert Gould's more pointed attack took on the sexual risks of her plays, which he had decried in "A Satyr Against the Play-House 1685," but which he now directly reviled in "The Female Laureat":

> What tho' thou bring'st (to please a vicious Age)
> A far more vicious widdow on the Stage,
> Just Reeking from a Stallions Rank Embrace,
> With Ruffled Garments, and disordered Face,
> T'acquaint the Audience with her Slimy Case?[39]

The barely offstage encounter between Wilding and Lady Galliard to which Gould refers is an unapologetically sexual and visual representation of female desire and sexual danger. Gould's crass summary of the scene reduces Behn's sexual strategy to a pornographic repetition of the Restoration sex comedy. While the scene plays on the voyeuristic impulses of her audience, it is also an urgent attempt to take female desire seriously.

Lady Galliard, a widow caught between her notions of propriety and her overwhelming desire for Wilding, struggles throughout the play with the social price she must pay for her desire. The irresistible attractions of Wilding, the "Tarmagant Tory," are politically coded, but the problem of female desire in the play has more to do with the disappearance of women in both Whig *and* Tory systems. When Lady Galliard contemplates the consequences of having slept with Wilding, she does so in terms of her arrival into a placeholder, "whore," which overrides her identity: "My word! And have I promis'd then to be A Whore? A Whore! Oh, let me think of that! A Man's Convenience, his leisure Hours, his Bed of ease . . . A loath'd Extinguisher of filthy flames, Made use of, and thrown by—oh infamous" (IV.i, 53). The epithets barely accord her status as a human being and disregard her desire for Wilding. Without his sincere desire in return, Lady Galliard cannot sustain her specificity or her agency. Though Wilding declares he will never love her, she cannot help herself and "*sinks into his Arms by degrees.*" When they reenter, in fewer than 100 lines, a weeping and furious Lady Galliard declares herself a "feeble woman," unable to reject him. In Behn's darker moments, female desire is not returned in the circuit of erotic exchange, as Ruth Salvaggio has argued elsewhere.[40]

In a strategy that balances her darker inquiry into the limits of female desire, Behn exposes the older male body to more exaggerated comic play. Sir Timothy, Whiggish sexual hypocrisy incarnate, provides explosive political comic material. His name, Treatall, links him to indiscriminate political excess, which Wilding laments in the first act: "You keep open house to all the Party, not for Mirth, Generosity, or good Nature, but for Roguery. You cram the Brethren, the pious City-Gluttons, with good Cheer, good Wine, and Rebellion in abundance, gormandizing all Comers and Goers, of all Sexes, Sorts, Opinions, and Religions . . . in hopes of debauching the King's Liege-People into Commonwealths-men" (I.i, 13). Sir Timothy secures his political authority through bribes and hospitality and keeps Wilding from his inheritance with the excuse that Wilding is a whoring, drinking, rich-living, and irresponsible Tory. But Sir Timothy's own reputation for feasting and his clandestine sexual activity is a mirror to Wilding's. At the beginning of the play, Sir Timothy hypocritically declares that good "Oliver" (Cromwell) did a great thing when he "by wholesome Act, made it death to boast; so that then a man might whore his heart out, and no body the wiser" (I.i, 12). In Behn's other plays, blood relation proves a better guarantee of political solidarity than it does here, but the association between Whiggish uncle and

Tory nephew still carries meaning; in spite of their politics, they share a propensity to replace one female love object with another.

Sir Timothy proves that he is the lesser man, alienated from the body, when he is duped by a woman-swapping scheme. Wilding's former mistress Diana poses as the kidnapped heiress Charlot at one of Sir Timothy's public suppers, where he proposes marriage in order to steal Charlot away from his Tory nephew. He explains that her faith and troth to Wilding mean nothing in the city: "I have known an Heiress married and bedded, and yet with the advice of the wiser Magistrates, has been unmarried and consummated anew with another. . . . Nay, had you married my ungracious Nephew, we might by this our *Magna Charta* have hang'd him for Rape" (III.i, 39). Civil law, which strengthened women's legal identity within marriage through the Chancery courts, proves to be only a codified system of sexual privilege for those with political power. Wilding, dressed as an ambassador from Poland, adds to the political content of the comic event. He has been sent to crown Sir Timothy as the next "elective" king, chosen by the Polish people for his business acumen and his contributions to English civil society. Sir Timothy is swept away by Wilding's fabricated offer and abandons his anti-monarchical politics. These jokes on civil law and monarchy, which play on hypocritical Whig ideas about power, also recycle a Tory propaganda piece that claimed Shaftesbury had sought the elective crown of Poland.[41] Behn also uses the mock crowning of a Whiggish dupe in her short story, "The Court of the King of Bantam," in which a foolish rich young man, "Woud-Be King," is offered the throne by friendly conspirators who want to get him out of the way of the romance plot. In both cases, the attractions of monarchy expose the hypocrisy of Whig poseurs who only want access to greater power and whose politics have no content. Politically speaking, there is nothing there.

Wilding's relationship to Charlot shifts between the economics of merchants and the erotics of libertines. He brags that he is "in possession" of Charlot, though Sir Charles reprimands him for having "arriv'd to that degree of Lewdness, to deal [his] Heart about" between Charlot and Lady Galliard (I.i, 14). When Charlot discovers that Wilding has a mistress, she uses economic language to express her fury: "Go ask my Lady *Galliard,* she keeps the best account of all your Sighs and Vows, And robs me of my dearest softer hours" (II.i, 23). The term "account," which carries a strong sense of both to count units and "to reckon moneys given and received," suggests that Wilding's Tory pleasure economy works like a Whig cash economy at Charlot's expense.[42] Wilding is too comfortable with dealing and accounts, financial concepts that were the domain of tradesmen and merchants in the late seventeenth century; he talks easily about percentages and does a fine impersonation of a Polish merchant. Wilding's language is somewhat specialized, considering that in 1682, Dryden's "Religio Laici" used "ALGEBRA" as an example of new vocabulary beyond the scope of most people.

Wilding's sexual desire and his repudiation of commercial gain are part of the Royalist psyche, but they are also forms of masculine cultural capital that he can bank and trade. By contrast, Charlot, without her Wilding, has no defense against either economy; both will devalue her as a fallen commodity. Charlot's tendency to explain her situation as serious or tragic keeps her on the margins of the comic world. She calls Wilding "A thing just like a Man, or rather Angel! / He speaks, and looks, and loves, like any God!" but sex is never a matter of play for her (V.i, 74). Charlot who, much closer to Angellica than to the more upbeat heroines Julia, Cornelia, and Hellena, does not have the mythical social space of freedom in which these other heroines explore the reciprocity of subjectivity and objectivity. As economic reality encroaches on Behn's comedy, her comic events begin to deflate, and heroines like Charlot are trapped objects waiting to be rescued.

At the close of the play, Charlot gets her man, but not by her plan; Wilding's other two mistresses have left him for more advantageous matches. Charlot enters the final scene hysterical, assuming that the wedding music at Lady Galliard's home means she has married Wilding, when in fact she has settled for Sir Charles, her would-be rapist. Behn forestalls Charlot's comic resolution until the last moments of the play, when Wilding assures her that he is hers and that he loves her "more than Life" (V, 74). Charlot can also take some comfort in Wilding's father's will, which he has robbed back into his possession. But their union at the end of the play is possible only once Wilding's other options have been married off. Charlot, like Lady Galliard and Diana, is at the mercy of Wilding and the circumstances that propel him through the plot. The parallels between Tory and Whig ideology in *The City Heiress* threaten women, even though the play officially maintains Tory loyalties. Wilding's closer relation (literally and legally) to Whig control and support, along with the failure of libertine ideology for Lady Galliard, shades Behn's sexual politics in this play.[43] The threat of being displaced, replaced, or abstracted looms larger and throws more women into more direct competition with each other. The shared situation of these three women is underscored by one last bad joke; Wilding carries syphilis. Lady Galliard, Diana, and Charlot are literally marked by the *dis*-ease of male sexuality, which determines the meaning of their bodies and desires without their consent.

One Last Chance

Behn's *The Lucky Chance* (1686) has received a great deal of attention from twentieth-century feminist critics, attention it deserves for its later revivals as well as for its content.[44] Although the play was rediscovered and rewritten by Hannah Cowley as *A School for Greybeards* later in the eighteenth century, a tightening market for new plays compromised the success of its original run. Technically, it was the least popular of Behn's "popular" plays, with only four productions, including Cowley's revision. In the late 1680s, the United Company was using old plays rather than supporting active playwrights, and Behn, who had likely mortgaged the play to Zachary Baggs for £6, was facing hard times along with her colleagues.[45] She had not written a play since 1682, having focused her energy instead on fiction and poetry in the hopes of scraping together a living. *The Lucky Chance* turns to more realistic theatrical description, which Rose Zimbardo has identified both as novelistic and as the dramatic mode that flourishes in the 1690s in less satiric comedies (161–63). Dark themes of inescapable bad marriage, unchecked avarice, and the generational powerlessness of young lovers reflect Behn's sense of disillusionment, out of which she launches her most severe test of her model of comic sexual agency. Her young lovers have to work their way out of the economic logic that shapes their material existence and their psychological realities. Behn's challenge to the substitution of one woman for another and her attempts to keep her heroines from collapsing into mere bodies through comic events lead her to a final distinction between marriage and the happy ending. She must finally go outside the generic script to make a place for women as subjects in their own right.

When the play opens, Julia has already married Sir Cautious Fulbank instead of her lover Gayman, whose fortune is ruined. In a parallel plot, Sir Feeble Fainwood has married but not yet bedded the much younger Leticia, after keeping her beloved Bellmour abroad with a false arrest warrant. Julia's explicable yet unadmirable need for financial security over love surpasses that of her namesake in *The False Count;* the first Julia could at least blame her father for the match. Gayman, who has mortgaged his estate to Sir Cautious in the interest of living rakishly and courting Julia, is a more pathetic kind of rake than even Behn's second Willmore. He lives in a filthy garret and must provide small sexual favors with his landlady Gammer Grime in exchange for his room and the goods she procures for him. The gravitational pull of Fulbank's and fellow alderman Fainwoud's wealth grounds the play's flights of comic fancy and reminds the audience that these rich men exert the power to make women and men objects, even though they are satirized as impotent buffoons.

Sir Feeble, played by the great comic Anthony Leigh in the original production, is a rich buffoon with no legitimacy. Like Isabella and Francisco in *The False Count,* Sir Feeble believes that he can buy everything and accordingly lives in a world of objects. When he finds that his bride has (allegedly) fainted in the arms of Bellmour/Francis, Sir Feeble says to Leticia, "Alas, poor Pupsey—was it sick—look here—here's a fine thing to make it well again. Come buss, *and it shall have it*" (II.ii, 240, my italics). His use of "it" for Leticia is part baby talk and part reference to his impersonal ownership of her body as a material artifact. She barely attains the status of a sexual object since Sir Feeble cannot support his claim to be a sexual subject. Sir Feeble Fainwoud's name, which recalls Lady Cockwood's and Lady Laycock's monikers, continues this sexual and political joke; his aging body and his childish speech patterns undermine his masculine authority, which, like Sir Cautious's failing "courage," cannot find its biological referent. The contrast of his infantilizing baby talk with the subsequent exclamation, "oh, how I long for the night," brings out a disturbing ring of father-daughter incest. This construction of incest plays a significant role in *Oronooko* two years later in 1688 as the grandfather of Oronooko takes Imoinda, asserting property rights that he would enforce by rape if he could. Behn's more tragic novelistic exploration of incest is still, however narrowly, under comic control in *The Lucky Chance.*

While male writers give us older men like Sir Sampson Legend in *Love for Love* and Old Bellair in *The Man of Mode,* both of whom have inappropriate desires for younger women, their bodies are not made into comic spectacles like those of the aging Lady Cockwood or Lady Laycock of Betterton's *The Amorous Widow, or The Wanton Wife.* Behn, conversely, is willing to put the aging male body on comic display in place of the aging female, a risk which Centlivre also takes a few years later in *The Busy Body,* though their representations of the male body are not simple reversals of gendered anxiety. Lady Laycock and Lady Cockwood never have the social or economic power of a Sir Sampson or an Old Bellair, an asymmetry reflected in Behn's portrayals of Sir Feeble Fainwoud and Sir Cautious Fulbank. These old men believe they can purchase subjectivity, but they only accentuate the sexual failure of their bodies; like Francisco, the more they buy, the closer they come to being objects themselves.

At the opening of the play, Julia teases Sir Cautious about the pending nuptials of Sir Feeble Fainwoud and the much younger Letitia:

> *Sir Cautious:* . . . a Wedding is a sort of an Alarm to Love; it calls up every Mans Courage.
> *Lady Fulbank:* Ay, but will it come when 'tis call'd?
> *Sir Cautious:* I doubt you'll find it to my Grief—(*aside*) . . . no, thou'dst rather have a young Fellow.
> *Lady Fulbank:* I am not us'd to flatter much; if forty Years were taken from your Age, 'twou'd render you something more agreeable in my Bed, I must confess. (V.ii, 274)

The wedding reinforces the exchange of women between men, but Julia questions the efficacy of this symbolic practice if her husband's "courage" will not "come when 'tis called," a jibe that puts his sexually inadequate body into comic play. Gayman gives us our first similarly hostile glimpse of Sir Feeble Fainwould, Sir Cautious's fellow geezer: "a jolly old Fellow, whose Activity is all got into his Tongue, a very excellent teaser; but neither Youth nor Beauty can grind his Dugion to an Edge" (I.i, 223). Sir Feeble, determined to prove his sexual authority in spite of the limitations Gayman describes, declares that all will be lawful once he has "Livery and Seisin of [Letitia's] body" (III.i, 245). The term, actually livery *of* seisin, designates a land transfer that takes place in person and on the land in question, but Sir Feeble needs a body that is able and willing to match his contractual intention.[46] Behn affirms power vested in the body in the legal transaction of marriage; the joke this time is on men who cannot produce the metaphor or the embodied substance of authority. Sir Feeble understands that his legal claim to Letitia must be materialized through a sex act, but he also confesses to Sir Cautious that, "wise old men must nick their inclinations (*singing and dancing)* for it is not as 'twas wont to be, for it is not as 'twas wont to be" (I.iii, 231). Sir Feeble can produce the illusion of good husbandry, but only with the help of legal convention and good timing; his body, like Sir Cautious's, is faulty, inadequate, and no longer fully present.

With the physical basis for his authority in question, Sir Feeble swears, "I'll in, throw open my Gown to fright away the Women, and jump into her Arms" (III.i, 246), to ensure that he is alone with Letitia on his wedding night. This moment in the play allegedly drew disapproval from the wits at Will's Coffeehouse, where it was decried after Leigh illustrated Sir Feeble's line on the stage. Behn quixotically deflected the charge by attributing the idea of the open gown to Leigh *and* by continuing to assert that she is attacked unfairly as a woman for bawdiness. The grumbling led to her famous preface, where she continues her comic play with bodies and gender by asking for "privilege for my masculine part." But that open gown takes the spectator too close to the revelation of a patriarchal authority, which cannot fulfill its phallic promises. Behn uses the idea of phallic failure to try to lead her characters and herself out of the symbolic economy, in which individuals can be abstracted or displaced through economic and social exchanges. If she can show that their authority is an economic ruse that wrongly substitutes money for bodies, she can argue for a more egalitarian sexual politics, with pleasure and power for all.

Behn tries to imagine how a reconstituted world of pleasures would look through Gayman and Julia. Their pleasures promise to banish the alienating function of money that overdetermines sexual subject and object positions. In such a world, the Platonic and Cartesian distinction between subject and object would not be calcified in terms of sex difference. Julia attempts to teach Gayman a lesson in this new sexual economics when she sends him enough gold to reclaim his lands on the condition that he meet his anonymous benefactress. That the gold was formerly his own, mortgaged to Fulbank, further illustrates that economic alienation can produce sexual alienation. Gayman is happy to have the money, but he is not yet prepared to imagine himself as both a sexual subject and object in the unfamiliar landscape of this proposal. At the meeting, he hesitates, so Pert prods him: "What do you fear a longing Woman Sir? . . . Why stand you gazing Sir, a Womans Passion is like the Tide, it stays for no man when the Hour is come" (III.i, 249). Pert's baiting remarks posit the validity and the difference of female sexual desire, which has its own rhythms and characteristics. The comic valence of her lines inheres in their inappropriateness, but she also normalizes Julia's desire by asking, "why stand you gazing," which makes Gayman's failure to understand female desire the unusual event.

Julia has prepared a surreal bedroom scene and enlists servants to provide the voices of singing spirits who bless him, "to keep him ever young in bed," and promise him "The joy of love without the pain" (III.i, 251). This is a gift economy of *jouissance* that works from displacement to presence; the gift is, at last, the body of the beloved. But to accept this gift, Gayman will need to leave his masculine anxieties at the door, which he cannot do. He assumes that a desiring woman must be revolting, and that her monetary gift only confirms the lack of natural worth that she seeks to supplement. When Julia questions him the next day about his assignation, he confesses that he slept with a woman but that she was a carcass "rivelled, lean, and rough" (IV.i, 259). His gendered logic dictates that if she is a purchaser of male sexuality, then she is compensating for what she cannot attract naturally as an object. Julia tests Gayman's ability to defy the logic of subjects and objects in favor of bodies and pleasures, but he fails her test when he insists on thinking about sex through monetary principles that equate female economic power with undesirability. In his economy, women are sexual commodities and cannot be self-determining purchasers or givers. Because Gayman is so persuaded that *real* (desirable) women are passive, he does not recognize his own lover in bed. Commodity fetishism strikes again, and the particular embodied woman, Julia, is lost in Gayman's reading of women as units of exchange.

Behn's fine distinctions about pleasure beyond the rubrics of subject and object prove too difficult for Gayman, who misrecognizes Julia as a faulty subject who "pays" while he must "endeavor to be civil," but he makes a more glaring mistake in the gambling scene:

> *Gayman:* You have Moveables Sir, Goods—Commodities—
> *Sir Cautious:* That's all one Sir; that's Moneys worth Sir; but if I had anything that were worth *nothing*—

> *Gayman:* You would venture it,—I thank you Sir—I wou'd your Lady were worth nothing. (IV.i, 266)

Jane Spencer and Catherine Gallagher have noted the slang association of female genitals with nothing, but Julia is also worth "nothing" to Sir Cautious because he can do little with her. When Julia asks what her husband has lost, he replies, "Only a small parcel of ware that lay dead upon my hands, sweetheart," to which Gayman enjoins, "But I shall improve 'em, madam, I'll warrant you" (IV.i, 268). This tendentious joke, a joke told between two men in the presence of a woman, parodies the patriarchal version of marriage. While the joke (or contract) involves two men, it cannot be accomplished without the presence and participation of a woman. Marriage is, among other things, the legal moment at which a woman's provisional subjectivity as a contracting individual is invoked, deployed, and then disappears. Once married, her potential *productivity* as a mother and guarantor of future heirs completes her redefinition as a possession, which could be improved (or not) like other properties. But Julia trumps Gayman's and Fulbank's model of exchange with yet another plot, one outside of marriage and beyond the domain of economics, "the joy of love without the pain." She imagines, however briefly, a third possibility, the rematerialization of the body beyond use or exchange values. No one but Julia, however, follows this thought, and she is left to express her disappointment to both her would-be owners. She insists that Gayman has made her "a base prostitute, a foul adulteress" (V.ii, 278) by continuing to relate to her as an exchange value within the patriarchal economy. The charge is even more fitting for Sir Cautious, whose only ostensible motive for offering Julia was to save £300.

What Behn glimpsed through Julia is an alternative sexuality, straight but not patriarchal, with radical economic and social implications. This sexuality is in the end untenable, but Behn can give such a glimpse because she assures her audience of another conclusion in advance with the label "comedy." The dominant social order, Frye's "community," will be restored and even strengthened with or without Julia. The tensions between Behn's comic events, which explore alternatives to anonymous exchange, and the demands of comic structure are most pronounced in this dark comedy. Although Letitia manages to escape the abuse of marriage law and contract *de futuro* that Sir Feeble uses to entrap her, Julia is already Lady Fulbank and already disappointed in Gayman's lack of vision. This ending, as Peggy Thompson and Paula Backscheider have noted, refuses formal closure, invokes *divorce a vinculo,* and leaves Julia's fate open to possibility (Backscheider 92; Thompson 83). By resisting the force of the marriage ending as the truth of closure, Behn holds open a realist's fantasy: Julia Fulbank, herself at last, in an imperfect world.

The perplexing conclusion of *The Lucky Chance* gestures to the future of Behn's sexual politics, which were running against the tide by the late 1680s. Her comic argument for mutual desire outside of a circuit of commodity exchanges grows historically less tenable as her most successful plays develop it. That the last of her plays to reach the theater in her lifetime, *The Emperor of the Moon,* was a wildly successful pantomime is strangely fitting. The play, second only to *The Rover* in popularity, takes elements from *commedia dell'arte* and blends them with Behn's gift for staging physical comedy that exploits theatrical spaces and bodies. She moved from politically challenging comedy to farce as a commercially successful resignation to changing theatrical taste. Even though Behn's plays enjoyed a life later in the eighteenth century, only *The Rover* would have a secure place among the transitional comedies of the late 1680s and '90s, the most prominent of which are Congreve's *Love for Love* (1695), Cibber's *Love's Last Shift* (1696), and Vanbrugh's *The Relapse* (1696). When Charles Gildon staged *The Younger Brother* (similar to *The Lucky Chance* in its psychologically complex account of female desire) in 1696, the audience hissed.[47] *The Lucky Chance* was revived briefly in 1697 and in 1718, but did not return again until 1786, a banner season for women playwrights that included revivals of Centlivre's *The Wonder, A Woman Keeps a Secret,* and *A Bold Stroke for a Wife;* Cowley's *Who's the Dupe?, The Belle's Stratagem, Which is the Man?,* and *A Bold Stroke for a Husband;* Harriet Hook's *The Double Disguise;* Sophia Lee's *The Chapter of Accidents;* and Inchbald's *The Mogul Tale* and *I'll Tell You What.* New plays that season included Inchbald's *Such Things Are, The Widow's Vow,* and *The Midnight Hour,* and Cowley's *A School for Greybeards; or, the Mourning Bride,* a revision of *The Lucky Chance.* But even Behn revised proved to be too spicy for her audience; the play managed nine performances in the 1786–1787 season but then dropped out of the active repertoire of Cowley plays.

In spite of these difficulties, Behn's comedies continued to be performed on the London stage well beyond the Restoration, an important corrective to the critical myth that her forthright sexual discussions appealed only to the pre–1700 audience. *The Rover, The Emperor of the Moon, The False Count,* and *The Feign'd Courtesans* all had successful later revivals, although Behn never lost her status as a dangerous character. She became both the standard of theatrical accomplishment and of moral depravity against which future women playwrights were judged. Sir Walter Scott, who was willing to procure a Behn novel for his great aunt when asked, still felt the need to send it in a brown wrapper.[48] The appeal across generations affirms Behn's cultural place as a creator of Restoration prose and comic romance narrative, second only to Dryden in her popularity, though her reputation for sexual adventure marked that legacy. Behn's popular arguments for the located, embodied identity of her characters makes visible the repressed truth of the marriage comedy: women have legitimate sexual desires, without which there is no comic ending.[49] Behn's model of female sexuality entails a willful blindness to the realities of late-seventeenth-century marriage and property law. But the sense of inevitable reconciliation with the law through marriage that the genre supplies makes the lovers' transgressions even more appealing and invites the audience to defy cultural gravity with them. Her plays asked audiences to identify with the comic couple and their *mutual* sexual desire rather than with the comic hero in his quest for sex and love. The emphasis on female desire animates her social critique of libertine values from within. Behn's egalitarian model of sexual desire is also at odds with an emerging bourgeois economic order that demands both female chastity and sexual objectivity. The focus on intricate plotting in these plays offers the specifically theatrical pleasures of following female characters through multiple identities and tracing in their movements a more surreptitious critique of the standard romance plot, which is built around male mastery.[50] The comic dividend of pleasure depends on the audience's ability and willingness to follow Behn's argument for a world of mutual pleasure and a female, if not precisely feminist, vision of women *and* men as active objects of desire.

CHAPTER FOUR

Coming To Market

Centlivre and the Promise of Contract

The world of finance looms large in Susanna Centlivre's *A Bold Stroke for a Wife*. Act IV begins with a scene in a "Change Alley" coffeehouse, where stock-jobbers call out their prices:

> *1st Stock: South-Sea at seven Eighths!* who buys?
> *2'd Stock: South Sea* Bonds due at *Michaelmas,* 1718. Class-Lottery Tickets.
> *3d Stock: East India* Bonds? (IV.i, 35)

Centlivre weaves stocks, bonds, lotteries, and other financial instruments into her romance plots as a way to appropriate the egalitarian possibilities of commercial contracts for her heroines. Centlivre had great faith in the emerging stock market and the South Sea Company, a sentiment shared by the women who controlled roughly 20 percent of major stock funds from 1690 to 1753.[1] Stocks were popular with middle- and upper-class women because they were not yet taxed like land and, more importantly, because Chancery courts (also known as equity courts) upheld the right of a married woman to act as a *feme sole* with respect to these financial instruments, as long as they were purchased out of pin money or other designated personal property. Stocks and other short-term financial contracts created highly mobile forms of ownership that subordinated other categories of legal identity to the functional and economic category of "shareholders": the stock market welcomed men and women equally as contractual agents, provided they could pay. Stocks also bridged the gap in the legal identity of women who moved from the category of *feme sole* to *feme covert* by preserving a woman's right of ownership in her married state.

Stocks, paper credit, bills of exchange, and other commercial contracts abstracted identity into owners and creditors, which permitted an equality of male and female persons. At the height of modern contract thought in early-eighteenth-century marriage law, such paper equality seemed almost tenable. In the cases of *Gore v. Knight* (1705) and *Wilson v. Pack* (1710), the equity courts decided in favor of a married woman's right to control contested property, both during her life and through her will, if it was purchased out of her separate money or pin money.[2] *Bennet v. Davis* (1725) affirmed that a wife could possess separate property without trustees, while *More v. Freeman* (1725) upheld the wife's contract to pay her husband £200 a year out of her separate estate "in consideration of his permitting her to live apart from him," even though her trustees were not a party to the agreement (Staves, *Married* 177). The extension of private contracts into the realm of the marriage contract affirmed the legal identity of women within marriage, and equity courts supported their actions as agents on their own behalf.

Centlivre used the extension of contracts into the domestic realm to support her heroines' claims to domestic authority, just as her position as a successful playwright shaped her imagined relationship to her husband. In 1720, Centlivre appealed to Charles Joye, a director of the South Sea Company, for a gift of stock in the ill-fated company to reward her efforts for the Whig cause. Her poem, "A Woman's Case," refers to the gamble she took in dedicating her comedy *The Wonder* to George ("Brunswick"), then electoral prince, whose claim to the throne Queen Anne resisted. She had put her husband's royal post as yeoman of the mouth (otherwise known as cook) to Queen Anne at risk without the reward of party support. Like her heroines, Centlivre links her domestic fate to her ability to secure cash as both a precaution against marital strife and a means to establish some domestic authority after the wedding day. Through the gruff voice of her husband, she illustrates the intertwined worlds of domestic felicity and stock ownership:

> Madam, said he, with surly Air;
> You've manag'd finely this Affair;
> Pox take your Schemes, your Wit and Plays.
> I'm bound to curse 'em all my Days . . .
> Two Years you take a Play to write,
> And I scarce get my Coffee by it;
> Such swinging Bills are still to pay,
> For Sugar, Chocolate, and Tea
> I shall be forced to run away
> You made me hope the Lord knows what
> When Whigs should rule, of This, and That,
> But from your boasted Friends I see
> Small Benefit accrues to me:
> I hold my Place, indeed, 'tis true,
> But well I hoped to rise by You.[3]

Centlivre casts Joseph Centlivre as a nag, a feminized man torn between obligations to his female sovereign and expectations of support from his playwright wife. He promises to be "as faithful as a Turtle-Dove" and that he "Never hereafter will offend/With either Male or Female Friend" if the money arrives. Her role as breadwinner switches the gender of public and private spaces as well as masculine and feminine roles in marriage, particularly in Joseph's promise to behave with his male *and* female friends. Financial power within the marriage reorganizes gender scripts and gives her power over her husband's behavior: Joseph Centlivre cajoles, while Centlivre tries to bring home big financial rewards.

Centlivre uses this intersection of public finance and private felicity in her comedies to make her heroines agents in both the public and the private dimensions of their lives. She seizes on the flexibility of contract and appropriates it for her heroines through misrecognized or lost letters, faulty contracts, slippery words, and withheld "writings" or legal instruments of inheritance. Jacqueline Pearson has noted the importance of language in Centlivre's plays in a more general sense. She argues that women gain power through silence while men are empowered through word play, and that written documents, deeds, and wills symbolize men's power over women. While her first point deserves attention, it is compromised by the fact that Centlivre's powerful, talkative heroines like Miranda, Patch, and Anne Lovely are all very effective rhetoricians. Even though Centlivre's heroines occasionally withhold speech, it is not their primary mode. Pearson's second point about writing is more tenuous. In these comedies, writing comes from many directions and rarely remains in the control of men. *Love's Contrivance* includes much writing by women as well as strategic silence. In *The Busy Body,* secret letters, charms, and missing papers create comic disruptions of fatherly prerogative that allow her heroines to make their own contracts. In all these plays, Centlivre maintains that words and contracts are not only the domain of men.

Centlivre's optimistic reading of liberalism and contract culture likely contributed to the staggering popularity of her plays for 200 years; no other English playwright of the eighteenth century, male or female, could boast as many plays in repertoire throughout the period.[4] But her arguments for contract within the private sphere led her into the heart of a contradiction in the marriage contract. The Enlightenment impulse to craft a rational system of law that could be abstracted and generalized did not extend to marriage, where contradictory laws and precedents made it impossible to establish clearly the legal situation of married women. The liberal fantasy of "equal freedom of everybody before the law and in the marketplace" (Atiyah, *Rise and Fall* 77) did not describe marriage contracts. While women were necessarily parties to the marriage contract, and while they had become in many cases parties to ancillary contracts for pin money and separate maintenances, women's legal difference from men was preserved in the property law that defined the terms of modern marriage. The mobility of property through contracts and the immobility of property through inheritance are opposing economic forces that animate marriage contracts, where women are both parties to and the condition of the transfer of wealth in marriage. The more women are perceived as conduits, the less their individual will or identity matters, but women who can articulate their position as parties to contract also have a basis for legal subjectivity, domestic authority, and an alternative erotics of mutuality. The tension between commercial contract and the traditional definition of the marriage contract comes out to play in comic scenes that have papers, words, and promises flying about the room. The comic symptom of the mobile word, the trope of the contract, proves radically unstable in these plots, which are nonetheless dedicated to finding every possible reason to believe in modern marriage.

Moral Money Management

Centlivre's first comedies were not her most successful. *The Perjured Husband* (1700), which she submitted as Susanna Carroll, blended tragedy with a comic subplot set in Venice at carnival time.[5] The play reaches back to the Restoration for its materials and its form, as does her other tragicomedy, *The Stolen Heiress* (1702). Both of these plays allude to her future as a comic playwright, but as individual efforts they are muddled, and they met with very limited success. *The Beau's Duel* (1702) moved closer to Centlivre's successful comic style, in which circulating letters play an important role. *Love's Contrivance, or, Le Medecin malgré Lui* (1703) similarly capitalizes on the device of outwitting bad fathers who withhold or reverse their consent out of greed. Both plays also include faithful lovers (Bellmie and Manley) who are model husbands for Centlivre's bourgeois fantasy of contractual equality in marriage. But *The Perjured Husband* was poorly received, and Bowyer surmises that it is unlikely that *The Beau's Duel* had a very long run (42–43). Notably, both *The Stolen Heiress* and *Love's Contrivance* appeared anonymously, with hints that the author was in fact male.[6]

Centlivre's first big stage success was *The Gamester* (1705), which ran to a sixth night under her own name. Centlivre used the theme of gambling to hit the moral tone of the newer "moral" comedies established by Steele in *The Lying Lover* (1703) and Cibber in *The Careless Husband* (1704). *The Gamester* shares the reformist impulse of Steele's *The Tender Husband* (1705) and Cibber's *The Lady's Lost Stake* (1707). But unlike Cibber's work, which was still engaged with what Allardyce Nicoll terms "the gallantries of the Restoration drama," Centlivre focuses on the social and personal need for reliable promises.[7] And unlike Steele's heroines, her female lead characters are very ready to act in their own defense and in the reformation of their wayward men. Centlivre borrowed from Jean François-Regnard's *Le Joueur* (1696), but she improves the fate of Valere, who loses his beloved in the original, and rewrites his rival Dorante as a less threatening, mercenary older uncle. She focuses on Valere and, to a lesser extent, Lady Wealthy, who must each give up their gambling habits to enjoy financially and romantically stable futures.

Gambling was a serious social problem in Centlivre's Whiggish estimation. Her dedication called for an end to gambling after the example of George, earl of Huntingdon, the play's dedicatee, the "Actions of [whose] Life File the Teeth of Satyr." George, the seventh earl of Huntingdon, became a soldier during a period of estrangement with his father before he inherited his title. Once he became earl, he went to great lengths to settle his mother's and aunt's property, which he had inherited, on his sister Elizabeth. He then began a Chancery suit, a way to mitigate the common-law principles that kept women out of the line of inheritance, to provide for his stepmother's children. His legal advocacy for women in his extended family, his identity as a soldier, and his death in February of 1704 make him a figure worthy of Centlivre's praise as an exemplar of good fiscal management and domestic responsibility.[8] Centlivre asserts optimistically that were gambling to be eradicated, "then wou'd the Distress'd be reliev'd, the Poor supported, and the Virtuous encourag'd, which would distinguish our Nobility as much above our Neighbours, as their Heroick Deeds have done" (*Gamester,* dedication). Centlivre holds that economic injustice is a function of illogic, in this case the risk of wealth through gambling. Conversely, a robust economy of stable, well-argued English contracts and a coherent legal system will lead to general plenty. But the certainty of her dedication obscures another question she pursues in the play: what counts as investment and what counts as gambling? Coffeehouses were centers both of legitimate commercial activity and gambling, a line blurred by the advent of stock funds. Valere, the compulsive gambler of the play, takes his gambling as seriously as a man of business would the stock market. He has ties to both the old order of landed rakes and libertines and the new order of paper credit.[9] Sir Thomas upbraids his wayward son in the tradition of Aristophanic comedy, but his references to "Reformation" and "estate" put the conflict in the context of early century anxieties about the new economic man. Sir Thomas wants Valere to abandon the pursuit of a bad form of paper credit and speculate instead for business gains that translate into the solid earth of estates.

Valere's gambler economy hides his real economic lack behind excess and display. Blind to the world of labor, Valere keeps tradespeople frozen in expectation and want. Galloon, the tailor, needs his money for coal during his wife's lying in, and Mrs. Topknot, the milliner, needs the money for her daughter's dower. Both debts constrain the lives of men and women who are tied to Valere through larger social networks of power and jeopardize their comic narratives of marriage and reproduction. Valere flatters Mrs. Security in an attempt to get her to loan him money, but unlike Gayman in *The Lucky Chance,* Valere's sexuality is useless as currency when he doesn't honor his other debts. Mrs. Security asks for collateral, but all Valere has to offer is his promise on paper, which she refuses. Valere cries out indignantly, "Refuse my Note! I scorn your Money," but his pride cannot hide the fact that his word is only a paper phallus, a representation without substance (I, 13). Valere's proto-bank note, a form that does not become legal tender in England until 1797, drew on what Peter Mathias has called "the web of credit supporting business" that allowed most eighteenth-century businesses to function with relatively little ready cash. Such notes also provided some stability during times of great confusion in the national money supply of silver and copper coin (Mathias 95). Valere's lack of money is not unusual, but his poverty becomes real when he loses credibility as both an economic and a moral agent; he cannot guarantee his bill.

The shift of value in Valere's world parallels the movement from aristocratic ideas of genealogical value (expressed in the precious metal content of the coin) to a bourgeois model of inner worth. Inner worth guarantees the credibility and solvency of the individual through the readable signs of virtue, such as hard work and seriousness, which were the bank notes of the new individual.[10] Valere's failure to signify his inner worth and thus be worth his word compromises his right to make contracts in the bourgeois world of the play. Laura Rosenthal has argued that the instability of his relation to contracts and money threatens Valere with the alienable sexuality usually associated with women, but without feminization per se (Rosenthal 235). But his sexuality also moves away from a Restoration-era royalism, in which sexual and political authority inhere in the person, and toward a social and civic model of identity, in which his credibility as a lover depends on the worth of his contracts. His unreliability poses the greater danger in the world of this play, where the realm of contract is the promise of sexual equality between women and men, who must be willing and able to negotiate.

Valere's lies, often joint productions with his valet Hector, culminate in the story that Angelica's picture is being copied at the painters, when in fact Valere has gambled it away to Angelica in disguise. Angelica, who presents the original and shames Valere, laments, "When a Man breaks all his Oaths to me, I know no reason I shou'd keep my Word with him" (V, 65). Unlike Behn's Angelica, Centlivre's heroine understands contracts and can manipulate them across the boundaries of private and public, erotic and commercial. She demands of Valere "Can you upon Honour (for you shall swear no more) forsake that Vice that brought you to this low Ebb of Fortune" (V, 67). Her role as agent and reformer puts her in charge of the marriage contract; her forgiveness is in effect the marriage proposal, and Sir Thomas promises her "a swinging Jointure" (V, 65). With this appeal to the power of the word, *The Gamester* set the tone for Centlivre's future comic successes, the greatest of which pressed further on the contractual nature of marriage and on her heroines' freedom of contract.

Follow the Bouncing Contract

After *The Gamester,* Centlivre followed up with *The Basset-Table* (1705), which has received recent attention from feminist scholars for its portrayal of Valeria, the female scientist.[11] Valeria's scientific experiments and her plan for rational love with Ensign Lovely unfold amid the gaming of other characters, where financial ruin (in the case of the merchant-class Mrs. Sago) and near sexual ruin (in the threat of rape for Lady Reveller) mark the dangers of this faulty economy. *The Basset-Table,* however, managed only a four-night run before it disappeared from the stage; it had a similarly limited life in print, with editions in 1706 and 1735. The next two attempts, *Love at a Venture* (1706), which drew materials from *Le Galand Doublé* (1660) and *The Platonick Lady* (1706), both show a concern with words and contracts. In the former, Bellair claims that his exploits "will make the prittiest Novel" when he is caught by Beliza in one of his multiple courting personas (I, 18). Wou'dbe, a social climber, writes down others' words and is compared to a poet who must gather witticisms for his plays because he has none of his own. Like Farquhar in *The Beaux' Stratagem* (1707), Centlivre explores the legal and social problem of the marriage of younger women to much older men. Unlike Mrs. Sullen, however, her Lady Cautious finds no magical solution to her legally contracted marriage and, "since [her] Marriage-Knot can never be dissolv'd" she must serve instead as the eponymous voice of caution (V, 55). In the latter, Mrs. Dowdy, a tradeswoman, provides a comic portrait of a country person aspiring to fashionable status. Her asides prefigure Frances Sheridan's Mrs. Surface, Richard Brinsley Sheridan's Mrs. Malaprop, and Frances Burney's Mrs. Voluble and sustain the comic appeal of the piece. Though all of these Centlivre plays are well-crafted, they did not please the theatergoing public.

These commercial failures and her marriage to Joseph Centlivre in 1707 led to a two-year hiatus, out of which Centlivre emerged with her greatest success. *The Busy Body* was, in fact, the seventh most successful play of the eighteenth century and the period's most popular play by a woman.[12] The play's history began, however, with a struggle between Robert Wilks, the original George Airy, and Centlivre that threatened its first run. According to John Mottley,

Wilks disliked his part so much that "in a Passion he threw it off the Stage into the Pit, and swore that no body would bear to sit to hear such Stuff."[13] The *Biographia Dramatica* lamented that audience sympathy for the playwright "forced a run of thirteen nights; while Mr. Congreve's *The Way of the World*, which perhaps contains more true intrinsic wit, and unexceptionable accuracy of language, than any dramatic piece ever written . . . could scarcely make its way at all" (99). Lord Byron, testily registering Centlivre's popularity in his own day, echoed this sentiment when he referred to her comedies as the "balderdash" that drove Congreve's far superior work off the stage (Bowyer 97). These moments suggest the degree to which her play struck a note that caused these men to object violently to its themes, as well as the continued resistance to female authorship. Centlivre's very popular comedies offered comic pleasures that were too volatile, or perhaps too populist, for some critics.

George was not a very masculine leading man by contemporary standards; Miranda controls the plot, tells George what to do, and releases herself from guardianship. George is wealthy with £4,000 a year, but he is subject to Sir Francis's control of Miranda and must beg and then pay for an audience with her. Miranda overhears this transaction and uses it against George in the famous dumb scene in which George implores her to "assume your self" by leaving her fortune to Sir Francis and becoming dependent on George's wealth (II, 20). Miranda refuses on principle; she will not sacrifice her fortune or become a dependent for love. As if subordination to Miranda were not enough, George must also play the straight man to the crowd-pleasing Marplot. Wilks's objections before opening night did not, however, impede the play's success or the approval by Steele in *The Tatler,* where he called it an "effect of nature and instinct," a compliment that keeps a safe distance between Centlivre and poetic genius.[14]

Centlivre uses xenophobia to serve the cause of female liberty early in the play. Sir Francis's wealth, gotten through international trade, falls under a pall after Charles's opening assertion that gold "buys even Souls, and bribes Wretches to betray their Country" (I, 2). Wealth and, more to the point, greed threaten the moral and political integrity of the nation. The suspicions of Sir Jealous, which spring from anxieties about reproduction and fidelity, become national issues when he turns his back on English customs:

> *Patch:* Oh, Madam, it's his living so long in *Spain,* he vows he'll spend half his Estate, but he'll be a Parliament-Man, on purpose to bring in a Bill for Women to wear Veils, and the other odious *Spanish* Customs—He swears it is the height of Impudence to have a Woman seen Bare-fac'd even at Church, and scarce believes there's a true begotten Child in the City.
>
> *Miranda:* Ha, ha, ha, how the old Fool torments himself! Suppose he could introduce his rigid Rules—does he think we cou'd not match them in

> Contrivance? No, no; Let the Tyrant Man make what Laws he will, if there's a Woman under the Government, I warrant she finds a way to break 'em . . . (I, 8)

Sir Jealous's anti-English sexual values come from his obsession with money; his fear about "true begotten" children is a concern about inheritance, and Miranda scoffs at the proposition that women could be reduced to conduits for heritable wealth. Miranda imagines a legal space for women "under the Government," whose forensic existence comes into being by breaking the laws of tyrants and championing true Englishness.

Centlivre's play bears some resemblance to Behn's *The Lucky Chance* in that the sexual pretensions of older men seeking younger women feed the play's jokes. But unlike Letitia, who cringes under Sir Feeble Fainwoud's baby talk, Miranda plays along with Sir Francis's pet names, calling him "Gardy" to her "Chargy," and pretending to prefer him to men her own age II, 14; 15). To his face she is fawning and flirtatious, but her asides make her purpose clear: her "Unconscionable old Wretch, Bribe me with my own Money" sets the tone for the remainder of the play (II, 15). Like Behn's Willmore, George makes himself a sexual object to underscore the motives of love and desire that trump financial interest. George Airy urges Miranda, "View me well, am I not a proper Handsome Fellow, ha? Can you prefer that old, dry, wither'd, sapless Log of Sixty-five, to the vigorous, gay, sprightly Love of Twenty-four? With Snoring only he'll awake thee, but I with Ravishing Delight wou'd make thy Senses Dance in Consort with the Joyful Minutes" (II, 20). The irrepressible Marplot exclaims in the following act, "Here's a Husband for Eighteen—Here's a Shape—Here's Bones ratling in a Leathern Bag. *[Turning Sir* Franci*s about.]* Here's Buckram, and Canvass, to scrub you to Repentance" (III, 38). Behn and Centlivre agree on the importance of bodily attraction, and they distinguish between erotic desire and other kinds of desire. Like Sir Feeble Fainwoud in *The Lucky Chance,* Sir Francis is unable to distinguish sexual desire from greed and cannot use his wealth to supply his lack of physical attraction. For Centlivre, however, the emphasis falls on the legal and contractual instruments through which Sir Francis attempts to secure Miranda's fortune and body. His full immersion in the logic of acquisition makes it impossible for him to see that Miranda might use similar contracts to resist his greedy and incestuous fantasy of "engross[ing] the whole" (III, 39).

Sir Francis's temporary control over Miranda comes from his legal guardianship, sustained by the literal papers that declare her inheritance. Sir Francis then superimposes another paper, the marriage contract, on their existing legal and economic relation. Miranda uses the materiality of these papers against him when she urges Sir Francis to "sign Articles" that will free her from the age restriction of her father's will and allow her to marry by choice. Sir Francis kisses and hugs Miranda and exclaims, "Adod, I believe I am Metamorphos'd; my Pulse beats high, and my Blood boils, me-thinks—." Miranda assures her overexcited sexagenarian that "the Market lasts all the Year," but after her exit, he rhapsodizes, "Well, *Franck,* thou art a lucky Fellow in thy old Age, to have such a delicate Morsel, and Thirty Thousand Pound in love with thee. . . . Some Guardians wou'd be glad to compound for part of the Estate, at dispatching an Heiress, but I engross the whole" (III, 39). In Behn's comedies, this sort of response from an older man creates a primarily sexual disgust, but Centlivre uses it to map her critique of real versus ideal contracts. Sir Francis fails to be part of the economy of good exchanges that Centlivre wants to support in her defense of contract. By "engrossing the whole," Sir Francis is both impeding the good flow of property and making Miranda disappear. As guardian, he would act the part of both father and husband in the marriage exchange, thus reducing Miranda's legal personhood to near invisibility. He anatomizes Miranda into "a delicate Morsel" and "Thirty Thousand Pounds," a thing and a signifier of value, ways of thinking that make her the object of the marriage contract rather than one of its parties. While George Airy has some interest in Miranda's money as well as her person, he does not equate them. She teases George that he fell in love when "your happy Ears rank in the pleasing News, I had Thirty Thousand Pound," but this bit of honesty reinforces the distinction between Miranda and her exchange value (IV, 52). She presents herself as possessor of her own fortune, which bolsters her status as a contractual subject. This status supports her interpretation of elite marriage as a contract in which affection and economic interest are mutual motives for bride and groom; the reality of marriage portions need not make an object of the bride, as long as she understands the business of marriage.

The second couple, Isabinda and Charles, both suffer under parents who are blocking characters; Sir Charles is Sir Francis's son, and Isabinda is Sir Jealous's daughter. Because of Sir Jealous's oppressive "Spanish" restrictions, they are forced to conduct a textual courtship. Their real and imagined love letters undergo dizzying comic displacements, evading the eyes of the father. Sir Jealous first suspects Whisper, a servant, of bringing a letter to Isabinda, and asks him his business. Whisper, who has come on Charles's behalf, must invent a story to escape Sir Jealous's wrath:

> *Whisper:* Nay, Sir, my Business—is no great matter of Business neither; and yet 'tis Business of Consequence too.
> *Sir Jealous:* Sirrah, don't trifle with me.
> *Whisper:* Trifle, Sir, have you found him, Sir?
> *Sir Jealous:* Found what, you Rascal.

> *Whisper:* Why *Trifle* is the very Lap-Dog my Lady lost, Sir; I fancy'd I see him run into this House. I'm glad you have him—Sir, my Lady will be overjoy'd that I have found him.
> *Sir Jealous:* Who is your Lady Friend?
> *Whisper:* My Lady Love-puppy, Sir. (II, 27)

Sir Jealous, who suspects Whisper is "some He-Bawd," tries to apprehend the scene in fiscal terms (II, 26). He rightly suspects some transaction, but Whisper's wordplay draws Sir Jealous off the trail. The imaginary dog Trifle transforms Sir Jealous's accusation into a thing. Whisper is a trifler in the sense that he is talking about nothing (trifles) and that he challenges Sir Jealous's authority; technically, Sir Jealous is right in both cases. There is *nothing* involved in the transaction he facilitates between Charles and Isabinda; Sir Jealous assumes Whisper is hiding a letter or other piece of evidence when in fact Whisper was there to signal a meeting that has not yet happened. But Whisper's trickster-servant facility with language also substitutes the invented thing, the dog, for the real message, the sign for the meeting and possible spousals between Charles and Isabinda, which temporarily satisfies Sir Jealous's demand for material evidence. Whisper leads Sir Jealous away from the world of real contracts and into the world of imaginary things, a comic inversion befitting his materialistic drive to use his daughter as a commodity in trade with Don Diego Babinetto. The transformation of the letter that isn't into the dog that isn't is the first of several comic displacements to protect the words of Charles and Isabinda from the intervention of Sir Jealous.

The lovers take to writing in characters, a language of their own invention, to keep them safely outside of the law of this literal father. The nonverbal, graphic message provides a more material form of communication, a system of representation that forgoes the alienation of proper language in favor of something between language and material presence. Patch collects one of these letters from Whisper at the beginning of act IV, but she mistakenly drops it on the stairs, where Sir Jealous finds it. He grumbles, "humph; 'tis *Hebrew* I think. What can this mean. . . . [T]his was certainly design'd for my Daughter, but I don't know that she can speak any Language but her Mother-Tongue. No matter for that, this may be one of Love's Hieroglyphicks" (IV.i, 44). His assumption that the letter is in Hebrew is both a graphic misrecognition and a socioeconomic one: his guess connects Hebrew, a suitor, and illicit trade as ways he could be cheated. He sarcastically encourages Isabinda to "write a Bill upon your Forehead, to show Passengers there's something to be Let" when she stands on her balcony (II.ii, 24). His desire to manifest his anxieties on her body calls up Wycherley's Pinchwife and his more cynical and violent threat to carve slut on Margery's forehead.

But Centlivre rereads Wycherley's dynamic and relocates the threat from husband to a father. Sir Jealous also deflects the violent writing on the body to the "Bill," the instrument of an economic transaction that, ironically, would benefit Sir Jealous. Centlivre's focus on the hieroglyphic and the correspondingly textual threat of the bill keep the question of sexual right in the realm of civil, public contract. Unlike Pinchwife, who is concerned about Margery's illicit circulation, Sir Jasper reads Isabinda's sexual identity and her potential sexual activity through legal instruments of trade and contract. He is, in that sense, a modern patriarch.

Patch, Isabinda's maid, sports a conventional name for a *fille de chambre,* but she also provides the literal patch in the ruptured strategies of her mistress. When Sir Jealous confronts Patch and Isabinda with the letter in "Hieroglyphicks," Patch calls on "Invention, thou Chamber-maid's best Friend" and proceeds with her fantastic story:

> *Patch:* Oh Lord, Oh Lord, what have you done, Sir? Why the Paper is mine, I drop'd it out of my Bosom. *[Snatching it from him.]* . . . Why, Sir, it is a Charm for the Tooth-ach—I have worn it this seven Year, 'twas given me by an Angel for ought I know, when I was raving with the Pain; for no body knew from whence he came, nor wither he went, he charg'd me never to open it, lest some dire Vengeance befal me, and Heaven knows what will be the Event. Oh! cruel Misfortune that I should drop it, and you should open it—If you had not open'd it—(IV, 46)

Patch's comic misreading of the letter distracts Sir Jealous from his purpose. She argues that the hieroglyphic is a kind of writing that is not to be read, an irrational signifier that escapes the linguistic law of the father. Patch interposes her body, all bosom and toothaches, as the meaning of the letter, while the imaginary, mysterious angel stands in for Charles. "Angel" circulates in the script as the sign of help for lovers; Marplot is Sir George's "better Angel" when he brings news of Miranda, and Patch is Charles's "Angel" for helping him impersonate Don Diego Babinetto (III, 41). Without rational, legal claim to agency in the marriage contract, these plotting lovers resort to the world of magic and irrationality. The text of the letter remains undeciphered in the realm of a material rather than fully linguistic sign. The letter does refer to a bodily problem, though not the proposed toothache; the embodiment that keeps women from full participation as legal and economic actors here becomes the alibi that translates the letter back into the language of the body. The dilemma of female embodiment shapes women's disadvantages in marriage contracts, though Centlivre points to the remedy of a more textual equality of contract in this comic event.

Miranda and George use their trysting time to plan their wedding in the most businesslike terms. Miranda, after assuring herself that Sir George is a good choice because he "is what I have try'd in Conversation, [and] inquir'd into his Character," pops the question to George thus: "Do you think we can agree on that same terrible Bugbear, *Matrimony*, without heartily Repenting on both sides?" (IV.ii, 52). Her assertive relation to language and contract culminates in this proposal scene. George excitedly agrees, but Miranda warns him that they will not be eloping. She explains that she has obtained Sir Francis's consent to marry and that she won't do anything until she is sure Sir Francis is away and she has her estate: "then I and my *Writings,* the most *material* point, are soon removed" (IV.ii, 53, italics mine). Miranda knows that her writings, the legal documentation of her wealth, are her point of access to subjectivity because they allow her to enter into the marriage contract as a property-owning party to the contract. As "the most material point," they signify her economic autonomy, the grounds of her equality within the marriage. Her plan puts George in a subordinate position (this must have been just the sort of thing that infuriated Wilks), but it is the culmination of Miranda's subjectivity as a female person capable of making her own deals.

Enter Marplot into this tenuous legal moment. His arrival with Sir Francis forces George to hide in the chimney, where he is nearly discovered until Miranda insists that the board can't be moved because she has a monkey within. Immediately, Marplot breaks into a childish rhapsody on monkeys.[15] "A Monkey, dear Madam, let me see it; I can tame a Monkey as well as the best of them all. Oh how I love the little Miniatures of Man" (IV, 54–5). The quote from Rochester has the dual effect of reinforcing Marplot's feminine status within the play (the long-winded Lady caricatured in Rochester's "A Letter from Artemiza in the Town to Chloe in the Country" speaks the line "the little Miniatures of Man") and calling into question George's status as a man. The fine line between human and animal, which has been used against women who are and are not fully conscious, rights-bearing persons, rebounds on George, trapped in the vaginal space of the chimney. Marplot echoes this comic displacement of monkey to man when he laments at the end of the scene, " . . . when you talk'd of a Blunderbuss, who thought of a Rendevous? and when you talk'd of a Monkey, who the Devil dreamt of Sir *George?*" (IV, 56). The linguistic displacements in the half-rhymed "blunderbuss" and "rendezvous" draw a connection between danger and love and give greater resonance to the displacement of man with monkey. The animal nature of Sir George, or any man, calls into question the sexual double standard of contract; if males can overcome their status as mere animals when they make contracts, why cannot women? It also poses a more immediate question for Miranda; can she trust George to be the rational, civil contractual partner she takes him to be?

Miranda responds to the alleged monkey as Sir George when Marplot asks if it has a pretty chain. She replies, "Not yet, but I design it one shall last its Life-time" (IV.ii, 55). George has already proven that he is willing to pay, connive, and submit to Miranda's direction in the hope of legal sexual access. But while Behn was more celebratory of sexual desire, Centlivre encounters it as an anxious aftereffect of contract. She acknowledges Miranda's desire for George (when George embraces her in the dumb scene she exclaims, "Oh Heavens! I shall not be able to contain my self") but Centlivre tends to suppose in Lockean fashion that the passions are a threat to reason, and that access to reason (and property) are the basis for the contractual self. The Lockean and even earlier Cartesian principles of rationality that grounded eighteenth-century philosophy depended on a disembodied model of the conscious mind as the locus of the rational self. *An Essay Concerning Human Understanding* provides a relatively gender-neutral phenomenological account of the Lockean consciousness that collides with the corporeal, nut-gathering political subject of *Two Treatises on Government,* with crucial implications for women. The constitution of Locke's political subject depends on reason, which seems universally available in the *Essay* just as it does in Descartes. The upshot, found in Locke's attitude toward servants, slaves, lunatics, children, and with only slight differences, women, is that the "we" who are "born free as we are born rational" (*Two Treatises* 150) does not include those who are naturally inferior. This tautology places minors by lack of reason (children, the mentally handicapped) in the same category as those for whom Locke posits a prior or pre-political inferiority, as he does for women, slaves, and servants. George and Miranda cannot accomplish their contract in the open because she is not "born free as [she is] born rational," a fact which impinges on his freedom to contract as well. The sexed body reasserts itself as a remainder within Locke's logic of subjectivity and Centlivre's chimney; the persistence of the body threatens to make monkeys of men and women alike.

The final scenes of the comedy deal with conventional blocking fathers and guardians in terms of the contractarian concerns of the plot. After Sir Jealous has threatened to beat Isabinda's eyes out and turn her out of doors to force her to agree to marry Don Diego (actually Charles), he suspects an imposter and tries to stop the wedding. Centlivre parodies Sir Jealous's paternal prerogative to use violence on his child in his abrupt change of mind, but the threat to which the joke refers is no less real. Sir George guards the passage to the church and reminds Sir Jealous that "the Act and Deed were both your own, and I'll see 'em sign'd, or die for't," and he stands ready to enforce the contract that is to Isabinda's advantage (V.iii, 69). Sir Jealous has arguably forced a betrothal, which has ambiguous but possibly binding consequences in 1709. The word and deed are, in the end, where authority is vested in contract theory, and a classically patriarchal mode of authority has a stake in their efficacy.

Miranda promises Sir Francis "if ever I marry, positively this is my Wedding Day," her sly but legally accurate vow to marry Sir George (V.i, 60). For her final contractual coup, she procures the title to Charles's estate, her own "writings," and the paper of the marriage license. Her wit and plotting during the play shape the conclusion, in which she, George, Isabinda, and Charles are all at liberty to marry for love *and* money, to unite the commercial contract with the romantic one. This conventional piece of stage business takes on additional force in relation to the bodily claims that Sir Francis tries to make. He insists that "my Estate shall descend only to the Heirs of her Body," but Sir George interposes "Lawfully begotten by me" (V, 70). The contest is ultimately over Miranda's body, a fact that reminds us of her Lockean and cultural definition as a biological woman with reproductive and "parental" potential. Pateman argues the point thus: "If Adam was to be a father, Eve had to become a mother. In other words, *sex-right or conjugal right must necessarily precede the right of fatherhood.* The genesis of political power lies in Adam's sex-right or conjugal right, not in his fatherhood. Adam's political title is granted *before* he becomes a father" (87). The line of estate, the transfer of property, and the legal status of Miranda's body overshadow her provisional contractual authority. Miranda's last acts manipulate the world of written contracts, but she must still face the "terrible Bugbear" of marriage. She encourages Sir George to reserve some of his love and tenderness "for our future Days, to let the World see we are Lovers after Wedlock; 'twill be a Novelty—" (V, 52). Her final wish expresses the instability of the contractual marriage of even the most reasonable lovers; once the contract is accomplished, even the most legally adept *feme covert* can only hope for the best.

Because She Can:
The Argument for Contractual Equality

In spite of her soft critique of marriage, Centlivre sustained her Habermasian faith in the ability of free markets to create a public sphere "not only as a sphere free from domination but as one free from any kind of coercion" that could guarantee civil society and civil liberties.[16] In this bourgeois discourse, free markets are part of a larger project of liberating English society from aristocratic modes of power. Centlivre spoke often of the "Publick Good," which she identified with free trade and the house of Hanover. She also declared that the arrival of George Augustus presented an economic boon of sorts in that it "raised the PUBLICK CREDIT of the British Nation."[17] Economic improvement, in Centlivre's decidedly Whiggish sense, depends on a public sphere guaranteed by contractual civil society of property owners. Her rhetorical appeal to an England at liberty in "A Poem Humbly Presented to His Most Sacred Majesty George, King of Great Britain, France, and Ireland" and the dedication to *The Wonder* situate the public sphere at the nexus of Protestant ideology, trade, and contractual civil society.

The Wonder: a Woman keeps a Secret (1714) begins with the question of a woman's ability to make and keep a promise, in this case a secret. The ironic title takes up the tautology of women and contract with a tautology of its own; women are trustworthy because they are. National identity, which supports her heroine's claims to be equal parties to marriage contracts, plays an even more important role in this comedy, which is set in Lisbon. Don Felix, the jealous lover of Violante, is in hiding because of a duel. He must also learn to overcome his jealous "Portuguese" tendencies and become a more rational "English" companion. This transformation, in light of both its political content and theatrical possibility, made Don Felix one of Garrick's favorite roles and the choice for his farewell performance in 1776.

Centlivre's dedication of *The Wonder* to "His Serene Highness, *George Augustus,* Electoral Prince of Hanover, Duke and Marquess of *Cambridge,* Earl of *Milford-Haven,* Viscount *North-Allerton,* Baron of *Tewksbury,* and Knight of the most Noble Order of the Garter" threw this comedy into the political fray over succession during the first run. After Queen Anne fell ill in December of 1713, the crisis began in earnest. While the Tories officially favored the Act of Settlement, which would bring the Hanoverian line to the throne, there was still support among Jacobites for James, half-brother of Anne, whose succession would preserve the hold of the house of Stuart. The politicized "Cambridge writ," the official call of the duke of Cambridge (George II) to the House of Lords, was opposed by Anne, but it quickly became a symbol of commitment to Protestant succession and to the principles of contractual civil society. Centlivre's dedication politicized *The Wonder*'s broadly nationalist themes. The dedication Anglicizes the German George I as true and royal Briton and stakes England's future on George Augustus, contractual patriarch: "*our Religion, our Laws, and Civil Rites can be in no Danger under a Prince, who from his Conversations with our Nobility, and his Presence at their most important Debates, will have a perfect Insight into all the Parts of our Constitution.*" George Augustus will guarantee the future of England by understanding what words mean, by listening to debate, and by understanding the promises of the constitution. Though she must fantasize away George's language barrier, Centlivre returns to the status of the word, and in particular the constitution, as the compact between the people and their ruler. She writes hopefully of "*the most accomplish'd of* Princes *[who] will perfect himself in the Arts of Government under the Eye, and Direction of the Greatest of* Queens." Her wishful revision of Anne as happy tutor to her Hanoverian successor allowed Centlivre to make the bold Whiggish claim that "every honest Briton" welcomed the Hanovarian line as a salvific preservation of the throne. She reflected on her political gamble six years later in "A Woman's Case" (1720), in which she has her husband comment "If out, I'm by your Scribbling turn'd, / I wish your Plays and you were burn'd." For her dedication, she earned the scorn of Pope and a few royal command benefit performances (not the pension for which she had hoped), but the political risk of the dedication insisted on her rhetorical (if not contractual) access to the political process.[18] The play proceeds on the basis of a similar syllogism; women can prove their contractual aptitude by making and keeping good contracts. The comedy locates the cultural dissonance in those comic characters who refuse to believe that women are trustworthy.

The Wonder stands apart from other popular comedies in the period in its presentation of sincere female friendship. Violante's title "secret" is that she harbors her runaway friend Isabella, who escaped an arranged marriage to Don Guzman through a leap out a window, only to fall (literally) into the arms of the irresistibly English Colonel Britton. As Virginia Woolf observed when she read that "Cloe liked Olivia," the effects of Violante's affection for Isabella change the dynamic of the plot's formula drastically. Centlivre prioritizes the relationship between the young women above the main romance, and it forces Felix to develop real trust in Violante. *The Perplex'd Lovers* and *The Busy Body,* as well as Behn's *The Lucky Chance,* show female friends who are cooperative and advance each other's causes, but very few other plays of the Restoration or early eighteenth century show friendly, much less sacrificial relationships between women.[19] The pretended and false friendships of *The Way of the World, The Beggar's Opera, The Man of Mode,* and *The Country Wife* are more common. These plays have also had a tremendous influence on the modern critical consensus about the Restoration, shaping the set of questions critics have tended to ask and answer. The critical construction of the rake-hero (Hume), the critical fascination with a carefully defined "comedy of wit" (Fujimura), and the selection of plays in otherwise evenhanded studies of the drama (Nicoll, Hume) make it difficult, if not impossible, to see bonds between women and to think about how those bonds develop female subjectivity on the comic stage. Here, Violante's claim to make good contracts has everything to do with her relationship to a woman, which Felix cannot see.

Violante is destined for a convent to consolidate her family's fortunes, although she and Felix are in love when the play opens. Flora reproaches Violante with reading Felix's love letter over and over when it is "always the same Language. . . . Nothing charms that does not change . . . except a Bank Note, or a Bill of Exchange" (II.i, 12). Flora's joke distinguishes between types of contracts (emotional and financial) even as it suggests the slippage between the two. Lissardo similarly laments that Inis and Flora move between registers of erotic and commercial value when they fight over him as "an Acre of Land, that they quarrel about Right and Title to me." In the context of this competition, Flora asks Inis, "has he given thee Nine Months earnest for a living Title? Ha, ha" (III.i, 30). In the second joke, the body of Lissardo becomes property, to which Inis could acquire title by giving birth to his child, the result of the "Nine Months earnest." The joke inverts the legal supposition that women are sexual property with the supposition that men are commodities to be acquired through children. While neither proposition is ideal, the joke raises concerns about the new economic man as feminized by fluctuating valuations and by women's economic agency, concerns that both Catherine Ingrassia and Jonathan Kramnick see in the rhetorical and material connections between professional writing and modern finance.

Jokes about men and wealth also write women more fully into the marriage plot as agents of their own destinies. Inis tells Isabella that were she in Isabella's position, she would take passage on the next ship "with all my Jewels, and seek my Fortune on t'other side the Water," the promised land of England where women can be fortune seekers (I.i, 9). Isabella believes that there, "Duty wears no Fetter but Inclination," unlike her own Portugal, where custom "inslaves us from our very Cradles, first to our parents, next to our Husbands; and when Heaven is so kind to rid us of both these, our Brothers still usurp Authority, and expect a blind Obedience from us, so that Maids, Wives, or Widows, we are little better than Slaves to the Tyrant Man" (I.i, 8). But in spite of Isabella's bold opening comparison between Portugal and England, she describes the legal status of Portuguese *and* English women, for whom an education in obedience shapes both social convention and the law. Women's status under the law is a function of widely held concepts of gender. Isabella returns to the core problem of the play, the assumed natural inferiority of women written into Locke and, to a lesser degree, Hobbes, which keeps women from full civil participation. But Centlivre meets the tautology of female inferiority on its own terms by showing that women can make contracts, keep secrets, and otherwise partake of civil society through Violante's and Isabella's examples.

While Isabella rhapsodizes on English freedom, Britton eroticizes immured Portuguese women and their fortunes. He finds nunneries that contain "such Troops of soft, plump, tender melting, wishing, nay willing Girls too, thro' a damn'd Grate, gives us *Brittons* strong Temptation to Plunder" (I.i, 6). The conflict between Isabella's imaginary England of freedom within monogamy and Britton's imaginary Portugal, with freedom from monogamy, turns on the interrelation of economics and sex. Britton boasts: "Women are the prettiest Play-things in Nature, but Gold, substantial Gold, gives 'em the

Air, the Mien, the Shape, the Grace, and Beauty of a Goddess. . . . *None marry now for Love, no, that's a Jest, / The self same Bargain, serves for Wife, and Beast*" (I.i, 7). Britton's crass materialism makes manifest the larger philosophical dilemma of the play; the status of women as negotiating subjects in the marriage contract has everything to do with their wealth. Wealthier women have more opportunities to make ancillary contracts for separate property and pin money that give them a degree of autonomy, but they are also more likely to be regarded as conduits for the transfer of wealth. The middle- and upper-class marriage arrangements that secured growing colonial profits and the title to England's real estate confirm the truth of Britton's cynical marriage policy. Estate consolidation became even more profitable as technical advances in agriculture encouraged landowners to cut labor costs between 1710 and 1750.[20] The perspectives of Isabella and Britton expose two competing realities for English women entering into marriage contracts: where Isabella finds an ideal of choice in English contract, Britton understands the contract as another economic transaction conducted between men that circulates wives and beasts as goods.

Britton needs to learn that women have understanding, economic interest, and intelligence, in addition to bodies. When he reads a letter from Isabella, he muses: "I suppose the Stile is frank. . . . *Very concise . . . first time I ever knew a Woman had any Business with the mind of a Man* . . . hope she takes me to be Flesh and Blood" (III.i, 28). Britton, who speaks of his desire in terms of urgent hunger ("Ah *Frederick*, the *Kirk* half starves us *Scotchmen.* We are kept so sharp at home, that we feed like Cannibals abroad" [I.i, 6]), here calls Isabella "a *Philosophical Wench*" for her desire to be "let into . . . [his] mind" before she is willing to marry him (III.i, 28). Isabella's letter, which expresses her interest in both legal security and sexual pleasure, leads to the meeting between a veiled Isabella and the colonel. He rakishly offers her breakfast, and then "My Heart, Soul, and Body into the Bargain" (III.iii, 41), but Isabella wants a "clear Title" with no encumbrances, and a lease for life. Her legal vocabulary cuts to the center of the marriage contract and its metaphorically solid real estate, his body, that must be guaranteed hers. She meets with resistance when she asks for a lawyer *and* a parson, civil and ecclesiastical authorities of "the word":

> *Colonel:* The Lawyer, and the Parson! No, no, ye little Rogue, we can finish our Affairs without the help of the Law—or the Gospel.
>
> *Isabella:* Indeed but we can't, Colonel.
>
> *Colonel:* Indeed! Why hast thou then trappan'd me out of my warm Bed this Morning for nothing! Why, this is showing a Man half famish'd, a well furnish'd Larder, then clapping a Padlock on the Door, till you Starve him quite.

> *Isabella:* If you can find in your Heart to say Grace, Colonel, you shall keep the Key.
> *Colonel:* I love to see my Meat before I give Thanks, Madam, therefore uncover thy Face, Child, and I'll tell thee more of my Mind.—If I like you—
> *Isabella:* . . . suspend your Curiosity now; one Step farther looses me for ever.—Show your self a Man of Honour, and you shall find me a Woman of Honour. (III.iii, 42)

The colonel reluctantly agrees to the "blind bargain," suspending his prodigious appetite for the sake of a social contract with Isabella. Legally binding words are Isabella's only assurance that his appetite as a "Man half famish'd" survives the more extended term of legal union. Honor and contract are the only ways to secure her from the whimsy of his carnal motives. Colonel Britton barely reforms—Centlivre writes him a brief moment of self-awareness before Frederick, in which he confesses, "I have a natural Tendency in me to the Flesh, thou know'st" (V, 66). He does ultimately contract a legal marriage with Isabella, but their future occupies the uncertain territory of Hellena and Willmore, whose predictable fate is announced at the beginning of *The Second Part of The Rover.*

Centlivre's jokes probe language itself, showing the necessity of words, even in their unstable form. As Samuel Butler lamented in *Hudibras,*

> *Oaths* are but *words,* and *words* but *wind,*
> Too feeble implements to *bind,*
> And hold with *deeds* proportion, so
> As *shadows* to a *substance* do. (Pt. 2, canto 2, lines 107–110)

The status of the word as comic symptom takes its clearest form in the joking of Lissardo, Don Felix's servant. Lissardo assures Violante that his master has thought of nothing but her since he left Lisbon, explaining: "By an infallible Rule, Madam. Words are the Pictures of the Mind, you know; now to prove he thinks of nothing but you, he talks of nothing but you—for Example, Madam, . . . the Priest came to make him a Visit, he call'd out hastily, *Lissardo* said he, bring a *Violante* for my Father to sit down on;—then he often mistook my Name, Madam, and call'd me *Violante* . . ." (II.i, 14). Centlivre's comic supposition that words are the pictures of the mind echoes the Lockean phenomenological premise that the mind is furnished with ideas from the senses; over time, these impressions acquire names. Memory has the "Power to revive again in our Minds those *Ideas,* which after imprinting have disappeared, or have been as it were laid aside out of sight." The ideas "which naturally at first make the deepest and most lasting Impression, are those, which are accompanied with *Pleasure* or *Pain*" (*Essay* 149–50). These linguistic spots of time create conscious experience and keep individuals in a world bound by affective meaning. Violante, in this comic version of the principle, is less a thing (even though she briefly becomes a chair) than she is the vocabulary of Don Felix's emotional experience, turned into spoken language.

Felix's involuntary confessions, which rename the world "Violante," suggest that private feelings, manifested in the symbolic, public language, can reshape public discourse. But Lissardo puts words (including "Violante") into an unstable play that catches up with him when, distracted by Flora, he absent-mindedly agrees that he and his master had attended balls and parties in their exile. He hastily retracts: "Balls, Madam! Odslife, I ask your Pardon Madam! I, I, I, had mislaid some Wash-Balls of my Master's t'other Day; and because I cou'd not think where I had laid them, just when he ask'd for them, he very fairly broke my Head, Madam" (I.i, 15). The instability of language is a general rhetorical characteristic of joking (displacement) that takes on a more critical function in light of Centlivre's concerns with contract. Linguistic displacement can threaten contracts, which depends on the fixity of language; the anxious pleasures of wordplay must be resolved in the clearer outcome of the ending, an example of what Alexander Leggatt calls the drive of comedy to make the audience stop laughing.[21]

Felix's jealous responses bring the most abiding cultural anxieties about women's sexuality and its relation to property into the dramatic conversation. Felix's predictable, caustic reply to Violante, "his Affairs are wondrous safe, who trusts his Secret to a Womans keeping" (II.i, 26), displays his a priori assumptions about women, which Violante's example must change. The rules of genre say that Felix and Violante must play out the gendered conflict about contract and come to an understanding as lovers by the end of the play. His anxieties, which all spring from sexual fears of infidelity, cannot be greater than his love. Yet he resists granting Violante the equal right to a sense of honor that is not defined only in relation to him. Violante elaborates her claim to honor and thereby to subjectivity with greater success as she and Felix spat their way through the plot. When he petulantly refuses to mend the rift in act III, Violante makes a legal argument about her relationship to Felix: "am I bound by aught but Inclination to submit and follow thee—No Law whilst single binds us to obey, but you by Nature, and Education, are oblig'd to pay a Deference to all Woman kind." Her claim invokes a version of conventional chivalric code, but the main assertion of her independence in a single state extracts her from any promissory relation to Felix. She successfully figures herself as an agent outside the terms of the marriage contract.

Violante's argument gains more focus once Flora is discovered in Felix's chamber where she has been hiding in the press. Violante charges Felix with hypocrisy, then proposes a truce, which he promptly rejects. His persistent assumption is that his words are worth more than hers; the same standards of ocular proof do not apply to Violante's and Felix's claims. But the plot mocks Felix's pretensions. As a character, Felix has no more real control over the plot than does George Airy, a fact that makes him ridiculous as he attempts to take control in the midst of his persistent errors. Felix fumes and brandishes weapons, but these are highly comic moments for an audience who knows he is too in love to execute his drastic plans, which would secure him at best another banishment from Violante.

Felix has one last extended bout with his suspicions when he hears Britton describe the details of Violante's room, her gardens, and her last meeting with Felix during which Britton was stashed in Violante's bedroom. Felix is almost incapacitated with rage and calls out, "Contagion seize her, and make her Body ugly as her Soul" (V.i, 62). Violante responds coolly to Felix's fury: "If I were in your Place, *Felix,* I'd chuse to stay at home, when these Fits of Spleen were upon me, and not trouble such Persons as are not oblig'd to bear with them" (V.ii, 67). Violante has worked to establish her authority as a person who makes and keeps promises, and she uses that authority to navigate this comic event, which is more about domesticity than courtship. The attraction of this couple and the representation of their trials work because it is so deeply rooted in the gendered question of modernity: how can women be both makers and objects of contract? Felix wants to believe in Violante as a reliable subject in his clearer moments, but his Portuguese passions (for which we can read the foreign and suspiciously Catholic enemies of individual bourgeois and Protestant contract) choke off his logic.

In the argument that follows, Felix pledges to quit her forever and Violante retorts that he cannot because she has already banished him. The scene is a modern comic masterpiece that anticipates the domestic realism of Ibsen with a Wildean comic pace. Felix, still persuaded that Violante should apologize, "*Walks about in a great Pet*" according to the stage directions and refuses to listen to Violante's defenses until she breaks into tears. Felix immediately becomes more gentle and, more importantly, begins to listen to Violante's words. The exchange that ensues I reproduce at some length:

Felix: Didst thou ever love me, *Violante?*

Violante: I'll answer nothing.—You was in haste to be gone just now, I should be very well pleas'd to be alone, Sir. *(She sits down, and turns aside.)*

Felix: I shall not long interrupt your Contemplation.—Stubborn to the last. *(Aside.)*

Violante: Did ever Woman involve her self as I have done?

Felix: Now wou'd I give one of my Eyes to be Friends with her, for something whispers to my Soul she is not guilty.—(*He pauses, then pulls a Chair, and sits by her at a little distance, looking at her some time without speaking—Then draws a little nearer to her.*) Give me your Hand at parting however

> *Violante,* won't you, (*Here he lays his open upon her Knee several times.*) won't you—won't you—won't you?
> *Violante:* (*Half regarding him.*) Won't I do what?
> *Felix:* You know what I wou'd have, *Violante,* Oh my heart!
> *Violante:* (*Smiling.*) I thought my Chains were easily broke. (*Lays her Hand into his.*)
> *Felix:* (*Draws his Chair close to her, and kisses her Hand in a Rapture.*) Too well thou knowest thy Strength.—Oh my charming Angel, my Heart is all thy own, forgive my hasty Passion, 'tis the transport of a Love sincere! (V.ii, 70–71)

The pacing of this love scene depends on the comic energy it draws from the play's larger concerns. Felix attempts one more time to conquer the paranoid question that shapes civil contract law: if women are allowed to be self-possessing individuals, then how can a patriarchal culture assure that a father's (or husband's) property is securely transmitted through women to his heirs? Fear of infidelity is Felix's *only* motive to doubt, but it structures his entire relation to Violante; it determines her validity as an interlocutor and a potential maker of contracts at the most basic linguistic level. After his recurrent doubting and rage, he must sue for her attentions in a more humble tone with his "won't you—won't you—won't you?" Significantly, the only new evidence Felix has is Violante's tears; the real and revolutionary change is that Felix has decided to trust her word.

Could We Get That in Writing?

In February 1718, Centlivre had her last big stage success with *A Bold Stroke for a Wife.* The dedication and prologue loudly proclaim its originality, which Richard Frushell and F. P. Lock have disputed on the grounds of similarities to plays by Abraham Cowley and Dryden.[22] Their perspectives echo eighteenth-century critical tendencies to see Centlivre as an imitator of technique, a distinction that renders her talents in terms of Steele's "effect of nature and instinct." Centlivre chose the dedication of this play to announce that "the Plot is entirely New, and the Incidents wholly owing to my own Invention; not borrowed from our own, or translated from the Works of any foreign Poet; so that they have at least the Charm of Novelty to recommend 'em." The prologue "By a Gentleman" echoes Centlivre's claim of originality and promises "not one single Tittle from Molliere." Her defensiveness was likely roused by the recent attack on female playwrights like the fictional Phoebe Clinket who borrows from foreign sources in *Three Hours After a Marriage,* as well as by the tenor of reviews that assumed female playwrights were less talented than male ones.[23] The *Biographia Dramatica* claims that Wilks, who had objected violently to *The Busy Body,* also wished aloud of *A*

Bold Stroke for a Wife that "*not only her play would be damned, but she herself be damned for writing it*" (99). These anxieties about authorship and plagiarism fit Laura Rosenthal's account of the ways that gender, class, and other social indexes of subjectivity shape the ways that Restoration and early-eighteenth-century authors could claim property in their work (Rosenthal 17–23).

Centlivre's turn away from her successful version of the active, plotting heroine and toward a still witty but ineffectual heroine reflects some resignation about contract as well as a broader turn in comedy to more domestic and sentimental themes. *A Bold Stroke for a Wife* is still an intrigue comedy, an example of what Nicoll identifies as "the comedy of wit," which betrays a more cynical perspective on social order (Nicoll II: 155–56). But unlike Wycherley's or Etherege's cynical rakes, Centlivre's cynicism comes through her less active heroine and fewer aggregate lines for female characters. *A Bold Stroke* tells the boy-gets-girl plot of romantic comedy from a disconcerting female point of view: Anne watches in impotent rage as her guardians deny her personal freedoms and make her marriage to anyone nearly impossible. *A Bold Stroke* notably has no subplot, a standard feature of Centlivre's other intrigue comedies and of the style in general. The contrast between Centlivre's heroines (Miranda and Isabinda, Violante and Isabella) assures the audience that women deserve to control their own destiny through their wits, while it also balances the threat of such independence with a slightly more quiescent female. *A Bold Stroke* dispenses with this contrast and with the female friendship theme and turns instead to one woman who can do little to free herself from the multiple faces of patriarchal authority. Her angry but coherent emotional life provides a sharp contrast to her lover Fainwell, the consummate actor, whose protean array of personae flaunts his social freedom and his ability to re-create himself in a range of contractual relations.

Anne Lovely's task is to find a way around the last will and testament of her father, known only as a man who hated progeny so much he would have castrated a son. His will, a bad contract meant to entrap Anne, has vested guardianship of her person and estate in the hands of four irreconcilable guardians. The father's will is the legal crucible through which Anne will either have or be property, but the meaning of the will fragments into the various domains of her guardians: the "word" of God for the Prims, the ability to speak and read in the language of worldly style for Phillip Modelove, the historical text for Periwinkle, and the commercial contracts of Tradelove. Like Miranda, Anne holds out for her money, which will be more important in a marriage to a soldier. *A Bold Stroke* does not recant Centlivre's earlier claims that women should have access to the public, civil dimensions of contract, but she does admit that the access women have to that realm is tenuous and must at some level be granted by men. Fainwell moves through the plot, gathering signed contracts from the guardians, while Anne waits for these contracts between men to determine her future.

Centlivre puts Anne's unromantic understanding of the economics of marriage into the play's opening scene. When Betty suggests that Anne should escape her guardians through a clandestine marriage, Anne replies, "So you wou'd advise me to give up my own Fortune, and throw my self upon the *Colonel's*. . . . [T]here are certain Ingredients to be mingled with Matrimony, without which, I may as well change for the worse as for the better. When the Woman has Fortune enough to make the Man happy, if he has either Honour or Good Manners, he'll make her easie. Love makes but a slovenly Figure in that House, where Poverty keeps the Door" (I.ii, 8). Anne Lovely's wealth is her matrimonial power in that it obliges her future husband to treat her well. Here is an even more forthright version of Miranda's insight in *The Busy Body* that "there's no Remedy from a Husband, but the Grave," an observation immediately smoothed over by Patch's hopeful "it is impossible a Man of Sense shou'd use a Woman ill, indued [*sic*] with Beauty, Wit and Fortune" (V.i, 58). Anne understands that the authority her wealth brings in marriage does not translate into full subjectivity thereafter, even in marriage to a well-chosen, enlightened man; Anne explains, "He promis'd to set me free, and I, on that Condition, promis'd to make him Master of that Freedom" (I.ii, 8). Centlivre's illusion of equality between her promisingly rational lovers that parlays the woman's authority at the moment of marriage into a broader civil claim to equality evaporates here.

The plot exposes the foibles of each of Anne's guardians, with varying degrees of satiric ire. Sir Phillip Modelove, the man of fashion who is the most easily duped of Anne's guardians, declares to Colonel Fainwell that he is averse to matrimony because it would disrupt his circulation as a man of fashion. In his first scene, he is trying to make arrangements with a prostitute, who assures him that she is "constant to [her] Keeper" (II, 10). The woman eventually leaves in disgust after hearing Fainwell flatter Modelove: "Coxcomb's, I'm sick to hear 'em praise one another; one seldom gets any thing by such Animals, not even a Dinner . . ." (II.i, 11). This nameless prostitute has, as Pearson has noted, the liberty to say things that the heroine cannot about men in general (210). Modelove, who put Anne Lovely into circulation by bringing her to Bath, understands the economics of sexuality, but he is obsessed with his own misogynist performance of his class and gender. Colonel Fainwell, who disguises himself as a foppish aristocrat of French extraction, slips in the Anglophilic point that England remains superior in both the ladies and the laws as the preface to his inquiry about Anne Lovely. As the only guardian who openly agrees to sign his consent and who informs Fainwell of the other guardians, Modelove is less of a blocking agent than the other guardians.

Periwinkle, the antiquarian guardian, articulates a more reprehensible misogyny: "Women are no Rarities.—I never had any great Tast that Way. I married, indeed, to please a Father, and I got a Girl to please my Wife; but she and the Child (thank Heaven) died together—Women are the very Gewgaws of the Creation; Play-things for Boys, which, when they write Man, they ought to throw aside" (III.i, 29). Periwinkle's sexist and Cartesian investments in the life of the mind over the body make him an easy target for Fainwell's tricks, which return agency to Anne and to the feminine world that Periwinkle's absurd science tries to escape. He is in awe of the wonders that Colonel Fainwell presents, including a magic "girdle" that will enable the wearer to disappear and to travel anywhere on the earth in an instant. Once he realizes he has been duped, Periwinkle swears that Fainwell will never get Anne's money, though Periwinkle knows his signature contractually binds him. An image of scholarly misogyny, Periwinkle finds no resolution in the play's ending, but for the same reasons, he is a face of patriarchy that is easily neutralized. Like Modelove, he poses little real threat.

The most problematic guardians, Tradelove and the Prims, anatomize Anne's persistent problems, economics and sexuality. Fainwell is particularly frustrated by Tradelove and his financial machinations: "The Duce of this Trading-Plot—I wish he had been an old Soldier, that I might have attack'd him in my own Way . . ." (III.i, 34). Tradelove, as a merchant with no civic consciousness, collapses the dynamic between trade and freedom that animates Centlivre's faith in free-market liberalism. Unlike Thorowgood in Lillo's *The London Merchant,* who believes that "merchants contribute to the safety of their country," Tradelove "hates every thing that wears a Sword" (I.i, 4) and finds only merchants useful.[24] Like the stockjobbers who establish the price of their stocks and bonds through open exchange, Tradelove operates in a world of pure equivalence. This system of equivalencies threatens to make Anne an exchange value. When Tradelove realizes that he will lose his two-thousand-pound bet to the Dutchman (Jan van Timtamtirelereletta Heer van Fainwell), he exclaims that he could "tear [his] Flesh," then brightens at the suggestion that Anne could serve as payment (IV.ii, 42). Tradelove's only concern is that it seems too easy. He tells Freeman to "extol her Beauty, double her Portion, and tell him I have the entire Disposal of her" then muses in self-satisfaction: "*If when Cash runs low, our Coffers t'enlarge,/ We can't, like other Stocks, transfer our Charge?*" (IV.ii, 43). This cynical couplet veils a greater threat than Sir Francis's plan to "engross the whole" of his charge Miranda; Tradelove wants to dispense Anne in an anonymous circulation of other pure values. There is no faulty exchange (as in the case of Sir Francis and Miranda) or misapprehension of identity (as in the case for Felix and Violante), only pure ratios of value distributed by verbal contract. Tradelove is the doppelgänger of Centlivre's contractual optimism. Without a stable grounding for her forensic, legal identity, a woman's will is subject to challenge from the canonical tradition, which emphasizes the exchange of obedience for protection, and from the secular and contractual discourse, where those with more contractual authority and facility can control the exchange. Tradelove's wish to "tear [his] Flesh" over financial loss introduces the body as somehow responsible for his failure to control financial exchanges. It is a reminder to Tradelove that he cannot convert all matter into "pure" monetary values.

Anne also threatens to tear her flesh, but her torment comes from the Prims and their religious plan to subdue sexuality, the ideological complement to Tradelove's mercenary denial of the humanity of the body. In the name of a spiritual higher good, the Prims deny Anne's desires unless they are transformed into Puritan spiritual aims. The Prims are Quakers, and treat men and women with relative equality. Their non-hierarchical use of first names and their attention to women's as well as men's spiritual experience elevates the status of women, at least in comparison to Periwinkle and Tradelove. But that equality does not recognize women as agents of their own desire. The Prims are the greatest frustration for Anne and "the hardest Task" for Fainwell (IV.iv, 50) because they renounce human agency in favor of the divine will of God, which they manipulate for their own ends. To gain their consent, Fainwell must pose as an agent of God, the only person who could make a claim on Anne's body.

The Prims read any of Anne's desires that do not conform to theirs as temptations from Satan, and they interpret Anne as the object of another (bad) agent rather than a subject in her own right. What little space they do allow for her choices is fodder for conversion arguments and moral reproofs. In this spirit, Mrs. Prim badgers Anne about sexy clothing:

> *Mrs. Prim:* . . . Thy naked Bosom allureth the Eye of the By-stander—encourageth the Frailty of Humane Nature—and corrupteth the Soul with evil Longings.
>
> *Mrs. Lovely:* And pray who corrupted your Son *Tobias* with evil Longings? Your Maid *Tabitha* wore a Handkerchief, and yet he made the Saint a Sinner.
>
> *Mrs. Prim:* Well, well, spit thy Malice—I confess *Satan* did buffet my Son *Tobias,* and my Servant *Tabitha;* the Evil Spirit was at that time too strong, and they both became subject to its Workings—not from any outward Provocation—but from an inward Call;—he was not tainted with the Rottenness of the Fashions, nor did his Eyes take in the Drunkenness of Beauty.
>
> *Mrs. Lovely:* No! that's plainly to be seen. (II.ii, 16)

Anne counters Mrs. Prim's Puritan objections to her sartorial sins with her understanding of sexual agency and sexual desire. In order to make her claim, Mrs. Prim has to posit Anne as a subject who makes choices that might elicit sexual responses from men. Mrs. Prim asserts that people (women) do things that have effects on other people (men); her disapproval makes Anne an agent, albeit an indirect one, whose will produces results. But, as Anne rebuts, by this same logic Tabitha must have tempted Tobias Prim with similar "outward Provocations" that drew them into a sexual contract with each other. Mrs. Prim rejects Anne's proposition and reduces Tabitha and Tobias to unfortunate objects of evil forces.

Centlivre sets up Anne as a critic of hypocrisy since she cannot be an agent of change under the Prims' restrictions. Anne's dialogue exposes the similar logical contradictions of Mrs. Prim's morality and the marriage contract; like marriage law, Mrs. Prim slides parties between subject and object positions, as it is convenient. Her world is just as much a threat to female subjectivity as Tradelove's commercial exchanges. Centlivre also turns her attack upon Mr. Obadiah Prim and the Foucaultian paradox of sexual purity that he embodies. Anne tells him she knows he "squeez'd *Mary* by the Hand last Night in the Pantry—when she told you, you buss'd so fiithily [*sic*]? Ah! you had no Aversion to naked Bosoms, when you begg'd her to show you a little, little, little Bit of her delicious Bubby . . ." (II.ii, 18). Obadiah can do nothing but deny the charges and wonder privately how Anne found out. He manifests his desire for the female body in a straightforward request to see what Puritan garments relegate to nonexistence. But this denial, like the Puritan talk about regulating desire, turns out to be a technology of desire itself.

In act V, Anne confronts Mrs. Prim with the Puritan restrictions that nurture her investment in the sexual body. Mrs. Prim brags of her own conquests, or more precisely the conquests of her breasts, in an account that misreads desire as modesty:

> *Mrs. Prim:* . . . I'd have thee to know, *Anne,* that I cou'd have catch'd as many Fish (as thou call'st them) in my Time, as ever thou did'st with all thy Fool-Traps about thee.—If Admirers be thy Aim, thou wilt have more of them in this Dress than thy other.—The Men, take my Word for't, are more desirous to see what we are most careful to conceal.
>
> *Mrs. Lovely:* Is that the Reason for your Formality, Mrs. *Prim?* Truth will out: I ever thought, indeed, there was more Design than Godliness in the pinch'd Cap. (V.i, 51)

The dialogue echoes Mandeville's *The Virgin Unmask'd* (1709), which opens with Lucinda imploring her neice, Antonia, to be more modest in her dress: "Here, Niece, take my handkerchief . . . to cover your Nakedness: If you knew what a Fulsome Sight it was, I am sure you would not go so bare: I cann't abide your Naked Breasts heaving up and down; it makes me Sick to see it" (1). In Mandeville's fictional dialogue, knowledge produces sexuality; Lucinda's sexual knowledge sexualizes the niece's body in the frame of the dialogue. The regulation of sexuality through modest dress, as in the case of Mrs. Prim, is yet another technology of power that produces more sexual desire.[25] But unlike Lucinda's pragmatic assessment of female sexuality, Mrs. Prim pretends not to know what she knows about sexual desire. Talk of sexual desire, enflamed passions, and immodesty is a sexual act that Mrs. Prim cannot acknowledge as such. When Mrs. Prim admits that the covered body is also a sexual strategy, Anne seizes on the moral contradiction. Mrs. Prim's outrage confirms Anne's direct hit; she calls Anne "corrupted" and "into the High Road of Fornication," while betraying the passion beneath her own prudish appearance (V.i, 51). Mrs. Prim's investment in the sexual body, once removed from sight by Puritan dress, reemerges at the level of discourse. Her biblically mediated talk makes sex threatening and justifies her Puritan policing of female sexuality. The words of biblical authority, transformed by Mrs. Prim as "allureth," "encourageth," and "corrupteth," play with the textual production of desire as part of the joke; the Prims are titillated by talk of voracious, overwhelming female sexuality (in the English of King James) with which they persecute Anne.

Fainwell and Anne's revenge plays on the Prim's hypocrisy and their displacement of agency. Fainwell poses as the traveling preacher Simon Pure and "converts" Anne to the Quaker doctrine. Fainwell reveals himself to Anne and reminds her of her promise to him: "Make me Mistress of my Fortune, and make thy own Conditions" (V.i, 57). Her actual submission to Fainwell subtends the performed submission to "the spirit" that sends Simon Pure to save the "Maiden . . . in vain Attire" he saw in a dream. The second half of Anne's conversion plays as high farce. Fainwell claims that his "Spirit is greatly troubled" in fear that he has "retrieved her, as if it were, yea as if it were out of the Jaws of the Fiend" only to lose her again to the "Evil Spirit" (V.i, 61). Anne plays along so well, quaking and struggling with "the Flesh—I greatly fear the Flesh, and the Weakness thereof," that the virtuoso actor Fainwell exclaims in an aside, "She acts it to the Life" (V.i, 61, 62). Anne finally persuades Obediah Prim to give his consent when she relates the vision of her submission to Simon Pure and her destined pregnancy: "Something whispers in my Ears, methinks,—that I must be subject to the Will of this good Man, and from him only must hope for Consolation,—Hum—it also telleth me that I am a chosen Vessel to raise up Seed to the Faithful, and that thou must consent that we two be one Flesh according to the Word—hum—" (V.i, 62). Anne successfully writes the script for the will of God, which makes both her and Fainwell "vessels" of a greater plan. Her desire for Fainwell becomes salvation, Fainwell's desire for her becomes mission work, and sexual desire becomes the sign of God's will for more little Puritans. Fainwell and Anne act out the Puritan displacement of agency in their spirit-filled mockery of courtship negotiations.

A Bold Stroke leaves Anne with only the security of the lengths to which Fainwell is willing to go; Fainwell is now the master of both her fortune and her self. Anne speaks only a throwaway closing line as a gibe to Tradelove; Fainwell, not Anne, has made these contracts with her guardians. Her complicity in Fainwell's scheme doesn't register in the dialogue of the ending, a reminder that her will is subsumed in the literal and binding will of her dead father. The situation is surprising only next to those of Centlivre's bolder heroines in *The Gamester, The Busy Body,* and *The Wonder.* Centlivre's *Bold Stroke* has more desperation than hope in it and provides a mirror to the frustrations to the reform of common-law notions of marriage. Neither the social compact, commercial contracts, nor the marriage contract fully accepts women as agents who are able to make and fulfill promises. The marriage contract, which comes the closest to formalizing female agency in the exchange of vows, undercuts whatever contractual ability women might have in the public sphere. Contract theory as the basis of, if not general equality, then property and the possibility of civil identity glosses over the ambiguous status of women in these three versions of contract in the name of a general economic and liberal world-view. Centlivre's attempt to write a happy, comic ending for contract theory at last collapses in the face of a legal system that has no compelling interest in the subjectivity of women as citizens, property owners, or cultural agents. Notably, *A Bold Stroke* achieved its greatest popularity later in the century, at a less optimistic moment in the negotiation of women's subjectivity in the marriage contract.

Centlivre's failure to resolve the Lockean crisis of female subjectivity is not, in the end, remarkable, for she fails within the logic of early liberal feminist thought. The post-Lockean, Whiggish argument for equality gambled on the ability of contract logic to provide a "paper" neutrality even as it preserved sex difference. Centlivre's box-office consciousness reinforced the generic, ideological claims of the marriage comedy; she delivers happy endings and affirms the triumph of young couples over the obstacles to their adulthood. But the more purely comic moments reveal what Bergson called the "saline base" that is also part of the appeal of comedy. The public responded enthusiastically to Centlivre's connections between economics, contract, and marriage as the nexus of a cultural trauma that England needed yet did not want to discuss. Contract is in this sense her comic *sinthome,* the symptom turned into the condition of pleasure. At the very least, Centlivre's contracts provide women with the chance to negotiate their own commodification, for better or worse, for richer or poorer.

CHAPTER FIVE

Rule, Britannia

Women and the National Community in Cowley's Comedies

Great Britain in the 1770s was coming to terms with its identity as a colonizer beginning to lose its colonies. In particular, the war with the American colonies, which had to be fought while England was already at war with France, raised questions about national identity and national futures. Playwrights responded to this crisis in definition with new plays like Cumberland's *The West Indian,* Coleman the Younger's *Inckle and Yariko* (1786) and *The Battle of Hexham* (1789), Burgoyne's *The Heiress* (1786), and Cowley's *The Belle's Stratagem* (1780), which defined the British nation and national character against an international backdrop. Evenings at the theater from 1776 to 1790 often heightened the nationalist flavor of main pieces with patriotic musical and entr'acte entertainment. In addition to Thomson's "Rule, Britannia," Henry Purcell's "Britons Strike Home," originally for the opera *Bonduca,* took on a life of its own as a musical interlude. Theater managers folded the following nationalist songs into evenings at the theater: "In Act II of mainpiece the grand chorus, *See the conquering Hero comes*" (October 7, 1776, CHR); "Mainpiece to finish with The Grand Naval Review, in which a *Dance of Sailors* by Blurton, Mrs. Sutton, &c., and *Rule Britannia* by Davies, Fawcett and others" (DL November 9, 1776); "End of mainpiece The Merry Sailors, as 6 Nov. 1776" (CG Jan. 10, 1777); music "from CORONATION ANTHEMS" (CG March 19, 1777); and "*O, What a Charming Thing's a Battle*" (DL April 21, 1777).[1] That these nationalist and militaristic musical offerings shared stage space with popular French operatic songs like *La Force de l'Amour* and *Les Amans Heureaux* only underscored the political stakes of representation and the public production of national identity.

The development of the idea of Britishness, as Linda Colley has argued, depends on the presence of a national other, a "them" to produce the "us," even when that "us" is not monolithic or exclusive of other identities (Colley 5). What the "imagined political community" of Great Britain meant, then, had to do with the perceived failures and shortcomings of its political and cultural others.[2] The singing of "Rule, Britannia" at the end of plays, which became a more common practice in this period, emphasized the "us and them" dynamic of nationalism. The song defines British identity through the inferiority of others: "Britons never will be slaves." James Thomson's original lyric, which first appeared in 1740, was included in afterpieces such as the "Grand Antigallican Procession in Honor of St. George's Day," on May 1, 1781, to close with "Britannia brought in a Triumphal Car, attended by Europe, Asia, Africa, America . . . and attended by Mars and Neptune."[3] The musical extension of the "never" in the line as it is sung emphasizes the oppositional thrust of identity as well as the most crucial point for late-century Britons: we are the ones who are not slaves. This negative representation of political liberty offers an anxious but viable national identity to Anglicans and Catholics, Scots and English, men and women, and to any group who can identity with Britishness and not its Others.

Hannah Cowley entered this nationalist theatrical environment as the last of Garrick's protégés during his Drury Lane tenure. From 1747 to 1776, he produced 15 new plays by 9 new women playwrights (Catherine Clive, Susanna Cibber, Frances Sheridan, Elizabeth Griffith, Dorothy Celisia, Henrietta Pye, Charlotte Lennox, Hannah Cowley, and Hannah More) whose careers he nurtured and whose productions he hand-picked and often edited. In the same period, Covent Garden produced only three.[4] There is little question that Garrick opened up the late-eighteenth-century stage to greater numbers of women, but according to Ellen Donkin, Garrick's sponsorship was a sword that cut both ways. The cost to female playwrights was the loss of control over their texts, whether through obligatory editing or the implication that Garrick was the real genius of the play (Donkin 60–62).

At a more intimate level, Garrick seemed hungry for adoration from his protégé-daughters. In a letter to Frances Cadogan, Garrick expressed outrage at Frances Brooke's depiction of him in *The Excursion.* "If my heart was not better than my head, I would not give a farthing for the Carcass, but let it dangle, as it would deserve, with It's brethren at ye End of Oxford Road. . . . [S]he Even says, that I should reject a Play, if it should be a Woman's—there's brutal Malignity for You—have not ye Ladies—Mesdames, *Griffith, Cowley,* & *Cilesia* spoke of me before their Plays with an Over-Enthusiastick Encomium?—what says divine Hannah More?—& more than all what Says the more divine Miss Cadogan?"[5] Garrick's emotionally complex outburst echoes Lear's need for daughterly approval ("What says our second daughter, our dearest Regan. . . ." I.i). In his anger, he clarifies both his support of women in the theater and his demand for absolute gratitude. When Frances

Brooke narrates another version of Garrick's mentorship that is less flattering, he imagines her as a dangling carcass of a traitor in an Oxford Road repopulated with regicides. But Garrick played both the betrayed and the betrayer in his relationships with his protégés. After Cowley's initial success with *The Runaway* (1776), which Garrick edited and placed, she was faced with what she perceived as Garrick's treachery. Another Garrick protégé, Hannah More, came out with *The Fatal Falsehood,* a tragedy suspiciously like Cowley's own *Albina,* which had been passed from Garrick to Sheridan to Harris.[6] The conflict made it to the public through the *St. James Chronicle,* where Cowley and More traded accusations and insults. Garrick's role in the possible plagiarism is ambiguous, but his response was not; he sided with More and left Cowley to make her own way. These emotional dramas drew lines between the "us" camp of Garrick's world and the "them" of outsiders who rejected or did not merit his help.

The twin disappointments of Garrick's withdrawal from the profession and the possible foul play regarding *Albina* crystallized Cowley's reliance on the theatergoing English public. Cowley's move from a Garrick-sponsored comedy to farce and more aggressive, women-centered comedy marks the most significant transformation of her career. She could no longer please Garrick, and instead had to please the nation. Cowley's successful recourse to public taste capitalized on a shift in theatrical audiences in the 1770s. Playwright Arthur Murphy called the theaters "a *fourth estate,* Kings, Lords, and Commons, and *Drury-Lane play-house,*" in light of the high attendance figures and the cultural importance that playhouses of the later eighteenth century enjoyed.[7] The theaters were large enough to seat the estimated 1,000 to 1,500 spectators who attended the four London playhouses on any given night.[8] Covent Garden expanded to 2,500 seats in 1782 and again to 3,013 in 1792, while Drury Lane grew from 2,300 seats in 1790 to 3,600 in 1794. These ample spaces created the largest indoor audiences in English history. In defiance of the distance these large spaces created, acting styles became more natural, and comic delivery became more lifelike, corresponding more closely to the lived experience of the audience (*London Stage* pt. 5, I: 109). An expanding population and declining numbers of seats restricted by royal monopoly testify to the increase of non-aristocratic and elite theater patrons as well as the larger audiences of the later century.[9]

A seat at the theater in 1776 was more accessible than it had been fifty years before, but the size and the populist turn of the theaters raised critical concerns about declining standards. Exhibitions from England's colonial territories as well as of mechanical wonders like Cox's Museum of Automata, which comes under scrutiny in Burney's *Evelina,* were evidence to many that public taste was on the decline. Comic operas like Miles Peter Andrews and William A. Miles's *Summer Amusement* (1779) and John Burgoyne's *The*

Maid of Oaks (1774), pantomimes, mimics, and short musical productions succeeded with the public but alarmed critics who saw in them the triumph of mere entertainment over dramatic art.[10] Garrick's own 1769 Stratford Jubilee, with its elaborate pageantry and its popularizing bent, is a part of the story of popular spectacle. Garrick's *The Jubilee* (1769) turned the muddy Stratford Jubilee into a theatrical spectacle for the London audience the fall after the event. *The Jubilee* invited audience members to sing along with the chorus, and it featured a procession that came through the audience.[11] The success of so much spectacle and musical entertainment prompted theater critics and pundits to take up the cry to reform the stage, particularly comedy, from the old evil of sexual impropriety and the new evil of populism.

The popularity of entertainments as well as the perceived delicacy of the age should frame Goldsmith's famous comments on the demise of comedy. Goldsmith argued in his preface to his 1768 *The Good-Natur'd Man* that the pursuit of humor "will sometimes lead us into the recesses of the mean" and hoped that "too much refinement will not banish humour and character from our's, as it has already done from the French theatre" (*Works* V: 13–14). Four years later in his *An Essay on the Theatre; or, A Comparison between Laughing and Sentimental Comedy,* Goldsmith put the case against sentimental comedy more starkly:

> In these Plays almost all the Characters are good, and exceedingly generous; they are lavish enough of their *Tin* Money on the Stage, and though they want Humour, have abundance of Sentiment and Feeling. If they happen to have Faults or Foibles, the Spectator is taught not only to pardon, but to applaud them, in consideration of the goodness of their hearts; so that Folly, instead of being ridiculed, is commended, and the Comedy aims at touching our Passions, without the power of being truly pathetic: in this manner we are likely to lose one great source of Entertainment on the Stage; for while the Comic Poet is invading the province of the Tragic Muse, he leaves her lovely Sister quite neglected. Of this, however, he is no-way solicitous, as he measures his fame by his profits. (*Works* III: 212)

The exemplary comedy, in which bourgeois sexual values and the good judgement of parents are usually affirmed, is part of a more gradual change in comic values than Goldsmith's diatribe against sentimental comedy would suggest. *Love for Love* and *The Conscious Lovers* are tarred with this brush, but they are repertoire pieces and not evidence of a recent turn in taste. His concern that new comedies cashier the manly spirit of their tradition (one almost hears Fielding's manly lash of satire crack in the background) in the rage for this new "weeping sister" is in part a puff for his *She Stoops to Conquer* and its comic sensibilities. Robert Hume has argued that twentieth-century critics have given this piece of Goldsmith's too much weight; it elides the variety of "laughing" comedies in repertoire and invokes the too-broad category "sentimental," which obscures rather than explains a wide range of comedies after the Restoration.[12] Though many new comedies turned to sentimental and pathetic subplots, the satiric edge of Restoration and early-eighteenth-century comedies could still be found in comic after-pieces such as Arthur Murphy's *The Way to Keep Him* (1760) and Samuel Foote's *A Trip to Calais* (1775) and *The Maid of Bath* (1771), and in comic operas like Sheridan's *The Duenna* (1775). The success of these more satiric comic forms complicates the critical commonplace of the sentimental tone of late-century theater. The gentler romantic comedy did not overtake the stage after 1760, but rather grew with the romantic New Comedy style of the period as one variation in a broad range of comedies.

Goldsmith's essay rehearses an old debate between the value of exemplary comedy and the less obviously pedagogical satiric comedy. In this debate, Goldsmith did labor against the tide of criticism, which favored the exemplary as a way to build the nation and improve its subjects. James Beattie's revised *On Laughter and Ludicrous Composition* (third edition, 1779) responds to Goldsmith indirectly in his preference for sentimental comedy, which comes from reflection and sympathetic emotions, over "animal" comedy, which comes from sudden impulses that can be destructive or hurtful. Beattie claims that when comedies lead audiences "only [to] laugh at our faults, without despising them, that is, if they appear ludicrous only, and not ridiculous, it is to be feared, that we shall be more inclined to love than to hate them . . ." (393). Richard Cumberland wrote in his 1806 *Memoirs* that he and all conscientious writers for the stage must strive "to give no false attractions to vice or immorality, but to endeavor, as far as it consistent with that contrast . . . to turn the fairer side of human nature to the public."[13] Cumberland's assessment of his "conscience and duty" as a playwright unites the long-standing critical supposition that comedies should instruct with a new sense of "the public," that wider audience that demanded a wider range of admirable characters.[14] The gentle approach of example over criticism encouraged a safely bourgeois vision of marriage to the stage. In plays like Colman's *The Jealous Wife* (1761) and Cumberland's *The West Indian* (1771), the more virtuous or "exemplary" strain of comedy recalls the domestic strategies of Cibber and Steele. These optimistic versions of bourgeois marriage helped to unify this heterogeneous audience.

While new comedies were not uniformly sentimental, late-century playwrights expressed a bourgeois hopefulness about marriage that coincides with the beginning of the legal retreat from liberal applications of contract thought to marriage. Chancery court judges reasserted the legal principle of coverture, which made husband and wife one person under the law and hence incapable of making contracts with each other, in a series of cases including *Lean v. Shutz*

(1778) and *Marshall v. Rutton* (1798–1800) (Staves, *Married* 178). The legal logic of separate maintenance contracts, which claimed women continued to be civil subjects after marriage, was dealt a substantial blow through rulings from Kenyon, Loughborough, and Arden, who all upheld the principle that husband and wife are one person, and hence cannot make contracts with each other. In *Marshall,* Kenyon reinforced the patriarchal prerogatives of husbands by insisting that it was legally impossible for husband and wife to be "in some respects in the condition of being single, and leave them in others subject to the consequences of being married."[15] The principle he asserts is flawed in that common law had always made provisions for the survival of one spouse or another, but it established as a matter of legal coherence a sentimental version of the family in which individuals are subsumed into the allegedly united, affective, and protective family.

At this conservative turn in the history of marriage law, Cowley used the romance conventions of stage comedy and the spirit of English nationalism to ground an ideal individual liberty that included her female characters as rights-bearing individuals. The discourse of nationalism, which pervaded the theater and the culture at large, balanced the more conservative arguments from Kenyon and others with the promise of liberty, independence, and self-determination. The conservative elements of duty and familial obligation remain features of her plays, but Cowley also exploits the discourse of freedom that merchants and military leaders adapted from the philosophical and political individualism of Enlightenment thought. Through this nationalist matrix, Cowley redeems her heroines from the role of obliging prop to male plots by allowing them to claim a share in those rights by virtue of their Englishness. The strategy presses on the cultural and legal inheritance of English Enlightenment thought, which, on the surface at least, underwrites the free choices of rational women *and* men. In this sense, she takes up where Centlivre left off in a proto-feminist argument for the value of contract. But her appeal to national identity illuminates the uneven conditions in which contracts are negotiated. Contracts themselves are not enough, since they always depend on the conditions of identity that either validate or invalidate the parties involved. The cynicism of the later plays represents an international Britannia mired in the slave trade, a domestic economic crisis, and the loss of the American colonies. Britain in this state was unequal to the task of making good on the claims of individual liberty for men or women.

"The Gallantry of the English Nation"

The Runaway appeared on the London stage the same year that the American Declaration of Independence appeared on the international political stage. Like the colonial rebels throwing off English rule, Cowley's heroine Emily rejects the mercenary governance of her uncle Morely. But Cowley, like her heroine, was careful to remain the dutiful daughter in distress rather than the public rebel. She wrote the prologue, which makes reference to the "not very common" fact that she is a female poet. Cowley's feminine spin on the prologue tradition of self-deprecation declares her lack of learning and her demi-professional status as a mother who writes for her children's sake. She is not as humble as she is in her dedication to Garrick, where she claims to be a pitiable "*Woman* tracing with feeble steps the borders of the Parnassian Mount," but she seeks the audience's sympathy for her domestic circumstances. If the audience approves of the play, "Then Tom shall have his kite, and Fan new dollies." Cowley includes, however, a Behn-like threat to the men in the audience: "Let him who hisses, no soft Nymph endure; /May he who frowns, be frown'd on by his Goddess, / From Pearls, and Brussels Point, to Maids in Boddice." Cowley's entrance into the theater world, like Behn's and Centlivre's, draws particular attention to her sex, here as the mother-turned-writer, in an attempt to use it to her advantage. The strategy appeals to the public's sense of justice, which seemed ready to support equality for sufficiently humble supplicants.

The play builds up a salubrious, good-hearted English patriarch, Mr. Drummond, through strategic contrasts and international references to lesser cultures and customs. The structure of nation- and character-building works, but because Mr. Drummond is the benefactor rather than the biological father of the main character George, it also introduces the possibility that the English ideal may be failing to meet its legal, international, and domestic responsibilities as "naturally" as it ought. The male characters of the play carry the plot, with the help of the eponymous Emily and her energetic friend Bella. Bella has the lion's share of women's lines (344 in all compared to Emily's 144), but she is not the heroine. Her love interest remains offstage, and she does not reap the main reward of comedy, the hand of the beloved, although much is made of Bella's promise from Belville, George's school friend.

International circumstances impose on the play in lighter jokes and asides that help to establish the political and ideological sovereignty of England. The opening line from a tired and hot George Hargrave exclaims "'twould be less intolerable riding post in Africa." The offhanded line calls up an international world where English people colonize and dominate others. George's comparison draws Africa and England together to berate the English weather for "going native," when it ought to be the pleasant and preferable standard against which colonial experience can be judged. Heat was no small issue to English nationals who took part in trade with Jamaica, India, and the American colonies, where it was associated with the fevers and tropical diseases that claimed the lives of as many as 100 times the number of sailors lost in combat.[16] England must live up to that standard of temperateness, a figure for social balance as well, in an increasingly international and colonial community that was willing to challenge British authority. Lest the audience take George's joke too much to heart, Emily assures in the same act that "surely 'tis in England that Summer keeps her court—for she's no where else so lovely" (II, 15). This rhapsody, her first speech in the play, introduces Emily as a woman who values the true England and who thus should share in its blessings and liberties.

All this talk about the weather sets the stage for other definitions of Englishness that celebrate fair play, freedom, and rationality. Jarvis, a servant, is in league with the matronly Lady Dinah to discredit Emily and thus further Lady Dinah's plan of marrying the much younger George. Jarvis refers to his qualms as function of national location: "the resolution with which I could go thro' an affair of this sort, would in another hemisphere make my fortune—but hang it, in these cold northern regions there's no room for a man of genius to strike a bold stroke—the fostering plains of Asia, for such talents as mine!" (IV, 47). Deception, if practiced in other countries without England's sense of social order or its criminal justice systems, presents Jarvis with no impediments. Similarly, the extremity of Lady Dinah's revenge against Emily's youth leads her to long for "France! for thy Bastile, for thy *Lettres de Cachet!*" (III, 39) to persecute her enemy. Rhapsodizing on France in late-century comedies is a familiar trick to make a character ridiculous, but Lady Dinah's emphasis on the Bastille and the machinations of the French elite brings us into the particular sphere of rights and due process under British law. Lady Dinah's lack of any sense of proportion puts her at odds with the play's basic presumption of the value of freedom. Her assumption that she could marry George (rather than his father) because Hargrave senior is willing to arrange it is another face of her failure to honor basic freedoms of choice in marriage. Foreign cultures can bring to bear a pleasurable exoticism, as is the case when an Italian love song unearths Bella's secret passion for Belville, but their main function is to celebrate the social superiority of English values.

Related to the problem of the foreign is the ambiguous situation of higher learning and ancient languages, a theme that explodes a few years later in her farce *Who's the Dupe?* As *The Runaway* opens, George has just returned from college, which leads Lady Dinah to wax rhapsodic about "the Antients" and sparks his father to mock his time with "musty old Dons" and his lack of interest in hunting. The unavailability of university education to women as well as the bluestocking craze for languages situate Lady Dinah's fascination with Greek and Latin, but her immediate interest is tied to cosmetics. She uses Roman precedent to justify her hair dye and "paints" and laments the need for secrecy in such practices. The excesses of the "Antients," including an empress who traveled with five hundred asses in order to bathe in their milk, become an easy joke in the hands of her maid, Susan: "Five hundred Asses in one Lady's train!—thank Heaven, we have no such engrossing now-a-days—*our* Toasts have all their full share" (II, 19). Susan's comparison maintains that England is a more egalitarian place, where no one woman could command all of the asses. The joke also depends on Lady Dinah's age and her diminished charms; she is past attracting a young suitor, much less five hundred of them, with or without cosmetics. Cowley situates the artificiality of her plan to trap George in a match "between fifty and twenty-one" (II, 20) against a more natural and native English erotic economy that eschews her stiff manners and classical pretensions.

Cowley also identifies blocking characters in this play as abusers of the law. They function as comic butts to warn against the litigious and greedy landowners and merchants who undermine true English customs. Hargrave and Justice, perhaps the most conventional of all the characters, lament the decline of true English vigor among young people, but their imaginary past in which body and spirit were more robust serves only their individual interests. Mr. Hargrave longs for "good old Bess's days—when our Men of Rank were robust, and our Women of Fashion buxom," yet he is happy to sacrifice George to Lady Dinah. The appeal to the past proposes a lost respect for "the jolly manners of their Ancestors," or a more substantial sense of English cultural history, but in fact it is an attempt to justify greater parental control over the sexuality of children (I, 9). The gesture *back* in time beguiles the fact that Lord Hardwicke's Marriage Act of 1753 had bolstered his parental control over marriage and the property transmitted through them.

Justice, who is a parody of a sexually vigorous middle-aged man, rouses at the thought of "a rosy buxom lass" rather than the "puny girls" that have diminished the great English race. But a mere 22 lines later, Justice finds even greater excitement; presented with the possibility of punishing a man "for breaking into farmer Thompson's barn last night," he is prepared to leave his drink with Hargrave after shirking all his other duties. He ignores his responsibility to license businesses and administer the care of paupers, but he takes pleasure in protecting private property at the expense the poor. When Hargrave receives a report that a poor man has taken a hare from a trap, the two men leave the comfort of the smoking room to prosecute this petty infraction. The comic logic of association between sexual desire and economic desire uncovers this larger truth: the real site of desire for these men is in proving the dominance of their property rights over the rights of others.

Emily Morley's situation strengthens an analogy between property rights established by the Enclosure Acts and parental rights strengthened by the 1753 Marriage Act. Emily's uncle has tried to marry her off to a man she regards as having an "effeminate" mind, and so she seeks shelter in the home of Mr. Drummond, a friend of her late father's. Emily tries to find a way to have some choice in marriage after the Marriage Act closed the loopholes that would have allowed her to evade a bad guardian in earlier times. Her situation parallels that of the poor man who tries to feed himself after the system of commons had been undermined by the expansion of private property; in both cases, the less powerful lose ground. When Justice accuses Drummond of breaking the law for releasing an alleged "poacher," Drummond assures Justice that the poor man had only found a rabbit in his own garden. Hargrave's paranoid response makes any "free" property a threat to (newly) private property. He speculates that as soon as he is dead, "my fences will be cut down—my meadows turned into common—my corn-fields laid open—my woods at the mercy of every man who carries an axe—and, oh—this is noble, this is great!" (IV, 53). By defining himself through his property (and the comic repetition of "my") he imagines himself as always in a potential state of loss. His possessiveness makes him the butt of the scene's joke; under these circumstances, one rabbit exposes him to endless lack. The similar sum-zero game of disposing children leads Hargrave to limit George's choices and Morley to limit Emily's. Hargrave and Morley both believe that the only way to protect themselves and their property as extensions of those selves is to limit the freedom and autonomy of those around him.

The comic struggle over property resolves through Drummond's good parenting and George's nationalism, both of which provide models of social selfhood that vest authority in an individual rather than in alienable property. For Emily, however, the specter of an older national femininity threatens to make her the property of others. Her uncle Morley claims that "in the days of your great Grand-mother, a Girl on the point of marriage had never dared to look above her lover's beard—and would have been a wife a week before she cou'd have told the colour of her husband's eyes" (V, 61). Morley's sense of history is off; depending on the precise age of the mothers of Emily's family at pregnancy, her great-grandmother would likely have been born between 1670 and 1700, which would make her a contemporary of either Behn or Centlivre.[17] From available accounts, courtship in the late seventeenth and early eighteenth centuries was a more flirtatious enterprise, laced with sexual innuendo, than courtship in the 1770's. Women in the Restoration and early eighteenth century could contract legal marriages without parental consent and make ancillary contracts with their husbands that extended their property rights as *feme soles.* Morley's notion of creeping sexual abandon in women, however, reflects a late-century bourgeois narrative of decline that supports parental control at the expense of history and daughters.

What timorous Emily does claim of her English heritage is a version of the freedom of speech. She agrees to talk to George "on my own terms," and explains, "I have no dislike to the charming freedom of the English manners" (III, 38). Communication is the cornerstone of Emily's freedom of choice in marriage and the horizon of her future happiness. But her ability to withhold speech is also an important liberty. When Lady Dinah uses her servant Jarvis in a plan to discredit Emily by identifying her as a traveling player, Emily again refuses to give her name. Justice mocks her supposed performance as a person of consequence who "stands upon Constitutional ground—a Patriot, I'll assure you—she refuses to answer Interrogatories" (IV, 58). He reads her resistance as an American Revolution in miniature. She and the American colonials claim liberties and rights that enable them to resist the institutions, modern patriarchy and Great Britain respectively, that demand their obedience. Emily can control the way Justice can use her identity by withholding speech; her situation is that of a political prisoner who faces hostile interrogation with silence. Emily's situation changes, however, with the arrival of her uncle Morley in a coach and six. Her visible class position rewrites her relationship to this community of inquisitors, and Justice is forced to backpedal: "So, so . . . we are got into a wrong box here—she can be no Patriot, our Patriots don't ride in coaches and six" (IV, 59).

While class is a mitigating circumstance, Emily's situation still requires the creative intervention of a man to secure her theoretical claims to English liberty. George has courted her before the play starts, so when he proposes to her in front of Morley and Hargrave as Morley in the fifth act, it is to enforce an earlier model of *contract de presenti,* which vests the power of contract in the two lovers. Emily's reply to his "Consent, my charming Emily, and every moment of my future life shall thank you" asserts her prerogative to make the marriage contract with George while it also acknowledges her more circumscribed lot as a woman in this system: "At such a moment as this, meanly to disguise my sentiments would be unworthy of the woman, to whom you offer such a sacrifice—obtain the consent of those who have a right to dispose of us, and I'll give you my hand at the altar" (V, 69). Forcing guardians and parents into postures of consent is standard comic fare, but this exchange is particular to Cowley's nationalist strategies. Drummond presents himself as a good father who will inherit the young people who have been cut off, thus keeping them in the system and the system in good favor. He reincarnates the will of Emily's deceased military father and declares that he would have defended Emily's choice in the matter. He cajoles Morley to relent, with the promise of national reward and virtue: "you shall come and live amongst us, and we'll reconcile you to your native country: notwithstanding our ideas of the degeneracy of the times, we shall find room enough to act virtuously, and to enjoy in England, more securely than in any other country in the world,—the rewards of virtue" (V, 71). His final lines depart from this jingoistic discourse of rights to try to cap the nascent argument for English women's natural equality when he reproves Bella for picking apart the marriage vow: " . . . *Love,* one might manage that perhaps—but *honour, obey,*—'tis strange the Ladies had never interest enough to get this ungallant form mended" (V, 72). Drummond quickly explains that love teaches duties beyond a vow and reminds her that she too will soon marry, but he overlooks the second point Bella raises: women have no real civic participation, no "interest," in a nation that prides itself on liberty, rationality, and rights, yet curtails their legal subjectivity through marriage law.

The question of whether the discourse of nationalism reaches beyond the terms of masculinity finds a partial, Drummond-like answer in Garrick's epilogue, delivered by Bella, played by Elizabeth Younge in the first run. Bella shares her fears that Belville may have been corrupted by Italian culture during his absence and transformed into "Sir Dingle Dangle":

> For me, no maukish creature, weak, and wan;
> He must be *English,* and an *English*—Man.
> To Nature, and his Country, false and blind,
> Shou'd *Belville* dare to twist his form and mind,
> I will discard him—and to Britain true,
> A Briton chuse—and, may be, one of *you!*

She assures her audience that "Free Men in Love, or War, should ne'er be press'd," no small assurance in 1776 when England was looking for both foot soldiers and sailors to fight the war with the colonies. The ideals of turgid English masculinity that opposes the Italian "*Dingle Dangle*" who would leave Bella "Wedded, tho' I am" to "still live *single*" depends on the feminizing valence of Italy and associations with Italian castrati. The castrati formed a substantial contingent in the non-dramatic entertainments that crowded the stage of the 1770s, but the "real" English man is part of a nationalism that can provide a "real" marriage plot, complete with the mutual marital authority that Bella proposes. The epilogue, penned by Garrick, imagines an Englishman so grounded and confident that he can indulge his good sense "to govern *me*—and let *me* govern him." Mutual authority, however comic its function in the epilogue, confirms natural male virility and female civil rights through the discourse of nationalism.

This paean to English manhood requires something of Englishwomen as well; Bella promises to keep Hymen's torch burning through kindness and sense. The epilogue then turns to harangue women for the outrageous hair and hat styles of the 1770s, which were no small problem for theatergoers in the 1770s and early 1780s, especially those seated in the pit or the galleries.[18] The comic excess of headgear is a formulaic complaint of the era. Articles and prints in *The Oxford Magazine* satirized the fashion for towering headdresses that threatened their surroundings and particularly the men in their orbit. Diminutive male hairdressers climb ladders to coif a fine lady in *The Female Pyramid* (*Oxford Magazine,* 1771) while S. H. Grimm's *The French Lady in London, or the Head Dress for the Year 1771* shows a woman with a head of hair that terrifies male onlookers and a menagerie of pets.[19] These visual and textual accounts of high fashion suggest that the problem of overdressed hair is a French import, a threat coded in psychosexual terms. Cowley's masculine Englishness is a careful and gendered balance between an international world and England (as well as between the abuse of rigid law and a more flexible ethic of justice), but immoderately dressed hair, as a sign of corrupt foreign taste, threatens to disrupt the gender balance. The array of styles includes "*fruits, roots, greens*" and "A *kitchen-garden,* to adorn my face!" The effect of the whole is farcical, but the "curls like Guns" give a phallic presence to women who defy "*Nature*" with the style and height of their hair. Coming from the mouth of the defiant Bella, Garrick's reproof settles on women the responsibility for maintaining the cultural climate in which English masculinity can flourish. Garrick's epilogue urges women to a natural, self-regulating obedience in the interest of English masculinity.

Alone with the Audience

Cowley's frustrating break with Garrick followed the hearty success of *The Runaway.* In the midst of professional uncertainties, she began work on *Who's the Dupe?,* a lively farce modeled on the comic subplot of Centlivre's *The Stolen Heiress,* which was promised a good early-season date in the 1778–1779 calendar but was delayed until April 1779, when late-season actors' benefits crowded its future. *Who's the Dupe?* had a fine run of 15 nights, but Cowley had to pay the managers of Covent Garden an inflated price of 100 guineas for the chance of a benefit night; the charge had been regularized to £105 (the amount she had to put up for the production), and it was unlikely she could make that figure back so late in the season. While the farce eventually netted her £70 that season and enjoyed 126 performances before 1800, the financial and professional uncertainties that surrounded her redefined Cowley's relationship to the profession.

Cowley's career was shaped by theatrical seasons, factors that by 1779 had become dominant personal issues. She found herself unable to time the market without the nod from the managers, particularly Sheridan, who was very interested in mounting his own plays, yet she was acutely aware of the market fluctuations of the theater. In *Who's the Dupe?* she translates these concerns into an opening scene with two flower girls lamenting the lack of customers in spring and worrying about summer, where the supply of flowers will outweigh the slight demand:

> *First Girl:* I *Vow* I ha'n't had a customer to-day. Summer is coming, and we shall be ruin'd. When flowers are plenty, no body will buy 'em.
> *Second Girl:* Aye, wery true—people talks of summer; but for my part, give me Christmas. In a hard frost, or a deep snow, who's drest without flowers and furs? Here's one of the Captains. [Enter Sandford] Flowers, Sir! (I, 1)

Without theatrical patronage, Cowley also found her wares out of season. *Albina* finally opened in July 1779 at the Haymarket, a time so unenviable in the theater calendar that the anonymous prologue commented, "What right has She upon our *Summer* stage?—/—With dismal Stories, and long Acts in verse,/ . . . As though we shiver'd in December snows!" As was the case for her flower girls, the advent of summer for playwrights meant the beginning of a dry season. The girls also find themselves conflated with their merchandise by Sandiford, who, when offered flowers, replies, "I'd rather have roses. What will you take for these?" and pinches one girl's cheek. She smartly replies, "I can't sell them alone—the tree and the roses must go together." Cowley would have to play her hand in a similar marginal space as a theatrical vendor but not as an Angellica, with "Roses for every Month." Cowley also borrows from *The Rover* when Sandiford resumes his pursuit of the "two fine Girls." He laments "the Women dress so equivocally, that one is in danger of attacking a Countess, when one only means to address a Nymph of King's-Place" (I, 3), echoing Blunt's confusion about expensive clothes and Frederick's caution, "'twoud anger us vilely to be trust up for rape upon a Maid of quality, when we only believe we ruffle a Harlot" (IV, 506). By appealing to Behn's precedent, Cowley aligns herself with a tradition of independent women in the theatrical marketplace, vulnerable but viable.[20] Like Cowley, the flower girls are economically unprotected and at the mercy of the seasonal consumption patterns of the wealthy. These reminders that there are no truly "free" markets or protected positions for female playwrights, even in these relatively good times, set the tone for the farce.

Who's the Dupe? is a brisk, funny story of a classic "cit," Mr. Doiley, who wants his daughter Elizabeth to marry a man of "Larning." Elizabeth, however, has already made up her mind to marry Granger, a penniless younger brother who matches her own temperament. The farce depends on Elizabeth's decisive plotting; she is an unambiguous agent, much closer to Centlivre's Miranda than *The Runaway*'s wilting Emily. The world of the farce accentuates her authority and mocks her father's city pretensions: "I was grieved—grieved to the soul, Betty, when thou wert born. I had set my heart upon a Boy—and if thou'd'st been a Boy, thou shouldst have had Greek, and Algebra, and Jometry enough for an Archbishop" (I, 5). Like Behn and Centlivre before her, Cowley was an outsider to the world of classical education. She shared Behn's scorn for "the learned cant of time and place" and ridiculed the idea that classical education or dramatic theory is necessary or even preferable for a writer whose main task is to communicate with and please the theatergoing public. The father and daughter refract this gendered debate about education through their competing definitions of English success, Doiley's vision of a university-educated grandson who will become lord mayor or Elizabeth's English freedom to marry Granger, whose name is redolent with associations to agriculture and land.

In contrast to her father's provincialism and double negatives, Elizabeth is self-possessed and well-educated. Elizabeth knows that Granger needs her money, a fact he confesses to Sandiford in the opening scene: "I had rather marry Elizabeth Doiley with Ten Thousand Pounds, than any other woman on earth with an Hundred"(I, 3). His comic pragmatism undercuts the high chivalry of suitors' promises without abandoning the possibility of real affection. Granger relies on Elizabeth's agency, however, to outwit her father, whom she says will marry them freely at St. James. She asks Granger to "be guided by me" and assures him "you have only to be obedient" (I, 6). Elizabeth includes touches of Centlivre's Miranda as well as Cowley's own Bella, but while the latter must be reproved by Mr. Drummond, no avuncular, paternal, or romantic voice contests Elizabeth's authority.

Granger's first exercise in "obedience" exceeds any of Miranda's directives to George Airy; he is to dress as a woman, the French mantua-maker Mrs. Taffety, in order to evade detection by Elizabeth's father. As Mrs. Taffety, Granger learns the freedoms of speaking from the margins, where a French outsider can attack the play's "man of learning." Gradus laces his opening address to Elizabeth with names of obscure sophists and overwrought metaphors. Granger as Mrs. Taffety replies "*Mon Dieu! Madame!* is dis de Gentilhomme for whom you vant de Bride Cloaths?—He speak like a Dictionary-maker, and look like a Physician" (I, 8). Granger's outburst is, in the first case, the content of what Elizabeth can't say directly; she is a late-century educated merchant class woman who needs to stay above the fray to preserve her class position. But Elizabeth, as the director of his drag act, secures her authority over Gradus and her father by creating a phallic woman who can do the work of comic exposure for her.

Both fake and real women can dominate Gradus, who is woefully out of touch with popular national culture. Elizabeth's cousin Charlotte sketches Gradus while recounting her successful flirtation that is designed to discredit him with Mr. Doiley: "Oh, that's the way of all your great Scholars—take 'em but an inch out of their road, and you may turn 'em inside out, as easily as your glove" (I, 13). Cowley expected her audience to gloat with Charlotte over Gradus's gullibility, a comic moment that depends on recognizing Gradus as a professional intellectual, in the pattern of Samuel Johnson, Garrick's good friend. Johnson is also another of the mid-century men famous for taking on women protégés, among them Charlotte Lennox, Frances Burney, and Cowley's rival Hannah More. Cowley knew well that mentorship was selective, and that women who did not receive it had slim chances of success in an increasingly crowded book and script market. The caricature of Gradus displaces feelings of abandonment from the deceased Garrick to the still living Johnson and thus avoids the psychological burden of resentment for a dead mentor. Gradus's appearance, which is "a provocative to mirth," and Elizabeth's plea that "'tis possible for a Man who does not move as if cut in wood, or speak as though he delivered his words by tale, to have Breeding" resemble Boswell's reports of Johnson's awkward physical appearance, his tics, and his speech patterns (I, 4). The direct hit is Granger's comparison of Gradus to "a Dictionary-maker." But the overall characterization of Gradus is not so much a pointed caricature of Johnson as a satire of the world Hannah Cowley knew she was missing and would have to do without. The comic contrast of elite education and "common sense," in which the latter triumphs easily, clears the space for Cowley as a producer of national mass culture in the tradition of Behn and Centlivre.

Cowley defeats the world of intellectual privilege through a comic fantasy of male capitulation to female charm and wit. Gradus, who is fascinated with Elizabeth's cousin Charlotte, is only too happy to play the fop for the sake of her kisses. Thrust a bit too far into the stream of life and dressed in tasseled satin, with spangles and a trendy *chapeau bras,* Gradus proclaims at the close of the play, "I have had enough of languages. You see I have just engaged a Tutor to teach me to read the World" (II, 26). His declaration falls into the pat formula of romantic comedy, but it also repudiates intellectual exclusivity for popular and populist culture. With fifteen performances in its first season, *Who's the Dupe?* showed Cowley's growing understanding of the ticket-buying public.[21] It also paints a world, however farcical, in which women negotiate with their suitors and future husbands for control over comic closure, which affirms their active role in their marriages.

The play of English liberty, economic contingency, and female authority proved to be profitable and intellectually animating for Cowley. Her next comedy, *The Belle's Stratagem,* which Inchbald praised in her *Remarks* (1806–1809) as "abounding in excellent satire, with a most perfect description of the modes and manners of the fashionable world," secured her fame with 28 performances in its first season. It opened on February 22, 1780, a time more conducive to full benefit nights and a healthy run than her previous starts.[22] The play was such a success that the Covent Garden manager paid Cowley to keep the play out of print and added a £100 honorarium for her loyalty.[23] Elizabeth Inchbald described *The Belle's Stratagem* as able to negotiate the attractions and social liabilities of comedy: "Its greatest charm is, that it is humorous, without ever descending to that source of humour, easy of access, and which is placed among characters in low life." *The Belle's Stratagem* makes direct nods to Etherege's *Man of Mode,* Farquhar's *The Beaux' Stratagem,* and most immediately Goldsmith's *She Stoops to Conquer,* but comic heroines in the style of Centlivre's and Behn's provide its comic energy.

The Belle's Stratagem recuperates elements of Bella from *The Runaway* in Letitia Hardy, a witty leading lady who knows of the ways of the world. The plot, like Goldsmith's, takes up the problem of generating erotic interest in a match determined by previous arrangements. Letitia has been betrothed to the quintessential man of the *ton,* Doricourt, since infancy, and whichever of the two should opt out of the bargain will forfeit a large estate. Cowley reflects somewhat cynically on the complicity of the 1753 Marriage Act with a model of marriage as merger in the age of companionate love-matches. At the same time, she stresses the mutuality of the marriage contract and the ability of both parties to determine the trajectory of property. The more immediate narrative problem, however, is that while Letitia is enamored of Doricourt, Doricourt responded to Letitia with indifference at their first meeting. She must remedy the situation if she is to have any influence over Doricourt, who is already as disenchanted as "a husband of fifteen months" (I.iv, 15). Letitia recuperates her erotic authority through the play of national and foreign identities in her Hegelian "stratagem." She performs both the exotic other and a debased, parodic form of English simplicity, then she reconciles Doricourt to the marriage by revealing herself as the author of both his fantasy girl and his worst nightmare. Letitia's mastery of the erotic economy is an advertisement for an Englishness that contains its foreign others. Letitia leads the play's other characters through the currents of erotic and international exchange to the Promised Land of English married love.

Doricourt revels in the pleasurable excess of the foreign supplement; indeed, it defines him. His porter argues that his master ought to rank with a lord because "*We* have traveled, man!" (I.ii, 6). Doricourt, sounding rather like Etherege's Dorimant, describes his grand tour as a progression of nations and stages of consciousness which culminates in a return to England, where "the sweet follies of the Continent imperceptibly slide away," leaving only the polished Englishman (I.iii, 8). Upon his return, Doricourt's French footman shows off his wardrobe for a fee: "*Allons, Monsieur,* dis way; I will shew you tings, such tings you never see, begar, in England!—velvets by Le Mosse, suits cut by Verdue, trimmings by Grossette, embroidery by Detanville" (I.ii, 6). This direct echo of Sir Fopling's attire comes through a comic French character who creates some distance between Doricourt and the devotion to the Parisian fashion designers he describes. Doricourt has "mastered" these fashions and made them his own. As Courtall reflects jealously: "His carriage, his liveries, his dress, himself, are the rage of the day! His first appearance set the whole *Ton* in a ferment, and his valet is besieged by *levées* of taylors, habit-makers, and other Ministers of Fashion, to gratify the impatience of their customers for becoming *á la mode de Doricourt*" (I.i, 3–4). But the catalogue and the focus on his attire commodify Doricourt and threaten to feminize him as an exotic other. Lady Frolic and "two sister Countesses" make muffs out of his waistcoat, both proving his popularity and reducing his fashionable authority to a feminine accoutrement. Doricourt needs more Britishness in his life to counter this foreign and feminine circulation.

The anchor of his Englishness, the friendship he reserves for men "born beneath a British sky" (a global proposition in 1780) is compromised when his footman mistakes Saville for another paying customer on the wardrobe tour. Saville chides Doricourt when they meet, saying he only expected "a *bon jour,* a grimace, and an *adieu* . . . judging of the matter from the rest of the family" (I.iii, 7). His British identity, while it is more secure than that of the fashion gossip Flutter or the rakish and cruel Courtall, could suffer the fate of being evacuated by his cosmopolitanism without the stabilizing force of the more John Bull-ish Saville. An art auction of pieces by continental masters in act two drives this point home. Puffers, professional bidders who undermine the "real" value of the works by driving up the bid, inflate the value of the auction pieces. The actual bidders have no knowledge of the historical or narrative context of the pieces, which makes it too easy for the sharpers to create inflated values. One bidder mistakes David and Bathsheba for Diana and Acteon, admitting that she "know[s] nothing of the Story" (II.i, 32). The auctioneer Silvertongue introduces another piece, an unnamed city in wax: "call it Rome, Pekin, or London, 'tis still a City: you'll find in it the same jarring interests, the same passions, the same virtues, and the same vices, whatever the name" (II.i, 32). The lack of specific characteristics leaves this replica city in a state of endless possible substitutions with other cities and nations. Silvertongue's ironic declaration that "this can be no English City" (II, I, 33) because he sees corruption behind its doors only underscores the point: in the new "global economy" of the late eighteenth century, cosmopolitan experience could mean the erasure of nation.

Doricourt's rhapsodies on continental women, who outshine the "insipidity" of English beauty, gender the erotic supplement of foreignness: "*l'air enjoué!* that something, that nothing, which, every body feels, and which no body can describe, in the resistless charmers of Italy and France" (I.iii, 9). Doricourt understands this beauty to be a performance rather than "real intrinsic beauty," but he insists that it is the indefinable space of the erotic, "that something, that nothing." In contrast, the curmudgeonly Sir George justifies his marriage to the English Lady Frances in terms of her foreign docility: "she has a simplicity of heart and manners that would have become the fair Hebrew damsels toasted by the Patriarchs" (II.i, 20). Sir George, a kindlier Pinchwife who tries to keep his innocent bride from the London world, eventually learns that English women cannot be locked up, even in a world with rakes like Courtall. The play's argument for freedom is rooted in ideas of the nation. Doricourt argues to Saville that he keeps French and German footmen for similar reasons, "as the Romans kept slaves; because their own countrymen had minds too enlarged and haughty to descend with a grace to the duties of such a station" (I.iii, 8). While technically separate from the discussion of the eroticism of foreign women, George's attitude toward footmen illustrates the logic of the foreign Other. Foreigners exist in the service of a dominating English masculinity. Doricourt's position on the naturalness of using foreign labor for menial tasks rests, according to him, on a single word: "*Obedience!*" The complete obedience of the Frenchman naturally makes him a better servant than the Englishman, who "the other, a being, conscious of equal importance in the universal scale with yourself . . . is therefore your judge, whilst he wears your livery" (I.iii, 8). This piece of jingoism, however, runs aground on the issue of gender. Doricourt would have all the English men free and equal, all foreign men feminized slaves, all the foreign women sexy, and all the English women invisible.

The comic logic of Letitia's "stratagem" works in the space of this "nothingness" to craft a positive legal and erotic identity for herself as a British woman with both English sense and foreign allure. Letitia has inherited her father's prescience in trade, and she uses it to bolster her erotic value. When Letitia seems credulous at his declaration that Doricourt fell in love with her at their first disastrous meeting, he boasts: "How did I foresee the fall of corn, and the rise of taxes? How did I know, that if we quarrelled with America, Norway deals would be dearer? How did I fortell that a war would sink the funds?" (I.iv, 16). The answers to all of these questions remain conspicuously absent, but Hardy's assurance suggests one for all: because I am a successful English merchant, and we know these things. He masters these international situations because he understands the British economy in relation to its colonial and foreign others. Hardy proves he is the "true Englishman" by understanding markets in an international context and using his knowledge to advantage. Letitia similarly understands her national identity in relation to an eroticized international world and negotiates between these two positions. Her split self embodies the economic problem that Doricourt's desire has constructed; the Englishwoman is debased in relation to her exotic other, yet she is also the means of securing national wealth through marriage. She uses this tension, like the international dilemmas her father describes, to create value. She prosecutes her paradoxical plan "as the most important business of my life" (I.iv, 18). Her freedom to act depends upon the will of her father, but he gives it as a function of his business-identified prescience: "I foresee Letty will have her way, and so I sha'n't give myself the trouble to dispute it"

(I.iv, 19). His position as the good father and master tradesman sanctions female liberty; he welcomes her into the fraternity of economic masters where she can execute her plan.

Letitia's first persona is a country bumpkin who giggles, thinks Swift's Houynhynmns are real, and uses homely expressions. Her performance parodies what Doricourt fears from her English modesty. Looking at her picture, he comments "*Ma foi!* the painter has hit her off.—The downcast eye—the blushing cheek—timid—apprehensive—bashful.—A tear and a prayer-book would have made her *La Bella Magdalena*" (III.i, 35). His reflection is a near quotation of *Evelina* and the poem that the rakish Sir Clement Willoughby writes to praise Evelina:

> SEE last advance, with bashful grace,
> Downcast eye, and blushing cheek,
> Timid air, and beauteous face,
> Anville,—whom the Graces seek.[24]

The domestic currency of Burney's heroine speaks to a bourgeois standard of femininity that both Doricourt and Cowley find too passive. In place of this demure and retiring ingenue, Doricourt fantasizes a woman with "A mind, a soul, a polish'd art" who will wound him with darts of "endless love" (III.i, 35). His Petrarchian conventions, as predictable as the sentimental tropes of Clement Willoughby's verse, locate the cosmopolitan woman as the source of "endless" desire, including a crucial term in Cowley's romantic lexicon, "mind." His desire for intelligence comes first, and provides the assurance that he does in fact want what he is about to get.

Letitia's next performance as the "incognita" catches Doricourt with a libertine song that invites him to "wake" to pleasure. Set up by the first bumpkin performance, Doricourt falls immediately for this international woman with "English beauty—French vivacity—wit—elegance" (IV.i, 58). She refuses to give her name (which, she points out, cannot last in marriage) but assures Doricourt that marriage's threatening chains are "possible to wear . . . gracefully,—Throw 'em loosely round, and twist 'em in a True-Lover's Knot for the Bosom" (IV.i, 58). The echo of *The Rover*'s "true-love's knot" brings a greater sexual charge to their banter. The mutual relationship, she promises, would make her: "any thing—and all!—Grave, gay, capricious—the soul of whim, the spirit of variety—live with him in the eye of fashion, or the shade of retirement—change my country, my sex. . . ." The promise of this national and, more strikingly, sexual multiplicity grounds her variability in her position of national privilege. The possibility of changing her sex suggests an erotic mutuality of English subject-partners as social, if not political, equals.

After her catalogue of the colonial territories where she would live with him (Esquimaux huts, Persia, Lake Ontario's tribes, Ceylon, Conconda) Letitia comes to the Mogul's seraglio, where she would "cheat him of his wishes, and overturn his empire to restore the Husband of my Heart to the blessings of Liberty and Love" (IV.i, 59). This return to true Englishness saves her husband from his polygamy as well as his internationalism. The English Letitia encompasses the eroticism of the foreign woman. Letitia is both nationally located ("English beauty" as "delightful wildness") and erotically elsewhere as both the disappearing incognita and the idiot "mistress" Doricourt tries to escape. Hardy provides the punch line to the comic scene after the incognita Letitia has left Doricourt in raptures. "Mr. Doricourt!— . . . I know who you are in love with . . . My Letty" (IV.i, 60). When Doricourt will only read this as the rebuke of a father-in-law, Hardy decides to join Letty in her plotting.

As the play winds to its climax, Cowley circulates her characters through a whirlwind of rehearsals, performances, and mistaken identities. Hardy pretends to be dying, which leads him to muse anxiously, "I foresee some ill happening from this making believe to die before one's time. But hang it—a-hem!—I am a stout man yet; only fifty-six—What's that?" (V.i, 66). Hardy senses intuitively the maxim of costume balls; you always come as yourself. His first disguise, Isaac Mendoza, was a version of Hardy as wily trader, but in the play's first run this was a thicker joke. Quick, who played Hardy, also created the role of Isaac the Jew in Sheridan's *The Duenna,* to which he refers directly. This referentiality, which locates Quick as actor *and* character, plays with the power of performance, a parallel to Letitia's virtuosity. Meanwhile, in order to avoid marriage to the bumpkin Letitia, Doricourt puts on a lunatic show, a monthly affliction that is the result of a poisoned box of sweetmeats from an Italian princess. His cyclical, feminized madness makes him the slave of a foreign woman, but it also makes him the butt of a joke. Mrs. Racket and Miss Ogle laugh openly at his antics and explain to him how to play a madman. Doricourt is still learning how to perform his national and his gender identity.

The greatest performance, the speech act of the wedding ceremony, proves that performances are, in the end, real. After the ceremony, Doricourt encounters his "incognita" and discovers that she is chaste, rich, and free. He raves at his misfortune until Letitia stops the torture and takes off the veil:

> *Letitia:* You see I *can* be any thing; choose then my character—your Taste shall fix it. Shall I be an *English* Wife?—or, breaking from the bonds of Nature and Education, step forth to the world in all the captivating glare of Foreign Manners?
>
> *Doricourt:* You shall be nothing but yourself—nothing can be captivating that you are not. . . . (V.iv, 81)

This closing promise of Englishness that is its own supplement draws together the realms of stability and pleasure under the sign of British nationalism. The echoes of Behn's "Hellena th'inconstant" and Cornelia, "the most mistress-like wife," are here tamed under the more stable sign of "English wife," which has successfully colonized its erotic others. She is the fantasy of endless variety ("I *can* be anything") and fulfillment ("nothing can be captivating that you are not") that affirms the nationalist terms of Letitia's authority. Letitia uses the play of national identity to produce her eroticism and her agency, both of which are happily in excess of Doricourt's expectations. His relatively submissive posture at the end of the play confirms her comic authority as an English woman who has mastered English liberties and her wayward English man.

Cowley's nationalist bent succeeded wildly with her public. *The Belle's Stratagem* was the fourth most performed play (excluding Shakespeare) in the last quarter of the eighteenth century and was part of active repertoire through the nineteenth century.[25] When her father, Philip Parkerhouse, wrote to his friend Lord Harrowby to appeal for a financial subsidy to support Cowley's writing, he used *The Belle's Stratagem* to advertise her accomplishments.[26] Elizabeth Inchbald, who praised the play as the best of Cowley's work, played Lady Frances Touchwood in the 1781 run, one of her highest profile mainstage performances.[27] But Cowley's sanguine sense of the egalitarian possibilities of a nationalist discourse turns sour in her next big success, *Which Is the Man?* (1782), in which political systems, social power, and women's claims to self-determination have broken down.

His and Hers Nationalisms

Which Is the Man? appeared February 9, 1782, only a few months after British troops had surrendered to American forces at Yorktown. It was the most popular mainpiece of the season at Covent Garden, with 25 performances. The only play that rivaled its success was *The Count of Narbonne,* a gothic tragedy with 21 performances that season and production assistance from Horace Walpole.[28] The popularity of these two pieces, one a dark comedy and the other a gothic exploration of psychic trauma in the family, reflects the unsettled political climate in the post-American and pre-French revolutionary period. The 1778 French alliance with the Americans and the loss of the war with the colonies threatened British pride as well as British trade. From 1707 to 1767, 95 percent of the increase in British exports went to colonial markets; chief among them was the American colonies. The colonies accounted for 20 percent of British exports and supplied 30 percent of its imports.[29] Although Britain continued to export to the newly formed United States, the end of British rule and the return of

French influence in the American colonies and French Quebec, part of the spoils of the Seven Years' War, challenged the sovereignty of British markets. The war with France continued until 1783 and added to the spiraling national war debt. In 1783, the national deficit stood at over £240 million, requiring £9.4 million annually in service payments alone.[30] The economic and ideological implications of this post-revolutionary but not yet postwar moment fracture Cowley's hardy nationalism. She seemed less certain about the ability of English nationality to provide meaningful civic identity to women or men.

One of the first indicators that something has changed in the world of this play is that foreign countries, in particular France, are very hospitable to women's concerns. The Republican lure of France is not represented as radical legal power, but as what English liberty should have been able to deliver on its own. Although her guardian Fitzherbert has sequestered Julia Manners in a convent in France, she has also taken advantage of legal differences to marry the man she loves, Belville, while out of the country. This secret marriage prompts the avuncular but stern Fitzherbert's desire to "punish" Julia's independence and her "want of confidence," even though he approves of her choice (II.ii, 20). Julia, unable to claim Belville as her husband, must reflect on the difference of English and French law for women. Her loss of control once back in England, encapsulated in her plaintive "I fear 'tis a wrong step; and yet what other can I take?" stands in contrast to the independence of her actions in France. While portions of French culture, in particular the convent, suggest a curtailed liberty for women, Julia finds that French law recognizes her as an agent where English law does not. William Alexander, in *The History of Women,* first published in 1779, claims that the matrimonial laws of France "as well as the customs which regard their personal liberty, seem more indulgent," as do the laws and customs of Italy, Prussia, and Spain.[31] The reality of matrimonial law in France was more complex. The French legal system had long regarded marriage as a civil contract, dating back to the late sixteenth century, during which the process of moving control over marriage from canonical law to French law began. The French used a procedural device called "appel comme d'abus" that took contested marital cases out of church courts and placed them in the jurisdiction of French courts, where legal separation was possible.[32] Usually, wives sued for legal separation; but husbands usually charged the suing wife with adultery just before or just after she brought her charges. If the wife won her case, she gained control over her dowry funds in addition to the separation. If she lost, she was forced to enter a convent; the husband was responsible for her pension there, but he retained control over the dowry.[33]

Divorce became an option after the French Revolution, when the Constitution of 1791 declared that marriage was nothing but a civil contract. The subsequent law of September 20, 1792, permitted divorce with few restrictions, leading to an explosion of divorces from 1792 to 1795 that panicked some and led to an amendment of the law in 1803 before its 1816 repeal.[34] While French Salique law did not permit women to inherit the crown, the more consistent civil definition of marriage and the provisions for separation suggest that France was more willing to recognize marrying and married women as individuals under the law. French law still required parental consent before the age of 25 for women, but the legal focus on the consent of the couple, affirmed by the Council of Trent, placed the emphasis on the contractual dimension of marriage.[35] Julia, who takes advantage of the gaps between the French and English legal systems by marrying an Englishman in Paris, fittingly makes her contract under these legal provisions.

Fitzherbert occupies the place of the benevolent patriarch in the play, but his severity undermines his moral authority. In spite of his convent design for Julia, Fitzherbert rails against the freedom of French culture. He proposes tollgates on the "great turnpike between Dover and Calais" to control the number of "travelling philosophers [who] have done more towards destroying the nerves of their country, than all the politics of France" (II.ii, 15). His condemnation of continental liberties dovetails with his implicit demand to control the exchange of Julia. This heavy-handed mastery puts him in the comically suspect position of the good guardian who is a danger to his female charge.

Once he learns that Julia has married in France, he tortures her by proposing the country booby, Bobby Pendragon, as his choice of a husband, with nearly disastrous consequences. Julia, trying to avoid Bobby's attentions, finds herself thrown into the company of Lord Sparkle, whose unscrupulous election procedures and sexual conduct signify a breakdown of the English political system. Sparkle fulfills none of his political duties to the House of Lords, unlike the fashionable Villars in *The Belle's Stratagem* who discretely slips out to tend to the opening of the budget in the House of Commons. Even the corrupt and comic Justice of *The Runaway* manages to attend to more civic duty than Sparkle. The Pendragons, a bumpkin brother and sister team, have supported his election, and they expect something in return. They wrongly believe that Sparkle regards them as true friends and that his hollow compliments to Sophy constitute lovemaking. He calls his compliments "the coin of conversation" and "hyperbole," eventually translated by Bobby as "a stretch." He tries to finesse Bobby's complaint about the empty promise of a colonel's post by reproving, "You thought it so valuable then, that you got me a hundred extra votes on the strength of it; and you are now a little ungrateful wretch, to pretend 'twas worth nothing" (V.i, 51). Words, like money, are only temporary values in Sparkle's economy, where he never pays. This malaise of meaninglessness is, as he explains to Beauchamp, the rule of his existence.

Sparkle: We love, hate, quarrel, and even fight without suffering our tranquility to be incommoded;—nothing disturbs.—The keenest discernment will discover nothing particular in the behaviour of *lovers* on the point of marriage, nor in the *married,* whilst articles of separation are preparing.
Beauchamp: Disgustful apathy!—What becomes of the energies of the heart in this wretched system? Does it annihilate your feelings? (III.i, 21)

Sparkle's meaningless life collapses into an apathy that he generalizes to all fashionable English people. His example, marriage and separation without feeling, puts the marriage contract at the center of this nihilism.

Sparkle's fiscal irresponsibility raises questions about national integrity and the relation of trade to land in this credit economy. When Bobby Pendragon declares that all Cornwall, "Tin-Mines and all," will know of Sophy's disappointment, he refers to the material wealth that supported Sparkle in the election. Sparkle's gambling, like Valere's in Centlivre's *The Gamester,* is another social threat, but Cowley represents it as a danger to the land itself. Sparkle brags in the first act that he gambles "for solid earth" rather than guineas, "a mercantile kind of wealth, passing thro' the hands of dry-salters, vinegar merchants, and Lord-Mayors.—*Our* Goddess holds a cornucopia instead of a purse, from which she pours corn-fields, fruitful vallies [sic], and rich herds. This morning she popp'd into my dice-box a snug villa, five hundred acres, arable and pasture, with the next presentation to the living of Guzzleton" (I.i, 4). He confesses that he and his gambling companions don't have many guineas, so they must use them for counters while they gamble for land, their inherited wealth. Flourishing paper credit in the 1770s and North's recoinage from 1773 to 1776, which recalled over £16 million worth of gold coins to remint (and reassert) their value, lie beneath Sparkle's flippant claim.[36] The newly valued gold coin of the day, complete with George III's imprint, marked an attempt to stabilize money value in a nation that seemed increasingly like a "Paperwealth" both to citizens and trading partners.[37] But Sparkle rejects this reaffirmed gold standard. He prefers his paper relation to land as Fitzherbert's heir apparent; his personal value is based on a promissory relation to the estate, presumably the same relation that many of his fellow gamblers try to sustain through their big talk of "solid earth." The lack of a meaningful tie to the land echoes in his plans to raise the rents of his tenants: "Upon my soul, I pity 'em! But how can it be otherwise, whilst one is obliged to wear fifty acres in a suit, and the produce of a whole farm in a pair of buckles?" (III.i, 25). He is an economically grotesque figure, a Gargantua of fashion with no notion of economic value, a lack that is directly tied to his faulty relationship to English soil.

As comic foils to Sparkle, the Pendragons are unable to play with empty words or empty economic values and fall instead into absurd literalism.

Once it becomes clear that Sparkle has no intention of courting or marrying Sophy, Bobby Pendragon challenges Lord Sparkle to a duel: "Miss *Pendragon* told me she was *dissatisfied:*—then says I, *I'll* demand *satisfaction*" (IV.i, 38). Similarly, Sophy's claim to Sparkle's affection depends on the fictions that she reads as real:

> *Sophy: "How would a Coronet become those shining tresses!"*—the very speech of Lord Rosehill to Miss Danvers; and these couples were every one married.
> *Sparkle:* Married! I never heard of 'em!—Who are they? Where the Devil do they live?
> *Pendragon:* (*strutting up to him*) Live!—Why in our county, to be sure.
> *Sophy:* No, no, *Bobby,* in *The Reclaim'd Rake,* and *The Constant Lovers,* and *Sir Charles Grandison,* and *Roderic Random* . . . (IV.i, 39)

Sophy, even less sophisticated than Lydia Languish, confuses imaginary and real people in farcical style, but Sparkle's response exposes a disjunction between national culture and English law that is especially serious for women: "Ha! ha! ha! you are a charming little Lawyer, (*to* Sophy) and might, perhaps, establish your proofs for *precedents,* if Sir Charles Grandison was on the Bench: yet I never heard of his being made Chief-Justice, tho' I never thought him fit for any thing else" (IV.i, 39). Sparkle mocks the rift between the representations of women's prerogatives and their legal status, particularly as they are made visible in literature. The gesture toward Sophy as lawyer confirms this hit: she can only have access to the legal system and be her own advocate in a fictional realm, where men like Sir Charles exist. His disregard for the legal system (as a member of the house of lords) is notable: that he never thought Sir Charles Grandison fit for anything else belittles both Richardson's virtuous man and the courts. Cowley poses a difficult question through Sparkle's self-reflexive joke: what good are representations of women's social power if they can't challenge the economic interests of men encoded in the law? The English good sense and justice that reign in literary representation, where women's moral authority carries more weight, are only empty signifiers in a national context where political and legal authority remain in the hands of a few unaccountable men.

Sparkle's empty value system culminates in the near rape of Julia. His motive for her capture has nothing to do with Julia herself. He wants her as a mistress because "'tis the fashion to have mistresses from higher orders than sempstresses and mantua-makers." He also uses her to gain revenge on her guardian Fitzherbert, who "will not suffer me to draw on his banker for a single guinea" though he has already taken advantage of his claim to the estates (II.i, 23). The connection between Fitzherbert and Sparkle in this passage raises a dark structural point; they *are* complicit in the legal and economic systems that threaten Julia's choices. Julia can be circulated in this way, like Florinda in *The Rover,* because she naively believes that patriarchal power is benevolent, when in truth, Fitzherbert remains more intent on teaching her lessons than protecting her interests. When Sparkle's plan becomes apparent, Fitzherbert accepts no blame, insisting that Julia's "rashness" was the source of her troubles, not his "little punishment" (V.i, 47). Threatened by Sparkle's and Fitzherbert's respective plans, yet legally married to Belville, Julia finds herself in a no-man's land. Julia enters act five with the selfish and plotting Clarinda, fainting and insisting that "Miss *Belmour* will tell you all she knows.—I am too wretched!" Feeling unable to speak from any position of authority, she surrenders her story to a suspect character. Julia's move outside of an English discourse of law to claim her English birthright of liberty has made it impossible for her to reenter English society without finding herself again entrapped by her guardian, who demands obedience and compels her stratagem. Fitzherbert, determined to punish those who do not stay within England's cultural and legal contradictions, creates the sexual dangers that Julia faces. She exclaims, "Oh Sir! had you reveal'd this to me this morning, what evils should I have escap'd," for which Fitzherbert will take no responsibility (V.i, 47). He refers to his desire to punish her or take revenge on her four times and calls her ungrateful and disobedient on three occasions. The quiet indictment of Fitzherbert does not keep him from administering the ending of the play, but his demand for control colors the conclusion, which is weighted down by his punishment schemes.

Insofar as Sparkle can take the fall for Britain's political and economic ills, he clears a space for the overly earnest Beauchamp and his virtuous military masculinity to save the day. That his name is French is only the first tendentious twist to his role. Beauchamp successfully (though accidentally) saves Julia from Lord Sparkle's advances because "as a *Man,* it is my duty to protect endanger'd innocence . . . as a *Soldier,* it is part of the essence of my character," even though he still believes he owes Sparkle for his commission (IV.ii, 37). Belville mocks his nationalist fire, fed by his unrequited love for Lady Bell, as "the gallantry of One Thousand One Hundred and One" (I.i, 7). Beauchamp's spirit of seriousness marks an extreme in the play that, like Lady Bell's fashionability, is hard to read. At times, he seems a comic butt. Beauchamp is also in a compromised financial situation, like Behn's Gayman, but declares "never can I submit to be quartered on a Wife's fortune, whilst I have a sword to carve subsistence for myself" (I.i, 8). His reluctance to accept a woman's financial bounty shadows the ending, in which Beauchamp faces just such a future. Beauchamp also commands very little dialogue for a male character. He does not match Lady Bell, even though he spends more time on stage, and he barely surpasses the retiring Julia, who is reluctant to make her own case.[38] Like Britain the nation, Beauchamp still carries the banner of the good society that can support women's claims to liberty and justice out of chivalry, but he is financially weakened and, at times, hard to take seriously.

Cowley makes it difficult to find a happy medium between British and other, virtue and vice, and liberty and duty in this cast of characters. The two remaining candidates, Belville and Lady Bell Bloomer, present significant problems. Belville takes moderate positions on nationalism, female liberty, and economics, but he is ignorant of the information regarding Julia, Fitzherbert, and the status of their marriage. He blurts out his marriage to Julia because he has no idea that Fitzherbert is the guardian, and he later assumes Julia has been unfaithful when he finds her rescued in Beauchamp's apartments. In contrast to his relative ignorance, Julia, Lady Bell, and the problematic Fitzherbert manage information and take the upper hand in the play's comic events. His lack of information keeps him from being a comic agent in the plot and undermines his sexual appeal in a genre where wit, or at least information, distinguishes desirable characters from undesirable ones.

Lady Bell provides a last problematic option for positive audience identification. Conscious of her social and erotic power over Beauchamp, she seems both shallow and cruel when she describes her entrance into a fête: "I ascend the stairs—move slowly thro' the rooms—drop my fan—incommode my bouquet—stay to adjust it, that the *little* gentry may have time to fix their admiration—again move on . . . and see nothing but spite in the eyes of the women, and a thousand nameless things in those of the men" (II.i, 13). After such asides, Fitzherbert must assure Julia (and the audience) that she really has a fine understanding and sensible heart underneath her fashionable exterior. Her manipulation of the poor soldier Beauchamp ("Now, how shall I receive him? It will be intolerable to be formal") directly echoes Lady Wishfort in The *Way of the World:* "Well, and how shall I receive him? In what figure shall I give his Heart the first Impression?"[39] Clarinda, who has been socially bested by Lady Bell, keeps her nemesis from looking as ridiculous as Lady Wishfort by being both older and more callous. Clarinda rejoices in Lady Squander's bankruptcy: "So Christie has her jewels and furniture at last!—I must go to the sale.—Mark that Dresden service and the pearls" and then comments callously, "It must be a great comfort to her to see her jewels worn by her friends" (I.ii, 8). She exemplifies the worst of French and English values, fashionable superficiality and greed, and preys on others whose social and economic stocks have fallen. The former possessions of her former friends now circulate anonymously through auction, where even the term "friend" is the mark of alienation. Her maid Tiffany, who laments that being the chambermaid "to a *Miss* on the brink of Thirty requires as good politics, as being Prime Minister!" anticipates Clarinda's own fall as a woman who has missed her moment on the market (I.i, 9).

Lady Bell sees significant liberties for women in French salon culture. She argues that English customs ruin men for conversation and advocates French qualities as a remedy: "Whilst we aukwardly [*sic*] copy the follies of the Parisians, we absurdly omit the charming part of their character. Devoted to elegance, they catch their opinions, their wit, and their bons mots from the mouths of the ladies.—'Tis in the drawing-room of Madame the Dutchess, the Marquis learns his politicks; whilst the sprightly Countess dispenses taste and philosophy to a circle of Bishops, Generals, and Abbés" (III.iii, 30). Englishmen, according to Lady Bell, are divided from women in the governance of the country. This split of national priorities contrasts with a more holistic model of national taste and policy that she finds in French culture, where women have a hand in national affairs, however indirectly. The possibility that France could have more to offer a woman than England does is the nervous tic of this play. Lady Bell's observations are only slightly comic, and their content was lent credence in the initial run by the casting of Elizabeth Younge, who also played Bella and Letitia Hardy, the latter Cowley's most vivacious pillar of good sense and judgment.

Lady Bell extends her power over Beauchamp in an uncomfortable last scene, where she punishes Sparkle's hubris at the expense of the heartbroken soldier. Her legal control over her money as a widow gestures to an earlier, darker marriage that "would have broken her heart else" (II.i, 10). Her joy at leaving her weeds suggests that the threatened broken heart had more to do with anguish during the marriage than with Lord Bloomer's parting. Once she does confess her love for Beauchamp, she exerts her widow's authority over economic arrangements. She counters Fitzherbert's offer to make Beauchamp his heir by insisting that he remain a soldier, lest she should "lose the credit of having done a mad thing for the sake of the man—my heart prefers" (V.i, 54). Her declaration not only keeps Beauchamp in a position of economic inferiority but also leaves Sparkle ambiguously open to the inheritance he stood to lose through Fitzherbert's change of heir.

The indeterminacy of this ending culminates in Beauchamp's closing speech: "Love and my Country! Yes, ye shall divide my heart!—Animated by such passions, our forefathers were invincible; and if we wou'd preserve the freedom and independence they obtain'd for us, we must imitate their virtues" (V.i, 54). The *division* of love (the more feminized, domestic territory) and country (figured here as British military might) keep the gendered terms of his future separate. The dialectical resolutions of Cowley's other comedies, where nationalism enables and animates egalitarian heterosexual arrangements, contrast with this more fractured solution, where "freedom and independence" are endangered. Cowley's ending cannot suture over the greater rupture that she has uncovered; a discourse of British nationalism, while it promises an ideology of liberty to women, cannot guarantee that liberty any more than England can guarantee its wartime national debt or its colonial future. Love and country are, in the end, separate terms that divide rather than unite. Women are on their own to guard against the loss of identity in the national and, here, international marriage market. Lady Bell can do it successfully, but Julia barely survives with her honor and will intact.

Nationalism and the unreliable prop of the foreign other unravel even further in *A Bold Stroke for a Husband,* which opened February 25, 1783. Cowley's *A Bold Stroke,* which hearkens back to Centlivre's play in name more than in spirit, enjoyed a good first two years before it began to fade from the boards. As the last and least of her comic successes, it marks the limits of Cowley's dialectic of foreign and British identity and exposes her dependence on extraordinarily supportive men and masquerading women. In this *Bold Stroke,* women plot, cross-dress, and rely on each other for help to secure, reclaim, and avoid husbands in a Spanish intrigue plot worthy of Behn. But in spite of their freedom of motion, there is no notion of natural law or nationalism to place that freedom in a larger context of rights. Instead, performance alone produces agency for women in this "foreign" Madrid play, Cowley's only popular full-length comedy set outside of England. (Cowley's *A Day in Turkey,* a comic opera first staged in 1791, lasted on the boards three years compared to *A Bold Stroke*'s five, plus revivals after 1800.) The anonymous prologue announces that England's greatest points of pride are its "Bold strokes in war," but that this play, in a "bold stroke of nature, not of art. / A female pen calls female virtue forth," and so convinces men of the attractions of marriage through a display of female sense and wit. This stroke will "rectify the age," which has not understood the worth and virtue of women. Reflecting on Centlivre's title, the play puts forth two bold strokes, one by the single Olivia to get the husband of her choice and one by Victoria to reclaim her philandering husband Don Carlos. But without a larger idea of liberty, made accessible through nationalism, their successes are merely "bold strokes" or lucky chances.

Olivia puts off the suitors her father introduces with tendentious jokes; she feigns a love for kittens before an ailurophobic general, a love of the Jew's harp for a concertmaster, and a common ancestry for a Castillian count. Her reputation as a shrew and her ability to read the specific anxieties of her suitors revolt each unfortunate man while she waits for Julio. The strategy works, but it almost collapses in the final revelation scene, in which no one can say whom or what Olivia really is. The national identity that had anchored previous heroines is missing; Julio alone can supply her meaning. In the last act, she can accept Julio's vows only "When you [father] command me" (V.iii, 83), a more deferential end that one might expect from a character who scorned the easily broken Katherine of *The Taming of The Shrew. The Taming of the Shrew* appeared 142 times from 1747 to 1779 in an abbreviated form as the afterpiece *Catherine and Petruchio* and would have been familiar as a short comic plot to Cowley and her audience.[40] Olivia spars with her father and his gentleman, but her devotion to Carlos and her affection for Donna Victoria ground her character in the midst of her shrewish performances.

A Bold Stroke's sentimental plot also gestures to the limits of nationalist discourse as an argument for female specificity. Like Amanda in Cibber's *Love's Last Shift* (1696), Donna Victoria begins the play as a patient Griselda, abandoned by a philandering husband for the beautiful Laura. But Victoria plots and schemes in the name of motherhood and marriage. When she discovers that Don Carlos has given her estate to Laura, Victoria has no recourse to the law. Similarly, Laura will have none when Victoria/Florio dupes her out of the deed. Donna Victoria impersonates a young man, Florio, in order to study Laura, "that I might, if possible, be to my Carlos, all he found in her" (I.ii, 21) and to reclaim her lands for her children. To get the lands back, she must reenact her husband's infidelities incognito and reproduce the scene of her own betrayal. The erotic end of this disguise is to displace herself further by becoming more like Laura. She successfully captivates Laura by being captivating, but she departs suddenly when she sees "love's arrow quivering in her heart" (21). The mirror of female identification and desire gives her erotic agency, which she rejects, leading Olivia to ask archly, "Would you have done so, had you been a man?" (I.ii, 21). Victoria's imitation of a careless lover, like Marcella's performance in *The Feign'd Courtesans,* highlights the theatrical quality of identity, in which the self is perpetually elsewhere.

Victoria plays with her theatrical mobility to cover her own legal mistake; she has signed over her estate to Carlos through "lavish love . . . without securing it to my children" (II.i, 21). Having surrendered her separate property, she has only a theatrical solution to compensate for her lack of legal subjectivity. While Victoria's particular dilemma is a function of her husband's philandering, her need to invent a subject position mirrors the trend in late-eighteenth-century rulings against the legal identity of women within marriage. Separate maintenance contracts applied only to marriages that did not work, but the legal principle involved in the reaction against contract suggests a shift in the culture's perception of women. Hardline rulings from Lord Chief Justice Kenyon overturned precedents for women's separate maintenance contracts in *Ringstead, Barnwell,* and *Corbett.* Kenyon asserted that allowing wives to make contracts with their husbands would dissolve "the bond of marriage" and "would introduce all the confusion and inconvenience which must necessarily result from so anomalous and mixed a character" (quoted in Staves 180). Victoria's queer solution suggests, among other things, that gender, law, and identity might have to be radically renegotiated when the domestic ideology of companionate marriage proves treacherous.

As a whole, the play retreats from the independent-minded Olivia in favor of Donna Victoria's story, which is both more challenging in its sexual possibilities and more conventional in its ideal of wifely devotion and sacrifice. In a final discovery scene, Donna Victoria throws herself at her husband's feet and cries, "Strike, strike it here! Plunge it deep into that bosom already wounded by a thousand stabs, keener and more painful than your sword can give" (V.i, 71). Victoria's physical and emotional risk contains her performances within the domestic, where "Virtue is our first, most awful duty" (V.i, 72) and where Victoria can be a better spokeswoman for wifely obedience. This sentimental conclusion gestures to Cowley's own repudiation of her early comedies later in life. She began rewriting them in her retirement, but not surprisingly, the bowdlerized versions are much less interesting than the originals, which held the stage into the nineteenth century. *A Bold Stroke for a Husband* moves the comic discourse closer to Inchbald's interest in law, divorce, and the limits of marriage. Audiences were willing and eager to follow Cowley's exploration of nation as a discourse open to women. Cowley used the relativity of rights to ground her heroines' agency in their Englishness, a marker of identity set against an international world of power relations. But as that world grew more international, and as Great Britain faced greater challenges to its international prerogative, the solid ground of nationalism began to melt. *A Bold Stroke for a Husband* probed the limits of nationalism or any other identity claim for women who were not full civil subjects under the law. In so doing, it set the tone for Inchbald's full-length comedies, which explore the struggles of married women to redefine themselves within failed relationships and beyond the law.

CHAPTER SIX

BEYOND THE LAW

Contract, Divorce, and Community in Inchbald's Comedies

As England faced the 1790s, Hannah Cowley's nationalist comedies as well as Centlivre's Whiggish *The Busy Body, The Wonder,* and *A Bold Stroke for a Wife* continued to appeal to audiences. *The Belle's Stratagem* enjoyed 40 performances in the decade; *Who's the Dupe?* had 41; *The Busy Body* 33; and *A Bold Stroke for a Wife* 42. *The Busy Body, Who's the Dupe?,* and *The Belle's Stratagem* were offered every year of the nineties, ensuring the presence of well-known female playwrights in the theatrical conversation. Their visions of assertive heroines, grounded in the economic and national heritage of Great Britain, implicitly linked domestic bliss in the home to good domestic policy for the nation. Newer comedies, however, particularly those of Elizabeth Inchbald, reflected the instability of domestic, national, and international law that shaped the cultural consciousness at the end of the century. Inchbald, who acted in Cowley's *The Belle's Stratagem* and her less successful *The World as it Goes,* emerged as the premiere female playwright of the 1790s with comedies about colonial corruption and divorce. This unlikely subject matter for comedies appealed to a public bombarded with bad news by translating some of their most pressing concerns into comic events that diffused some of the anxieties of *fin de siècle* England. The Hastings trial represented the colonial authority of England in a negative light, providing perhaps the most important piece of late-century theater that lasted from 1788 to final acquittal in 1795. The abolitionist movement, the Regency Crisis occasioned by George III's illness and the dissolute behavior of the prince regent, and eventually the French Revolution also unsettled the idea of the rule of law, while rendering lawlessness a chilling alternative.[1]

Inchbald expresses concerns about the abuse of power and the terror of life without the law in popular plays such as *The Mogul Tale* (1784), *I'll Tell You What* (1785), *Such Things Are* (1787), *Every One Has His Fault* (1793), and *The Wise Man of the East* (1799), which deal with specifically colonial questions. In *The Mogul Tale,* which was staged 74 times before 1800, Inchbald mocks the apprehensions of three English balloonists blown off their course and into the seraglio of a philosophical sultan. In *Such Things Are,* performed 36 times during the same period in addition to a strong print circulation in the 1780s and 1790s, she interweaves a sentimental with a farcical plot as she explores the corrupt colonial community of Sumatra, an unforgiving sultan, and the influence of reformer Haswell, a character modeled on John Howard. Although Inchbald comments on British imperialism in these plays, as Betsy Bolton and Katherine Green have discussed, she raises more general questions of law and power that take her subsequent comedies to the domestic dilemmas of marriage and divorce in England.[2]

Inchbald's exploration of marriage law and divorce as both a cultural crisis and a generic dilemma unfolds in her three other original popular comedies, *I'll Tell You What* (1785), *Every One Has His Fault* (1792), and *Wives as They Were, and Maids as They Are* (1797). *Every One Has His Fault* and *Wives as They Were, and Maids as They Are* were each performed annually to the end of the century, with 47 and 28 performances respectively. *I'll Tell You What* fell off somewhat after 1794, but went into four print editions and enjoyed a healthy 50 performances before that fade. In these comedies, Inchbald shifts her attention away from the nubile heroine and the courtship plot and toward the adult married woman, who must negotiate the terms of her civil and personal existence from within the marriage contract. Her plays give an account of the messy, imperfect, legally flawed state of marriage at the end of the century. The narrative question is no longer how to get to a happy marriage ending, but what modes of relationship and identity are available for the heroine after a marriage has imploded.

A Divorcing England?

The rise in the number of divorces from 24 in the years from 1715 to 1759 to 102 between 1760 and 1799 reflects both a growing population and slowly changing attitudes toward marriage. After the Marriage Act of 1753, unhappy unions were less contestable based on spousals, clandestine ceremonies, and contracted states, intermediate claims that could dissolve a marriage without divorce.[3] Leah Leneman speculates that shifting attitudes toward personal freedom, as well as the marriages interrupted by the wars to which Britain was committed from 1776 to 1782 and 1794 to 1815, are the best explanations for the rise in divorce rates. Divorce had become more visible on the international front as well. In post-revolutionary France, divorce rates temporarily exploded with the collapse of ecclesiastical authority and the introduction of more libertarian Continental legislation. The public records of the nine main urban centers in France document 20,000 divorces between 1792 and 1803. Working-class people filed most of these divorces, and women pursued 71 percent of the cases.[4] Divorce proceedings in Scotland, where divorce had a legal and ideological place in the culture, provide a complementary picture of rising divorce rates. Scottish judges presided over 904 divorce proceedings between 1684 and 1830, 786 of which occurred after 1771. Men and women sued evenly (54.5 percent by men and 45.5 percent by women), and in contrast to English legal history, commoners initiated most of these suits.[5] The surge in post–1770 divorces extended to the American colonies, with an increase in suits in Massachusetts and Connecticut.[6] These trends in France, Scotland, and the colonies put divorce in the domain of the cultural Other. Divorces abroad created a sense of distance from the growing number of divorce cases while they also presented a mirror to the nation's marriage dilemma.

Katherine Binhammer argues that the British press's interpretation of these statistics, which in fact show that domestic divorce rates were quite low in consideration of population growth, constituted a "sex panic" in England in the 1790s. Divorce statistics in conservative arguments linked a supposed sexual crisis to national security, which depended on men, laws, and the nation at large to protect British women from sexual corruption.[7] As democratic pamphleteer and biographer John Corry cautioned, "female chastity is the true foundation of national honour; . . . licentiousness, should it become universal among us, would, like an earthquake, overturn the social edifice."[8] The threat of depravity, writ large in the behavior of *French* women during the revolution, had to be policed in English women. But these women's sexual lives were made increasingly public by criminal conversation trials collected in anthologies like *Trials for Adultery . . . at Doctor's Commons* (1779–1780), *The Cuckold's Chronicle: Being Select Trails for Adultery, Incest, Imbecility, Ravishment, &c.* (1798), and in the *London Times'* Law Reports. The *London Times* section, "Law Reports" featured extensive reporting on prominent trials, which helped to sell papers. *Town and Country Magazine* and *Bon Ton Magazine* also printed reports of the legal proceedings, often tailored into pornographic narrative, such as the trial of Major Archibald Hook, "for Adultery with his own Niece."[9] Women in these arguments and narratives are both sexually vulnerable and potentially voracious, a familiar paradox with new legal implications in a world where divorce and political revolution were realities.

Divorce reshaped the meaning of marriage in general and of the wife in particular. Under canon law, the first stage of divorce, a separation called *divortium a mensa et thoro* (divorce from bed and board) implicitly penalized women, as the parties without direct legal access to property. Civil divorce, restricted to those who could pursue the parliamentary *divortium a vinculo matrimonii,* still favored men legally and economically. Full divorces usually hinged on criminal conversation suits, in which the husband sued the wife's lover for damages from the "criminal conversation" that alienated the wife from the husband. The suits, known in newspapers and legal reports as "crim. con." cases, made public the cuckolding of the husband, but they also necessarily assigned a monetary value to the wife—damages over loss of use, as well as emotional and mental anguish. This legal remedy reversed the argument of contract as an agreement between husband and wife in favor of the older common law discourse of chattels and property. The rupture of marriages exposed the legal tenets that late-century courts were inclined to maintain: the principle of coverture, the economic rights of the husband, and the insubstantiality of women's civil identity.

The legal retreat from contract logic in marriage set the political stage for Inchbald's less powerful comic heroines in her divorce comedies, where the idea of a valid contract between husbands and wives proves to be a cheat. Staves, summarizing the legal shifts of the long eighteenth century, explains that "efforts to apply contract ideas to the marital relation in the mid-eighteenth century led to results which were found socially intolerable. Thus, by the end of the period the courts retreated from contract ideology in this field and reimposed . . . deeper patriarchal structures" (*Married* 4). These legal structures maintain the validity of contracts between a husband and trustees for the wife, but not those between husband and wife. Divorces in Inchbald's comedies trace out the retreat from marital contract logic and the renewed emphasis on the powers of the father to dispose of the daughter and the husband to possess the wife.

In light of these late-century social and political anxieties, stage comedy had some explaining (or at least reassessing) to do. Comedy historically had been the form that brought together social and psychic fantasies of community in the marriage plot, but Inchbald's comedies displace courtship and marriage with legal evidence and divorce. *The Provok'd Wife, The Relapse, The Beaux' Stratagem,* and *The Innocent Mistress* are only a few of the comedies that had raised the topic almost 100 years earlier.[10] Inchbald's thoughtful comic insights, however, indicate that the institution of marriage is not open to the heartier joking of the Restoration and the earlier eighteenth century. Divorce and domestic crisis gained fresh social and political urgency in the late 1780s and 1790s, though these topics were more likely to reach the stage in gothic dramas, such as Robert Jephson's popular *The Count of Narbonne* (1781), based on Walpole's *The Castle of Otranto.*[11] Some late-century comedies, including Sheridan's *A School for Scandal* (1777), Isaac Jackman's musical afterpiece *The Divorce* (1781), and George Coleman the Elder's *The Separate Maintenance* (1779), also mention divorce, but they tread lightly on its consequences. Coleman engages in the most substantial discussion of this group. He represents the separate maintenance of the title as a pitfall of the fashionable world but evades both divorce and separation by reconciling the couple in question. The play premiered August 31, 1779, but the script never made it into print, and its popularity waned significantly by the 1786–1787 season.[12] In contrast, Inchbald's substantive explorations of the social implications of divorce continued to appeal to audiences well into the nineteenth century. She probed dilemmas of the family and the community which, according to Paula Backscheider, "Ibsen and Shaw might have been reluctant to stage," yet she kept her audience.[13] Coleman, who later produced *I'll Tell You What,* wrote to her, "I know your whole thoughts are at present engrossed by divorces, separate maintenances, &c.," his teasing acknowledgment that she had found a way to write a comedy that could engage the public in these substantial questions.[14] Her comedies bring the emotional dimensions of bad marriages and divorce into public discourse and allow audiences to identify with the imperfect parties involved. The effect both demystifies divorce and argues that under English law, women tended to suffer harsher economic and social consequences than men did, regardless of fault.

Inchbald's handling of divorce brings a generic as well as a social problem to light. Wives in her plays must negotiate the terms of their civil and personal existence in the shadow of a marriage contract that is under stress or already ruptured. The situation provides a wealth of anxieties as fodder for comic events, but it puts great strains on the comic plot. The comic structure of marriage no longer holds against the comic events, which repeat anxieties about marriage in its compromised state. Inchbald builds her main plots around troubled and defunct marriages, with little comic relief from courting couples. She asked a fundamental generic question in these plays: What did it mean to write in the seemingly romantic, Greek New Comedy style and *begin* a play with a divorce? Inchbald's investigation of marriage itself drew attention to the provisional status of the comic structure in an era preoccupied with the failures of the law. The law failed to provide stability or definition for the human relationships and communities it purported to regulate. In this unsettled generic and historical landscape, comic events provide clues to help audience and playwright reconstruct a meaningful sense of community beyond the legal arrangements of marriage.

Inchbald wrote her most popular comedies between 1785 and 1797, a time of legal retreat from the more egalitarian court cases that had vested the power of contract in married women earlier in the century. In this climate, Inchbald saw divorce as a dangerous legal remedy to bad marriages and a threat to the futures of wives whose husbands sue for divorce. In Inchbald's socially cautious assessment, divorce undermines the one contract that women can make, which proves that marriage was not a just contract in the first place. Although the wives in the plays are not entirely blameless, male characters such as George Euston in *I'll Tell You What* and Robert Rambler in *Every One Has His Fault* compel divorces and alienate women from wealth, family, and children. These situations echo some of the most notorious divorce cases of the later eighteenth century. In *Grafton v. Grafton,* the duke of Grafton divorced the Duchess Anne for her adultery after he had separated from her and kept a public mistress. The duchess lost her title and access to her children. *Middleton v. Middleton* and *Cadogan v. Cadogan* similarly turn on the wife's sexual conduct, husband's adultery notwithstanding.[15]

Inchbald's stance on divorce challenges the validity of contract relations as a means of regulating and strengthening human relationships.[16] In the face of contract's failures, Inchbald proposes that affective bonds between individuals who are not equals could be the basis for an ethical liberal community. Her Catholicism colors her assessment of divorce, just as her own stormy marriage did, but her approach is not a simple conservatism. Her affective formula, which promises to recognize individuals *within* a failing or corrupt system, is an antidote to the instability of marriage law. *I'll Tell You What* gestures to this problem by basing its main comic events on the shifting female identity of "Lady Euston." Depending on the period, "Lady Euston" could be Harriet, George Euston's first wife, or the present Lady Euston, his second. In *Every One Has His Fault,* Lord Norland asks of the divorced Miss Woodburn, "What are you now? Neither a widow, a maid, nor a wife" (III.i, 56), and he uses her unstable legal position as an argument for his governance. In both cases, the words meant to define the place of women and secure their relationship to a legal system prove empty. Where legal subjectivity fails, Inchbald extends social subjectivity to her fallen and mistreated female characters. That the bulk of these plays were so often funny in the midst of their serious business is a testament both to Inchbald's talent and the cultural anxieties about women and marriage law that she taps. These plays press on the limits of the marriage plot to explore the nature of civil community and the place of women within it. While there are hopeful moments, her comic logic suffers the same fate as that of her fellow female playwrights. The comedies darken with time as she continues to probe the relationship between law, gender, and marriage in search of a more stable place in a community that recognizes women as members.

Unanswered Questions

Inchbald's first successful stage piece, the farce *The Mogul Tale,* launched her first full-length production, *I'll Tell You What,* a comic inquiry into divorce and familial alienation. Colman already had the play, either as *Polygamy* or as an unnamed manuscript submitted under the pseudonym "Mrs. Woodley," when *The Mogul Tale* appeared.[17] According to Boaden, Coleman had to be "reminded" that he admired Inchbald's *I'll Tell You What* after *The Mogul Tale* inspired him to give it a second reading.[18] The title and the content of the play present the audience with a risqué question: what will the adulterer, Major Cypress, tell about his illicit encounter with Harriet, the first Lady Euston? The implicit question is indecent, both in Slavoj Žižek's psychoanalytic formulation and in a more moralistic late-eighteenth-century vocabulary. In a late-eighteenth-century context, the answer would include the details that courts and magazines sought to prove adultery in criminal conversation suits. Evidentiary standards included hair powder in the carpet, moved furniture, or, a favorite of the magazines, a detailed confession from one of the guilt-ridden parties. For Žižek, "The basic indecency of the question consists in its drive to put into words what should be left unspoken, as in the well-known dialogue: 'What were you doing?' 'You know what!' 'Yes, but I want *you* to tell me!' Which is the instance in the other, in its addressee, that the question is aiming at? It aims at a point at which the answer is not possible, where the word is lacking, where the subject is exposed in his impotence. We can illustrate this by the question of the subject-child to his father: the stake of such a question is always to catch the other who embodies authority in his impotence, in his inability, in his lack" (Žižek, 179). There is no answer to its implicit question, "What?" Major Cypress tells nothing but the framework of a story. As in Žižek's assessment, Major Cypress's ambiguous answer "aims at a point at which the answer is not possible, where the word is lacking, where the subject is exposed in his impotence."

The "I'll tell you what" story of *I'll Tell You What* has taken place before the play opens. In the first scene, Mr. Euston returns from St. Kitts to find his nephew George Euston divorced and remarried, and the first Lady Euston (Harriet) also remarried. George had discovered Major Cypress stashed in a closet in Lady Euston's room one day, and the fateful tête-à-tête hastens the divorce. Major Cypress spends most of the play repeating this scene of discovery, which ended Harriet and George's marriage. Fascinated by his own verbal failure ("Faith it was an odd speech, and has been laughed at since in a thousand fashionable circles"), Major Cypress repeats the scene for Colonel Downright: "'Dear Sir George,' said I (half stifling a laugh, for by my soul I could not help it, though I pitied the poor devil too), 'Dear Sir George,' said I, 'I'll tell you what'—you will find *nobody* to blame in this affair—I protest my being in that closet was entirely owing to 'I'll tell you what'—In short to an—an *undescribable something*—There I made a full stop" (I.iii, 18). Major Cypress's exclamation on being caught in Lady Harriet's closet by her husband is a deliberate non-answer; his only gloss is "an *undescribable something.*" Colonel Downright replies skeptically, "But I hope you keep the key of the closet." The joke, which becomes the title of the play as well as the story of the divorce, is tellingly incomplete. Nevertheless, the scene, in which other men congratulate Major Cypress before Harriet's then-husband George, is clear about the value of female sexuality, the combative model of male sexuality it generates, and the relationship of divorce to patriarchal power. The public revelation of the closet scene leads to an exchange between men, through which Harriet is transferred from George to Cypress by divorce and remarriage, which George and Harriet's brother compel. The possibility of divorce lulls Major Cypress into the belief that he can exercise a joker's mastery over the system of marriage while he participates in it.

Inchbald builds the plot around the competition between men that such sexual values create. Compared to the "cuckolding comedies" of the Restoration, such as Betterton's *The Amorous Widow* (1670), Wycherley's *The Country Wife* (1673), Leanerd's *The Rambling Justice* (1678) and Ravenscroft's *The London Cuckholds* (1681), Inchbald has little patience with sexual rivalry and tends to represent it as childish. Cypress, who claims to have planted thorns in George's bosom, is corrected by Downright, who calls them "horns." Cypress likes the joke, taking pleasure in the witty play that makes him feel he is the victorious rake, but Downright wishes him joy "*Ironically.*" Cypress's mastery of George through this sexual transaction is neither self-evidently funny nor true mastery. Both parties lack the mythologized masculinity asserted in the legal principle of coverture. Coverture annuls the legal identity of the wife and absorbs her into the husband's identity. Neither man can successfully define Harriet in the terms that the law demands. The unnamed, the "I'll tell you what" is Inchbald's attempt to speak about the social and legal meaning of female sexuality. Harriet's meaning has come loose of the system that was designed to contain it, and her reentry into the sexual economy as a self-determining commodity poses a challenge to the system that is, it seems, hard to describe.

Major Cypress's desire to repeat the "I'll tell you what" story as a joke strikes his friend Colonel Downright as risky if not perverse behavior. Major Cypress jokes on, in spite of Downright's observations that Major Cypress may be an object of pity, or the butt of the joke, as Harriet's husband. Downright also points out the temporal confusion surrounding the phrase "my wife":

> *Major Cypress:* . . . —"Dear Major," cried my wife—
> *Colonel Downright:* Your wife?—Sir George's you mean.
> *Major Cypress:* Yes, Sir George's *then*—but my wife *now.*
> *Colonel Downright:* Ay, ay, and I most sincerely give you joy! (*Ironically*) (I.iii, 16)

The joke takes its form from the displacement of Harriet from "his wife" to "my wife," but the anxiety of the displacement refers to the unstable territory of female sexuality. The jokes of this comedy, coupled with its unusual closure (no marriages, one separation), challenge the conventional wisdom of the comic festival ending. Harriet poses a problem of meaning that remains a problem for the Major: "I'll tell you what" and the "*undescribable something*" remain blanks that the Major is unable or unwilling to fill. The "*undescribable something*" that put him in the closet was Harriet's desire, however short-lived it was. Major Cypress doesn't seem to understand that his victory over George, his favorite joke, is a function of Harriet's sexual agency.

Cypress repeats the "I'll tell you what" joke in an attempt to exert social mastery. He promises to tell Colonel Downright about his most recent intrigue ("—I'll tell you another time, on purpose to make you laugh; no other design whatever" (I.iii, 19), but other jokes grow out of the first, giving voice to social concerns about marriage and its limits. Harriet's brother compels her to marry Major Cypress, "convinced that nothing less than a soldier, should undertake the guard of a Lady's honor!" (I.ii, 9). Cypress repeats this point as a joke that Bloom, Harriet's maid, relates: "your Ladyship's honor would require the guard of a file of musketeers" (I.ii, 9). This joke brings to consciousness what Cypress should be blind to: he has helped to produce Harriet as an unstable value through his seduction, though he insists "she had been to this hour an example to wives, if I had not tempted her to stray" (I.iii, 15–16). His disregard for the marriage contract has already undermined his place in the community and his role as a husband, yet he tries to shore up his own contract by repeating the moment of crisis. The other irony here is historical; as a soldier, Major Cypress could easily be called away to duty, one of the leading factors in adultery according to the divorce and separation statistics (Stone, *Broken Unions* 6–10). His jokes turn on him as the repressed content of his attempt to locate Harriet's constancy in spite of her past and his present.

Cypress's jokes backfire several times in the play. The first instance is when Colonel Downright tries to repeat the "I'll tell you what" story to Mr. Anthony Euston, Harriet's former uncle in marriage, who does not yet know of the divorce and remarriages. Major Cypress, who cannot stop the naïve Colonel Downright's insinuations about the "good story of a—a—zounds 'I'll tell you what:' and 'an *undescribable something*—'" must then explain to Mr. Anthony the revolution of spouses. Mr. Anthony, who first assumes that George must be dead, eventually exclaims against "the depravity of the times" (II.iii, 39), though he remains certain of George and his principles. Major Cypress then confesses to the Colonel: "Rat me if I have not an appointment for to-morrow evening with Euston's *other* wife!—Is it not the most impudent thing of me—" (II.ii, 42). Cypress needs an audience, like Freud's tendentious joker, but the larger frame of the play casts this temporary authority as his weakness. His joke economy feeds on new indiscretions, which destroy the fabric of relationships in the play's community. Major Cypress's compulsion to make jokes and his one-upmanship leaves Colonel Downright, who had finally accepted the first joke, confused. He is unable to laugh at Cypress's *new* joke, the supposed seduction of the second Mrs. Euston, and leaves the scene "thinking on the happiness—of a married man" (II.ii, 43). Downright's reaction brings the taste of humor's saline base to the surface of the play. The Major's hysterical jokes, as much the object of his affairs as the sexual satisfaction itself, point to the tears in the social fabric that he has created. These moments of temporary mastery give the audience a sense of his lack of community with other characters and foreshadow his pending isolation.

In contrast to Major Cypress's destructive joking, Lady Euston's productive jokes preserve her marriage and stand out in a play in which women do very little plotting. Lady Euston argues to Sir George that "There is as severe a punishment to men of gallantry (as they call themselves) as sword or pistol; laugh at them—that is a ball which cannot miss; and yet kills only their vanity" (III.i, 49). Her elaborate jokes on her unwanted suitors keep George out of duels, alive and well for her sake; "Nay, Sir George, in a year or two, I may, perhaps, have no objection to your fighting a duel—but only three months married—I do wish to keep you a little longer" (III.i, 48). She explains to Sir George how she mocks her suitors to keep their advances from developing into seductions. She promised Lord Bloomly the requested lock of her hair, but asked "a few hairs from one of his eye-brows in return," which he refused on the grounds that "he valued that little brown arch more than the lock he had been begging for" (III.i, 50). Lady Euston then told this story as a joke in fashionable company to humiliate the lord and keep him from further advances. Her interaction with Lord Bandy explores the power struggles of fashionable lovemaking in detail:

> "You are the most beautiful woman I ever saw," said Lord *Bandy;* "and your Lordship is positively the most lovely of mankind"—"What eyes," cried he; "What hair," cried I; "what lips," continued he; "what teeth," added I; "what a hand and arm," said he; "and what a *leg* and *foot,*" said I—"Your Ladyship is jesting," was his Lordship's last reply; and he has never since even paid me one compliment. Prudes censure my conduct—I am too free—while their favorite, Lady Strenuous, in another corner of the ball room, cries to *her* admirer—"Desist, my Lord, or my dear Sir Charles shall know that you dare thus to wound my ears with your licentious passion—if you ever presume to breath it again, I will acquaint him with it—depend on it I will. (*Sighs and languishes*) Oh! you have destroyed my peace of mind for ever." (III.i, 50–51)

Through her joking, Lady Euston not only makes an object of Lord Bandy by talking about his body, but she also mimics in an Irigarayan sense as someone who can "assume the feminine role deliberately. Which means already to convert a form of subordination into an affirmation and thus to begin to thwart it" (Irigaray 76). Her mimicry of gender roles exposes the master/slave struggle of flattery, then trumps the struggle by translating it into *her* joke. By refusing to play the woman in this game, she averts the potential confrontations between suitor and husband that could endanger her beloved and that could make her the object of erotic transactions.

While the comic plot untangles relationships between married people and the social order they inhabit, a serious subplot details the dire circumstances of Charles Euston's family. After Charles married a poor woman against his father's wishes, Mr. Anthony Euston disinherited his son and forced him and his family into a life of poverty. Anthony later encounters his daughter-in-law Mrs. Euston as a stranger who is about to prostitute herself to provide for her hungry children. He is already prepared to save her from poverty and prostitution when he discovers her identity and claims her as a daughter. Colonel Downwright then reunites father and son by intimating that Sir Anthony has taken advantage of Mrs. Euston; Charles challenges the "vile purchaser" of his wife's honor to a duel, only to discover his father and her savior. As Charles kneels, Mr. Anthony Euston declares "as your father, you might pursue your purpose—But, as your wife's friend and preserver, still kneel to me; and receive her, virtuous, from my hands" (V.ii, 76). The mistaken identities and the relationships beyond blood ties suggest that compassion can create community where conventional familial and legal arrangements (which can demand an impossible obedience) have failed. Like the comic plot, the sentimental plot creates relationships of accountability and community beyond the law and the family.

Inchbald's willingness to lodge a critique of marriage puts her in company with her friend William Godwin as well as other liberals who found the institution a corrupt form of contract. Where Godwin sees marriage's failure as a rejection of rational agreement, Inchbald imagines the problem as a failure of feeling. Inchbald maintains throughout the play that marriage is only a legal echo of human feeling, and as such, it succeeds only when people honor it. In her defense of stage romance, she asserted "there is too *little,* not too *much* of that tender and delicate attachment . . . it would, next to religious principles, be the best possible preservative against those frequent violations of the marriage vow, which are the disgrace of an enlightened age, and a Christian nation."[19] Her sentiment contrasts the instability of contractual marriage vows with the antidote of affection, which theater can foster through the pedagogy of its plays. Elizabeth Farren, who played the destitute Mrs. Charles Euston, spoke Coleman's epilogue. She appealed to the audience to allow a woman playwright to instruct them through her heartfelt representation of the "Critical Minute," the crisis of the impoverished wife faced with wrenching poverty or prostitution:

> Alas, what a Minute! Ah! What can be done?
> All Means must be tried, and our Drama shews one.
> Let Papa in that Minute, that so frowns upon her,
> Redeem the vile Debts that encumber her Honour!
> Let Papa in *that* minute that teems with undoing
> Step in like my father, and marr a Lord's wooing. (*Plays,* vol. I)

The father's entrance is less the triumph of the patriarch than the reinvention of paternal authority. Anthony Euston earns emotional credibility when he rescues Mrs. Euston; he discovers her legal relation to him after the fact. The appeal to the fathers in the audience ("Let Papa") is thus a call to affection and compassion rather than power. The sentiment, however, echoes the increasing paternalism of the courts that was eroding the precedents for married women's separate property.

The play ends with one last repetition of the title joke through a reenactment of the original closet scene that shames the philandering Major. Harriet intercepts what seems to be a letter from Lady Euston to Major Cypress, which turns out to be another of her jokes. When she summons Sir George to show him the letter, Major Cypress comes home unexpectedly and George must hide in the same closet that Cypress had used. Cypress, in a foul mood after Lady Euston has humiliated him at the masquerade, resolves to torment Lady Harriet and requests French horns while she naps. George then pops out of the closet, repeating Major Cypress's stumbling excuse, only to be interrupted by Bloom, who announces that "The horns are ready, Sir—would you choose to have them?" (V.iii, 85). After this tightly constructed visual and verbal joke, Cypress and Harriet resolve to end a relationship "formed on vice."

The closing excises Cypress from the community with his own joke, while Lady Harriet looks forward to a life of reform. The newly separated Harriet wonders how she can "retrieve my innocence, my honour, forever lost!" but Mr. Anthony assures her that she still has "that in-born virtue which *never perishes*—which never leaves us but to return" (V.iii, 87–88). This model of an individual who is defined by moral interiority rather than the legal consequences of her actions is particularly important for Harriet, who could be exiled for her sexual choices. Mr. Euston completes Mr. Anthony's liberal but morally demanding model of identity with his appeal to the more gentle claims of community: "we are all *relations,* you know—the whole company are related to one another.—Though it is in an odd kind of jumbled way—I wish some learned gentleman, of the law, would tell us *what* relations we all are—and what relation the child of a first husband is to his mother's second husband, while his own father is living. . . . [F]or fear the gentlemen of the long robe shou'd not be able to find out the present company's *affinity,* let us apply to the *kindred ties* of each others passions, weaknesses, and imperfections; and, thereupon, agree to part, this evening, not only *near relations* but *good friends*" (V.iii, 88). The possibility of a world of "*kindred ties*" not dependent on blood or legal relation but on affinity is Inchbald's powerful final gesture to relationships beyond the legal definition of the family. By subordinating the claims of the law to the bonds of affection, Inchbald holds open the possibility that Harriet could still exist as a moral being and as a recognizable member of a community of relations *and* friends. The true kindred tie is beyond the law. Mr. Anthony and Mr. Euston displace the generic pull of the marriage ending in favor of a focus on an irregular but inclusive community that is more than the sum of good and bad sexual choices. The jokes of *I'll Tell You What* and its unconventional ending present hopeful comic vision of honest social relations, which include a place for Harriet in the community.

Harmony and Dissonance

In the years between 1786 and 1793, Inchbald brought out four translations for the stage and her highly successful novel *A Simple Story.* The plays and the novel allowed her to investigate father-daughter relationships as the second tier of patriarchal authority that underwrites marriage. The persistence of paternal power in the erotic and social relationships of *A Simple Story* and the near-incestuous *The Child of Nature* (1788) shadows the discussion of marriage in *Every One Has His Fault,* a play so popular that Boaden declined to summarize it in his *Memoirs* "since every body has seen it, or read it" (310).[20] The play appeared in 12 print editions before 1805, 7 of which appeared in 1793. Between the opening on January 29, 1793, and April 16, 1793, Covent Garden presented the play 31 times, with an additional 4 performances later in the year. The play was also popular in the United States in print and on the stage.[21]

The play begins with a discussion of sexual differences in a prologue that mentions Wollstonecraft's *A Vindication of the Rights of Woman,* printed a full year earlier. Her hostile relationship with Wollstonecraft, which did not preclude her friendship with William Godwin, likely grew out of their different sexual mores.[22] The prologue, written by the Reverend Robert Nares, reflects that hostility as well as an understanding of the justice of Wollstonecraft's argument. The opening joke of the prologue about the author's great fault ("A fault, in modern Authors not uncommon, / It is—now don't be angry—He's—a *woman*") draws attention to the still-current question of the gender of authorship. Wollstonecraft's sustained argument for the intellectual equality of men and women squares with Inchbald's insights in the comedies as well as *A Simple Story,* though she distinguishes sharply between gender roles. Like Aphra Behn, Inchbald was uncomfortable with the implication that equality might mean the erasure of difference. The prologue moderately advocates that men should not force women into ignorance and fear, "producing only children, pies, and tarts," but it stops short of the claim that women can "do everything as well as Men." Gender equality taken too far leads to the paranoid specter of Amazonian women in combat, an uncannily familiar trope for the dangers of an equality that undermines the "natural" claims of sex. In spite of its moderate plea not to force literate and intelligent women "back . . . [w]ithin the pale of ignorance and fear," and its protest against confining women "entirely to domestic arts," the prologue keeps its distance from Wollstonecraft on egalitarian marriage:

> I grant, as all my City friends will say,
> That Men should rule, and Women should obey;
> That nothing binds the marriage contract faster,
> Than our—a "Zounds, Madam, I'm your lord and Master."

William Farren, who played Lord Norland, the severe patriarch of the play, delivered the prologue. The baldness of the "lord and Master" claim filters through this character, but it also adds a sense of resignation that weighs on the play's consideration of contract and justice. The stern fathers of Inchbald's comedies and novels cannot be wished away. They also serve as guarantors of a social order under grave challenge in the 1790s. The prologue questions whether comedy, the form that both advocates and refines the terms of marriage, can continue to speak to English audiences in this troubled *fin de siècle.* Nares's prologue turns to comedy as a fading muse whose "lovers, you well know, are few and cold./'Tis time then freely to enlarge the plan/ And let all those write Comedies—that can." His appeal to make more comedies and to "enlarge the plan" implies that a revision of the form, such as Inchbald provides, may be necessary to its continued success. The stakes of this theoretical question extend beyond Goldsmith's distinction between laughing and crying comedy to the possibility of meaningful comic pedagogy in the marriage stories it has to tell. In this case, the content of the comedy takes us back to the abuse of overstern power, the function of divorce, and a story about marriage without the comic guarantee of an exuberant ending.

Inchbald opens *Every One Has His Fault* in a fallen world, where the bachelor Solus laments his single state to the harried husband Mr. Placid. Solus longs for the comic plot ("Oh! I wish a wife and half-a-score children would now start up around me") and admits that he has fathered children, but he has neither maintained them nor been able to come to terms with marriage. "But as it is, in my present state, there is not a person in the world

I care a straw for; and the world is pretty even with me, for I don't believe there is a creature in it who cares a straw for me" (I.i, 2). Inchbald focuses the opening on his lost opportunity for relationships with children and with a wife, but she balances his longing with the cautionary example of Mr. Placid, who fears his wife. She navigates throughout the play between these evils, the social dissolution she fears in a society that rejects marriage and the failure of meaningful and intimate relationships within it.

Every One Has His Fault, like *I'll Tell You What,* has a comic main plot and a sentimental subplot. In the main plot, Sir Robert Ramble has compelled Miss Woodburn to divorce him under Scottish law simply because he has grown tired of married life. Miss Woodburn still loves Sir Robert and wants him to be able to keep her property to relieve him of his gambling debts, though she is now living under the stern guardianship of Lord Norland. Lord Norland disregards her feelings for her ex-husband and wants her to remarry according to his wishes, without the right to know the groom. Miss Woodburn agrees, on the sacrificial condition that she can give her portion back to Sir Robert. The Placids, a couple governed by the domineering Mrs. Placid, balance Inchbald's main plot with a farcical critique of marriages based on faulty premises. Harmony, a single character who spends all his time trying to repair broken relationships, holds the plot together. Contemporary reviewers hailed Harmony as a type "new to the stage" and an "original" character exemplifying simple good will.[23] He is both a matchmaker and a social diplomat on a mission to create communities, though he must lie to do his work. The relationships he orchestrates under false pretenses reveal the fragile nature of social communities and comic closure.

The more serious plot of *Every One Has His Fault* mirrors the sentimental plot of *I'll Tell You What.* Lord Norland cut off his daughter, Lady Eleanor, after she married against his wishes. Her family is destitute, and her husband Mr. Irwin steals Lord Norland's wallet in a fit of desperation to provide for them. Lord Norland strikes out to prosecute fully of the law, even after Irwin returns the wallet, while Edward, Lord Norland's young charge, puzzles over the superiority of justice to mercy. Edward is in fact the son whom the Irwins left behind when they went to the American colonies to seek their fortunes. Lord Norland eventually forces the boy to choose between himself as grandfather guardian and his mother in act five, but the entire family is reconciled at the end of the play when Harmony rouses Norland to feeling by making him believe that Irwin has committed suicide. Harmony unites the comic and the sentimental plots to make them speak to the same problem; the ties of marriage and family must be ties maintained with love and commitment, or they will destroy communities.

The high farce comes from the Placids who, in opposition to their name, are in constant conflict. Their characterization draws on a long legacy of feuding couples, including the Oakleys in Colman's *The Jealous Wife* and Inchbald's Lord and Lady Tremor in *Such Things Are,* though the fault in this couple is all on Mrs. Placid's side. Mrs. Placid torments Mr. Placid for being inclined to help the destitute Irwin family, their former neighbors in America. Her power over him extends to an absurd degree. In act I, she ruins his appetite by her cruelty to the Irwins, then she demands that it return:

> *Servant:* Dinner is on table.
> *Placid:* Ah! I am not hungry now.
> *Mrs. Placid:* What do you mean by that, Mr. Placid? I insist on your being hungry.
> *Placid:* Oh yes! I have a very excellent appetite. I shall eat prodigiously. (I.i, 8–9)

The physical immediacy of her control parodies the ideals of shared feeling in the ideal companionate marriage. Mrs. Placid torments the submissive Mr. Placid into contemplating Sir Robert Ramble's solutions, separate maintenance and divorce. Once Mr. Placid realizes that Sir Robert has secured a divorce under Scottish law, he says wistfully, "I have no such prospect. Mrs. Placid is faithful, and I was married in England" (II.i, 24). In contrast to Sir Robert, who has made a technical and unethical provision for divorce by marrying in Scotland, Placid is trapped by English law in a marriage that divorces feeling from legal tie. Inchbald's appeal in both cases is to the preeminence of feeling and its relationship to conscience, through which, like Milton, she hopes to avoid binding couples to lives of deceit and misery in unhappy marriages.

Sir Robert Ramble praises the Scottish laws that have made possible his divorce from Miss Woodburn. As Sir Robert puts it, "Blessed, blessed country! that will bind young people together before the years of discretion—and, as soon as they have discretion to repent, will unbind them again!" (II.i, 21). Scotland is the place to evade English marriage law with a hasty trip to Gretna Green for a marriage with provisions for divorce, in which a wife or husband can sue over infidelity. The potentially egalitarian provisions of Scottish law, however, do not change the fact that Sir Robert, not Lady Ramble, controls the legal discourse in this relationship. Lord Norland, who is intent on asserting his authority over Miss Woodburn, exemplifies Inchbald's concerns about the abuses of marriage law that penalize women. When Miss Woodburn discovers that Mr. Harmony is to be her mystery husband, she explains to Norland that Mr. Harmony must be "sensible he would not be the man I should choose." While Miss Woodburn respects Harmony, he is secretly helping her to convey the title of her estates to Sir Robert. Norland leaves no allowance for Miss Woodburn's opinion and explodes:

Lord Norland: And where is the woman who marries the man she would choose? You are reversing the order of society; men, only, have the right of choice in marriage. Were women permitted theirs, we should have handsome beggars allied to our noblest families, and no such object in our whole island as an old maid.

Miss Woodburn: But being denied that choice, why forbid to remain as I am?

Lord Norland: What are you now? Neither a widow, a maid, nor a wife. If I could fix a term to your present state, I should not be thus anxious to place you in another. (III.i, 56)

The dialogue ventures into dangerous territory under the cloak of comedy. Lord Norland exposes the fallacy of a woman's freedom of choice in marriage when under the care of a stern guardian or father. Their conversation, which is much more thoughtful than similar encounters in Behn or Centlivre, acknowledges Norland's real social power while it exposes its abuse. Norland's need to place Miss Woodburn, to "fix a term to your present state," reveals the foundations of his identity in hers. He is anxious to place her because both of the women supposedly under his control, his daughter and guardian, have compromised his authority as patriarch and guardian. He is uncomfortable with Miss Woodburn's liminal state as neither widow, maid, nor wife, just as the law is. Miss Woodburn is similarly between Scottish and English marriage law as an English wife with a Scottish divorce; she is fully within neither system.

According to Lord Norland, masculine prerogative ("men, only, have the right of choice in marriage") needs no moral justification. In comedy, where playwrights create plots that honor the desires of nubile female characters, Lord Norland's rigor is suspicious, but his authority finds support in the law and cannot be wished away. Lord Norland tries to explain to his grandson Edward that his rigor is rooted in the law and so is justice itself. Norland argues that he will be just to his attacker (Irwin, his son-in-law) but that he has no obligation to be merciful. Edward gently dismantles Norland's logic by questioning the possibility of justice independent of social considerations:

Lord Norland: I will be just.

Edward: And that is being merciful, is it not, my Lord?

Lord Norland: Not always.

Edward: I thought it had been.—It is not *just* to be unmerciful, is it?

Lord Norland: Certainly not.

Edward: Then it must be *just,* to have mercy.

Lord Norland: You draw a false conclusion. Great as is the virtue of *mercy, justice* is greater still. *Justice* holds its place among those cardinal virtues which include all the lesser—(IV.i, 77)

Young Edward elaborates a Jacobin liberalism in response to his austere grandfather's model of justice that threatens both familial and, by analogy, national community. The balance of mercy against justice in this dialogue allies Inchbald's liberal politics with Godwin's. Godwin shared Inchbald's concern that positive law provides an incomplete model of civil society by sacrificing true understanding to parroting obedience.[24] As Godwin details in *Caleb Williams,* a legalistic model of justice is prone to corruption and abuse. Inchbald's interest in the affective, however, departs from Godwin's concern with duty and rationality. Her moral argument turns from law to intimate relationships and, here, to the example of the merciful child. She reinvests the roles of wife, daughter, father, and husband with affective authority that will sustain relationships when the law and abstract justice threaten to erase identity and break the bonds of communities.

Harmony, who lies to do good, offers the only viable challenge to Norland's control over the terms of justice and the law. Harmony's function is opposite to Marplot's in *The Busy Body,* although like Marplot, he is not personally concerned in the romantic plot. While Marplot kept lovers apart long enough to produce an intrigue plot, Harmony wants to unite lovers, married couples, and the community in general against the centripetal force of social alienation. In strictly narrative terms, his actions hurtle toward closure, but his function within the genre is more complex. He combats the social forces of divorce and possessive individualism that pose threats to the Greek New Comedy and the model of community it creates. Once the marriage ending is subject to question (through either divorce or individual rejection of marriage), the comic plot that depends on marriage for its conclusion loses force. Harmony's manipulations keep marriages together, but his efforts are transparent frauds, which also call the ending into question. Harmony lies about the hidden good will of estranged lovers, hostile in-laws, and grumpy spouses, claiming instead that they compliment their adversaries behind their backs and reconciling the parties under false pretenses. His happy ending is a lie. The open deception of Inchbald's closure, Wildean in its cynicism, shifts the register of the comic from a social fantasy of affective community to conscious machination in a fallen world. Harmony's tag line, "but provisions are so scarce," casts his interest in helping others in terms of financial distress. He operates in an economy of emotional scarcity rather than plenty, where he metes out love and kindness to the less fortunate. While his projects are only occasionally fiscal, Sir Robert's and Irwin's situations prove that money (and the power behind it) is the overwhelming force in the structure of social relations.

Warm-hearted Harmony is moved to greet and shake hands with strangers out of his "unbounded affection for all my fellow creatures" (I.i, 9). He wistfully explains to Miss Spinster his vision of a connected community:

"I sincerely lament that human beings should be such strangers to one another as we are. We live in the same street, without knowing one another's necessities; and oftentimes meet and part from each other at church, at coffee-houses, play-houses, and all public places, without ever speaking a single word, or nodding 'Goodbye!' though 'tis a hundred chances to ten we never see one another again" (I.i, 10). When he calls for all the day's newspapers, however, in act II, the porter would have brought him three dozen papers that, at the time of the play's first run, were brimming with criminal conversation suits and divorce proceedings. These pieces of domestic theater became mainstays for papers like the *London Times* and magazines like the *Bon Ton.* Earlier, in Coleman's 1779 *The Separate Maintenance,* Lord and Lady Oldcastle learn of their daughter's alleged divorce suit in the newspapers, and Snake in *The School for Scandal* (1777) lauds Mrs. Clacket's "work" in making a divorce that supplied "a Tête á Tête in the *Town and Country Magazine*" (act I). The print media reports thrived on cases with detail and conflict, such as the case of Campbell v. Hook provided. *The Cuckold's Chronicle,* an anthology of the most famous and salacious crim. con. suits of the day, reprinted parts of Hook's trial from the *Bon Ton* magazine. The wronged husband, Mr. Campbell, claimed that Major Hook had debauched his own niece Harriet with "books to inflame her passions, prints most indecent to be exhibited by any body to any body." When he raved that she was "a wh——e, a d——d wh——e, the worst of wh——es, she replied, she became a wh——e through his means . . . that he who ought to have been her father and her protector, had been the ruin of her and her family."[25] In Hook's version of the events, he collected Harriet from a seaside resort and traveled with her to Edinburgh to conduct business. The case merited an illustration in the *Bon Ton,* "The Marrow Bone Uncle & the deluded Niece," which showed the uncle Hook cutting a portion of a phallic marrow bone to share with the niece.[26] The cartoon depicts the uncle tempting his niece to sexual misconduct through her appetites, but it also provides the readers with the object of their desires: an illustration of the acts that occasioned these divorces. The cartoon niece presents her ankle and calf in the foreground as she reaches for the representational "marrow bone."

Newspapers and magazines, through which the dissolution of marriages became public, point to the false boundary between public and private exchanges. Juicy news stories sold newspapers by making private affairs public. The content of crim. con. trials made clear that the legal culture was prepared to put a price on sex, particularly on female sexuality, and thus bring it fully into a public and commercial sphere. The logic of civil divorce furthered the abstraction of human feeling into cash penalties by dividing wealth in the divorce according to a sense of damages, which often left women in uncharted territory. Inchbald's observation that divorces tended to benefit philandering husbands like Sir Robert and to penalize the women who lose their place and their reputation in the process shaped her conservatism. Harmony orchestrates happy endings in this world where they do not come of their own accord and where, counter to comic fantasy, women have difficulty managing plots that give them viable places in the community.

The play's conclusion is a shaky peace. Sir Robert confesses his love for Miss Woodburn privately and publicly; the second confession returns to the legal tradition of *contract de praesenti,* which, as Behn and Centlivre understood, vested agency in the man *and* woman as makers of the marriage contract. Sir Robert declares himself "ready to take another [marriage] oath; and another after that, and another after that—And, Oh, my dear Maria, be propitious to my vows . . ." (IV.i, 85). Miss Woodburn refuses him in a brief assertion of her right of refusal but then runs to him in the last act when Harmony intimates that Sir Robert has been wounded in a duel. The reaffirmed mutuality of their promise marks the beginning of their reconciliation, in which the desires of both parties have a place. Sir Robert's plea, "—I cannot live without you.—Receive your penitent husband, thus humbly acknowledging his faults—" confirms Solus in his desire for a wife. He decides to "procure a special license, and marry the first woman I meet" (IV.ii, 86). Like the characters in Jane Austen's satiric *The Visit,* Solus's desire to marry is without a specific object; the wedding comes as a function of comic closure rather than the culmination of a romance plot. Harmony's testimony of Mrs. Placid's loving concern also persuades Mr. Placid to be happy with his termagant wife. With the help of two bottles of wine, Mr. Placid publicly declares, "I will henceforth be master," but his attitude softens when his wife cries, "I never saw it before, and it has made me sober in an instant" (V.iii, 107). Harmony's last dramatic story (another lie, of course) about Irwin's death softens all hearts and reconciles Lord Norland to his estranged son-in-law and daughter, who form a final tableau before the curtain.[27]

Harmony gets the last, dark laugh when he almost confesses his compulsive lying: " . . . it weighs so heavy on my conscience, I would confess what it is, but that you might hereafter call my veracity in question" (V.iii, 113). The more cynical implication of this ending is that social harmony, if not social justice, cannot be achieved naturally. Harmony's lying and the rapid succession of marriages and reconciliations foreground the artificiality of the ending. Sir Robert declares that "we should never have known half how well we all love one another, if you had not told us," innocent of his irony (V.iii, 113). Mr. Solus, who bounds in wearing all white clothes from his marriage, adds to the absurdist spirit of an ending that must patch up the questions about the law, justice, and marriage that the play's events have raised. He declares: "I cannot say she was exactly my choice. However, she is my wife now; and that is a name so endearing, I think I love her better since the ceremony has been performed" (V.iii, 108). Through Harmony's method, Inchbald proposes that marriages depend on deceptions. To reach her revised comic closure, the reconfirmed marriage, couples must trick themselves rather than their guardians as they stumble toward endings that preserve their marriages and the communities that anchor them. Harmony's desire to change a world of strangers and enemies into a community of friends succeeds, but to echo *I'll Tell You What,* a relationship founded on vice never can last. Generically and socially, the ending of *Every One Has His Fault* is provisional, preserving the form of the comic plot in the hope of reviving its content.

Holding on to the Past

Most of Inchbald's growing fame in the 1790s came from her two novels *A Simple Story* (1791) and *Nature and Art* (1796), but she continued to have stage success with translations and original plays. In addition to *Every One Has His Fault* (1793), Inchbald wrote *Cross Partners* (1792), *The Wedding Day* (1794), and the unperformed *The Massacre* (1792), her response to the Reign of Terror. Her other original plays, farces, and translations continued to hold the stages of Covent Garden and the Haymarket. Drury Lane, though not a venue for her new plays, staged revivals of *The Child of Nature* and *The Wedding Day.* Her last successful original play, *Wives as They Were, and Maids as They Are,* extends the concerns of *A Simple Story,* but this time, genre demands a happier ending. As in *A Simple Story,* the plot features a problematic father and a controlling husband, both of whom demand submission from young women.

The entangled plot and subplot raise questions about which is the focus.[28] Inchbald confessed in her *Remarks for the British Theater* that "the first act promises a genuine comedy" but that the play fails to deliver on the promise, veering instead between the burlesque, the serious, the pathetic, and the refined comic. The play splits its attention between the legal trials of a daughter, Miss Dorrillon, and the sexual trials of a wife, Lady Priory. Miss Dorrillon, modeled after the charming but doomed Miss Milner, gambles and lives extravagantly, though she avoids sexual improprieties of any sort. Her father Sir William left her in the care of Mr. Norberry and his sister while he pursued business abroad. As the play opens, he has returned, posing as Mr. Mandred in order to glimpse the true character of his daughter, in whom he is very disappointed. Inchbald imports gothic anxieties about fathers and their relationship to daughters into her comic plot through his name, both the "dreaded man" and an echo of the obsessive Manfred in *The Castle of Otranto.* Mandred tries to compel Miss Dorrillon's dutiful obedience to him as male authority incarnate and is frustrated by her refusal to respond. When she is dunned for her gambling debts, Sir William exerts his fatherly right to dispose of the daughter, first to jail and then to Sir George in marriage, which she finally accepts with daughterly submission. As plot summary, Miss Dorrillon's story is hardly comic. Inchbald confines her agency as a comic heroine to a few comic events, in which she negotiates in the language of the law. Inchbald replaces generic tricks, happy accidents, and bumbling guardians with a tough-minded realism about domestic authority and the limits of female agency.

Lord and Lady Priory are at the center of the play's other plot. Lord Priory has kept Lady Priory under his complete control, but like Wycherley's Pinchwife, he finds he must eventually introduce her to a larger community at Mr. Norberry's home. Lady Priory, who has no clear counterpart in *A Simple Story,* exemplifies good wifely behavior under duress. Lord Priory, who seems more interested in testing her than in preserving her safety, deliberately exposes her to sexual danger in the form of the rake Bronzley. Both Lord Priory and Sir William crave submission, and both get it, though in an unsettling comic closure that shows the strain of comic events on the ideal of the companionate marriage.[29]

The psychologically dense material of this play leads Inchbald to use exaggeration, farce, and unlikely situations in order to discuss divorce, infidelity, and paternal authority in a post-revolutionary era. In Katherine Rogers's assessment, "no dramatist writing for the conventional theater of 1797 could deal realistically with such actual social problems" ("Britain's First" 287). Inchbald does, however, with this very serious and unusual comedy, which, according to the *Critical Review* of 1797, is "rather sentimental than lively" and "has more moral than wit."[30] Somewhat unfairly, Inchbald critiqued her play in the third person in her *Remarks for the British Theatre:* "in the dearth of true comic invention, she has had recourse at the end of her second act, to farce . . . and wanting humour to proceed in the beaten track of burlesque, she then essays successfully, the serious, the pathetic, and the refined comic; failing by turns in them all, though by turns producing chance effect."[31] Put more charitably, Inchbald questions her comic impulses and reimagines stock comic situations as ethical dilemmas. Relationships that might otherwise be vehicles for comic events have a psychological depth more common in tragedies. Her serious approach to comic form in *Wives as They Were* makes impossible the disinterestedness that Susan Purdie, working from Bergson, Hobbes, and Freud, calls comedy's hallmark, but it opens up the comic structure itself to social critique (116). The direct look at patriarchs and their power makes it difficult to locate the comic as the play slips between farce, satire, and sentimental reform. Perhaps the final joke of the play is that there is no joke that can moderate the power of husbands and fathers.

The play opens with two suspicious policy statements by the managing patriarchs. When Mr. Norberry accuses Sir William of treating women with excessive rigor, Sir William replies, "True—for what I see so near perfection as woman, I want to see perfect. *We,* Mr. Norberry, can never be perfect; but surely women, women, might easily be made angels!" (I.i, 3). Nevertheless, to make angels, Sir William instills the fear of God. Sir William's temper explodes when his daughter disappoints him. Stage directions often indicate that he delivers his lines to her *"with violence,"* and he vows "I will instantly teach you how to respect *me . . ."* when Miss Dorrillon begins to tease him for his "austere looks" (III.i, 50). His outburst leads Lord Priory to exclaim, "How strange, that a man can't command his temper" (III.i, 51), a joke that rebounds on Lord Priory, who "used to be rather violent in [his] temper" according to the more objective Mr. Norberry (I.i, 6). Lord Priory, the dominating husband, explains that his violent temper leads his wife to obey "without hesitation—no liberty for contention, tears, or repining" (I.i, 6). His domestic management includes mandatory rising at five o'clock A.M., if not earlier, to ensure an early bedtime and to keep Lady Priory from public entertainments. If his wife does not rise on time, he locks her in the room for the whole day, at which point, "for not having seen a single soul, she is rejoiced even to see *me*" (I.i, 8). Lord Priory's and Sir William's authority depends on the threat of violence, a situation that usually speaks to comic ineptitude in the lexicon of stage comedy; here, it occupies a more ambiguous space. Their anger marks comic events like jokes in their explosive truth telling, but the jokes are not necessarily funny. They ride the line between comic expression and realism, calling on the audience to provide the definitive answer. That they are so difficult to assess is an indication of their psychological complexity and their potentially subversive function in a play uneasy with patriarchal power, yet anxious about the cost of revolution.

Sir William expects an acknowledgment of his authority generally as a man rather than specifically as Miss Dorrillon's father. He opines that his daughter has grown disrespectful, but as Mr. Norberry points out, Sir William has hidden his identity. Sir William's overwhelming need for acknowledgment through a show of obedience keeps him from seeing Miss Dorrillon's basic goodness in spite of her failings. She righteously refuses her suitor Sir George's financial help: "What part of my conduct, sir, has made you dare to suppose I would extricate myself from the difficulties that surround me, by the influence I hold over the weakness of a lover," a principled stand that her friend Lady Raffle abandons when confronted with similar gambling debts (I.i, 20). Sir William's search for some "proof of discretion" from her leads him to ignore her affection for him. Inchbald laces Miss Dorrillon's behavior to Sir William with flirtatious overtures. She explains to him in act one, "Sometimes indeed I have traced a spark of kindness, and have gently tried to blow it to a little flame of friendship; when, with one hasty puff I have put it out" (I.i, 17), an echo of the incestuous strain in *A Simple Story* and *Matilda.* Even Bronzely can report that her affection for her father, confessed in private, "is totally unconnected with any interested views. . . . I believe she loves her father sincerely" (III.i, 47). Sir William's masquerade has forced her into a relationship with the father as "the law" rather than with the absent object of affection, her father Sir William. Sir William refuses her proofs of love and instead demands that Miss Dorrillon confirm her relationship to patriarchal authority through obedience alone.

When pressed, Lord Priory and Sir William both have difficulty justifying their austere demands for obedience from the women in their lives. Lord Priory appeals to the model of the ancients, in which a husband "seldom gave them liberty to do wrong" (I.i, 5). His paranoid need to secure his authority and her chastity justifies what the moderate Norberry calls cruelty. Priory explains, "Did you ever observe, that seldom a breach of fidelity in a wife is exposed, where the unfortunate husband is not said to be 'the best creature in the world! Poor man, so good-natured—Doatingly fond of his wife!—Indulged her in everything!—How cruel in her to serve him so!' Now, if I am served *so,* it shall not be for my good-nature" (I.i, 6). He consoles himself after he has agreed to let the rakish Bronzely "test" his wife: "I have no command over my temper.—However, if a man cannot govern himself, yet he will never make any very despicable figure, as long as he knows how to govern his wife" (IV.iii, 63). The moral pretense for his control over Lady Priory evaporates in this admission, in which he declares both his self-interest and his instability.

While Lord Priory struggles to maintain his authority through traditional conjugal right, Miss Dorrillon, with the energy and irreverence of *A Simple Story*'s Miss Milner, seizes on the contractual dimension of marriage law in her comic discussion of contract and desire. As a desirable woman pursued by many men, she fits the type of the nubile comic heroine who manipulates the plot by her wit. When Sir William seems to have taken Sir George's interest in her to heart, Miss Dorrillon rebuts with a comic performance that pits passion against the law as Ovid meets Blackstone:

> *Miss Dorrillon:* . . . Have you, with all that solemn wisdom of which you are master, studied Ovid, as our great lawyers study Blackstone? If you have—shew cause—why plantiff has a right to defendant's heart.
>
> *Sir William:* A man of fortune, of family, and of character, ought at least to be treated with respect, and with honour.
>
> *Miss Dorrillon:* You mean to say, "That if *A* is beloved by *B,* why should not *A* be constrained to return *B*'s love?" Councellor for defendant—"Because, moreover, and besides *B* who has a claim on defendant's heart, there are also *C, D, E, F,* and *G;* all of whom put in their separate claims—and

> what, in this case, can poor *A* do? She is willing to part and divide her love, share and share alike; but *B* will have all or none: so poor *A* must remain *A* by herself *A*." (II.i, 27)

Miss Dorrillon's interpretation of the law, which designates suitors as alphabetical placeholders, shows that marriage contracts are not like other contracts. As "*A*," she imagines competing claims which might lead her into a range of contractual relationships with B, C, D, and others, but marriage does not work this way. It posits a single relationship between two parties that will exclude all other similar relationships. As a party to that contract, "*A*" ought to have free choice, but her choices are constrained by the economic and social claims of her father and guardian. "Poor *A*" cannot remain a *feme sole* once cut off from financial support from her father, a fact which underscores the urgency of marriage for a woman in Miss Dorrillon's position. Miss Dorrillon's choices are limited beyond the letter of the law, and those extralegal considerations create her more pressing social realities.

Only in the space of the prison, and only after she has confirmed her affection for her father by returning the bail money when she hears of his distresses, does he reveal himself to her relief and confusion. The revelation silences her until the very end of the play, when she agrees to marry Sir George in order to find a milder governor. She delivers the ambiguous closing prophecy that "a maid of the present day shall become a wife like those—of former times" (V.iv, 95). While Inchbald insists on female virtue, she also suspects the system of paternal authority that moves seamlessly from father to husband. The comic event of Miss Dorrillon's courtroom scene weighs on the comic structure of the compelled marriage that concludes this plot line, in which her narrative interest and energy collapses into silence. She becomes the "*B*" of her legal argument, subsumed into the person of George as a legal and theatrical actor who no longer speaks for herself.

Lady Priory, who represents "wives as they were," has a relationship to the law that is clearer but still vexed. She explains her relationship to her husband to Mr. Bronzely: "he *is* myself . . . to the best of my observation and understanding, your sex, in respect to us, are *all tyrants.* I was born to be the slave of some of you—I make the choice to obey my husband" (IV.ii, 58–59). Whether audiences laughed nervously or at all at this line, the statement works like a joke in its connection of categories (husband and tyrant) that are supposed to be separate. Lady Priory's truthfulness casts her husband as merely a chosen tyrant. She describes the fractured subject position of married women as *femes coverts* under the law: he is myself. The ancient notion of marriage trumps the modern, in which women are parties to a contract. The theoretical persistence of patriarchy, argued variously by Carole Pateman, Susan Staves, and Michael McKeon, is here cynically oversimplified as timeless tyranny. The historical gesture of the title tends to collapse temporal difference even as it hints at historical change; marriage preserves the past as the living legacy of women. Lord Priory's response to Lady Priory's assessment, dependent as it must have been on performance, reiterates this continuity that clashes with the revolutionary discourse of rights and self-determination: "Yes, Mr. Bronzely; and I believe it is more for her happiness to be my slave, than your friend—to live in fear of me, than in love with you.—Lady Priory, leave the room" (IV.ii, 59). In the displacements of Lord Priory's revealing declaration, love, fear, slavery, and marriage become indistinguishable for married women.

Lady Priory's statement about tyranny raises interpretive questions about the role of the comic in this comedy. The Priorys are at the center of what would seem to be the farcical subplot of a sentimental comedy. Inchbald's willingness to deal openly with divorce and remarriage in her other plays, coupled with the fact that the great comic actor Quick played Lord Priory in the first run, adds to this expectation. Quick played a range of comic parts in Inchbald's plays, including Sir Luke Tremor in *Such Things Are,* Mr. Solus in *Every One Has His Fault,* and the General in *The Midnight Hour.* In all of these roles, error or hubris meets with some correction, if not humiliation. Comic logic all but demands that the jealous Lord Priory be taught a lesson when his oppressed wife bursts forth into a wider community, where she can escape into the arms of a worthier man. This plot, however, never emerges, in spite of a string of opportunities for Lady Priory's revenge. For the first run, Quick's presence kept the role of Lord Priory in an interstitial space between comedy and domestic tragedy. His reputation for full-blown comic characters balanced the role of the stern husband who governs with Inchbald's blessing.

Bronzely forces Lady Priory into defensive action when he steals a kiss in a dark room. Lady Priory cuts off a piece of his coat for evidence, a symbolic castration that provides the evidence she needs to bring him under the rule of law. Bronzely evades these consequences when he trades coats with Sir William and draws the austere father into guilty proximity to his rival, Lord Priory. Later, Lord Priory is easily tempted into a test of her honor and sends Lady Priory to Bronzely's home. When he threatens her with rape, she manages to save herself though the unlikely strategy of performative knitting:

Bronzely: . . . By heaven she looks so respectable in that employment, I am afraid to insult her. [*After a struggle with himself*] Ah! don't you fear me?
Lady Priory: No—for *your* fears will protect me—I have no occasion for my own.
Bronzely: What have I to fear?
Lady Priory: You fear to lounge no more at routs, at balls, at operas, in Bond-street; no more to dance in circles, chat in side boxes, or roar at

> taverns: for you have observed enough upon the events of life to know—that an atrocious offence like violence to a woman, never escapes condign punishment. (V.i, 78)

Although her first recourse is to the public judgement of the law, the principle of coverture and the symbolic union of husband and wife cannot protect her in the private space of Bronzely's home. The punishment for rape also fails to deter Lord Bronzely, who seizes Lady Priory's hand and declares, "Oh! for once, let your mind be feminine as your person—hear the vows—." Bronzely, who admits he feels shame for his actions, desists only after she explains that she will resent Lord Priory for exposing her and that he will make an impression on her heart if he returns her safely. In both cases, bonds of affection *beyond* the law save Lady Priory. Marriage law may provide the structures of these relationships, but it cannot provide the content. Lady Priory continues to believe in the power of the law, but sexual danger has forced her to recognize the limited protection it offers.

The "respectable" vision of Lady Priory at her knitting was enough to make Bronzely quake, but Inchbald's own experience of sexual assault proved that an attacked woman rarely could claim such composure or authority. According to John Taylor's account, when theater manager Thomas Harris attempted to "take the fort by storm," Inchbald pulled his hair violently and escaped into the green room, where she informed her colleagues with her characteristic stutter, "Oh! if he had wo-wo-worn a wig I had been ru-ruined."[32] Although the Harris story was not made public until 1834, *Wives as They Were* went up under Harris's management at Covent Garden. Her representation of a thwarted rape gives Lady Priory the power to defend herself by romanticizing the ability of women to protect themselves with their virtue, a much more composed version of her response to Harris's attack. In the midst of these tensions between rape, blame, and victimization, Inchbald is unsettlingly canny about the motives of sexual violence as the last resort of frustrated men trying to control women.

The final opportunity for the Priory plot to turn comic is in Lady Priory's confession after her abduction and return. Once reunited, Lord Priory's only interest is in her public confirmation of his prediction: "I said she'd preserve her fidelity! Did not I always say so? Have I wavered once?" and he repeats "do you hear?" to all who will listen. When he realizes Bronzely and Lady Priory have arrived in a post-chaise, he threatens: "Instantly explain, or I shall forfeit that dignity of a husband to which, in those [sic] degenerate times, I have almost exclusive right" (V.iv, 91). This failure of care, if not love, fractures the confession he wants her to make. Lord Priory demands that she "boldly pronounce before this company that you return to me with the same affection and respect, and the self-same contempt for this man—[*to* Bronzely]—you ever had. [*A short pause.*]" Her reply is a conspicuous silence, the same silence that greets his "can you be at a loss to say you love me?" When he thunders, "How! Don't you fear me?" he gets a yes, but she never amends and says she loves. Her final confession is double; she argues that "to preserve ancient austerity, while, by my husband's consent, I am assailed by modern gallantry, would be the talk of a Stoic, and not of his female slave." She then explains that gratitude is the only thing she feels for Bronzely for her safe return, but he cannot hear the critique and declares simply "Then my management of a wife is right after all!" (V.iv, 94).

Bronzely's highly unlikely reform follows Lady Priory's ambiguous response. Lady Priory's virtue genuinely impresses Bronzely, but he still reduces the attractions of marriage to his "legal authority" over Lady Raffle. She submits to him as chief magistrate, "rather than have no chief magistrate at all" (V.iv, 95). The explicitly political term for a husband, which Locke uses to *distinguish* civil authority from the natural authority of the husband and father, is a fitting end to a comedy torn between cynicism and conservatism. The collapse of the civil realm into the natural or familial provides some conceptual relief from the work of distinguishing between the authority of fathers, husbands, and magistrates. Inchbald's comic explorations of the law's private and public features drove her into the arms of Kant's paradox of enlightenment: "freedom to make *public use* of one's reason in all matters" is contained by the political maxim: "*Argue* as much as you like and about whatever you like, *but obey.*"[33] Inchbald exercises her freedom to write comedies, to challenge comic forms, and even to critique the letter of the law, but these freedoms, like comic events, are contained within a larger script that conserves the past. Obedience to the law through marriage preserves women and communities that Inchbald believed were at risk from the aftermath of an international revolutionary spirit and from smaller domestic revolutions in British law. Marriage law moved slowly toward modern civil divorce, but it retreated from the more egalitarian claims earlier in the century that had vested in married women the power to make contracts with husbands.

Suspicious of contract, Inchbald instead reaches toward a model of community and relationship in these plays that can keep women safe when the law denies them a place as agents and subjects. Inchbald's affective politics take seriously the importance of feeling and community in the fluid public/private domain of the law. Given the revolutionary challenges to law for law's sake among her Jacobin associates, the French revolutionaries abroad, and her own Catholicism, Inchbald's position is subject to misreading as simply reactionary. Nevertheless, as she anatomizes the power of fathers and husbands, splitting it into the power to circulate women and the power to possess them, she sees little place for a Hellena, a Miranda, or a Letitia Hardy. The late-century shift in women's legal status, represented for her in the disappointing economics and power politics of divorce, threatens the one contract women can make, even if that is only to "choose a tyrant."[34]

Returning to Žižek's gloss on Kant's *On Enlightenment,* I read Inchbald's disenchantment with contract as the logical limit of her liberal hopes: "Reason about whatever you want and as much as you want—but *obey!* That is to say: as the autonomous subject you can think freely, you can question all authority; but as part of the social 'machine,' as a subject in the other meaning of the word, you must obey unconditionally the orders of your superiors" (Žižek 79). For Inchbald, the problem with the autonomous subject is that he or she is never autonomous. The only remedy is an affective individualism that could be the supplement to the law, which will always fail as a substitute for morality. Her last plays, including *To Marry, or Not to Marry,* do not challenge the religious ideology of wifely obedience, but they do gesture to the space outside of marriage, the social world Inchbald herself inhabited most of her adult life. Inchbald had, by 1798, amassed a small fortune of almost £6,000 from her literary work and was secure enough to enjoy the privilege of the "widow's vow" to live independently. She turned down suitors and marriage proposals to live alone and control her own money. She also claimed that she avoided all "unmarried women," Mary Wollstonecraft in particular, out of the demands of propriety. Her politics are hardly feminist, but her plays express her passionate concern for the legal status of women in a world where promises, it seems, were made to be broken.

CONCLUSION

The Repetitive Future of Comedy

"If she had been a Man, she would have made a great figure in Parliament, and Speeches might have come perhaps to be printed in time."

(Sir Charles, describing Arabella in *The Female Quixote,* 311)

My inquiry into the popular plays of these four remarkably successful playwrights has considered the public negotiation of the meanings of marriage at the moment in English culture when, for political, legal, and economic reasons, marriage began to take on its modern outlines. In this process of change, the status of women shifted significantly away from the older, common-law understanding of chattels and closer to what Stone and others have called its companionate form. But this process was vexed by the persistence of old ideas such as coverture in common law and the emergence of new gendered dilemmas in the rationalization of marriage law. The arc of these changes moves from the first arguments for a modified, libertine individualism, which Behn adapted to her heroines; to the height of the exuberance for contract in the early eighteenth century captured by Centlivre; and finally to Cowley's later-century attempts to prop up the shaky claims of women to civil autonomy, which grew less tenable as the century progressed. Inchbald's resignation in *Wives as They Were, Maids as They Are* captures the sense of both historical change and historical repetition that women lived through their experiences of marriage; the modern moment was bound to repeat the legal past of matrimony, whether it liked it or not. As Inchbald and Staves have suggested, the Enlightenment narrative of progress was not obviously true for women.

The position of women in relation to marriage contracts was arguably diminished by the end of the century, after which generations of nineteenth-century fathers and husbands asserted their patriarchal authority with renewed vigor in the name of the affectionate, private family. English law reflected the diminished hopes that the principles of the social compact extended to women until the Divorce Act of 1857 legalized civil divorce and, more importantly, the Married Women's Property Acts of 1870 and 1882 recognized the separate legal identity of women as property owners. The arguments for the legal subjectivity of women in general and the separate existence of married women in particular derailed in early nineteenth-century England, a fact reflected in the changing relation of women to the stage. After Inchbald's success, few women writing comedies saw their work on stage.

The most successful comedies by women until the 1870s were by three eighteenth-century women in this study; Behn, alas, proved too racy for the stage, though a complete edition of her works was reprinted in 1871. Centlivre's *A Bold Stroke for a Wife* was revived in 1840, *The Busy Body* was revived six times from 1840 to 1859, and *The Wonder: A Woman Keeps a Secret* appeared in twelve different productions from 1837 to 1868. Cowley's *A Bold Stroke for a Husband* had one revival in 1850, but *The Belle's Stratagem* went into eleven productions between 1838 to 1881. Inchbald's plays, which successfully hit the darker, thoughtful tone of both stage and closet comedy for the nineteenth century, reappeared often until the 1850s. Her most popular original works in the nineteenth century, *The Wedding Day, Everyone Has His Fault,* and *Wives as They Were, Maids as They Are,* were revived in four different productions apiece.[1] The surrounding stage fare, following the general Romantic move to dramatic poetry and closet drama, included more tragedy and, after mid-century, melodrama. Comedy in the eighteenth-century style, whether witty or more sentimental, continued on the stage in revivals, but the robust era of new comedies by women and men was largely over. Alicia Lefanu's *The Sons of Erin* (1812), Catherine Gore's *The School for Coquettes* (1831) and her *King O'Neil; or, the Irish Brigade* (1835), and Mrs. Virginia Vaughn's *Outwitted* (1871), *Monsieur Alphonse* (1875), and *Mated* (1879) were some of the only original comedies by women staged in the period. Gore and Vaughn are also remarkable because they had more than one comedy staged. The fate of the more widely read male playwrights, like Edward Bulwer-Lytton and Dion Boucicault, illuminate the rule; the next golden era of comedy would have to wait until the end of the century for Wilde, Pinero, and Shaw, accompanied by lesser-known playwrights such as Tom Robertson and Henry Arthur Jones.

For women new to the stage in the Romantic period, the gains made by former female playwrights gave way to new anxieties about publicity. What Baillie erroneously called the "newfound path" was, to many, a closed road.

Anne Hughes complained in 1790 that the stage "is accessible to few," while Felicia Hemans lamented in 1832 that "dramatic triumph seems of all the others the most difficult." Sophia Lee cynically reflected that theater managers were a tremendous problem. She lamented that "as I had neither a prostituted pen or a person to offer Mr. Harris, I gave up, without a trial, all thoughts of the drama. . . ."[2] Harris alone, according to Inchbald's and Lee's accounts, may have kept many women from attempting the stage with the most palpable sexual threats. Notably, American women enjoyed more stage success with their comedies, which took advantage of a broader range of theaters as well as a cultural environment somewhat more hospitable to women's rights activists and to progressive gender scripts. British women who did see their plays staged, including Mary Russell Mitford, Sophia Lee, and Joanna Baillie, tended to succeed with tragedies or adaptations of their novels, and their runs were not especially long.[3] Women who wrote comedies were overwhelmingly drawn to short home theatricals and plays for children; how many of these plays were stageworthy is a question for another study.

Baillie craved more than the provincial production of her tragedy *De Monfort,* and she hinted at the ways several of her plays might be produced in the preface to her second volume of *Plays on the Passions* published in 1821 (Burroughs 88). While denied the larger audiences of the professional theaters, Baillie published her plays for readers and produced them in elaborate private theatricals, which took advantage of smaller performance spaces to explore her theory of "Characteristic Comedy." Her focus on emotional struggle and domestic complication continues the project of Inchbald's comedy and moves further to develop character-driven plots rather than eccentric characters and repartée wit comedy. She examines the complications of domestic spaces and performance in the meta-theatrical *The Trial* (1798) and with attention to the problems of inheritance (*The Election,* 1802) and marriage (*The Second Marriage,* 1802 and *The Alienated Manor,* 1836). Baillie's thoughtful and subtle comedies proved popular with readers, but they did not enter the public sphere of performance. As a consequence, Baillie did not encounter the attendant struggles or the forms of cultural authority that shaped Behn's, Centlivre's, Cowley's, and Inchbald's careers. Like them, Baillie explored the possibilities and limits of sociality in comedy, but unlike them, she worked through her domestic pedagogy and critique in largely private circumstances for private readers.

My belief that comedies, as both narrative forms and as moments of humor, could both stage and publicly contest gender scripts, grew out of my readings of the long eighteenth century's comedies and women's contributions to the genre. I also see in comedy a mode rife with possibilities for the expression of dissenting points of view that do not entail radicalism *and* that can be undone within the text as part of the comic operation of plot. I believe it is worthwhile to read those moments and differences as a way to consider the expression and incorporation of popular dissent in the developing conceptions of marriage and of the good woman. Paula Backscheider, describing the Gramscian negotiation of the meaning of popular artifacts, argues that both established ideological positions and counterhegemonic strategies can be read in the same text. She celebrates the transgressive possibilities in Behn for her audience and for future playwrights: " . . . the most original aspect of Behn's work is that she opens a new discourse of sexuality, admitting not only women's experience of love but also their knowledge of sexual difference. These aspects of her work and her transgressive characters can be set beside texts that follow hers to demonstrate the importance for hegemonic processes of the tendencies either to protect or to appropriate."[4] I have located the struggle between appropriating new strategies and protecting old gender values in the tension between comic events and comic structures to foreground the historical struggles within the plays themselves. The plays were, I believe, an important part of creating hegemonic gender scripts that included these oppositions. My reading attends to the contributions these playwrights made to larger conversations about the status of women, but it does not make revolutionary claims for those contributions. Rather, my focus on repertoire plays paints a historical and generic dialectic that waxes comic and tragic in turns with respect to the plots of heroines, a dialectic that continues to shape the legal and literary scripts of the present.

My study also grew from my general observation that women (or any other power minority) have used humor as a way to speak the unspeakable. Taboo material can explode into public discourse through jokes and wordplay, bribing the hearers to assent to its wicked logic when direct speech would be ineffective or impossible. Women writing comedy did not (and do not) have a magical power to see the effects of ideology, but their position on the margins of both a professional community and a legal culture seems to have provided a space for reflection on its limits and failures. Through their heroines, who take part in the negotiation of marriage's meanings, they exploit the contradictions that surrounded women for the purposes of (or perhaps with the alibi of) a laugh, which garnered the assent of the audience.

This project is, finally, a political intervention at a strange moment in academic feminism. While first-rate studies that include "gender" in the title proliferate, employing a range of theoretical tools from post-structuralist accounts of gender, queer theory's insights about sexuality, and feminism's long engagement with popular images, studies on women writers can seem suddenly old fashioned. The theoretical separation of sex and gender, which has been so productive for a range of critical approaches, has perhaps also the less desirable dividend of calling into question the coherence of "women" as a category. In this study, I have argued for that coherence across the long eighteenth century with some sense of urgency. The category "woman" has been invoked to justify monolithic and ultimately untenable conclusions about what a woman is and, implicitly, what she ought to be. But there is no need to essentialize what we mean by "woman," even for the relatively defined domain of the London stage in the long eighteenth century, to suggest that women writing about middle- and upper-class marriages might bring shared experiences and shadings to their narratives. While placing male and female authors in entirely separate spheres misrepresents the public life of the period, dispensing with author's gender as an important critical category can, as Catherine Burroughs cautions, "cause us to overlook how particulars of women's material conditions may persist across historical periods."[5] Some attention to women writers is also in order when scholars look only to the usual canonical suspects, Dryden, Pope, Richardson, and Fielding (or, in the theater world, Wycherley, Congreve, Etherege, Farquhar, Garrick, and Goldsmith), to ask questions about masculinity, sexuality, and the rise of modern gender. In a 1999 issue of *Eighteenth-Century Studies* entitled "Constructions of Femininity," all five featured articles were written by women, but none featured the works of women writers, a striking absence in the period that gives birth to the professional woman writer.[6]

Studies of women writers such as Nancy Cotton's *Women Playwrights in England: c. 1363–1750* (1980), Angeline Goreau's *Reconstructing Aphra* (1980), and Jacqueline Pearson's *The Prostituted Muse* (1988) labored to reclaim lost or underrepresented authors from the injustices of literary history. Because of these books, critical work on women writers has moved well beyond the recovery stage to raise questions about women's relationship to philosophy, history, and literary genre. Recent studies, including Mary Trouille's *Sexual Politics in the Enlightenment: Women Writers Read Rousseau,* Devoney Looser's *British Women Writers and the Writing of History, 1670–1820,* Josephine Donovan's *Women and the Rise of the Novel, 1405–1726,* and Paula Backscheider's *Revising Women: Eighteenth-Century "Women's Fiction" and Social Engagement,* continue to yield critical insights about the past and the present of gender relations. These analyses of history and gender are usefully organized around the category of the woman writer, and their insights about gender need not be subsumed to the claims of a "larger" political or economic history to maintain their validity.

Acknowledging the circumstances in which women wrote stage comedies in the long eighteenth century is important at the opening of the twenty-first century, when studies of women writers are subject to new scrutiny. Wendy Brown, summarizing post-structuralist feminist arguments about the construction of gender, maintains that an exclusive focus on women impoverishes the theoretical and historical insights of feminist scholarship.[7] But her caution, which is in the context of late-twentieth-century curricula, should not keep scholars from returning to women as a group in historical analysis. The historical category "woman," marked by the variables of personal experience, economic position, cultural heritage, legal status, religious commitment, sexuality, and ethnic identity, still organizes the experience of people in female bodies. The situation of women shapes Behn's erotic arguments, Centlivre's contract strategies, Cowley's nationalism, and Inchbald's conservative communities. And while women are not the only group of writers who take an interest in the possibilities for gender critique and narrative revision that the comic form presents, they were and continue to be well-positioned comic observers of cultural contradictions that crop up in the experience of women.

Popular culture, then and now, calls critics to triangulate between the archive of audience desire that popularity outlines, the ideological limits of gender scripts expressed as generic demands, and the possibilities for the authorial inflection of difference or experience. While women writing for the stage have never regained the share of theatrical performances that they enjoyed in the eighteenth century, women writers in general have flourished. The novel remains the dominant form in which women have been able to write for profit, and more recently, Hollywood has welcomed large numbers of women as screenwriters for romantic comedies. In the stage comedies of these women writers as well as in popular romantic comedies on film in the late twentieth century, I see a common thread that can illuminate recurrent patterns in the experiences of Western women without erasing historical differences or making those experiences transhistorical.

The subgenre "chick flick" came into being at some point in the late 1980s. Its precise definition is elusive, but it seems to describe late-twentieth-century films concerned with female characters, often as they renegotiate the popular romance plot. It includes films like *Beaches* (1988), *When Harry Met Sally* (1989), *Thelma and Louise* (1990), *Sleepless in Seattle* (1993), *My Best Friend's Wedding* (1997), *You've Got Mail* (1998), *How Stella Got Her Groove Back* (1998), *Runaway Bride* (1999), *The Wedding Planner* (2001), and *Bridget Jones' Diary* (2001). I group these films together because they foreground the concerns and fantasies of women more than other popular films, even though they are by no means calculated to appeal to women only or, with the exception of *Thelma and Louise,* to express feminist sentiments. I also make no pronouncements about the quality or politics of these films; they simply represent mainstream box-office successes. While this specious category does not necessarily refer to screenplays by women, a significant number of the above were written by women as either original screenplays or novels: *Beaches* (screenplay by Mary Agnes Donoghue, novel by Iris Rainer Dart); *Thelma and Louise* (by Callie Khouri); *When Harry Met*

Sally, Sleepless in Seattle, and *You've Got Mail* (by Nora Ephron); *How Stella Got Her Grove Back* (by Terry McMillan with Ronald Bass); *Runaway Bride* (by Josanne McGibbon and Sara Parriott); *The Wedding Planner* (by Pamela Falk); and *Bridget Jones' Diary* (by Helen Fielding).[8] Without making essentialist claims about women writers now or then, it remains true that some stories get identified as women's stories within a broader popular milieu, and that many of those stories are created by women. Most of those stories are heterosexual in their main plot, interested in marriage or partnership above other concerns, and fit snugly to a set of generic expectations that most moviegoers bring with them. These expectations are not the same expectations that Restoration and eighteenth-century audiences brought with them, but they do correspond in the broadest terms to them. The basic question, then as now, is one of autonomy within a relationship that has the psychological and legal capacity to diminish a woman's autonomy more than a man's. Late-twentieth-century female screenwriters produce decidedly more optimistic versions of this dilemma than earlier female playwrights for good legal and cultural reasons. But they are still drawn in significant numbers to the story and to the struggle. Women writers of the Restoration and eighteenth century, who were even more visible to their audiences as women than screenwriters of the present, broke important ground, though their contributions did not lead to a permanent revolution for women in the theater. But, in spite of real differences, their dramatic reflections on marriage and gender bear an instructive resemblance to our own.

Notes

Notes to the Introduction

1. Nicole Hollander, "Gender Based Differences in Humor," reprinted in *Last Laughs: Perspectives on Women and Humor* 1.
2. Hazlitt, *Lectures on the English Comic Writers* (1818) 1.
3. Staves, *Married Women's Separate Property in England, 1660–1833.* My debt to Staves's study, which delves into the body of English common law and the archive of case histories in the period, is difficult to calculate. I will refer to this work in the body of the text in subsequent references.
4. *The Wives' Excuse* was a failure in popular terms; it was performed only three times in the 1691–92 season, in spite of a stellar cast, which included Thomas Betterton, Edward Kynaston, Elizabeth Berry, and Anne Bracegirdle. *The Soldier's Fortune* fared better, with 43 performances between 1677 and 1779. The later plays of Farquhar and Vanbrugh correspond more favorably to audience taste for indirect attacks on marriage, which are closer to the successful formulae of Centlivre and Cowley. *The Provok'd Wife* was a huge success, with 308 performances between 1697 and 1796, and *The Beaux Stratagem* was the most successful comedy of the period, with 656 performances between 1707 and 1800. These figures are drawn from *Index to the London Stage, 1660–1800,* ed. Ben Ross Schneider, Jr.
5. Eileen Gillooly's *Smile of Discontent: Humor, Gender, and Nineteenth-Century British Fiction,* and Audrey Bilger's *Laughing Feminism: Subversive Comedy in Frances Burney, Maria Edgeworth, and Jane Austen* are two of the finest recent studies on women and comedy in the eighteenth and nineteenth centuries. In particular, Gillooly's brilliant analysis of a feminine comedy at work in the novel draws on psychoanalytic ideas of motherhood, connection, and a culturally feminine desire to protect. These critical insights illuminate the qualities of the novel, a form that fosters narrative intimacy. The stage, however, must appeal to a broad audience quickly and cannot make use of such strategies. It becomes more difficult to speak of a feminine mode of stage comedy, but it is possible to speak of strategies that appeal to women, and to think about modes of reading that can make those strategies more available.

6. Frushell, introduction to *The Works of Susanna Centlivre* xi.
7. Centlivre refers to the "publick good" in "AN EPISTLE TO Mrs. WALLUP, Now in the TRAIN of Her Royal Highness, The Princess of WALES," printed in the *Daily Courant,* October 1714.
8. Staves defines this period as 1675 to 1778, but the cases that illustrate her argument best are *Williams v. Callow* (1717), *Angier v. Angier* (1718), *More v. Freeman* (1725) and *Cecil v. Juxon* (1737), all of which are historically proximate to Centlivre's career. See Staves, *Married Women's Separate Property* 175–77.

Notes to Chapter One

1. Jameson, *The Political Unconscious* 106.
2. Clayton Koelb cautions that a critic cannot "talk about all comedy at all times and all places and say anything sensible" in a less Marxist argument in "The Problem of 'Tragedy' as a Genre" 262.
3. See Glynne Wickham, *Early English Stages 1300 to 1600: III Plays and Their Makers to 1576.*
4. Discussions of humor, such as Norman Holland's *Laughing, A Psychology of Humor,* occupy an adjacent intellectual field that occasionally reaches out to the comedy of a period, but they begin with psychological questions about response rather than literary or aesthetic questions about form.
5. *The Rambler,* no. 194, Saturday, 25 January 1752, reprinted in *The Yale Edition of the Works of Samuel Johnson,* ed. W. J. Bate and Albrecht B. Strauss, vol. V.
6. Horace, "The Art of Poetry" line 343. Hume notes that while there is no such thing as a standard "theory of comedy" in this period, almost all critics argued for the moral utility of plays. He summarizes what he can of the varieties of comic theory by subdividing the question into debates about satirized and exemplary characters, the realism of comedies, and the relationship of plot, satire, humor, and wit to the comic form. See "Theories of Comedy" 32–62 in *The Development of the English Drama in the Seventeenth Century.*
7. Congreve, "Essay Concerning Humour in Comedy," in *The Complete Works of William Congreve* 3: 163, and Dryden, *Works* XVII: 60–61.
8. William Congreve, *Amendments to Mr. Colliers False and Imperfect Citations* 7.
9. George Farquhar, "A Discourse Upon Comedy" in *The Works of George Farquhar,* ed. Shirley Strum Kenny, vol. II: 378.
10. Althusser's theory of interpellation is a productive synthesis of Lacanian psychoanalytic insights about the formation of the self as a subject and Marxist notions of social determinism as they relate to the production of false consciousness in individuals. See Louis Althusser, *Lenin and Philosophy and Other Essays,* trans. Ben Brewster 162–65.
11. Tillotson, *Sermons on Several Subjects and Occasions* (London, 1757), XI, 110. This sermon, entitled "The Evil of Corrupt Communication," was originally delivered shortly after the accession of William and Mary and published with 54 other sermons in 1701.

12. Richard Baxter, *A Christian Directory* (London, 1673), 467.
13. Shadwell, *The Royal Sheperdess* (London, 1669).
14. Collier's rant, which expressed a trend away from the overt sex comedies of the Restoration, was not the final word on stage comedy. Many of the plays he excoriates, including *The Rover, The Plain Dealer,* and *The Man of Mode,* continued in repertoire. See *A Short View of the Immorality and Prophaneness of the English Stage* 10–11.
15. Canfield, in *Tricksters and Estates,* makes the similar claim that Restoration comedy is about class warfare and the transfer of estates between elite families.
16. Boyer, *Letters of Wit, Politics, and Morality,* London, 1701.
17. For various accounts of the "damning" audience, see Beavis, *The Laughing Tradition: Stage Comedy in Garrick's Day* 17–25, Hughes, *Drama's Patrons* 37, and Michael Booth's *The Revels History of Drama in English,* vol. VI: 21.
18. See Todd, *Sign of Angellica,* 35. Laurie Finke's argument in "Aphra Behn and the Ideological Construction of Restoration Literary Theory" takes up the issue of Behn's relation to a primarily masculine tradition of literary criticism and the ideological position of pragmatic outsider and proponent of aesthetic pleasure in greater argumentative detail. Notably, near the end of her career, in the preface to *The Lucky Chance,* Behn did align herself with the Greek and Latin traditions of dramatic comedy.
19. *Jokes and Their Relation to the Unconscious* 6–8.
20. Freud's focus on the joke has admittedly limited applications for the broader category of the comic: "The problems of the comic have proved so complicated and all the efforts of the philosophers at solving them have been so unsuccessful that we cannot hold out any prospect that we should be able to master them in a sudden onslaught, as it were, by approaching them from the direction of jokes" (181). Freud's point is well taken as a warning against hubris in comic theorists, but it also underscores the fact that what he does have to say about the comic is in relation to a theory of jokes.
21. *The Pocket Magazine,* 1795, 108–109.
22. *The Artist,* vol. I, no. 14.
23. This essay was originally a letter addressed to John Dennis. *The Complete Works of William Congreve* 3: 166.
24. Reginald Blythe, *Humour in English Literature* 14.
25. Hegel, *The Philosophy of History* 302–305.
26. No. 1, Thursday, March 1, 1711. *The Spectator,* ed. Donald F. Bond, vol. I: 1.
27. Catherine Gallagher, in *Nobody's Story: The Vanishing Acts of Women Writers in the Marketplace, 1670–1820,* argues that Behn exploited the connection between female playwrights and prostitutes to establish "a continuous but mysterious authorial identity—never actually embodied on the stage but persisting and transforming itself from play to play—and aligned this idea of authorship with the 'no thing' of female sex" (8). My reading of Behn's comic strategies, both in her public defenses and in the plays themselves,

draws on the connections between embodiment, professionalism, and sovereignty that Gallagher's argument makes.

28. Quoted in Todd, *Critical Fortunes* 6, 12.
29. Attributed to Gildon, 26. While the treatise has been attributed to Charles Gildon, it is by no means certainly his. S. B. Wells discusses the problems of attribution in "An Eighteenth Century Attribution."
30. Catherine Gallagher has argued that Behn cultivated the playwright/prostitute insult as a way to make a space for an authorial persona that thematized female self-division in the literary marketplace. See *Nobody's Story* 7–34.
31. See Todd, *Critical Fortunes,* "Cautious Memory" 30–43.
32. Stanton, "This New Found Path Attempting," in *Curtain Calls* 327.
33. Backscheider, *Spectacular Politics* 71, and Donkin 186–88. Donkin points out that the 1788–1790 seasons feature the same percentage of plays by women in a comparable timespan, 1988–1990, in the twentieth-century theater communities of London and New York. Notably, the percentage is much lower on Broadway than in London's West End theaters.
34. John Wilson Bowyer provides the £10 estimate as an average sale price in *The Celebrated Mrs. Centlivre.* Deborah Payne, in "'And Poets Shall by Patron-Princes Live': Aphra Behn and Patronage," explains that the unrecorded amounts for dedications, ranging from £10 to £50, as well as the influence a patron might have with publishers, provided other sources or guarantees for income to which Behn had some access after 1679. See Payne 108–109 and Gallagher 7–12.
35. St. Vincent Troubridge claims that the first modern benefit was a special concession for Elizabeth Barry in 1686. See *The Benefit System in the British Theater* 17. The estimates of Behn's profits are culled from Gallagher, *Nobody's Story* 8–10; John Wilson Bowyer's *The Celebrated Mrs. Centlivre* 98; and Maureen Duffy's *The Passionate Shepherdess* 204.
36. Link 18–19. *The London Stage* lists one benefit night for *The Gamester,* two benefit nights for *The Busy Body,* and two for *The Wonder.*
37. No receipts were listed for the benefit nights of these last two plays. The estimate is an average of what the most recent performances had garnered, minus the standard house charge of £105.
38. These figures are drawn from Inchbald's private records, printed in Boaden, *Memoirs.*
39. *The Revels,* vol. VI: 53. While other authors of the early nineteenth century, such as Scott, Byron, and Southey, earned tidy sums for their labors in various genres, the profits for eighteenth-century novelists, particularly for women, were considerably less. Burney only got £30 for *Evelina,* Austen first sold *Northanger Abbey* as *Susan* for £10, and Maria Edgeworth made £100 from *Castle Rackrent.* These figures, drawn from transactions from 1778 to 1803, tell a different tale than those of the higher paid male writers of the early nineteenth-century. See also Halperin, *The Life of Jane Austen* 101 and 201.
40. See also Todd, *The Sign of Angellica* 220.
41. Margaret Doody, *Frances Burney: The Life in the Works* 143 and 159.

42. Behn's sex is identified and discussed in the ancillary materials as follows: *The Forc'd Marriage,* prologue; *The Amorous Prince,* epilogue; *The Dutch Lover,* epistle; *Abdelazer*, epilogue; *The Debauchee,* prologue; *Sir Patient Fancy,* epistle; *The Feign'd Courtezans,* dedication; *The Rover,* post-script; *Second part of The Rover,* dedication; *The False Count,* prologue; *The Roundheads,* dedication; *The City Heiress,* dedication; *The Young King,* epistle (signed Astrea); *The Emperor of the Moon,* dedication; *The Lucky Chance,* dedication and preface; *The Widow Ranter,* posthumous dedication and prologue.
43. *Biographia Dramatica; or, a Companion to the Playhouse,* ed. David Erskine Baker and Isaac Reed, 1812, vol. I: 99.
44. *The Dramatic Censor, or The Critical Companion,* (London, 1770): 470, 380.
45. Rosenthal argues that shifting meanings of authorship in the eighteenth century made the category of plagiarist a gendered site in which ownership of ideas and of self were contested. Behn hotly disputes the construct in works like *The Rover* and *Oroonoko,* where she shows that male bodies and property are as alienable as their female counterparts. Centlivre attempted to inhabit the position of the masculine liberal individual in what Rosenthal terms "feminist individualism," with mixed results. The plays, in particular *The Platonic Lady, The Gamester,* and *The Basset-Table* show the strain of women declaring self-ownership under modern patriarchy, which undermines their efforts.
46. Many feminist scholars have explored the tricky matter of literary property, ownership, and self-representation for women writers in the period. In addition to Rosenthal's *Playwrights and Plagiarists in Early Modern England,* see Todd, *The Sign of Angellica;* Patricia Parker, *Literary Fat Ladies: Rhetoric, Gender, Property;* Ruth Perry, *The Celebrated Mary Astell: An Early English Feminist;* and Angeline Goreau, *Reconstructing Aphra: A Social Biography of Aphra Behn.*
47. Centlivre, Dedication to *The Platonic Lady,* 1707, *Works,* vol. II.
48. Jonathan Kramnick, in *Making the English Canon: Print-Capitalism and the Cultural Past, 1700–1770,* argues that "Initially, the reading of women illustrated the opening up of national culture for a wider public. Feminine taste would educate the public to enjoy polite subjects instead of the rough matters of older writing. By midcentury, however, the specter of female literacy was often understood to be the beginning of the end of national, masculine fortitude. Critics at this point frequently overlapped or combined the question of women readers and consumer culture: the commodification of culture was metaphorically expressed as its attenuated emasculation while the latter was literalized in the specter of domestic woman armed with books" (39–40). Clifford Siskin (*The Work of Writing: Literature and Social Change in Britain, 1700–1830*) and Catherine Ingrassia (*Authorship, Commerce, and Gender in Early Eighteenth-Century England*) also connect anxieties about professionalism and commercial writing to gender. Ingrassia argues at length that the link between early modern finance, authorship, and femininity

structured the experiences of professional writing and the stock market in ways that identified their dangers in feminine terms.

49. James Boaden, *Memoirs of Mrs. Inchbald,* vol. I: 223.
50. From "Lines to Agnes Baillie on Her Birthday," part of Baillie's "Miscellaneous Poems" collected in *Fugitive Verses* and reprinted in *The Dramatic and Poetical Works of Joanna Baillie,* 811. Baillie wrote the poem for her sister Agnes, who read most of Baillie's work in manuscript. My thanks to Judith Slagle for her conversations about Baillie and her help in navigating the works.
51. *The Plays of Frances Sheridan* 41.
52. Horace refers to the "unwarlike lyre" in Ode 1.6, line 10. He also represents Sappho lamenting the loss of the girls of her home on Lesbos in Ode 2.13. My thanks to Elizabeth Sutherland for drawing my attention to these odes and for additional background information on Sappho.
53. Freud, *Jokes and Their Relation to the Unconscious* 100.
54. Alleman's historical point, that "young people separated by the whims of parents, maidens deserted by their fiances, and unfortunate women seduced on promises of marriage all had more of a legal case than one might suspect today" (30), shapes his view of the comedies with an emphasis on the readable social fates of the characters.
55. The statistical average of clandestine marriages for the manners group, 23 percent, is inflated by the fact that 2 of Wycherley's 4 comedies include them. Behn's output of 16 plays, and Centlivre's of 13, provide more telling averages according to Alleman's *Matrimonial Law and the Materials of Restoration Comedy* 82. Subsequent tables identify the particular plays and characters in question. Behn's plays with clandestine marriages are *The Dutch Lover, The Debauchee, The Rover, Sir Patient Fancy, The Second Part of the Rover,* and *The Younger Brother.* Her plays with tricked marriages are *The Dutch Lover, The Town Fopp, The City Heiress, The False Count, The Lucky Chance,* and *The Younger Brother.* For Centlivre, the clandestine marriage plays are *The Beau's Duel, The Stolen Heiress, Love's Contrivance, The Gamester, The Bassett Table, The Busy Body, The Man's Bewitch'd, The Perplex'd Lovers,* and *The Wonder.* Her tricked marriage plays are *The Bassett Table* and *The Platonick Lady.*
56. See Pearson, *The Prostituted Muse* 63–65 and Alleman 82.
57. Pearson's statistics show that plays by women had a 9:6 ratio of male to female characters while plays by men had a ratio of 9:4.5. There are two plays by men (Dryden's *Secret Love* and Banks's *The Unhappy Favorite*) in which women speak more than half of the lines.
58. These line counts were prepared from the following plays: *The Recruiting Officer* (Farquhar), *The Beaux' Stratagem* (Farquhar), *The Committee* (Howard), *The Spanish Friar* (Dryden), *Love for Love* (Congreve), *The Old Batchelor* (Congreve), *Love Makes a Man* (Cibber), *The Busy Body* (Centlivre), *The Careless Husband* (Cibber), *The Amorous Widdow* (Betterton), *The Rover* (Behn), *The Constant Couple* (Farquhar), *The Relapse* (Vanbrugh), *Rule a*

Wife (Fletcher), *Love's Last Shift* (Cibber), *The Squire of Alsatia* (Shadwell), *The Pilgrim* (Fletcher), *Sir Courtly Nice* (Crowne), *She Stoops to Conquer* (Goldsmith), *The Rivals* (Sheridan), *The School for Scandal* (Sheridan), *Miss in Her Teens* (Garrick), and *The Jealous Wife* (Coleman). These plays represent, in decending order, the most popular repertoire pieces for the eighteenth century, not including Shakespeare.

59. Performance figures are drawn from Frances M. Kavenik, *British Drama, 1660–1779: A Critical History,* and *The London Stage.*
60. Corman, *Genre* 14–20.
61. The reinvention of the Greek New Comedy line foregrounds the love story which, in the words of Paul Goodman, "excites an independent interest, with feelings of desire, anxiety, fulfillment; it gives the audience something to latch on to. This sympathetic line, with which the audience can identify, is crossed by the malicious and resentful accidents of the comic intrigue." *The Structure of Literature* 101.
62. Among the most important of these studies are Elizabeth Bennett Kubek's "'Night Mares of the Commonwealth': Royalist Passion and Female Ambition in Aphra Behn's *The Roundheads,*" Robert Markley's "'Be Impudent, be saucy, forward, bold, touzing and leud': The Politics of Masculine Sexuality and Feminine Desire in Behn's Tory Comedies," and Susan J. Owen's "Sexual Politics and Party Politics in Behn's Drama, 1678–83." See also Todd, *Critical Fortunes* 107–110.
63. See *Shakespeare's Festive Comedy: A Study of Dramatic Form and its Relation to Social Custom.*
64. Barecca, *Untamed and Unabashed* 19.
65. Frye's structuralist assumptions set up as truths what are at best norms and at worst parts mistaken for wholes. Even Susan Purdie's *Comedy: The Mastery of Discourse* asserts that the exchange of women is a transhistorical feature of romantic comedy without asking what it might mean for comedies to challenge such a defining transhistorical feature.
66. Leggatt's study is a fine one, but it is nonetheless devoted to generic similarities at the expense of history, a position he announces (2).
67. Jameson's circularity on this point comes in part from the post-structuralism of his plan, which seeks a cultural motor and finds it, not surprisingly, in Marxist-inflected psychoanalysis. See *The Political Unconscious* 116.
68. Canfield gestures to the difficulty in his opening to *Tricksters and Estates* by clarifying his own categories, subversive and social comedy, against the range of traditional literary categories that precede his study (6–7). Hume, in *The Development of the English Drama,* claims that the proliferation of categories within the Restoration and early eighteenth-century body of criticism, such as the supposed distinction between wit and humor, anticipates the difficulty of later critics who seek to categorize the plays into exemplary, satiric, wit, and humors comedy and urges his reader to "beware of all-inclusive statements about this drama" (62). And Corman, whose interest in genre history demands that he address the problem, labors to avoid prescriptive

definitions that obscure the changing nature of genre and the variety of comic plays that the era produces (6–10).

69. The most satiric comedies of the 1670s tended to have as many virtuous characters as the less satiric plays of the turn of the century, and a play like *The Kind Keeper* (1678) was acknowledged a satire (rather than a sex farce) by its first audiences. See Salvaggio's *Mirror* 20 and 205.
70. Corman, who skips over Aphra Behn but includes Susannah Centlivre as a representative playwright in his three cross-sections of stage comedy, discusses the differences between farcical, more Jonsonian definitions of comedy and the more "sympathetic" vision, "one that in England is expressed for the first time, I believe, by such critics as Dryden and Congreve (though they both continued to accept much in the Jonsonian view) focuses instead on the love-plot tradition of Greek New Comedy" (10).
71. Backsheider, *Spectacular Politics* 91.
72. Nicoll writes that, "Mrs. Behn, we may say, holds, in relation to the development of the comedy of intrigue, much the same position that Shadwell holds in relation to the development of the comedy of humours." *History of the English Drama, 1660–1900,* vol. I: 220.
73. Hume claims that Behn's writing caters to popular taste and, while not without merit, exists principally to "occasion extensive sword play" (284). Similarly, he says that Centlivre's *The Busy Body* is "ultra-formulaic," made of stock materials, and concludes the "the merest pretence at a comic resolution" (117; 119). Scouten declares that *The Rover* is not a comedy of manners because it does not take place in a London drawing room, overlooking the international and intrigue settings of *Marriage A-la-Mode, The Plain Dealer,* and *The Country Wife* (see Hume, *Development* 336). Similarly, Hume's 1982 discussion of comic heroes overtly excludes Behn's *The Rover* because he claims its characters do not fit his model of the comic hero, which he revises as comedies set in London once the essay is under way. In *The Rakish Stage* (1983), which surveys the drama from 1660 to 1800, Behn and Centlivre are again represented, but Eliza Haywood, Charlotte Lennox, and Hannah Cowley never merit mention.
74. Lacan, "Of the Subject of Certainty," *The Seminar of Jacques Lacan,* Book XI: 31.

Notes to Chapter Two

1. Reprinted in *Catherine and Other Writings,* ed. Margaret Anne Doody and Douglas Murray.
2. Staves maintains that even though many forms of married women's property allowed women to claim wealth within and after marriages by asserting their legal identity through contract, deeper patriarchal structures asserted themselves over the course of the period: "A principle feature of these deeper patriarchal structures was that women functioned to transmit wealth from one generation of men to the next generation of men" (Staves, *Married* 4). Car-

ole Pateman's thesis in *The Sexual Contract* focuses on the slippage in the political theories of Locke and Hobbes between the public, civil realm in which contracts are made and the private realm of the family, where women are rhetorically sequestered. Michael McKeon's "Historicizing Patriarchy" uses the theoretical tools of post-structuralist gender studies to argue that the same system that proposes to distinguish sex from gender and thus provide a more egalitarian model of the self is also the system that ties gender and sex more closely to one another, affirming the naturalness of female submissiveness and reinventing patriarchal authority for the modern age. In each of these studies, the dialectic of female liberty and female submission to a patriarchal order that animates the historical struggle, and not a simple account of oppressive patriarchy.

3. These terms come from Carole Pateman's analysis of the late-seventeenth-century rise of contract and the reconsideration of kinship networks in *The Sexual Contract.*
4. Thompson, *Models of Value* 157.
5. Margaret Ezell claims that evidence in diaries, letters, and other historical documents of seventeenth-century English women does not support "the current model of domestic patriarchalism as a pervasive, restrictive blanket of strictly male control over women's education and marriage" (34–35) She argues persuasively that this approach is rooted in a Marxist strain of early British and American feminist criticism that identifies oppression. Her thesis about the private forms of power wielded by the "patriarch's wife" of the seventeenth century finds additional support in recent work by Amy Erickson on English law from the fifteenth to seventeenth centuries. These accounts, however, precede the major legal sea changes of the eighteenth century, in which the reconciliation of regional and canonical variations of the law affirmed the principle of coverture in common law. These legal reforms, as I will illustrate below, provided the legal mechanism for consolidating the tremendous wealth produced in the eighteenth century through elite marriages.
6. Although Garrick sponsored many women writers, they tended to have only one successful play before they faded from the active community of playwrights. Ellen Donkin discusses this phenomenon at greater length in *Getting Into the Act: Women Playwrights in London, 1776–1829* 60–65.
7. Quoted in Staves, *Married* 17. The list of treatises appears on 15.
8. *Harvey v. Ashley* (1748) 3 Atk. 607, at 612, quoted in Staves, *Married* 118.
9. Catherine Ingrassia, Bridget Hill, and others have shown that many women participated in businesses and owned property as *feme soles* or as *feme coverts* with specially designated property. My generalization here refers to the inconclusive status of women as contractual agents, which kept them from full participation in public fiscal ventures, including in some cases their ability to trade, without the consent of husbands or fathers.
10. In *The Alchemy of Race and Rights,* Patricia Williams speaks of three rhetorical features of Anglo-American jurisprudence that establish simple, exclusive categories such as rights versus needs and private versus public. The

logic of these binaries proposes the existence of "transcendent, acontextual, universal legal truths or pure procedures," and the existence of "objective, 'unmediated' voices by which those transcendent categories find their expression" (8, 9). Williams challenges the law's desire to ignore the complications of people's lived experience by insisting on these categories. In contrast to them, she imagines "the possibility of a collective perspective or social positioning that would give claim to the legal interests of groups" and that would validate the claims of women, minorities, and others whose experiences are invalidated by the law's purported neutrality (13).

11. Staves, *Players' Scepters* 117.
12. John Zomchick, *Family and the Law* 25.
13. Antonia Fraser relates this story in *The Weaker Vessel* 12–19.
14. C. B. Macpherson makes this argument at greater length in *The Political Theory of Possessive Individualism* 95–106.
15. *A Vindication of the Rights of Man,* in *The Vindications* 44.
16. The treatise lists three publishers, "E. and R. Nutt, and R. Gosling (Assigns of E. Sayer, esq.;) for B. Lintot, and sold by H. Lintot." The Lintots were father Barnaby Bernard Lintot, who printed works by Gay, Farquhar, Rowe, and Steele, as well as the first edition of Pope's *The Rape of the Lock,* and son Henry Lintot, who managed the father's business after 1730, when the *Treatise* was published. The 1737 edition reverses title and subtitle, which leads most to refer to it as *The Lady's Law.* E. Nutt and R. Gosling are also listed as printers of the second edition of *Baron and Feme* in 1719. The first edition, in 1700, was printed by R. and E. Atkyns.
17. Quoted in Staves, *Married* 152. Staves argues that in the early-eighteenth-century heyday of separate property, married women often acted as independent financial agents. Lord Chancellor Thurlow's ruling in *Fettiplace v. Gorges* (1789) similarly upholds that "personal property, where it can be enjoyed separately, must be so with all its incidents, and the *jus disonendi* is one of them." Similar points undergird the legal logic of *Grigsby v. Cox* (1750), 1 Ves. Sen. 518, and *Fettiplace v. Gorges* (1789), 3 Bro. C.C. 8, at 10, though a more rigorous common-law understanding of coverture was legally dominant by the end of the century.
18. Locke, in the *Second Treatise of Civil Government,* argues that property is created by the addition of labor. But his example, as C. B. Macpherson and others have pointed out, "naturally" alienates the labor of the poor person, which leaves him or her unable to claim that to which his own labor is added as property. This presumed alienation destroys the basis for his or her independent personhood: "Thus the grass that my horse has bit, the turfs my servant has cut, and the ore I have digged in any place where I have a right to them in common with others, become my property without the assignation or consent of anybody" (section 28: 135).
19. Locke, *Two Treatises* 162.
20. Patricia J. Williams, *The Alchemy of Race and Rights* 13.

21. Erickson draws evidence from probate wills and demographic estimates to describe the likely realities of marriage negotiations and settlements for early modern women. As she points out, "throughout the early modern period one child in three lost at least one parent before the age of 21. (The modern rate is only 3 per cent.) Probably at least half of all the young women had lost their fathers by the time they married" (93). Erickson also points to evidence that some married women conducted the marriage negotiations for their children with their husband's apparent blessing.
22. In *Married Women's Separate Property,* Staves details the role that equity courts played in the establishment of married women's separate property (175–76). Equity or Chancery courts were able to address cases in which justice would not be served through traditional or common law. Equity courts were thus able to enforce contracts about pin money and separate maintenance agreements, although their influence also eroded dower's traditional legal protections for women in favor of more contractual arrangements for jointure, a legal conveyance to wives that was open to manipulation by husbands (30–33). As a phase in the cultural movement toward contract as the legal logic of all social relations, it vested more power in the hands of husbands in the name of adjusting "the legal rules of dower to make them fit better with modern society and the forms of property which characterize it" (35).
23. Erickson asserts that Chancery litigation was an option only for a privileged few, and that most of the subjects of her study (the large group she deems "ordinary people") could not have afforded it (230). Erickson's argument illustrates the variation in the English legal system, but it also does not account for the later consolidation of competing legal jurisdictions into common law that it the background for this study of the drama.
24. P. S. Atiyah, *The Rise and Fall of Freedom of Contract* 77.
25. Armstrong makes this argument in *Desire and Domestic Fiction.* Pateman similarly argues that Locke's distinction between private and public establishes the domain of civil society: "The private, womanly sphere (natural) and the public, masculine sphere (civil) are opposed but gain their meaning from each other, and the meaning of civil freedom of public life is thrown into relief when counterposed to the natural subjection that characterizes the private realm" (11).
26. Michael McKeon, "Historicizing Patriarchy" 297, 301.
27. Quoted in Porter, *English Society* 26.
28. See Bevis, *English Drama: Restoration and Eighteenth Century, 1660–1789* (32); Avery and Scouten, *London Stage* I: clxii–clxvii; Arthur H. Scouten and Robert D. Hume, "Restoration Comedy and its Audiences," in Hume, *The Rakish Stage* 80; and *British Dramatists from Dryden to Sheridan* xiv.
29. Pedicord argues that the coterie audience assumption about seventeenth- and early-eighteenth-century theater is hard to sustain in light of the range of ticket prices and refund schemes for those who left early or came late.
30. Pedicord also notes that regular working hours would have kept journeymen from attending the theater until later in the evening (20–28).

31. Sam Vincent's *The Young Gallant's Academy* (1674) begins with a prologue reference to the playhouse, which makes room for "the Farmer's Son as to a Templer's." Quoted in *A Source Book in Theatrical History* 213.
32. Scouten reports the early-eighteenth-century figures in *The London Stage* as weekly totals of 25,000, with the patent theaters accounting for 17,200. My figures modify his to illustrate the parallel, based on the six-night week that most theaters observed (*London Stage,* pt. 3: clxi).
33. Joseph Massie's figures are reprinted in Peter Mathias, *The Transformation of England: Essays in the Economic and Social History of England in the Eighteenth Century* 186–87.
34. Paul Langford discusses these estimates in *A Polite and Commercial People: England 1727–1783.*
35. Bridget Hill's *Women, Work and Sexual Politics in Eighteenth-Century England,* and Ivy Pinchbeck's *Women Workers and the Industrial Revolution, 1750–1850* are indispensible studies in the history of women's work. Hill recounts the history of the Lackingons on 153.
36. "Women Without Men: Widows and Spinsters in Britain and France in the Eighteenth Century" 365.
37. Hill surveys a range of trades besides publishing, in which women had owned and administered print-related businesses for centuries. She notes a Mrs. Higginson, who was "a dealer in Timber," Elizabeth Montagu's involvement in her husband's farm and collieries, a Mrs. Vicars who ran a lead smeltery, and a group of anonymous widows in Coventry who took over for their deceased husbands as "barbers, grocers, tallow-chandlers, bricklayers, cordwainers, and even, in one instance, as a cutler and gunsmith" (246).
38. Erickson notes this general division on 19, but she emphasizes throughout her study that the treatment of boys and girls was relatively equitable, and that the personal preferences of parents seem to have been expressed often in special bequests to daughters. She also notes that there were plenty of inheriting women, especially among "ordinary men," who preferred "lineal females to collateral males" (63). In general, high mortality rates meant that property changed hands rapidly, and that some of those hands were female.
39. Burnett 288; quoted in Staves, *Players'* 116.
40. The problem of determining patrimony, while an issue, can be exaggerated to justify the anxieties of marriage law as natural rather than legal-cultural. The materiality of pregnancy marks the female body, to be sure, but the reality of offspring, the confessions of mothers, and the possibility of continued relations between the unmarried mother and father provide some insight into the mysteries of paternity. My thanks to Mark Schoenfield for helping me develop this insight.
41. This erotic dynamic does not, however, draw on an *uber*-feminism of sexual equality. The conflicts in Behn's plays between her interest in female desire and the economic demands of a landed ideology, which is not particularly interested in female agency, are substantial. Susan J. Owen discusses Behn's

shift away from more empowering portraits of women as she finds it politically necessary or desirable as a Tory propagandist.

42. Staves makes this generalization about what she terms the first phase in the legal elaboration of separate maintenance contracts, which stretched from 1675–1778. In this period, "equity courts were increasingly hospitable to the idea of separate maintenance and contract logic" (*Married* 175).

Notes to Chapter Three

1. The exact date of the first performance of *The Amorous Widow* remains unknown, although it was printed for the first time in 1706. For a brief discussion of this matter, see Robert D. Hume, *The Development of English Drama in the Late Seventeenth Century* 264–65.
2. Rochester, "Love a woman! Y'are an ass!" in *Rochester: Complete Poems and Plays* 45.
3. Warren Chernaik, *Sexual Freedom in Restoration Literature* 4.
4. In *The First English Actresses: Women and Drama, 1660–1700,* Elizabeth Howe argues that the rise of the actress in the public theater of the restoration elaborated the earlier seventeenth-century court trend toward ladies at court acting in masques under Queen Anne and Henrietta Maria. As part of the public discourse, the actress created the occasion and the means for a strong critique of the Restoration's sexual double standard and the asymmetry of men's and women's legal rights in relation to marriage. Similarly, Sandra Richards observes in The *Rise of the English Actress* that the actress gave shape to the sexy and witty comedies of the Restoration while also breathing life into older plays. Dawn Lewcock reads Behn's expert exploitation of the actress and the physicality of theatrical space to draw energy from the spectacle of sexual difference and its reinterpretation through the presence of women on stage.
5. Diamond, "*Gestus* and Signature in *The Rover*" 522.
6. The differences between Julia and Lady Laycock reflect the misogynist strain in late-seventeenth- and eighteenth-century satire and comedy that has been well documented by Felicity Nussbaum, Ruth Salvaggio, and Sandra Gilbert, all of whom have argued that femaleness represented a cultural or psychological threat to a culture in the throes of change. See Salvaggio, *Enlightened Absence;* Nussbaum, *The Brink of All We Hate;* Katherine Rogers, *The Troublesome Helpmate: A History of Misogyny in Literature;* Gilbert and Gubar, *Madwoman in the Attic;* and Gubar, "The Female Monster in Augustan Satire." More recently, Jacqueline Pearson, *The Prostituted Muse* (1988); Patricia Gill, *Interpreting Ladies* (1994); and Paula Backscheider, *Spectacular Politics* (1993) have all taken up the sexual politics of Behn as a cultural response to specific historical events and changes involving women.
7. The brief description comes from the characterization in the Dramatis Personæ of *Epsom Wells. A Comedy,* London: 1673, in *The Complete Works of Thomas Shadwell,* vol. II, ed. Montague Summers.

8. See Corman 14. His list also includes Lee's *The Princess of Cleve,* Southerne's *Sir Anthony Love,* and Burnaby's *The Ladies Visiting Day.*
9. Janet Todd attends to the differences between Behn and her fellow playwrights in *The Critical Fortunes of Aphra Behn* 1–2.
10. The cascade of Behn scholarship that emphasizes her gender in the context of the Restoration theater includes Pearson 146–68; Catherine Gallagher, "Who Was That Masked Woman? The Prostitute and the Playwright in the Comedies of Aphra Behn"; Susan J. Owen, "Sexual Politics and Party Politics in Behn's Drama, 1678–83"; and Robert Markley, "'Be Impudent, be saucy, forward, bold, touzing, and leud': The Politics of Masculine Sexuality and Feminine Desire in Behn's Tory Comedies."
11. Gill 137. Gill's *Interpreting Ladies* is a comparative study of Restoration comedy that establishes Behn's difference from her fellow male playwrights through close readings of their plays. Though she is not bound to the populist terms of my study, her argument solidly demonstrates the differences that I imply.
12. Gallagher also argues that Behn uses the theory of "possessive individualism," C. B. Macpherson's term, "in which property in the self both entails and is entailed by the parceling out and serial alienation of the self. . . . Aphra Behn's, however, is a gender specific version of possessive individualism, one constructed in opposition to the very real alternative of keeping oneself whole by renouncing any claim in the self" (25). I share Gallagher's understanding of the tension between women as alienable and as inalienable property in Behn's comedies, but my focus is on the philosophical concepts of subject and object that provide the gendered structure of feeling on which both libertine and bourgeois culture depended. I approach Behn anxieties about commodities and sexuality through this philosophical lens to avoid replicating the language of economics that Behn challenged in nuanced comic events, and yet to provide a way to discuss the alternative economy of desire she crafts. Behn's production of women as "active objects" is an erotic strategy that keeps them present in elite marriage narratives, which necessarily use women as the conduits for familial property and which often regard women as commodities. See Gallagher 24–26.
13. See Markley, "'Be Impudent, be saucy, forward, bold, touzing, and leud,'" Hutner, "Revisioning the Female Body: Aphra Behn's *The Rover,* Parts I and II," and Green, "Semiotic Modalities of the Female Body in Aphra Behn's *The Dutch Lover.*"
14. In "'And Poets shall by Patron-Princes Life': Aphra Behn and Patronage," Payne makes a more general point about the dynamics of patronage that takes up the gender of Behn and Gwyn in relation to the economics of dedications.
15. Robert Adams Day, in "Aphra Behn and the Works of the Intellect," reads Behn's "Essay on Translated Prose," the introduction to her translation of Fontenelle's *Discovery of New Worlds,* as an example of "mother wit," producing the first version of what came to be known as Higher Criticism in biblical scholarship. Day maintains that Behn's theatrical background gave

her unique liberties and experiences that compensated for the conventional learning she lacked as a woman. While his analysis overlooks the scientific and experimental writings of other women like Margaret Cavendish, who also found a way to compensate for her female education, it captures the renegade intellectualism that Behn's *Defense of the Female Sex* (London: 1695) celebrated: "I have often thought, that the not teaching Women Latin and Greek, was an advantage to them, if it were rightly consider'd, and might be improv'd to a great height."

16. Case discusses the legal ramifications of reading gender as a set of characteristics apart from sex in "Disaggregating Gender from Sex and Sexual Orientation: The Effeminate Man in the Law and Feminist Jurisprudence" 16.
17. A few of the recent studies that devote considerable attention to *The Rover* include Catherine Gallagher's "Who Was That Masked Woman? The Prostitute and the Playwright in the Comedies of Aphra Behn"; Jessica Munns's "Barton and Behn's *The Rover,* or, the Text transpos'd"; Jacqueline Pearson's *The Prostituted Muse;* Elin Diamond's "*Gestus* and Signature in Aphra Behn's *The Rover*"; Frances Kavenik, "Aphra Behn: The Playwright as 'Breeches Part'" and her *British Drama, 1660–1779: A Critical History;* Paula Backscheider, *Spectacular Politics;* Margaret J. M. Ezell, *Writing Women's Literary History;* Heidi Hutner, "Revisioning the Female Body: Aphra Behn's *The Rover,* Parts I and II"; David Sullivan, "The Female Will in Aphra Behn"; Jane Spencer, "*The Rover* and the Eighteenth Century"; Robert Markley, "'Be Impudent, be saucy, forward, bold, touzing, and leud': The Politics of Masculine Sexuality and Feminine Desire in Behn's Tory Comedies"; Derek Hughes, *English Drama 1660–1700;* Laura Rosenthal, *Playwrights and Plagiarists in Early Modern England;* J. Douglas Canfield, *Tricksters and Estates: On the Ideology of Restoration Comedy;* Dagney Boebel, "In the Carnival World of Adam's Garden: Roving and Rape in Behn's *Rover*"; Peggy Thompson, "Closure and Subversion in Behn's Comedies"; Anthony Kaufman, "The Perils of Florinda: Aphra Behn, Rape, and the Subversion of Libertinism in *The Rover, Part I";* Anita Pacheco, "Rape and the Female Subject in Aphra Behn's The Rover"; Linda R. Payne, "The Carnivalesque Regeneration of Corrupt Economies in *The Rover*"; and Nancy Copeland, "'Once a Whore and Ever'? Whore and Virgin in *The Rover* and Its Antecedents." This extensive list is not complete, but it represents the critical obsession with Behn's most popular stage comedy.
18. Shadwell's *The Virtuoso,* which remained in repertoire in the early eighteenth century, included the rough whoremonger Snarl and the cuckolding of Lord Gimcrack by the rake Bruce, who is himself married at the play's close (V.i).
19. Quoted in Regina Barreca, *They Used to Call Me Snow White, But I Drifted* 14.
20. Rose Zimbardo makes a similar argument in *A Mirror to Nature* when discussing satiric comedies of the 1670s. She notes that both *The Man of Mode* and *The Virtuoso* extoll "old-fashioned virtue and simplicity" through the adherence of Harriet, Miranda, and Clarinda to virtue and duty above love (119–23).

21. Ruth Salvaggio describes Behn's "writing of desire" as an expression of a specifically female desire for sexual pleasure that is outside the circuit of the marriage exchange. See "Aphra Behn's Love: Fiction, Letters, and Desire" 253–70.
22. Late-twentieth-century scholars have tended to see Angellica Bianca as an unreconciled figure of female vengeance who reminds the reader of the uncomic underside of the Restoration's sexual politics. Some of the best work on her importance has been done by Kavenik, Gallagher, Diamond, and Todd.
23. Suz-Anne Kinney, "Confinement Sharpens the Invention: Aphra Behn's *The Rover* and Susanna Centlivre's *The Busie Body*" in *Look Who's Laughing: Gender and Comedy* 95. In this claim, Kinney is working from Elin Diamond's earlier argument.
24. Jean Marsden notes that the advent of the actress on the Restoration stage was the occasion for more graphic and symbolically dense representations of rape, including the graphic tableaux of plays like Nicholas Brady's *The Rape; or, The Innocent Imposters* (1692) and D'Urfey's *The Injured Princess* (1682).
25. Jane Spencer discusses the Kemble revision as well as a 1757 prompter text of *The Rover* in "*The Rover* and the Eighteenth Century" 84–106.
26. See Beverly Lemire, *Fashion's Favorite: The Cotton Trade and the Consumer in Britain, 1660–1800* (9). McKeon also notes that the presence of sumptuary legislation from the fourteenth to the seventeenth centuries, "signalled not the strength but the instability of a once-tacit aristocratic ideology that now required explicit reinforcement" in "Historicizing Patriarchy" 305.
27. Spencer notes that "despite Behn's continued reputation among theater historians for an unusual degree of indecency, *The Rover* was much more suited to eighteenth-century tastes than many other Restoration comedies" ("*The Rover*" 87).
28. The bed-swapping narrative has a prospective mother-in-law, Lady Fancy (a stepmother), in bed with the prospective groom, Lodwick. The play's libertine Wittmore, who barely restrains himself from sex with Isabella, is also having an affair with her stepmother (again Lady Fancy). Sir Patient's final cynical renunciation of puritan asceticism to "turn spark and . . . keep some City Mistress" is a fitting benediction for a comedy that holds less real hope for a sexually and socially just ever-after than *The Rover.* Those who don't have sex want to, and those who do make little objection to casual or even mistaken sex partners.
29. Janet Todd notes that there is no record of his reaction to *The Second Part of the Rover,* if the Duke did see it. The play had some initial success, but it did not continue, "despite . . . its music and spectacle of platforms, dancers, horse and horseplay" (*Secret Life* 272).
30. Jane Spencer, "Deceit, Dissembling, and All That's Woman," and Lewcock, "More for seeing than hearing: Behn and the Use of Theatre" 66–83. I am also grateful to my students in English 422 at the University of Tennessee, whose reading of portions of *The Feign'd Courtesans* for the 1998 SEASECS meeting in Knoxville, Tennessee taught me much about the play's visual possibilities.

31. In *The Prostituted Muse,* Jaqueline Pearson notes a similar linguistic displacement of "ruined," which means lost virginity for women and lost wealth for men (69).
32. Jane Spencer first made a point of Marcella's multiple masks in "Deceit" 94–96.
33. Todd, *The Secret Life* 275.
34. John Wilmot, Second Earl of Rochester, "The Disabled Debauchee," in *Rochester: Complete Poems and Plays,* ed. Paddy Lyons 33.
35. Todd, *The Secret Life* 260.
36. Robert Markley and Molly Rothenberg argue in "Contestations of Nature: Aphra Behn's 'The Golden Age' and the Sexualizing of Politics" that Behn's representation of a sexually free and pristine nature fails to move beyond the ideological terms in which nature and sexuality are constructed in late seventeenth-century discourse. Their reading, which focuses on the conservative nature of Behn's vision of labor, also shows the supple connection between the gender of scientific discourse in Fontenelle, Bacon, and Hobbes and the ideology of sexual repression. See 301–21.
37. Dedication to *The City Heiress, Works* 7: 7.
38. *The City Heiress* borrows from Massinger's *The Guardian* and Middleton's *A Mad World, My Masters,* but Behn's reinterpretation of those materials is in the Italian spirit of *commedia dell 'arte.* The scenes and characters that she borrows could have come from Attic comedy or Italian *lazzi* as easily as from her more immediate English sources. The critical charges of plagiarism from her contemporaries and later critics like George Woodcock must be read against the history of comic stage practice. William R. Hersey has pointed out that the actual borrowed speeches are only two from *The Guardian* (71–80). She also notably expands the roles of all the female characters.
39. "The Female Laureat," Dyce Collections, Victoria and Albert Museum 607, quoted in Todd, *The Secret Life* 287.
40. Ruth Salvaggio, writing about the representation of Behn's love affair with John Hoyle in *Love-Letters to a Gentleman,* argues that "Behn's desire . . . follows a heterosexual plot that is undermined by the homosexual and/or homosocial plot of men ultimately desiring each other. . . . Far from being perverse, such an attitude about love was quite common and in fact accounts rather precisely for the heterosexual attitudes of men during the Restoration: Whether their sexual exchanges were with wife or prostitute, they enjoyed the position of control and freedom" ("Aphra Behn's Love" 257).
41. Janet Todd recounts the story of Shaftesbury's alleged opportunity in *The Secret Life of Aphra Behn* 283.
42. The OED lists 12 definitions of the term account (out of 39) that deal specifically with money, all of which are in use in the seventeenth century.
43. See also Todd, *Secret Life* 284.
44. *The Lucky Chance* is reprinted in the Oxford collection, *The Rover and Other Plays,* and James Coakley prepared a critical edition of it for Garland in 1987. Jacqueline Pearson discusses it at length in *The Prostituted Muse,* and it is the

subject of the following journal articles: Jane Spencer, "Adapting Aphra Behn: Hannah Cowley's *A School for Greybeards* and *The Lucky Chance*"; Robert Erickson, "Lady Fulbank and the Poet's Dream in Behn's *Lucky Chance*"; Peggy Thompson, "Closure and Subversion in Behn's Comedies"; Lynne Taetzsch, "Romantic Love Replaces Kinship Exchange in Aphra Behn's Restoration Drama"; Catherine Gallagher, "Who Was That Masked Woman? The Prostitute and the Playwright in the Comedies of Aphra Behn."

45. Todd, *The Secret Life* 365.
46. "An early form of conveyance of land requiring a transfer of ownership to occur on the land in question; the donor and the donee in person or by attorney must come on the land, and the donor must say the words of gift." Susan Staves, Glossary, *Married* 238.
47. Gildon, Epistle Dedicatory to *The Younger Brother.*
48. Gallagher opens her *Nobody's Story* with this anecdote (1–3).
49. Žižek identifies a strong parallel between the operations of joking and of sexual pleasure in *Enjoy Your Symptom!* He argues that the connection of sexual acts operates psychically like jokes, which also allow the individual to make connections that are repressed.
50. The appropriation of the intrigue plot was Behn's formal answer to what Spencer has called, "the typical sex comedy of the 1670's [which] was a story of masculine dominance and sexual success" (89). Pat Gill has observed this same focus on masculinity, which has been naturalized through generations of critical approaches to the genre in *Interpreting Ladies.*

Notes to Chapter Four

1. This figure is drawn from statistics in P. G. M. Dickson, *The Financial Revolution in England: A Study in the Development of Public Credit,* 282.
2. In *Gore v. Knight,* the equity court decided that the wife's separate estate was hers to dispose of after her death, thus affirming that as a woman "has a Power over the Principal, so she may dispose of the Produce or Interest." In *Wilson v. Pack,* a judge determined that a wife's jewels, purchased out of an allowance to her contracted before the marriage, are not assets liable to her husband's debts (Staves, *Married* 148–49).
3. "A Woman's Case: In an Epistle to Charles Joye, Esq: Deputy-Governor of the South-Sea," London, 1720.
4. Frushell, introduction to *The Works of Susannah Centlivre,* xi.
5. There is great biographical confusion about Centlivre's maiden name and the sequence of married names thereafter. F. P. Lock assesses the four major available accounts left by Giles Jacob, Abel Boyer, John Mottley, and William Rufus Chetwood and concludes that her father's name was likely Freeman, that she may or may not have married a nephew of Stephen Fox, that she certainly did marry a Mr. Carroll and then Joseph Centlivre. See Lock 13–18.
6. Rosenthal points out the masculine pronouns in the prologue of *The Stolen Heiress* and in the preface to *Love's Contrivance* 208.

7. Allardyce Nicoll, *A History of the English Drama,* 2: 185. Nicoll compares the blending of intrigue and manners elements in Centlivre's style, which he places in the tradition of Behn, with the "moral-immoral" comedies of Cibber and others, who aimed to incorporate both risqué and sentimental elements in their plays (184).
8. Steele also praised Elizabeth, the earl's sister, in the *Tatler,* nos. 42 and 49. The family was well-connected in political circles, and Lady Elizabeth was a friend of Mary Astell's. George's position as a soldier allied him with the Whig cause, which may have caused or exacerbated the familial rift with his father. See Edwin Welch, *Spiritual Pilgrim* 7–19.
9. Ingrassia 21. See also J. G. A. Pocock, *The Machiavellian Moment: Florentine Political Thought and the Atlantic Republican Tradition.*
10. James Thompson explores this point in "'Sure I Have Seen That Face Before': Representation and Value in Eighteenth-Century Drama" (1995) which is a prelude to his book-length study, *Models of Value* (1996).
11. Jacqueline Pearson seizes on *The Basset-Table* as an optimistic play and sees in Valeria a "sympathetic learned feminist, scientist and philosopher" (213). Rosenthal is interested in it as an intervention in the debate about women and gambling, which illustrates the possibilities and the limits "of her feminist individualism" (237). It is also reprinted in the Paddy Lyons collection *Female Playwrights of the Restoration: Five Comedies.*
12. This figure is drawn from the total number of performances for plays in the Augustan period according to Robert D. Hume, "Making of the Repertory."
13. Mottley, *A List of All The Dramatic Authors,* quoted in Bowyer, 96. The event was also reported by *The Female Tatler,* no. 41 (October 7–10, 1709) by Mrs. Cavil, who claims that "the *Treatment Authors* meet with from the *Play'rs,* is too gross for a *Woman* to bear, since at the getting up of so successful a *Comedy* as the *Busy Body,* Sir *Harry Wild-Air* in a great *dudgeon* flung his *Part* into the *Pitt* for damn'd *Stuff,* before the *Lady's Face* that wrote it" (quoted in Bowyer, 96). *Biographia Dramatica* repeats a version of the story in which Wilks suggests that the play should be damned, and Centlivre damned as well.
14. *The Tatler,* no. 19, Tuesday, May 24, 1709, 154. F. P. Lock notes: "Steele's point is not very convincing. . . . But it was traditional to praise women writers for their natural talent rather than their acquired art" (64).
15. Jaqueline Pearson in *The Prostituted Muse* claims that Marplot as a character who often acts like a woman is a satire on women. While I agree with her initial claim, the sex of the character disrupts the satiric trajectory and instead keeps Marplot more in the realm of the comic, where the dissonance between sex and gender can still have critical social implications. The polyvalence of satire does not permit such direct translation.
16. Jürgen Habermas, *The Structural Transformation of the Public Sphere: An Inquiry into a Category of Bourgeois Society,* trans. Thomas Burger with Fredrick Lawrence (Cambridge: MIT Press, 1989), 79.

17. Centlivre refers to the "publick good" in "AN EPISTLE TO Mrs. WALLUP, Now in the TRAIN of Her Royal Highness, The Princess of WALES," printed in the *Daily Courant,* October 1714.
18. Lock notes that Centlivre's jaunty complaint in "A Woman's Case," which was addressed to Charles Joye, a director of the South Sea Company, makes clear that she thought she "deserved more than the royal command benefit performances she was given" (129–30).
19. Suz-Anne Kinney makes a similar observation in her "Confinement Sharpens the Invention: Aphra Behn's *The Rover* and Susanna Centlivre's *The Busie Body*" in *Look Who's Laughing: Gender and Comedy,* vol. I, ed. Gail Finney.
20. The primary studies I have used to establish the shifting face of agriculture and capital in the period are Joan Thirsk, *Economic Policy and Projects: The Development of a Consumer Society in Early Modern England,* and Joyce Appleby, *Economic Thought and Ideology in Seventeenth-Century England.*
21. Alexander Leggatt, *English Stage Comedy, 1490–1990: Five Centuries of a Genre,* 4.
22. Lock notes that Centlivre seems to have borrowed bits from Cowley's *Cutter of Coleman Street,* Dryden's *Sir Martin Mar-All,* Dilke's *The Lover's Luck,* and Hamilton's *The Petticoat Plotter,* while Frushell summarizes that the play is her own, though endebted to "the plays of Hamilton, Cowley, Dryden, Shadwell, Dilke, or Cibber." Lock 109–10, and Frushell, *The Plays of Susanna Centlivre,* vol. I, lxix.
23. Bowyer argues that Finch is the real target of *Three Hours After a Marriage,* but the satire on intrigue plots and women writing comedies includes space for Centlivre in the satiric mirror.
24. George Lillo, *The London Merchant, or the History of George Barnwell,* in *The Beggar's Opera and Other Eighteenth-Century Plays,* introduction by David W. Lindsay, London: J. M. Dent/Everyman, 1993, reprinted 1995 (I, 269).
25. McKeon sees a similar strategy at work elsewhere in Mandeville's oeuvre. Mandeville's discussion of "The Lessons of [modesty]" in *The Fable of the Bees* "unmasks as an acculturation the apparent naturalness of female modesty." This demystification, McKeon is quick to point out, depends on the physical basis of what is truly given (the body), "without which the demystification loses all coherence" (302–03).

Notes to Chapter Five

1. These directions for the noted performances are all quoted in *The London Stage,* pt. 5, I: 23; 35; 51; 66; 74.
2. The phrase "imagined community" comes from Benedict Anderson's *Imagined Communities: Reflections on the Origin and Spread of Nationalism* (London: Verso, 1991) 6.
3. This particular description, from *The London Stage,* pt. 5, I: 427, is characteristic of the theatrical records of additional musical performances after a play. The attention to the musical afterpiece, which would have been seen

by greater numbers of people than the mainpiece, suggests the sense of importance that surrounded these performances.

4. Covent Garden was willing to produce plays by Behn, Centlivre, and Pix, but proved much more reticent to launch new careers. See Ellen Donkin, *Getting Into The Act* 60.
5. *The Letters of David Garrick,* ed. Little and Kahrl, 3: 1172, no. 1109. The letter is dated July 17, 1777.
6. Ellen Donkin's *Getting Into the Act* details the struggle between Cowley and More through private letters and public articles in *The St. James Chronicle,* which she situates in terms of Garrick's complex mentorship and his departure from the stage.
7. Quoted in John Pike Emery, *Arthur Murphy: An Eminent English Dramatist of the Eighteenth Century* 164.
8. These statistics were gathered by Pedicord and summarized in *The London Stage,* pt. 1, V: 209–10.
9. Paul Langford discusses this shift briefly in *A Polite and Commercial People, England 1727–1783* 611–13.
10. *Summer Amusement* was a three-act comic opera by Miles Peter Andrews and William A. Miles (Larpent MS 485). *The Maid of Oaks* was first performed in 1774.
11. See Frances M. Kavenick's discussion of *The Jubilee* in *British Drama, 1660–1779: A Critical History* 169–71.
12. Hume explains that the "flood" to which Goldsmith alludes "turns out to amount to about one new production a year, and some of those arguable. Few afterpieces are sentimental, but if we count them in, roughly seven of ninety new productions are "sentimental comedy"; counting mainpieces alone, approximately seven of forty." See *The Rakish Stage: Studies in English Drama, 1660–1800* 331.
13. Cumberland, *Memoirs* 141, quoted in Kavenick, *British Drama,* 184.
14. Martha England argues that the seemingly placid comedies of the later eighteenth century include radical elements in their very democratic appeal that link this theatrical moment to its revolutionary history.
15. *Marshall v. Rutton* (1800), 8 T. R. 545, at 546–47, quoted in Staves, *Married* 180.
16. While it is difficult to re-create accurate figures, Paul Langford estimates the ratio at close to 100:1, based on 1763 calculations. See Langford 630, and Arnold Zuckerman, "Scurvy and the Ventilation of Ships in the Royal Navy: Samuel Sutton's Contribution."
17. This estimate puts the age of the Morley women at conception at a range between 18 and 25.
18. See *The London Stage,* pt. 5, I: ccxii.
19. Diana Donald reprints these cartoons and discusses them in *The Age of Caricature: Satirical Prints in the Reign of George III* 85–90.
20. The contemporary supply and demand arguments of Smith's 1776 *An Inquiry into the Nature and Causes of the Wealth of Nations,* which put economic

agents at the mercy of markets, also situate their vulnerability as women in the marketplace.

21. *Who's the Dupe?* had 15 performances in the 1778–79 season and reigned as the second most popular afterpiece of the season. The first, *The Wonders of Derbyshire,* was a pantomime with many musical interludes. There is some speculation that the author was Sheridan.
22. *London Stage,* pt. 5, I: 227, notes the performance date; my general inference about the seasons concurs with Donkin's reading of Cowley's career.
23. Frederick Link notes that "The initial run was twenty-eight nights. Cowley received the usual three benefits, which probably netted her well over £400, and was paid an additional £100 on 16 June to delay publication. The play became a part of the standard repertory, though nearly half of the century's London performances cam in the first two seasons." See Link, "Introduction" in *The Plays of Hannah Cowley,* vol. I: xxiv.
24. *Evelina,* ed. Kristina Straub 367.
25. Katherine Rogers, *Meridian Anthology of Women Writers,* 408, and *London Stage* pt. 5, I, clxxii.
26. Quoted in Donkin 59.
27. Katherine Rogers discusses pantomimes and the practice of showing actresses' legs, which seems to have extended to Inchbald, in the preface to her edition of *Such Things Are* in *The Meridian Anthology of Restoration and Eighteenth-Century Women Dramatists* 487.
28. "Mr. Horace Walpole, with a Fondness nothing less than fatherly, directs that part of the Affair which respects the scenes and the Dresses, while Henderson takes Charge of the Rehearsals and casting of the inferior Parts . . ." *Public Advertiser,* Nov. 1, quoted in *London Stage,* pt. 5, I: 476.
29. Linda Colley, *Britons* 69; 137.
30. These figures stand in contrast to a less than £80 million debt in 1757. Langford 640–41.
31. Alexander, *The History of Women, from their earliest antiquity, to the present time; giving an account of almost every interesting particular concerning that sex, among all nations, ancient and modern,* third edition (London, 1782) 2: 475.
32. Sarah Hanley, "Engendering the State: Family Formation and State Building in Early Modern France," *French Historical Studies* (1989): 14.
33. Sarah Hanley, "Social Sites of Political Practice in France; Law, Litigation, and the Separation of Powers in Domestic and State Government, 1500–1800." I am very grateful to Sarah Hanley, Allan Pascoe, and Mary McAlpin for their kind instruction on French marriage law.
34. Roderick Phillips, *Family Breakdown in Late Eighteenth-Century France: Divorces in Rouen, 1792–1803.*
35. For a discussion of the age of consent in French law, see William F. Edminston, *Diderot and the Family: A Conflict of Nature and Law,* and Jean-Louis Flandrin, *Families in Former Times,* trans. Richard Southern.
36. See Langford, *A Polite and Commercial People* 568–69.

37. *London Magazine,* 1777, 469. In *Models of Value,* James Thompson argues that the paradigms of identity and aubjectivity available to eighteenth-century Britons were transformed by the logic of abstraction necessary to the modern economy. As Great Britian becomes more of a paperwealth, the logic of identity becomes more entwined in the personality of an individual, a shift that is both compensatory and that follows the general move from coin to paper value.
38. Beauchamp speaks 187 lines, Lady Bell speaks 252, and Julia 162. Lines spoken by men for the whole play total 1,165, while women's account for 786 lines.
39. Act IV, scene 1 in *The Comedies of William Congreve,* ed. Anthony G. Henderson (Cambridge: Cambridge UP, 1982) 369.
40. Garrick edited *The Taming of the Shew* into this comic afterpiece, which was first presented on March 18, 1756. The piece appeared under the alternate title *Katherine and Petruchio,* and it remained popular to the end of the century.

Notes to Chapter Six

1. While Inchbald 's initial liberal sympathies were with the revolutionaries, her politics, which Gary Kelly termed more feeling than thinking, couldn't support the aftermath. Inchbald's unstaged tragedy *The Massacre* (1792), in which she traces the fate of a bourgeois family attacked by a mob, expressed her horror at the reign of terror.
2. Betsy Bolton (7) has argued that Inchbald pokes fun of British "colonial paranoia" in *The Mogul Tale* while Katherine S. Greene discusses colonial politics in "You Should Be My Master: Imperial Recognition Politics in Elizabeth Inchbald's *Such Things Are.*"
3. Colin S. Gibson, *Dissolving Wedlock* 28.
4. Roderick Phillips, *Putting Assunder: A History of Divorce in Western Society* 257.
5. Leah Leneman, *Alienated Affections: The Scottish Experience of Divorce and Separation, 1684–1830* (11–17).
6. See Nancy Cott, "Eighteenth-Century Family and Social Life Revealed in Massachusetts Divorce Records," and Samuel S. Cohen, "'To Parts Unknown': The Circumstances of Divorce in Connecticut, 1750–1797."
7. Katherine Binhammer's "The Sex Panic of the 1790s"summarizes the tone of the divorce literature in the 1790s and sees it as an extension of political instabilities translated into the discursive field of marriage rather than a reflection of a real rise in divorces. Her statistical evidence stands, though it is important to note that the amount of publicity that magazines like *Bon Ton* and *Town and Country* gave to divorces legitimated the panic for many English people.
8. John Corry, *A Satirical View of London at the Commencement of the Nineteenth Century* 181.

9. The case of Major Archibald Hook and his niece, which was published in both the *Bon Ton* and *The Cuckold's Chronicle*, was a particularly spectacular report that joined the spectre of familial incest to adultery. Hook was an in-law rather than a blood relative. See Binhammer 424–27 and Peter Wagner, *Eros Revived: Erotica of Enlightenment in England and America* 128, and Staves, "Money for Honor: Damages for Criminal Conversation" 280.
10. For a discussion of divorce in earlier plays, see Paula Backscheider, "Endless Aversion Rooted in the Soul: Divorce in the 1690–1730 Theater."
11. Judith Pascoe discusses these plays in *Romantic Theatricality: Gender, Poetry, and Spectatorship.*
12. *The London Stage,* pt. 5, III: xxvii.
13. Introduction to *The Works of Elizabeth Inchbald* xvii.
14. Boaden, *Memoirs* 214.
15. While the majority of divorces were suits brought by men, Paula Backscheider notes two cases earlier in the period in which women initiated bills of divorce and succeeded. She documents the cases of Mary Wharton and the countess of Anglesey, Catherine Darnley Annesley, in "Endless Aversion Rooted in the Soul: Divorce in the 1690–1730 Theater." See also Lawrence Stone, *Broken Lives: Separation and Divorce in England, 1660–1857* (139–161).
16. Ian Balfour makes a similar point in his reading of *A Simple Story,* in which he claims that Inchbald "finds them [contracts] wanting as vehicles for truth and social justice." See "Promises, Promises: Social and Other Contracts in the English Jacobins" 244.
17. Inchbald had sent an unnamed farce to Harris on February 13, 1782, which he had turned down. Inchbald, who often submitted plays rejected by one manager to the other, may have resubmitted or worked the materials of the lost *Polygamy,* a title mentioned in Boaden, into a new, full-length form. The play that became *I'll Tell You What* was christened so by Colman, who could not resist the joke, "If you will call, *I'll tell you what* the title shall be." See Boaden 1: 140.
18. Boaden, *Memoirs of Mrs. Inchbald* 1: 199.
19. *The Artist* 2: 151.
20. *The Child of Nature* (1788), a translation of Mme. de Genlis's *Zelie,* brought the tropes of the romance plot to the relationship between the Marquis of Almanza and his beautiful, naive young ward Amanthis, the child of his exiled friend. Almanza loves her, and she him, but the distance in age and the custodial nature of their relationship supplies some difficulty. They are united at last, but not before Almanza can speak the uncomfortable truth of their relationship: "I was her father, before I was her lover" (24).
21. *Everyone Has His Fault* was performed and printed in Philadelphia in 1794. The subtitle reads: "A Comedy in Five Acts: As it is Performed at the New Theatre, Philadelphia: Mark'd with alterations (by permission of the managers) by William Rowson, prompter. Philadelphia: Printed for H & P Rice and Matthew Carey, 1794."

22. On Wollstonecraft's death, she wrote to William Godwin: "Against my desire you made us acquainted. With what justice I shunned her, your present note evinces, for she judged me harshly." Reprinted in C. Kegan Paul, *William Godwin: His Friends and Contemporaries* 1: 277.
23. See *Elizabeth Inchbald and Her Circle* 75.
24. Godwin railed against the formulaic operation of the law, which he felt destroyed the ability of individuals to reason for themselves. "Men are so successfully reduced to a common standard by the operation of positive law that, in most countries they are capable of little more than, like parrots, repeating what others have said." Godwin, *Political Justice* 206.
25. *The Cuckold's Chronicle: Being Select Trials for Adultery, Incest, Imbecility, Ravishment, &c.* vol. I: 60.
26. The Marrow Bone Uncle and the deluded Niece" was part of a tête á tête, a more narrative representation of a crim. con suit begun in *The Town and Country Magazine* (1769–92) that included a picture of the parties involved. Marilyn Morris observes, "Like its predecessor, the *Bon Ton* included a visual reputation of the pair, but instead of segregating them in chaste oval portraits, it depicted them engaged in some way, sometimes at the moment of being caught in the act of adultery." See *Bon Ton Magazine* (Feb. 1793) 2: 447. I am grateful to Marilyn Morris for sharing her work on these magazines. From Marilyn Morris, "Crim. Con. in *The Bon Ton* (1791–96) and the Promiscuity of Genre," unpublished manuscript.
27. Backscheider comments on the earlier tableau, in which Edward takes leave of Lord Norland to go with Eleanor his mother to live in poverty, as emotionally effective both because of the contrast with other stage business and because it "momentarily leads the audience to believe that Edward has chosen Lord Norland." *Works,* introduction, xxiii.
28. Catherine Craft-Fairchild notes this confusion in *Masquerade and Gender: Disguise and Female Identity in Eighteenth-Century Fictions by Women.* While the confusion was significant enough for Inchbald to lament in her *Remarks,* Miss Dorrillon carries the generic freight of the comic heroine in the more sprightly tradition of Restoration and eighteenth-century comedy, while the real confusion is in reading the Prims, who shuttle between comic and sentimental or pathetic registers.
29. My reading departs significantly from Backscheider's, who describes Lord Priory as a "firm but trusting patriarch" who questions his own high-handedness in the final scene. Inchbald, *Works,* introduction, xxxii.
30. Review of *Wives as They Were, Maids as They Are,* in the *Critical Review,* ns., v. 20 (1797): 36.
31. Inchbald, *Remarks, Wives as They Were, Maids as They Are* 3.
32. John Taylor, *Records of My Life,* vol. I: 399.
33. "An Answer to the Question: 'What is Enlightenment?'" in *Kant's Political Writings,* 55.
34. George Haggerty has discussed the conservative and liberal elements of Inchbald's work in "Female Abjection in Inchbald's *A Simple Story,*" as has

Claudia Johnson, *Equivocal Beings: Politics, Gender, and Sentimentality in the 1790s.*

Notes to the Conclusion

1. These statistics come from the introduction to *Drama by Women to 1900: A Bibliography of American and British Women Writers,* comp. by Gwenn Davis and Beverly A. Joyce.
2. Hughes, "To the Reader," *Moral Dramas, Intended for Private Representation.* London: William Lane, 1790; Hemans, cited in Henry Chorley, *Life of Mrs. Hemans,* vol. I: 229; and Lee, "Preface, *The Chapter of Accidents,* vol. 24 of *Bell's British Theatre,* iv. All cited in Burroughs, *Closet Stages: Joanna Baillie and the Theater Theory of British Romantic Women Writers* 75.
3. Mitford's *Charles the First* (1834), *The Foscari* (1826), *Inez de Castro* (1841), *Julian* (1823), and *Rienzi* (1828) were all tragedies. Lee's *The Chapter of Accidents* (1780) was a comic adaptation of her novel, and Baillie's *De Monfort* (1800), *The Family Legend* (1810), and *The Homicide* (1836) were all tragedies. The only known public production of one of her comedies was an 1817 production of *The Election* at the English Opera House.
4. Backscheider, *Spectacular Politics* 86.
5. Catherine B. Burroughs makes this point in *Closeted Stages: Joanna Baillie and the Theater Theory of British Romantic Women Writers.* She subsequently argues that

   > The fact that we may feel we know all we want to know about how gender operates as a category (in conjunction with the categories of class, race, and sexuality) does not entail that we ignore how the concept of gender (specifically) affects the material conditions of women throughout theater history or apologize for privileging it as one's analytical framework. . . . To do so would be to misrepresent the fact that gender ideologies have dominated the reception of British women on the stage from the time female performers made their debut in the middle seventeenth century to the current age. Although there is no need to posit "woman" or "gender" as a coherent category, the historical manifestations of this sex-gender system on the lives of women (and men) in the theater arts during the British Romantic period merit serious consideration. (24–25)

6. See *Eighteenth-Century Studies* 32, 3 (Spring 1999).
7. Brown does, however, advocate "the practice of a historiography quite different from that expressed by notions of cause and effect, accumulation, origin, or various intersecting lines of development, a historiography that emphasizes instead contingent developments, formations that may be at odds with or convergent with each other, and trajectories of power that vary in weight for different kinds of subjects" ("Impossibility" 94). To the extent that my interest is in the simultaneous generic convergence and difference

within women's comedies, I take up Brown's challenge. Her remarks are also oriented to the present state of women's studies and the present historical moment in which she asserts that a feminist academic "we" has been brought into being but can no longer sustain itself by the same strategies that produced it through oppositional struggle.

8. Ronald Bass also collaborated with McMillan on the screenplay for *Waiting to Exhale* (1995), based on her book by the same name. Bass has written a string of hits on his own, several of which would belong on a longer version of the list above, including *My Best Friend's Wedding* (1997), *Stepmom* (1998), *Snow Falling on Cedars* (1999), and *What Dreams May Come* (1998).

Bibliography

Addison, Joseph, and Richard Steele. *The Spectator.* Ed. Donald Bond, 5 vols. Oxford: Clarendon Press, 1965.

Alexander, William. *The History of Women.* 2 vols. Third edition. London: 1783.

Alleman, Gellert Spencer. *Matrimonial Law and the Materials of Restoration Comedy.* Wallingford, Pennsylvania: n.p., 1942.

Althusser, Louis. *Lenin and Philosophy and Other Essays.* Trans. Ben Brewster. New York and London: Monthly Review Press, 1971.

Appleby, Joyce. "Consumption in early modern social thought." In *Consumption and the World of Goods.* Ed. John Brewer and Roy Porter. New York: Routledge, 1993: 162–73.

Aristotle. *Poetics.* Trans. W. Hamilton Fyfe and W. Rhys Roberts. Loeb Classical Library. Cambridge: Harvard University Press, 1927: 1991.

———. *The Works of Aristotle,* vol. V. Trans. J. A. Smith and W. D. Ross. Oxford: Clarendon Press, 1912.

Armstrong, Nancy. *Desire and Domestic Fiction: A Political History of the Novel.* New York: Oxford University Press, 1987.

———. "The Rise of Domestic Woman." In *The Ideology of Conduct.* Ed. Nancy Armstrong and Leonard Tennenhouse. New York: Methuen, 1987: 96–141.

Astell, Mary. *Some Reflections upon Marriage. The Third Edition. To Which Is Added a Preface, in Answer To Some Objections.* London: R. Wilkin, 1706.

Atiyah, P. S. *An Introduction to the Law of Contract.* 4th ed. Oxford: Clarendon Press; New York: Oxford University Press, 1989.

———. *The Rise and Fall of Freedom of Contract.* New York: Oxford University Press, 1979.

Austen, Jane. *Catherine and Other Writings.* Ed. Margaret Anne Doody and Douglas Murray. New York: Oxford University Press, 1993.

Backscheider, Paula. "Endless Aversion Rooted in the Soul: Divorce in the 1690–1730 Theater." *The Eighteenth Century: Theory and Interpretation* 37.2 (1996): 99–135.

———. *Spectacular Politics: Theatrical Power and Mass Culture in Early Modern England.* Baltimore: Johns Hopkins University Press, 1993.

———, ed. *Revising Women: Eighteenth-Century "Women's Fiction" and Social Engagement.* Baltimore: Johns Hopkins University Press, 2000.

Baker, David Erskine. *Biographia Dramatica; or, a Companion to the Playhouse.* With Isaac Reed. London: Rivington, 1782.

Baillie, Joanna. *The Dramatic and Poetical Works of Joanna Baillie.* London: Longman, 1851.

Balfour, Ian. "Promises, Promises: Social and Other Contracts in the English Jacobins." In *New Romanticisms: Theory and Critical Practice.* Ed. David L. Clark and Donald C. Goellnicht. Toronto: University of Toronto Press, 1994: 225–50.

Ballaster, Rosalind. "Fiction Feigning Femininity: False Counts and Pagent Kings in Aphra Behn's Popish Plot Writings." In *Aphra Behn Studies.* Ed. Janet Todd. Cambridge: Cambridge University Press, 1996: 50–65.

Barber, C. L. *Shakespeare's Festive Comedy: A Study of Dramatic Form and Its Relation to Social Custom.* Princeton: Princeton University Press, 1959.

Barker-Benfield, G. J. *The Culture of Sensibility: Sex and Society in Eighteenth-Century Britain.* Chicago: University of Chicago Press, 1992.

Baron and Feme: A Treatise of the Common Law Concerning Husbands and Wives. London: Richard and Edward Atkyns, 1700.

Barreca, Regina. *They Used to Call Me Snow White, But I Drifted: Women's Strategic Use of Humor.* New York: Penguin, 1991.

———. *Untamed and Unabashed: Essays on Women and Humor in British Literature.* Detroit: Wayne State University Press, 1994.

Baxter, Richard. *A Christian Directory.* London, 1673.

Beasley, Jerry C. *Novels of the 1740s.* Athens: University of Georgia Press, 1982.

Beattie, James. *Essays. On the Nature and Immutability of Truth, in Opposition to Sophistry and Scepticism. On Poetry and Music, as They affect the Mind. On Laughter and Ludicrous Composition. On the Utility of Classical Learning.* Edinburgh: W. Creech, 1776.

Beavis, John. *English Drama: Restoration and Eighteenth Century, 1660–1789.* London: Longman Group, 1988.

———. *The Laughing Tradition: Stage Comedy in Garrick's Day.* Athens: University of Georgia Press, 1980.

Behn, Aphra. *The Works of Aphra Behn.* Ed. Janet Todd. 7 vols. Columbus: Ohio State University Press, 1992.

Bergson, Henri. *Laughter: An Essay on the Meaning of the Comic.* Trans. Cloudesley Brereton and Fred Rothwell. New York: Macmillan, 1917.

Betterton, Thomas. *The Amorous Widow, or The Wanton Wife.* London: 1714.

Bilger, Audrey. *Laughing Feminism: Subversive Comedy in Frances Burney, Maria Edgeworth, and Jane Austen.* Detroit: Wayne State University Press, 1998.

Binhammer, Katherine. "The Sex Panic of the 1790s." *Journal of the History of Sexuality* 6.3 (1996): 409–34.

Blackstone, Sir William. *Commentaries on the Laws of England in Four Books,* vol. I, 1753, London: W. Strahan, 1783.

Blythe, Reginald. *Humour in English Literature: A Chronological Anthology.* Tokyo: The Folcroft Press Inc., 1959.

Boaden, James. *Memoirs of Mrs. Inchbald, Including her Familiar Correspondence.* London: Richard Bently, 1833.

Boebel, Dagney. "In the Carnival World of Adam's Garden: Roving and Rape in Behn's *Rover.*" In *Broken Boundaries: Women and Feminism in Restoration Drama.* Ed. Katherine Quinsey. Lexington: The University of Kentucky Press, 1996: 54–70.

Bolton, Betsy. "Farce, Romance, Empire: Elizabeth Inchbald and Colonial Discourse," *The Eighteenth Century: Theory and Interpretation,* 39.1 (1998): 3–24.

Bon Ton Magazine. Or, Microscope of Fashion and Folly, 5 vols. London: W. Locke, 1791–95; D. Brewman, 1795–96.

Booth, Michael. *The Revels History of Drama in English,* vol. VI, 1750–1880. London: Methuen, 1975.

Bordo, Susan. "The Cultural Overseer and the Tragic Hero: Comedic and Feminist Perspectives on the Hubris of Philosophy." *Soundings: An Interdisciplinary Journal* 65.2 (1982): 168–205.

———. *The Flight to Objectivity: Essays on Cartesianism and Culture.* Albany: SUNY Press, 1987.

Boswell, James. *Boswell's Life of Johnson,* vol. V. Ed. G. B. Hill. Revised L. F. Powell. London; New York: Oxford University Press, 1953.

Bowyer, John Wilson. *The Celebrated Mrs. Centlivre.* Durham: Duke University Press, 1952.

Boyer, Abel. *Letters of Wit, Politicks and Morality.* London: J. Hartley,1701.

Braverman, Richard. *Plots and Counterplots: Sexual Politics and the Body Politic in English Literature, 1660–1730.* Cambridge: Cambridge University Press, 1993.

Brooks, Peter. *Reading for the Plot: Design and Intention in Narrative.* Oxford: Clarendon Press, 1984.

Brown, Laura. *English Dramatic Form 1660–1760.* New Haven: Yale University Press, 1981.

Brown, Wendy. "The Impossibility of Women's Studies." *differences: A Journal of Feminist Cultural Studies* 9 (1997): 79–101.

———. *States of Injury: Power and Freedom in Late Modernity.* Princeton University Press, 1995.

Burnet, Bishop Gilbert. *An Exposition of the Thirty-Nine Articles of the Church of England.* London, 1699.

Burney, Frances. *Evelina.* Ed. Kristina Straub. New York: Bedford Books, 1997.

Burroughs, Catherine R. *Closet Stages: Joanna Baillie and the Theater Theory of British Romantic Women Writers.* Philadelphia: University of Pennsylvania Press, 1997.

Butler, Judith. *Bodies That Matter: On the Discursive Limits of "Sex."* New York: Routledge, 1993.

———. *Gender Trouble: Feminism and the Subversion of Identity.* New York: Routledge, 1990.

Butler, Marilyn. *Romantics, Rebels and Reactionaries: English Literature and Its Background, 1760–1830.* Oxford: Oxford University Press, 1981.

Butler, Samuel. *Hudibras.* Ed. John Wilders. Oxford: Clarendon Press, 1967.

Canfield, J. Douglas. *Tricksters and Estates: On the Ideology of Restoration Comedy.* Lexington: The University of Kentucky Press, 1997.

———. *Word Is Bond in English Literature from the Middle Ages to the Restoration.* Philadelphia: University of Pennsylvania Press, 1989.

Carlson, Susan. *Women and Comedy: Rewriting the British Theatrical Tradition.* Ann Arbor: University of Michigan Press, 1991.

Case, Mary Anne "Disaggregating Gender from Sex and Sexual Orientation: The Effeminate Man in the Law and Feminist Jurisprudence." *Yale Law Journal* 105: 1 (1995): 1–105.

Centlivre, Susanna. *The Plays of Susanna Centlivre.* Ed. and intro. Richard Frushell. 3 vols. New York: Garland, 1982.

———. "A Woman's Case: In an Epistle to Charles Joye, Esq: Deputy-Governor of the South-Sea." London, 1720.

Chernaik, Warren. *Sexual Freedom in Restoration Literature.* Cambridge: Cambridge University Press, 1995.

Chorley, Henry. *Life of Mrs. Hemans,* vol. I. London: Saunders and Orley, 1836.

Cohen, Samuel S. "'To Parts Unknown': The Circumstances of Divorce in Connecticut, 1750–1797." *Canadian Review of American Studies* 11 (1980): 275–93.

Colley, Linda. *Britons: Forging the Nation 1707–1837.* New Haven: Yale University Press, 1992.

Collier, Jeremy. *A Short View of the Immorality and Prophaneness of the English Stage: A Critical Edition.* Ed. Benjamin Hellinger. London: 1698; New York: Garland, 1987.

Congreve, William. *Amendments to Mr. Colliers False and Imperfect Citations &c. from the Old Batchelour, Double Dealer, Love for Love, Mourning Bride.* London: J. Tonson, 1698.

———. *The Comedies of William Congreve.* Ed. Anthony G. Henderson. Cambridge: Cambridge University Press, 1982.

Connery, Brian A., and Kirk Combe, eds. *Theorizing Satire: Essays in Literary Criticism.* New York: St. Martin's Press, 1995.

Cooper, Anthony Ashley, Third Earl of Shaftesbury. *Characteristics of Men, Manners, Opinions, Times, etc.* Ed. John M. Robertson. Gloucester: Peter Smith, 1963.

Copeland, Nancy. "'Once a Whore and Ever'? Whore and Virgin in *The Rover* and Its Antecedents." *Restoration* 16 (1992): 20–27.

Corman, Brian. *Genre and Generic Change in English Comedy, 1660–1710.* Toronto: University of Toronto Press, 1993.

Corry, John. *A Satirical View of London at the Commencement of the Nineteenth Century.* London: 1801.

Corrigan, Robert W. *Comedy: Meaning and Form.* 2nd ed. New York: Harper, 1981.

Cott, Nancy. "Eighteenth-Century Family and Social Life Revealed in Massachusetts Divorce Records." *Journal of Social History* 10 (1976): 20–43.

Cotton, Nancy. "Aphra Behn and the Pattern Hero." In *Curtain Calls: British and American Women and the Theater, 1660–1820.* Ed. Mary Anne Schofield and Cecilia Macheski. Athens: University of Ohio Press, 1991: 211–19.

———. *Women Playwrights in England, c. 1363–1750.* Lewisburg: Bucknell University Press, 1980.

Cowley, Hannah. *The Plays of Hannah Cowley.* Ed. and intro. Frederick M. Link. New York: Garland, 1979.

Craft-Fairchild, Catherine. *Masquerade and Gender: Disguise and Female Identity in Eighteenth Century Fictions by Women.* University Park: Pennsylvania State University Press, 1993.

The Cuckold's Chronicle: Being Select Trails for Adultery, Incest, Imbecility, Ravishment, &c., vol. I. Boston: 1798.

Cumberland, Richard. *The Plays of Richard Cumberland.* 6 vols. Ed. and intro. Roberta F. S. Borkat. New York: Garland Press, 1982.

The Daily Courant. London: 1702–1735.

Davidoff, Lenore, and Catherine Hall. *Family Fortunes: Men and Women of the English Middle Class, 1780–1850.* London: Hutchinson, 1987.

Davidson, Cathy. "No More Separate Spheres!" *American Literature: A Journal of Literary History, Criticism, and Bibliography* 70.3 (1998): 443–64.

Davis, Gwenn and Beverly A. Joyce (eds.). *Drama by Women to 1900: A Bibliography of American and British Women Writers.* London: Mansell Publishing Ltd., 1992.

Day, Robert Adams. "Aphra Behn and the Works of the Intellect." In *Fetter'd or Free? British Women Novelists, 1670–1815.* Ed. Mary-Anne Schofield and Cecilia Macheski. Athens : Ohio University Press, 1986: 372–82.

Descartes, René. *Descartes Correspondance.* Ed. Charles Adam et Gérard Milhaud. 6 vols. Paris: Presses Universitaires de France, 1951.

———. *The Philosophical Writings of Descartes,* vol. II. Trans. John Cottingham, Robert Stoothoff, and Dugald Murdoch. Cambridge: Cambridge University Press, 1984.

deVries, Jan. "Between Purchasing Power and the World of Goods: Understanding the Household Economy in Early Modern Europe." In *Consumption and the World of Goods.* Ed. John Brewer and Roy Porter. New York: Routledge, 1993: 85- 132.

Diamond, Elin. "Gestus as Signature in Aphra Behn's *The Rover.*" *ELH* 56: 3 (1989): 519–41.

Dickson, P. G. M. *The Financial Revolution in England: A Study in the Development of Public Credit.* New York: St. Martin's Press, 1967.

Donald, Diana. *The Age of Caricature: Satirical Prints in the Reign of George III.* New Haven: Yale University Press, 1996.

Donkin, Ellen. *Getting Into the Act: Women Playwrights in London, 1776–1829.* New York: Routledge, 1995.

Donovan, Josephine. *Women and the Rise of the Novel, 1405–1726.* New York: St. Martin's Press, 2000.

Doody, Margaret A. *Frances Burney: The Life in the Works.* New Brunswick: Rutgers University Press, 1988.

———. "Gender, Literature, and Gendering Literature in the Restoration." In *The Cambridge Companion to English Literature, 1650–1740.* Ed. Steven Zwicker. Cambridge: Cambridge University Press, 1998: 58–81.

Dryden, John. *The Works of John Dryden,* vol. 17. Ed. Edward Niles Hooker and H. T. Swedenberg, Jr. Berkeley: University of California Press, 1956.

Duffy, Maureen. *The Passionate Shepherdess: Aphra Behn 1640–1689.* London: Cape Press, 1977, rev. 1989.

Eccles, Audrey. *Obstetrics and Gynecology in Tudor and Stuart England.* Kent, Ohio: Kent State University Press, 1982.

Eco, Umberto. "The Frames of Comic Freedom." In *Carnival, Approaches to Semiotics.* Ed. Thomas A. Sebeok. Mouton: New York, 1984.

Edminston, William F. *Diderot and the Family: A Conflict of Nature and Law.* Saratoga: ANMI Libri, 1985.

Emery, John Pike. *Arthur Murphy: An Eminent English Dramatist of the Eighteenth Century.* Philadelphia: University of Pennsylvania Press, 1946.

England, Martha Winburn. *Garrick's Jubilee.* Athens: Ohio State University Press, 1964.

English, James. *Comic Transactions: Literature, Humor, and the Politics of Community in Twentieth Century Britain.* Ithaca: Cornell University Press, 1994.

Erickson, Amy Louise. *Women and Property in Early Modern England.* London; New York: Routledge, 1993.

Erickson, Robert. "Lady Fulbank and the Poet's Dream in Behn's Lucky Chance." *Broken Boundaries: Women and Feminism in Restoration Drama.* Ed. Katherine M. Quinsey. Lexington: The University Press of Kentucky, 1996: 89–112.

The European Magazine and London Review. London: John Fielding, 1782–1826.

Ezell, Margaret J. M. *The Patriarch's Wife: Literary Evidence and the History of the Family.* Chapel Hill: The University of North Carolina Press, 1987.

———. *Writing Women's Literary History.* Baltimore: Johns Hopkins University Press, 1993.

Farquhar, George. *The Works of George Farquhar.* Ed. Shirley Strum Kenny. 2 vols. Oxford: Clarendon Press, 1988.

Ferguson, Margaret. "The Authorial Ciphers of Aphra Behn." In *The Cambridge Companion to English Literature, 1650–1740.* Ed. Steven N. Zwicker. Cambridge: Cambridge University Press, 1998.

Fielding, Henry. *Joseph Andrews.* Ed. Martin C. Battestin. Boston: Houghton Mifflin, 1961.

Finke, Laurie. "Aphra Behn and the Ideological Construction of Restoration Literary Theory." In *Rereading Aphra Behn: History, Theory, and Criticism.* Ed. Heidi Hutner. Charlottesville: The University Press of Virginia, 1993: 17–43.

Finney, Gail (ed.). *Look Who's Laughing: Gender and Comedy.* Langhorne, PA: Gordon and Breach, 1994.

Flandrin, Jean-Louis. *Families in Former Times.* Trans. Richard Southern. Cambridge: Cambridge University Press, 1979.

Flieger, Jerry Aline. *The Purloined Punchline: Freud's Comic Theory and the Postmodern Text.* Baltimore: Johns Hopkins University Press, 1991.

Fordyce, James. *The Character and Conduct of the Female Sex.* London, 1776.

Foucault, Michel. *The History of Sexuality,* vol. I. Trans. Robert Hurley. New York: Random House, 1978.

Franseschina, John. "Shadow and Substance in Aphra Behn's *The Rover:* The Semiotics of Restoration Performance." *Restoration: Studies in English Literary Culture, 1660–1700* 19: 1 (1995): 29–42.

Fraser, Antonia. *The Weaker Vessel.* New York: Knopf and Random House, 1984.

Freud, Sigmund. *The History of an Infantile Neurosis* (1918). In *Three Case Histories.* Trans. Philip Rieff. New York: Macmillan, 1963.

———. *Jokes and their Relation to the Unconscious.* Trans. James Strachey. New York: W. W. Norton, 1960.

Frye, Northrop. *Anatomy of Criticism: Four Essays.* Princeton: Princeton University Press, 1957.

Gallagher, Catherine. *Nobody's Story: The Vanishing Acts of Women Writers in the Marketplace, 1670–1820.* Berkeley: University of California Press, 1994.

———. "Who Was That Masked Woman? The Prostitute and the Playwright in the Comedies of Aphra Behn." In *Rereading Aphra Behn: History, Theory, and Criticism.* Ed. Heidi Hutner. Charlottesville: The University Press of Virginia, 1993: 65–85.

Garrick, David. *The Letters of David Garrick.* Ed. David Little and George M. Kahrl, with Phoebe deK. Wilson. Cambridge: Harvard University Press, 1963.

Gentleman, Francis. *The Dramatic Censor, or The Critical Companion.* London, J. Bell, 1770.

Gibson, Colin S. *Dissolving Wedlock.* London: Routledge, 1994.

Gilbert, Sandra M., and Susan Gubar. *The Madwoman in the Attic: The Woman Writer and the Nineteenth-Century Literary Imagination.* New Haven: Yale University Press, 1979.

Gildon, Charles. *A Comparison Between the Two Stages.* Pref. Arthur Freeman. London: 1702. Rpt. New York: Garland, 1973.

———. "Epistle Dedicatory to *The Younger Brother.*" London: J. Harris, 1696.

Gill, Patricia. *Interpreting Ladies: Women, Wit, and Morality in the Restoration Comedy of Manners.* Athens: University of Georgia Press, 1994.

Gillooly, Eileen. *Smile of Discontent: Humor, Gender, and Nineteenth-Century British Fiction.* Chicago: University of Chicago Press, 1999.

Godwin, William. *Memoirs of the Author of a Vindication of the Rights of Woman.* Pref. John Middleton Murry. New York: Richard R. Smith, 1930.

———. *Political Justice.* Ed. Isaac Kramnick. Harmondsworth: Penguin Books, 1976.

Goldsmith, Oliver. *Collected Works of Oliver Goldsmith.* Ed. Arthur Friedman. Oxford: Clarendon Press, 1966.

Goodman, Paul. *The Structure of Literature.* Chicago: University of Chicago Press, 1954.

Goreau, Angeline. *Reconstructing Aphra: A Social Biography of Aphra Behn.* New York: The Dial Press, 1980.

Green, Susan. "Semiotic Modalities of the Female Body in Aphra Behn's *The Dutch Lover.*" In *Rereading Aphra Behn: History, Theory, Criticism.* Ed. Heidi Hutner. Charlottesville: University of Virginia Press, 1993: 121–47.

Greene, Katherine. "'You Should be My Master': Imperial Recognition Politics in Elizabeth Inchbald's *Such Things Are.*" *Clio* 27: 3 (1998): 387–414.

Gregory, John. *A Father's Legacy to His Daughters.* London, 1774.

Grosz, Elizabeth. *Volatile Bodies: Toward a Corporeal Feminism.* Bloomington: Indiana University Press, 1994.

Gubar, Susan. "The Female Monster in Augustan Satire." *Signs* 3 (1977): 380–94.

Habermas, Jürgen. *The Structural Transformation of the Public Sphere: An Inquiry into a Category of Bourgeois Society.* Trans. Thomas Burger with Fredrick Lawrence. Cambridge: MIT Press, 1989.

Haggerty, George. "Female Abjection in Inchbald's *A Simple Story.*" *SEL* 36 (1996): 655–71.

Halperin, John. *The Life of Jane Austen.* Baltimore: The Johns Hopkins University Press, 1984.

Hanley, Sarah. "Engendering the State: Family Formation and State Building in Early Modern France." *French Historical Studies* 16: 1 (1989): 4–27.

———. "Social Sites of Political Practice in France; Lawsuits, Civil Rights, and the Separation of Powers in Domestic and State Government, 1500–1800." *American Historical Review* 102: 1 (1997): 27–52.

The Hardships of the English Laws in Relation to Wives. London: George Faulkner, 1735.

Harth, Erica. *Cartesian Women: Versions and Subversions of Rational Discourse in the Old Regime.* Ithaca: Cornell University Press, 1992.

Hays, Mary. *Appeal to the Men of Great Britain in Behalf of Women.* London: 1798 Rpt. New York, London: Garland Publishing, 1974.

Hazlitt, William. *Lectures on the English Comic Writers,* 1818. Intro. R. Brimley Johnson. Oxford: Oxford University Press, 1951.

Hegel, G. W. F. *The Philosophy of History.* Trans. J. Sibree. New York: Dover Publications, 1956.

Hentz, Gary. "'An Itch o Gaming': The South Sea Bubble and the Novels of Daniel Defoe." *Eighteenth-Century Life* 17 (1993): 32–45.

Hersey, William R. *A Critical Old-Spelling Edition of Aphra Behn's* The City Heiress. New York: Garland, 1987.

Hill, Bridget. *Eighteenth-Century Women: An Anthology.* London: George Allen and Unwin, 1984.

———. *Women, Work and Sexual Politics in Eighteenth-Century England.* Oxford and New York: Blackwell, 1989.

Hobbes, Thomas. *Leviathan.* Ed. C. B. Macpherson. New York: Penguin, 1981.

Hoare, Prince (ed.). *The Artist: A Collection of Essays.* 2 vols. London: John Murray, 1810.

Holland, Norman. *Laughing: A Psychology of Humor.* Ithaca: Cornell University Press, 1982.

Hollander, Nicole. "Gender Based Differences in Humor." In *Last Laughs: Perspectives on Women and Humor.* Ed. Regina Barreca. London: Gordon Breach, 1988.

Horace. *Satires, Epistles, and Ars Poetica.* Trans. H. Rushton Fairclough. Cambridge: Harvard University Press, 1938.

Howe, Elizabeth. *The First English Actresses: Women and Drama, 1660–1700.* Cambridge: Cambridge University Press, 1992.

Hughes, Derek. *English Drama 1660–1700.* Oxford: Clarendon Press, 1996.

Hughes, Leo. *The Drama's Patrons: A Study of the Eighteenth-Century London Audience.* Austin: University of Texas Press, 1971.

Hughes, Anne, Mrs. *Moral Dramas, Intended for Private Representation.* London: William Lane, 1790.

Hufton, Olwen. "Women Without Men: Widows and Spinsters in Britain and France in the Eighteenth Century." *The Journal of Family History* 9.4 (1984): 355–76.

Hume, Robert D. *The Development of English Drama in the Late Seventeenth Century.* Oxford: Clarendon Press, 1976.

———. "The Making of the Repertory." In *The London Theater World, 1660–1800.* Ed. Robert D. Hume. Carbondale: Southern Illinois University Press, 1980.

———. *The Rakish Stage.* Carbondale: Southern Illinois University Press, 1983.

Hutner, Heidi (ed.). *Rereading Aphra Behn: History, Theory, and Criticism.* Charlottesville: The University Press of Virginia, 1993.

———. "Revisioning the Female Body: Aphra Behn's *The Rover* Parts I and II." In *Rereading Aphra Behn: History, Theory, Criticism.* Ed. Heidi Hutner. Charlottesville: University of Virginia Press, 1993, pp. 102–20.

Inchbald, Elizabeth. *The Plays of Elizabeth Inchbald.* Ed. Paula Backscheider. New York: Garland, 1980.

———. *Remarks for the British Theater 1806–1809.* Intro. Cecilia Macheski. Delmar, New York: Scholars' Facsimiles and Reprints, 1990.

———. *A Simple Story.* Ed. J. M. S. Tompkins. Oxford: Oxford University Press, 1998.

Ingrassia, Catherine. *Authorship, Commerce, and Gender in Early Eighteenth-Century England: A Culture of Paper Credit.* Cambridge: Cambridge University Press, 1998.

Irigaray, Luce. *This Sex Which is Not One.* Trans. Catherine Porter and Carolyn Burke. New York: Cornell University Press, 1985.

Jameson, Fredric. *Marxism and Form.* Princeton: Princeton University Press, 1971.

———. *The Political Unconscious: Narrative as a Socially Symbolic Act.* Ithaca: Cornell University Press, 1981.

Johnson, Claudia L. *Equivocal Beings: Politics, Gender, and Sentimentality in the 1790s, Wollstonecraft, Radcliffe, Burney, Austen.* Chicago: University of Chicago Press, 1995.

Johnson, Nancy E. "Law And Literature: Women, Agency, and the Law: Mediations of the Novel in the Late Eighteenth Century." *Harvard Women's Law Review* 19 (1996) 269.

Johnson, Samuel. *The Yale Edition of the Works of Samuel Johnson.* Ed. W. J. Bate and Albrecht B. Strauss. New Haven: Yale University Press, 1969.

Johnstone, Albert A. "The Bodily Nature of the Self, or What Descartes Should Have Conceded Princess Elizabeth of Bohemia." In *Giving the Body Its Due,* Ed. Maxine Sheets-Johnstone. Albany: SUNY Press, 1992: 16–47.

Kant, Emmanuel. "An Answer to the Question: 'What is Enlightenment?'" In *Kant's Political Writings.* Trans. H. B. Nisbet. Ed. Hans Reiss. Cambridge: Cambridge University Press, 1970.

Kavenik, Frances M. "Aphra Behn: The Playwright as 'Breeches Part.'" In *Curtain Calls: British and American Women and the Theater, 1660–1820.* Ed. Mary Anne Schofield and Cecilia Macheski. Athens: University of Ohio Press, 1991: 177–92.

———. *British Drama, 1660–1779: A Critical History.* New York: Twayne Publishers, 1995.

Kaufman, Anthony. "'The Perils of Florinda': Aphra Behn, Rape, and the Subversion of Libertinism in *The Rover, Part I.*" *Restoration and Eighteenth Century Theatre Reserarch* 11.2 (1996): 1–21.

Kinney, Suz-Anne. "Confinement Sharpens Invention: Aphra Behn's *The Rover* and Susanna Centlivre's *The Busie Bodie."* In *Look Who's Laughing: Gender and Comedy.* Ed. Gail Finney. Langhorne, PA: Gordon and Breach, 1994: 83–101.

Koelb, Clayton. "The Problem of 'Tragedy' as a Genre." *Genre* 8 (1975): 248–66.

Kraft, Elizabeth. *Character and Consciousness in Eighteenth-Century Comic Fiction.* Athens: University Georgia Press, 1992.

Kramnick, Jonathan. *Making the English Canon: Print-Capitalism and the Cultural Past, 1700–1770.* Cambridge: Cambridge University Press, 1998.

Kristeva, Julia. *Powers of Horror: An Essay on Abjection.* Trans. Leon S. Roudiez. New York: Columbia University Press, 1982.

Kubek, Elizabeth Bennett. "'Night Mares of the Commonwealth': Royalist Passion and Female Ambition in Aphra Behn's *The Roundheads.*" *Restoration* 17 (1993): 88–103.

Lacan, Jacques. *Ecrits. A Selection.* Trans. Alan Sheridan. New York: Norton, 1977.

———. *The Four Fundamental Concepts of Psychoanalysis.* Trans. Alan Sheridan. Ed. Jacques-Alain Miller. New York: W. W. Norton, 1978.

———. "Of the Subject of Certainty." *The Seminar of Jacques Lacan. Book XI.* Ed. Jacques-Alain Miller. New York: W. W. Norton, 1988.

Lacquer, Thomas. *Making Sex: Body and Gender from the Greeks to Freud.* Cambridge: Harvard University Press, 1990.

Langer, Susanne K. *Feeling and Form: A Theory of Art.* New York: Scribner, 1953.

Langford, Paul. *A Polite and Commercial People: England 1727–1783.* Oxford: Oxford University Press, 1989.

Lanser, Susanne Sniader. *Fictions of Authority: Women Writers and Narrative Voice.* Ithaca: Cornell University Press, 1992.

Lee, Sophia. "Preface." *The Chapter of Accidents.* Vol. 24 of *Bell's British Theatre.* London: George Cawthron, 1796: iii-vi.

Leggatt, Alexander. *English Stage Comedy, 1490–1990: Five Centuries of a Genre.* London: Routledge, 1998.

Lemire, Beverly. *Fashion's Favorite: The Cotton Trade and the Consumer in Britain, 1660–1800.* Oxford: Oxford University Press, 1991.

Leneman, Leah. *Alienated Affections: The Scottish Experience of Divorce and Separation, 1684–1830.* Edinburgh: Edinburgh University Press, 1998.

Lévi-Strauss, Claude. *Structural Anthropology.* Trans. Claire Jacobson and Brooke Grundfest Schoepf. New York: Basic Books, 1963.

Lewcock, Dawn. "More for Seeing than Hearing: Behn and the Use of the Theatre." In *Aphra Behn Studies.* Ed. Janet Todd. Cambridge University Press, 1996: 66–83.

Lillo, George. *The London Merchant.* Reprinted in *The Beggar's Opera and Other Eighteenth-Century Plays.* Ed. David W. Lindsay. London: Everyman, 1993.

Little, Judy. *Comedy and the Woman Writer: Woolf, Spark, and Feminism.* Lincoln: University of Nebraska Press, 1983.

Littlewood, S. R. *Elizabeth Inchbald and Her Circle.* London: O'Connor, 1921.

Lock, F. P. *Susanna Centlivre.* Boston: Twayne, 1979.

Locke, John. *An Essay Concerning Human Understanding.* Ed. Peter H. Nidditch. Oxford: Clarendon Press, 1975.

———. *Two Treatises of Government.* Ed. Thomas I. Cook. New York: Harper Macmillan, 1947.

The London Magazine or, Gentleman's Monthly Intelligencer. London: R. Baldwin, 1747–1783.

The London Times. London: R. Nutkins, 1788 -.

Looser, Devoney. *British Women Writers and the Writing of History, 1670–1820.* Baltimore: Johns Hopkins University Press, 2000.

Lyons, Paddy (ed.). *Female Playwrights of the Restoration: Five Comedies.* London: J. M. Dent/Everyman, 1991.

Macaulay, Catharine. *Letters on Education. With Observations on Religious and Metaphysical Subjects.* Intro. Gina Luria. New York: Garland Publishing, 1974.

Macpherson, C. B. *The Political Theory of Possessive Individualism: Hobbes to Locke.* Oxford: Clarendon Press, 1962.

Mandeville, Bernard. *The Virgin Unmask'd,* 1709. Delmar, New York: Scholars' Facsimiles and Reprints, 1975.

Markley, Robert. "'Be Impudent, be saucy, forward, bold, touzing, and leud': The Politics of Masculine Sexuality and Feminine Desire in Behn's Tory Comedies." In *Cultural Readings of Restoration and Eighteenth-Century English Theater.* Ed. J. Douglas Canfield and Deborah C. Payne. Athens: University of Georgia Press, 1995: 114–40.

———. *Two Edg'd Weapons: Style and Ideology in the Comedies of Etherege, Wycherley and Congreve.* Oxford: Clarendon Press, 1988.

Markley, Robert, and Molly Rothenberg. "Contestations of Nature: Aphra Behn's "The Golden Age" and the Sexualizing of Politics." In *Rereading Aphra Behn: History, Theory, and Criticism.* Ed. Heidi Hutner. Charlottesville: The University Press of Virginia, 1993: 301–24.

Marsden, Jean. "Rape, Voyerism, and the Restoration Stage." In *Broken Boundaries: Women and Feminism in Restoration Drama.* Ed. Katherine M. Quinsey. Lexington: The University Press of Kentucky, 1996: 185–200.

Marx, Karl. *Das Capital,* vol. I. Trans. E. Aveling and S. Moore. London: Lawrence and Wishart, 1967.

Mathias, Peter. *The Transformation of England: Essays in the Economic and Social History of England in the Eighteenth Century.* New York: Columbia University Press, 1980.

McKendrick, Neil, John Brewer, and J. H. Plumb. *The Birth of a Consumer Society: The Commercialization of Eighteenth-Century England.* Bloomington: Indiana University Press, 1982.

McKeon, Michael. "Historicizing Patriarchy: The Emergence of Gender Difference in England, 1660–1760." *Eighteenth Century Studies* 28.3 (1995): 295–322.

Mendelson, Sara Heller. *The Mental World of Stuart Women: Three Studies.* Amherst: University of Massachusetts Press, 1987.

Miller, Nancy. *Subject to Change: Reading Feminist Writing.* Columbia: Columbia University Press, 1988.

Moi, Toril. *What Is A Woman.* Oxford: Oxford University Press, 1999.

Morris, Marilyn. "Crim. Con. In *The Bon Ton* (1791–96) and the Promiscuity of Genre." Unpublished manuscript, 2001: 1–24.

Munns, Jessica. "Barton and Behn's *The Rover,* or, the Text transpos'd." *Restoration and Eighteenth Century Theater Research* 3: 2 (1988): 11–22.

———. "Theatrical Culture I: Politics and Theatre." In *The Cambridge Companion to English Literature, 1650–1740.* Ed. Steven Zwicker. Cambridge: Cambridge University Press, 1998.

Nagler, A. M. (ed.). *A Source Book in Theatrical History.* New York: Dover, 1952.

Nettleton, George Henry, Arthur E. Case, and George Winchester Stone, Jr. (eds.). *British Dramatists from Dryden to Sheridan.* 2nd ed. Boston: Houghton Miflin, 1969.

Nicoll, Allardyce. *History of the English Drama, 1660–1900.* Vols. I-III. Cambridge: Cambridge University Press, 1952–59.

Nussbaum, Felicity. *The Brink of All We Hate: English Satires on Women, 1660–1750.* Lexington, Kentucky: University of Kentucky Press, 1984.

O'Brien, Patrick. "Agriculture and the Home Market for English Industry, 1660–1820." *English Historical Review* 100: 397 (1985): 773–800.

Otway, Thomas. *The Works of Thomas Otway; Plays, Poems, and Love Letters.* Ed. J. C. Ghosh. Oxford: Clarendon Press, 1968.

Owen, Susan J. "Sexual Politics and Party Politics in Behn's Drama, 1678–1683." In *Aphra Behn Studies.* Ed. Janet Todd. Cambridge: Cambridge University Press, 1996: 15–29.

Pacheco, Anita. "Rape and the Female Subject in Aphra Behn's *The Rover.*" *ELH* 65: 2 (1998): 323–45.

Parker, Patricia. *Literary Fat Ladies: Rhetoric, Gender, Property.* London: Methuen, 1987.

Pascoe, Judith. *Romantic Theatricality: Gender, Poetry, and Spectatorship.* Ithaca: Cornell University Press, 1997.

Paster, Gail Kern. *The Body Embarrassed: Drama and the Disciplines of Shame in Early Modern England.* Ithaca: Cornell University Press, 1993.

Pateman, Carole. *The Sexual Contract.* Stanford: Stanford University Press, 1988.

Paul, C. Kegan. *William Godwin: His Friends and Contemporaries,* vol. I. London: H. S. King and Co., 1876.

Payne, Linda R. "The Carnivalesque Regeneration of Corrupt Economies in *The Rover.*" *Restoration: Studies in English Literary Culture, 1660–1700* 22: 1 (1998): 40–49.

———. "'And Poets shall by Patron-Princes Live': Aphra Behn and Patronage." In *Curtain Calls: British and American Women Writers and the Theater, 1660–1820.* Ed. Mary Anne Schofield and Cecilia Macheski. Athens: Ohio University Press, 1991: 105–19.

Pearson, Jacqueline. *The Prostituted Muse: Images of Women and Women Dramatists 1642–1737.* New York: Harvester Wheatsheaf, 1988.

Pedicord, William. *The Theatrical Public in the Time of Garrick.* Carbondale: Southern Illinois University Press, 1954.

Perry, Ruth. *The Celebrated Mary Astell: An Early English Feminist.* Chicago: University of Chicago Press, 1986.

Peters, Julie Stone. *Congreve, The Drama, and the Printed Word.* Stanford: Stanford University Press, 1990.

Pilkington, Laetitia. *Memoirs of Laetitia Pilkington.* Ed. A. C. Elias, Jr. Athens: University of Georgia Press, 1997.

Pinchbeck, Ivy. *Women Workers and the Industrial Revolution, 1750–1850.* London, Cass, 1969.

Phillips, Roderick. *Family Breakdown in Late Eighteenth-Century France: Divorces in Rouen 1792–1803.* Oxford: Clarendon Press, 1980.

———. *Putting Assunder: A History of Divorce in Western Society.* Cambridge: Cambridge University Press, 1988.

The Pocket Magazine or, Elegant Repository of Useful and Polite Literature. London: Harrison and Co., 1794–1795.

Pocock, J. G. A. *The Machiavellian Moment: Florentine Political Thought and the Atlantic Republican Tradition.* Princeton: Princeton University Press, 1995.

Porter, Roy. *London Life in the Eighteenth Century.* New York: Penguin, 1990.

Purdie, Susan. *Comedy: The Mastery of Discourse.* Toronto: University of Toronto Press, 1993.

Ravenscroft, Edward. *The Careless Lovers. Edward Ravenscroft's "The Careless Lovers" and "The Canterbury Guests": A Critical Old-Spelling Edition,* 1–209. Ed. Edmund S. Henry, gen. ed. Stephen Orgel. New York: Garland, 1987.

Rawson, Claude J. *Satire and Sentiment, 1660–1830.* Cambridge: Cambridge University Press, 1994.

Reiss, Timothy J. *The Discourse of Modernism.* Ithaca: Cornell University Press, 1982.

Richards, Sandra. *The Rise of the English Actress.* New York: St. Martin's Press, 1993.

Rogers, Katherine. "Britain's First Woman Drama Critic: Elizabeth Inchbald." In *Curtain Calls: British and American Women and the Theater, 1660–1820.* Ed. Mary Anne Schofield and Cecilia Macheski. Athens: University of Ohio Press, 1991: 277–90.

———. *The Troublesome Helpmate: A History of Misogyny in Literature.* Seattle: University of Washington Press, 1966.

Rogers, Katherine, and William McCarthy (eds.). *The Meridian Anthology of Early Women Writers: British Literary Women from Aphra Behn to Maria Edgeworth, 1660–1800.* New York: New American Library, 1987.

Rosenthal, Laura. *Playwrights and Plagiarists in Early Modern England: Gender, Authorship, Literary Property.* Ithaca: Cornell University Press, 1996.

Rousseau, Jean-Jacques. *Emile or On Education.* Trans. Allan Bloom. New York: Basic Books, 1979.

Salvaggio, Ruth. "Aphra Behn's Love: Fiction, Letters, and Desire." In *Rereading Aphra Behn: History, Theory, and Criticism.* Ed. Heidi Hutner. Charlottesville: The University Press of Virginia, 1993: 253–70.

———. *Enlightened Absence: Neoclassical Configurations of the Feminine.* Chicago: University of Illinois Press, 1988.

Schneider, Ben Ross, Jr. (ed.). *Index to the London Stage, 1660–1800.* Carbondale: Southern Illinois University Press, 1979.

Schouls, Peter A. *The Imposition of Method: A Study of Descartes and Locke.* Oxford: Clarendon Press; New York: Oxford University Press, 1980.

Scott, Joan Wallach. *Gender and the Politics of History.* New York: Columbia University Press, 1988.

Sedgwick, Eve Kosofsky. *Between Men: English Literature and Male Homosocial Desire.* New York: Columbia University Press, 1985.

Shadwell, Thomas. *The Complete Works of Thomas Shadwell.* Ed. Montague Summers. London: The Fortune Press, 1927.

Shell, Alison. "Popish Plots: *The Feign'd Curtizans* in Context." In *Aphra Behn Studies.* Ed. Janet Todd. Cambridge: Cambridge University Press, 1996: 30–49.

Sheridan, Frances. *The Plays of Frances Sheridan.* Ed. Robert Hogan and Jerry C. Beasley. Newark: University of Delaware Press, 1984.

Siskin, Clifford. *The Work of Writing: Literature and Social Change in Britain, 1700–1830.* Baltimore: Johns Hopkins University Press, 1998.

Smith, Adam. *An Inquiry into the Nature and Causes of the Wealth of Nations.* Eds. R. H. Campbell and A. S. Skinner. Oxford: Clarendon Press, 1976.

Smollett, Tobias (ed.). *Critical Review or, Annals of Literature.* London: W. Simpkin and R. Marshall, 1756–1817.

Southerne, Thomas. *The Works of Thomas Southerne.* Ed. Robert Jordan and Harold Love. Oxford: Clarendon Press, 1988.

Spencer, Jane. "Adapting Aphra Behn: Hannah Cowley's *A School for Greybeards* and *The Lucky Chance.*" *Women's-Writing: The Elizabethan to Victorian Period* 2: 3 (1995): 221–34.

———. "'Deceit, Dissembling, and all that's Woman': Comic Plot and Female Action in *The Feigned Courtesans.*" In *Rereading Aphra Behn: History, Theory, and Criticism.* Ed. Heidi Hutner. Charlottesville: The University Press of Virginia, 1993: 86–101.

———. "*The Rover* and the Eighteenth Century." *Aphra Behn Studies.* Ed. Janet Todd. Cambridge: Cambridge University Press, 1996: 84–106.

Stallybrass, Peter, and Allon White. *The Politics and Poetics of Transgression.* Ithaca: Cornell University Press, 1986.

Stanton, Judith Phillips. "Statistical Profile of Women Writing in English from 1660–1800." In *Eighteenth-Century Women and the Arts.* Ed. Frederick M. Keener and Susan E. Lorsch. New York: Greenwood Press, 1988.

———. "'This New-Found Path Attempting': Women Dramatists in England, 1660–1800." In *Curtain Calls: British and American Women and the Theater, 1660–1820.* Ed. Mary Anne Schofield and Cecilia Macheski. Athens: University of Ohio Press, 1991: 325–54.

Staves, Susan. *Married Women's Separate Property in England, 1660–1833.* Cambridge: Harvard University Press, 1990.

———. *Player's Scepters: Fictions of Authority in the Restoration.* Lincoln: University of Nebraska Press, 1979.

———. "Money for Honor: Damages for Criminal Conversation." *Studies in Eighteenth Century Culture* 11 (1982): 279–97.

Steele, Sir Richard. *The Tatler.* Ed. George A. Aitken. Hildesheim, New York: G. Olms, 1970.

Stone, Lawrence. *Broken Lives: Separation and Divorce in England, 1660–1857.* Oxford: Oxford University Press, 1993.

———. *The Family, Sex and Marriage in England, 1500–1800.* New York: Harper and Row, 1977.

Stout, William. *The Autobiography of William Stout of Lancaster, 1665–1752.* Ed. J. D. Marshall. Manchester: Manchester University Press, 1967.

Sullivan, David. "The Female Will in Aphra Behn." *Women's Studies* 22: 335–47.

Taetzsch, Lynne. "Romantic Love Replaces Kinship Exchange in Aphra Behn's Restoration Drama." *Restoration: Studies in English Literary Culture, 1660–1700 17:* 1 (1993): 30–38.

Tasch, Peter. *The Dramatic Cobbler: The Life and Works of Isaac Bickerstaff.* Lewisburg: Bucknell University Press, 1971.

Tave, Stuart M. *The Amiable Humorist; A Study in the Comic Theory and Criticism of the Eighteenth and Early Nineteenth Centuries.* Chicago: University of Chicago Press, 1960.

Taylor, John. *Records of My Life.* 2 vols. London: E. Bull, 1832.

Thirsk, Joan. *Economic Policies and Projects: The Development of a Consumer Society in Early Modern England.* Oxford: Clarendon Press, 1978.

Thompson, James. *Models of Value: Eighteenth-Century Political Economy and the Novel.* Durham: Duke University Press, 1996.

———. "'Sure I Have Seen That Face Before': Representation and Value in Eighteenth-Century Drama." In *Cultural Readings of Restoration and Eighteenth-Century English Theater.* Ed. J. Douglas Canfield and Deborah C. Payne. Athens: University of Georgia Press, 1995: 281–308.

Thompson, Peggy. "Closure and Subversion in Behn's Comedies." In *Broken Boundaries: Women and Feminism in Restoration Drama.* Ed. Katherine M. Quinsey. Lexington: The University Press of Kentucky, 1996: 71–88.

Tillotson, John. *Sermons on Several Subjects and Occasions.* London, 1757.

Todd, Janet. *The Critical Fortunes of Aphra Behn.* Columbia, S.C.: Camden House, 1998.

———. *The Secret Life of Aphra Behn.* London: André Deutsch Limited, 1996.

———. *The Sign of Angellica: Women, Writing and Fiction, 1660–1800.* New York: Columbia University Press, 1989.

Todd, Janet (ed.). *Aphra Behn Studies.* Cambridge: Cambridge University Press, 1996.

The Town and Country Magazine or the Universal Repository of Knowledge, Instruction, and Entertainment. London: A. Hamilton, 1769–1796.

A Treatise of Feme Coverts: Or the Lady's Law, 1732. Intro. Lance E. Dickson. South Hackensack: Rothman Reprints, 1974.

Troubridge, St. Vincent. *The Benefit System in the British Theater.* London: Society for Theater Research, 1967.

Trouille, Mary. *Sexual Politics in the Enlightenment: Women Writers Read Rousseau.* New York: SUNY Press, 1997.

The Universal Magazine. London: H. D. Symonds, 1804–1814.

Vanbrugh, John, Sir. *The Provoked Wife.* Ed. Curt A. Zimansky. Lincoln: University of Nebraska Press, 1969.

Van Lennep, W., E. L. Avery, G. W. Stone, and A. H. Scouten (eds.). *The London Stage, 1660–1800.* 5 pts. Carbondale: Southern Illinois University Press, 1960–68.

Walker, Nancy A. *Feminist Alternatives: Irony and Fantasy in the Contemporary Novel by Women.* Jackson: University Press of Mississippi, 1990.

———. *A Very Serious Thing: Women's Humor and American Culture.* Minneapolis: University of Minnesota Press, 1988.

Wagner, Peter. *Eros Revived: Erotica of Enlightenment in England and America.* London: Secker and Warurg, 1988.

Weatherill, Lorna. *Consumer Behaviour and Material Culture in Britain, 1660–1760.* 2nd ed. London: Routledge, 1988.

Welch, Edwin. *Spiritual Pilgrim: A Reassessment of the Life of the Countess of Huntingdon.* Cardiff: University of Wales Press, 1995.

Wells, S. B. "An Eighteenth Century Attribution." *Journal of English and Germanic Philology* 38 (1939): 239–46.

Wickham, Glynne. *Early English Stages 1300 to 1600.* 2nd ed. London: Routledge and Kegan Paul; New York: Columbia University Press, 1980.

Williams, Patricia. *The Alchemy of Race and Rights.* Cambridge, Massachusetts: Harvard University Press, 1991.

Wilmot, John. *Lord Rochester.* Ed. Paddy Lyons. London: Everyman–J. M. Dent, 1996.

Wilt, Judith. "The Laughter of the Maidens, and Cackle of the Matriarchs: Notes on the Collision Between Humor and Feminism." *Women and Literature* 1: 173–96.

Wollstonecraft, Mary. *A Vindication of the Rights of Men,* 1790. Rpt. in *The Vindications.* Ed. D. L. Macdonald and Kathleen Scherf. Ontario: Broadview Press, 1997.

Zimbardo, Rose. *A Mirror Up to Nature: Transformations in Drama and Aesthetics, 1660–1732.* Lexington: The University Press of Kentucky, 1986.

Žižek, Slavoj. *The Sublime Object of Ideology.* Verso: London, 1989.

Zomchick, John. *Family and the Law in Eighteenth-Century Fiction: The Public Conscience in the Private Sphere.* Cambridge: Cambridge University Press, 1993.

Zuckerman, Arnold. "Scurvy and the Ventilation of Ships in the Royal Navy: Samuel Sutton's Contribution." *Eighteenth Century Studies* 10: 2 (1976): 222–34.

Index